Ellis House

Maria Channell

Ellis House

Helm Publishing

For information address:
Helm Publishing
3923 Seward Ave.
Rockford, IL 61108
815-398-4660
www.publishersdrive.com

ISBN -978-0-9801780-9-8

Printed in the United States of America

ACKNOWLEDGMENT

To Shawn, my family, friends and all the former clinical, residential and administrative staff at NAI – Cabrillo in San Diego. But most of all, to Andrew and Mattie – my beautiful sons.

REVIEWS

Elements in Maria's novel appeal to the type of readership which loves the dream sequence that creates suspense, dialogue conflict (between rigid director and sympathetic protagonist), conflict between professional psychologist and student husband, conflict between Emily and her troubled Mother, conflict in staff between controlling director and staff in group home. The point of view of narrator is handled very well. All in all, a great first novel.

Pat McColl, Freelance Editor

Well developed characters help create a rich storyline which draws you in and continues to entice you. The writing is crisp and confident, that of a seasoned writer; a riveting story from an author who knows her subject.

Peter Zoubek, Speech writer, Federal Government, Ottawa Canada

Chapter 1

I'm on my hands and knees in darkness, desperate to find my way in silence. There is no power, no dial tone, and I can hear footsteps above me - pacing, stopping, pacing, stopping. There are two people arguing. I recognize the voice of my husband. The voices crescendo to shouting. Screams. Shattering of glass. No more voices. Only silence.

My chest is so tight it aches. My heart pounds like a violent caged animal against my ribs. I feel the dampness of sweat pooling under my arms and hugging the curve of my spine. It collects on my brow. I wipe it away making my palms slick. I try not to panic. I tell myself to regulate my breathing - slow, deep, and even. I tell myself not to hyperventilate. I need to stay in control. Stay in control. No matter what - stay in control.

Slowly and silently, I ascend the steps, five, six, seven . . . I stop. I hold my breath and listen. Nothing. I continue, - ten, eleven, twelve. At the top of the stairs, I pause, listen and wait. I wait until my body starts to stiffen and my legs begin to cramp. I force myself to continue. Then, I hear it. A faint moan followed by muffled laughter. Damn it! Goddammit! My husband! I've got to get out. I've got to get help. I crawl through the kitchen, the ceramic tile cool to my touch. I reach the sliding glass door, raise my hand to flip the latch, gently pushing it open, - just enough, and holding my breath I squeeze outside. My body stiff with tension, I struggle to my feet. I start sprinting, the dry leaves crunching under my feet. The cool, damp wind chills my skin and tangles my hair. I repeatedly stumble and lose my footing on the uneven ground, but manage to regain my balance. The night is black as pitch, but I know where to go. I navigated these woods hundreds of times as a kid. There's a shortcut which avoids the road as it curves around the lake. I focus on the rhythmic movement of my legs. They are heavy, quivering; they may buckle beneath me at any moment, but I force myself to keep going. There is no other choice. I have several miles to go. I have to get there as fast, as fast as I am able.

I see the lake in the distance, a sheet of black glass, two symmetrical circles of light, reflecting from the marina and guiding me, like glowing beacons of hope - a life raft in this shoal of misery. As I get closer, I can see the boats tethered to the weathered pier. Almost there, my lungs on fire, I have to stop. I'm running on fumes. My body is devoid of energy and full of pain, when I finally allow myself to stop. Immediately, my body reacts. I double over from the cramping in my side and greedily gulp the cool night air. I stay stationary for what seems eternity, hands on my knees, my energy reserves depleted.

Eventually, I muster up the strength I need and forge ahead. Just then, I'm grabbed from behind, tackled to the ground, air bursting from my lungs. He's straddling me now his thick, muscular legs twisted around my waist. The black mask covers his face, but I can see his meager lips form a thin smile and I can smell his breath, sour like curdled milk. He puts his face next to mine and I can feel the rough, scratchy mask on my skin. I start to gag as he slithers his warm tongue into my mouth.

My breathing becomes erratic and labored as he tells me,

"Let's go see your husband. I know you must be worried about him." I close my eyes and try to focus on something other than the intense throbbing pain in my head and ringing in my ears . . .

"Grace. Grace. Wake up." I could feel my body being shaken and hear my name being called repeatedly.

"Wake up Grace. The phone's for you. It's someone from work. She says it's an emergency." My husband Elliot mumbled as he passed me the phone.

I took the receiver, my voice hoarse as I answered.

"Hello." I managed.

"Dr. Morgan, this is Ana. Sorry to call so late, but it's an emergency." The oversized, red numbers on the clock read 2:10 a.m. Otherwise the room was dark, nothing visible except outlines in varying shades of grey and black.

"What emergency?" I asked, suddenly becoming more alert and pushing my hair behind my ear so I could clearly hear what she was saying.

"Our new admit somehow sneaked out of the building and climbed onto the roof. She claims she has a knife and is going to kill herself if she can't go back home with her mom."

"How the hell did that happen?"

"Things were really crazy today and we were short staffed on the units to start with. Then two of the kids AWOLed..."

"Who?" I interrupted.

"Amanda and Jasmine," she responded.

Ana continued, "We sent everyone looking for them, which left us with a skeleton crew. But, we found them two hours later trying to buy cigarettes at a 7-Eleven."

"So you got them back, but the new admit managed to somehow get a knife and make it to the roof?" I knew I sounded exasperated and was making Ana uncomfortable, but I felt unsettled myself, the nightmare still running through my head.

"Yeah, I'm sorry Dr. Morgan. Emily must have slipped out while I was gone. I don't really know how long she's been up there...maybe thirty, forty minutes. She must have climbed up the fire escape."

"What's Emily's story?" I asked.

"We got her in earlier this evening. She got kicked out of her foster home because of noncompliance. Her social worker, Kim Howe, you know her? She's real nice. Anyway, Kim tried to find her another placement, but couldn't."

"Noncompliance meaning what exactly?" I asked. "Has she ever hurt herself, anybody else?"

"She cut herself up pretty good about eight months ago." Ana replied.

"Jesus," I said, climbing out of bed and wandering into the living room so as not to disturb Elliot any more than I already had. As my feet touched the smooth hardwood of the living room, I felt something beneath them. The floor was gritty, like tiny stones mixed with damp earth. Where did it come from? Why was it all over the floor?

"Dr. Morgan?" Ana asked into the phone line.

Distracted by the grit under my feet, I tried to refocus on Ana's voice. "Yes..." I mumbled, and recovered. "Yeah, sorry Ana. I was just thinking. Who's with her now?" I asked.

"Drew's talking to her. He's the only staff person she'll talk with."

"Was he able to keep her safe?"

"For now, but he believes she's already cut her arms and legs." Ana answered.

"God!" I exclaimed. Scenarios raced through my head. Foremost was my concern for the girl, but closely behind that was a concern for my reputation and my job. This was bad. "OK, I'm on my way." I said, now quickly walking back toward the bedroom and heading for the closet. "Just make sure you follow the new suicide protocol, the revised one. I'll be there as quickly as I can."

"Yeah, we will. I'm sorry Dr. Morgan." Ana apologized.

"Don't worry about it. You've got my cell number? Call me if there is any change."

"Yeah, I've got it."

I hung up the receiver and efficiently rummaged around in the bottom of the closet, retrieving a pair of jeans and sweatshirt I had worn yesterday evening. I pulled on my clothes, made my way to the bathroom and turned on the light, careful not to disrupt Elliot. I threw some cold water on my face and swept my honey blonde hair into a ponytail. Good enough, I thought, looking at the reflection staring back at me. I looked tired. My green eyes, framed by my gold rimmed glasses, seemed dull. Maybe it was the puffiness and dark circles around them. My skin seemed pale, my lips bloodless, under the unforgiving light. I no longer had that rosy hue of health which had always been so typical.

I knew I hadn't been sleeping well for the last couple months and physically it was starting to take its toll. My diet had suffered too, leading to some weight loss which made me look gaunt since I had always been thin. It made my face appear hollow, more angular, losing the softness around my chin. Even worse, my exercise routine had essentially been stopped in its tracks given my increased responsibilities at work. But work was no excuse. I really had to start taking better care of myself.

"Where are you going?" Elliot mumbled.

"Work." I answered.

"Jesus, why?" he responded irritably, sitting up in bed.

"We've got a kid who's threatening to kill herself."

"OK, so let someone else handle it for a change. It's not like it's unusual. There's a crisis at that place almost every night."

"I can't, they've screwed up on this one. I have to handle it."

"Right." He growled. "You can have someone else handle it, you just won't. Just because you're the clinical director doesn't mean you have to do it all yourself. Some things never change. You can't ever let anyone else be responsible."

He rolled over and continued. "Make sure you don't wake me when you get in. I've got to be at the lab by seven...and by the way, you look like shit."

"Yeah, well screw you too." I muttered to myself and stormed out the door into the chilly, autumn night. I didn't need Elliot to point out the obvious.

It wasn't until I was in the car that I remembered the floor in the living room when I was talking on the phone. The feeling against my feet, like walking across a forest floor. Pebbles? Sand? Dirt? What exactly? Maybe the African violet fell off the end table? Did Snowy knock it over? Our cat was always sniffing and eating our plants. Either way, it would have to wait until later.

Chapter 2

Ellis House was a stately three story Tudor building, which for many years had been home to a very well-to-do family. Specifically, it had belonged to an elderly man, Colin Kemper, who had been raised as an only child at Ellis House in the early 1950s, heir to a chocolate factory and an extremely successful catering company. He had demonstrated no interest in pursuing the family businesses and sold the companies at his earliest opportunity, investing his money. Instead, he pursued a lengthy and well respected career as a diplomat. Thus, the house remained vacant for decades given his postings abroad, barring the occasional return to his home state of Michigan.

When retirement presented itself, he returned to live out his final years on the estate. However, after surviving his initial winter, he had donated Ellis House to the state, a farewell gift to his community, and moved to Barbados where the more forgiving, temperate climate was better able to satisfy his desire to play golf and to ameliorate his arthritic pain. Originally, it had functioned as a halfway house for adults recovering from addictions, but given the growing need for child and adolescent placements, it had been turned into a group home in 1998.

The building was creamy yellow stucco outlined with dark maple beams. The generous, bright windows and sheer white curtains made the facade more welcoming than it otherwise would have been. The roof was shingled in brown with a tall, red brick chimney erupting from its center. Over the years, thick dark green ivy had thrived, masking most of its exterior and adding to its charm. The house was bordered by a circular driveway and set back from the street on a well-manicured lawn dotted with maple trees.

This particular group home was short term. Some children remained for several days, while others remained for approximately a year. The length of stay typically depended on whether or not a suitable placement could be found, though a fair share of kids ended up being hauled to Juvenile Hall, or "juvie", because of any number of criminal acts. While we saw a number of malcontents who were unwilling to change their behavior at any price, it always amazed me how many kids made progress and followed the rules, despite the fact they knew a move to another placement was inevitable and had little to do with how they conducted themselves at Ellis House.

Most of the time I was involved in an admission, but sometimes, in cases such as Emily's, we had a client "dumped" on us by social services and we were essentially forced to take him or her. Typically, when admitted, clients were first required to meet with the residential intake coordinator to be oriented to the facility. This was necessary to learn the daily routine and to understand what was expected of them. Within twenty four hours of admission, they were evaluated by a staff therapist to determine what clinical treatment was indicated. Most clients received group therapy daily, medication management and individual therapy at least once a week. Sadly, family therapy which was always indicated rarely occurred because most of the clients did not have any family willing or able to participate.

Many of the children and teenagers who circulated through Ellis House, and most group homes for that matter had parents who were incarcerated or deceased. If living parents existed, they almost always had a reason why they couldn't attend scheduled therapy sessions. They couldn't afford gas, their license had been revoked, they were residing in a drug treatment facility; the list went on and on. Of course, there were always exceptions and some parents participated in treatment despite extraordinary circumstances.

When I pulled up to the facility, I could see Drew shivering in his jeans and t-shirt with a flashlight in his hand. Drew was a shift supervisor who had come in on his day off to help with the initial AWOL crisis and had wound up on suicide watch. He was also one of the few residential staff who had managed to remain at Ellis House for more than a year, tolerating high staff turnover, inadequate pay and minimal benefits.

Drew, considered handsome by anyone's standard, was tall, with an athletic build and short, dark, brown hair. He was at ease on the units and had strict boundaries with the clients. This served him well given most of the female clients and staff members had a crush on him.

"Hey! Doc! How's it going?" He asked, flashing a knowing smile. She's up there." He said, shining the flashlight towards the roof and briefly picking out a human form. "Been up there for about forty minutes."

"Get that goddamn light out of my face asshole!" the girl shrieked.

"Sounds like a charmer." I said. "What's been going on? Ana told me she hurt herself earlier?"

"Yeah. Well, she promised me and said she wouldn't kill herself as long as no one tried to get her off the roof. That's why I left her up there. I didn't want to push her. Excuse the pun." Again with the smile. "I do know from what the foster mom told us when she dropped her off that she's fourteen. She said she

9

couldn't take having Emily around anymore because she had become so noncompliant and argumentative. Apparently she was refusing to attend school and was isolating herself from everyone in the house. Foster mom said she seemed more and more apathetic and irritable." Drew responded.

"Sounds bad, a lot of red flags. She ever been hospitalized?" I asked.

"I think she was hospitalized at least once before, but I don't know the details. Also, she was restrained tonight. My guess is that's what brought this on."

"Restrained? Nobody called me."

"Really? Well, it wasn't anything really unusual. Threatening to hurt herself, arguing with staff, told Danny he looked like a water buffalo. You believe that?" Emily was dead on, but it provoked Danny since the description fit.

Drew turned towards the roof and yelled loudly, "Emily, Dr. Morgan is here."

"Good for her. Now you'll have someone else to fuck with and maybe you'll leave me alone." Emily replied.

"Sounds motivated, huh Doc?"

"What do you want Emily?" I asked looking in the direction of the screaming voice.

"I'll tell you what I'm sure you already know given that everyone here has a damned big mouth including that dickless prick you are talking to."

"Dickless prick..." Drew mumbled. "Is that possible?"

"I want out of this fucking hole and I want to see my mom!" Emily shrilled.

"I hear what you're saying." I responded, hoping she would understand I was listening.

"Good. You know those bitches restrained me tonight? Threw me against the wall and then kept me in that room that smells like piss. They wouldn't let me out."

"Honest Doc, we didn't have her in your office," Drew said, smiling.

"Shut up Drew." I said quietly.

10

"I told them I'd be good, but they kept me in there. All I wanted to do was call my mom." Emily screamed.

"Is any of that true?" I asked.

"I doubt it. Yeah she was restrained, but the rest? I don't see how that would be possible. I never heard her say anything about calling her mom, but I wasn't around for the restraint. I didn't get here until after the AWOLs happened. When Ana was calling people to get extra staff to come in and help out. I've pretty much been out here most of the evening."

I yelled to Emily, "I'm really sorry you've had such a difficult time here."

"Yeah, lot of fuckin' good that does. You don't even know me."

"You're right. I don't know you, but I would like to get to know you."

"The guy I met when I got here said I could call my mom whenever I wanted to. Then when I wanted to they wouldn't let me."

"It sounds like there were some communication problems." I said.

"Yeah, you think so?" Emily replied sarcastically. "And I got bruises and scrapes from where that one peroxide blonde hose bag dug her nails into me. You expect me to stay here when I gotta deal with shit like that?"

"Look Emily, I don't know everything that went on here tonight, but I'm willing to help you out however I can. Maybe we can come up with a plan, get things sorted out and find a way for you to talk to the people who are important to you."

"Yeah, right. That'll never happen. All I get is being shipped from home to home. You know those bitches tonight wouldn't even let me call my mom during phone hours. They said that I wasn't on a good enough level, but when I got here earlier the staff said I could always call my mom. Fucking liars."

"OK Emily, I'm sure we can at least figure out something with your phone calls."

"I should be able to call my mom whenever. I want to call my attorney to file a complaint against the supervisor for violating my fucking personal rights."

"That's your right. You can call your attorney if that's what you want to do."

"Here we go..." Drew said and this time I silenced him with a stare. We had been outside for a while now and it was dark and it was cold. I could see big, white puffs of smoke forming from my mouth as I spoke. I wondered if Emily had anything on besides pajamas. Even if she had a blanket, she'd been up there a long time. She was probably freezing.

"Emily," I said, "I know that we just started talking, but I need to ask you something and I need you to be honest with me."

Silence. I waited for a few seconds and asked, "Emily, did you hear me?"

"Yeah."

"Emily, are you still thinking of hurting yourself? My understanding from Drew is that you have a knife and have threatened to kill yourself."

"Yeah."

"Do I still have to worry that you are going to try to hurt yourself?"

"I don't want to go to the hospital. I hate that place. I was sent there one time before and they did nothing to help me. Injected me with shit..."

"We're not talking about going to the hospital, but I need to know if you're still thinking of hurting yourself."

"You don't understand. I never want to hurt myself. I didn't the last time either. I don't want to die, but sometimes I can't take it anymore. It's too hard and I feel like it'll never get any better."

I'd heard this before, a common complaint. Sometimes the cutting relieved the emotional pain. "Emily, it may seem like that now, but things can get better. If I could promise you we would try to call your mom right now, would that help?"

"Yeah."

"OK, can you promise me you won't try to hurt yourself anymore?"

12

"Yeah."

"Emily, I'm going to come up there now and help you down. I've got a coat and a blanket and I bet you're freezing. I also want you to give me the knife when I get up there. Do you understand?"

"Yeah."

"OK then."

I tucked the coat and blanket under my right arm and moved in the direction of the ladder putting the small flashlight Drew had given me in my pocket. I started to climb the aluminum ladder which had been propped against the bottom platform of the old, black, metal fire escape. The rungs felt icy. I blew on my hands before I started my ascent somehow believing this would help keep them warm. The climb up the ladder was slightly awkward, given I was maneuvering with a coat and a blanket and talking to Emily as I went. However, the ladder was stable. Drew had anchored it solidly to the ground.

Once I climbed onto the first platform of the fire escape, it was an easier climb. Now my hands were free for the remaining two flights of stairs. I readjusted what I was carrying and pulled the flashlight out of my pocket so I could see where I was going. There was some ambient light from the house itself, the remainder coming from the flickering, yellow street lights in the distance. The several street lamps which stood nearby cast minimal light. They were obscured by the massive, maple trees, dead leaves still clinging to their branches. I reached the first floor continuing to talk, hearing the occasional one word response as I went. By the time I got halfway up the stairs, I could see where Emily had ensconced herself. She was huddled in a corner, under the gable where the platform ended.

When I reached the top of the stairs, I shone the light in her direction. I could see her hugging herself, arms wrapped tightly around her legs. As I got closer, I could see her face was puffy and stained with dried tears. The dark circles under her eyes were partially masked by her blonde, stringy hair. Her left pant leg was rolled up and it had numerous evenly spaced superficial cuts from where she had used the knife. She was shivering and I

13

immediately pushed the jacket and blanket in her direction. She quickly put on the jacket and wrapped the blanket around her legs.

"Hey, I said. Thanks for letting me come up."

She looked exhausted.

"I'm going to sit down beside you if that's OK. But could you please give me the knife?"

She looked at me suspiciously, but her face also betrayed relief and with some reservation she pushed the kitchen steak knife, in my direction.

"Thanks, I said. "You made a good decision. Now, let's go back to my office and try calling your mom."

Chapter 3

I returned home several hours later and was careful not to wake Elliot. I was surprised to find the carpet cleaned and the plant gone. Elliot appeared to still be in the same position as I left him in the middle of the night, his head awkwardly hanging over the edge of the bed. I removed my clothes and climbed into the cool sheets. Normally, I had difficulty falling asleep, but this morning I did not. I drifted quickly into a sound sleep. The sleep of the dead.

A few hours later, the alarm clock roused me, far too early. The morning was cold and bitter, much too cold for October. The sky was grey and snow had begun to fly, the first snow of winter. The snowflakes were fluffy and light, dusting the earth temporarily before melting into the ground still warm from the summer's sun.

I had spent the majority of my childhood in Ontario and was painfully familiar with the sub-zero temperatures which turned the land to ice during the long winter months. I dreaded the arrival of winter, no matter how mild, and already yearned for the return of summer's heat. I shivered as I walked across the yard, climbed into the dented, black ford Escort I had owned since starting graduate school, and turned on the ignition. I put the heat on full blast and climbed back out to scrape clean the windshield where an intricate pattern of ice crystals had formed. I rubbed my frosty hands together, climbed back in and slowly backed out of the driveway.

I felt stiff and groggy and dreaded the drive to work. It was no more than a twenty minute ride to Ellis House, but it afforded me time to think about life, an activity I had avoided lately. I put on "Goodbye Yellow Brick Road" to provide some distraction from my thoughts as I drove along the I-94 corridor.

There had been numerous changes at the group home since I had accepted my position six months ago. Budgets were being cut for both the residential and clinical programs, a practice not uncommon in the social services. I myself had recently been asked by administration to begin carrying a small caseload, despite my position as clinical director. This had not been part of the job description, but everyone had been called on to increase their duties and I was willing to do my part. Further, it was a welcome diversion from my administrative responsibilities.

Historically, there had been friction between the residential and clinical staff. The budget cuts and hiring freeze had only exacerbated the problem. The core conflict between the two sides resulted from the belief that neither did enough work. The residential staff believed the therapists did paperwork to avoid being present on the units; whereas, the therapists believed that if residential staff were better organized, they could complete their responsibilities easily. The unfortunate result was that tensions were running high and the clients were caught in the crossfire.

The warm air hit my face as I entered the reception area.

"Hi Susan," I said, as I shook the dampness from my coat. "How are you?"

Susan was one of several support staff who were indispensable to our agency. Pretty much any time from nine to five she could be found sitting in the warm and welcoming entrance of the facility, an atmosphere she had created. She reminded me of the ideal grandmother, short and heavy set with curly, grey hair and a contagious smile.

"Fine thanks." She said smiling. "Barry just called to let you know one of your children wants to see you and your husband is on line two." Children. She referred to all the clients as such and was always so friendly with them and their respective families. Friendly and nonjudgmental to a fault; it was good she was not a therapist. She'd never be able to confront clients about their behavior.

"Right," I said. "Nice to get a little oriented before the day starts, don't you think? Please let Barry know I'm on my way."

Susan nodded an affirmative and I walked back to my office. My office was a windowless shoe box. It had become even more cramped recently given I had been forced to share it with a graduate student. I threw my briefcase on my desk and picked up the phone.

"Hey, how's it going El?" I asked.

"Grace. I've got to get to work. Where did you put my car keys? I can't find them anywhere."

"I don't know Elliot. Where'd you have them last?"

"I didn't have them anywhere. They were on the kitchen table. You must have moved them."

"Did you check the kitchen counter, hall table? Say, did you notice the-"

"Yeah. Not there." Elliot interrupted. "Look, I'm going to be late. I left them on the kitchen table. They're not there. Where'd you put them?" He demanded angrily.

"I don't know. I haven't-"

"Sure, whatever you say." He replied and there was a click as the line went dead.

Things had been increasingly tense between Elliot and me over the last few months. I attributed it to our impending separation. He had been accepted for an internship in San Diego and given our ballooning student loans, it was agreed I would remain in Michigan and work. It was the practical option, but difficult on an emotional level. I decided it was better not to call him back. There was nothing I could do anyway. Instead, I walked up to the unit to see Emily.

Ellis House had three distinct units. The younger girls and boys resided together on the top floor. The administrative offices were located on the first level. I trudged up to the second floor where the adolescent girls and boys were housed.

This former home had been nicely renovated to reflect its new purpose, but managed to retain much of its original character. The ceilings were high and arched to accommodate long broad windows. The hardwood floors were dark cherry, including the curved banisters which gracefully connected all three floors.

All three units had a similar floor plan with clients sharing rooms. This not only doubled the amount of clients able to be admitted to the program, but gave them increased opportunity for socialization. However despite some of the benefits, it posed a problem for client confidentiality. Specifically, therapy space was already at a premium with treatment rooms frequently being used for clients' visits with county social workers, attorneys and family. With the kids doubling up, meeting with them in their room, even for an informal discussion was typically out of the question. Since the therapists were now sharing office space as well, the all too common result was some time would be spent looking for a place in which a confidential discussion could be conducted. I knocked as I entered Emily's room.

"Emily?" I asked.

"She's in the bathroom". Her roommate gestured to the left. Moments later, Emily appeared looking significantly better than she had the night before. She appeared younger than her fourteen years. Her light hair was pulled back in a pony tail and her pale skin highlighted the dark circles under her eyes. She wore jeans and a black turtleneck sweater which appeared several sizes too large for her small frame.

"Hi." I said. "I got your message."

"Hi. I just wanted to make sure you didn't forget," She responded, yawning as she spoke.

"No, I didn't." I responded. "Let's go to one of the family rooms, so we can speak privately. Is that alright with you?"

"Definitely."

As we were leaving the unit, the residential manager, Barry Shore, motioned me in his direction. He had been employed at the group home since it opened five years ago. He was tall and lanky, his raven curls creating a gloomy aura around his head. He'd graduated with a B.A. in psychology several years earlier and believed no one should question his decisions given the length of time he'd been employed at Ellis House.

"You know you can't take her off the unit." He commanded.

"Why?" I retorted, instantly becoming irritated.

"First of all, she's on suicide watch and secondly, because she was restrained last night and was incredibly disruptive to the unit."

"I don't see your point. You think I'm going to allow her to kill herself while I'm talking to her?" I said, my anger apparent.

"No, it's just-" Barry began before I interrupted.

"So, if that's not it, you're telling me you believe confidential discussions between therapist and client are somehow a privilege?"

"Well yeah," He stumbled. "I don't see why you have to reward her bad behavior. Just talk to her in her room. According to the rules, she shouldn't leave the unit until she's on a good level."

"That's ridiculous. That could take weeks." I said.

Ellis House followed a level system. Upon admission, clients were initially placed on an introductory level. If a client made good choices, he or she could advance to higher levels which brought with them privileges such as leaving the units to use the lounge, later bed times, and attending activities off grounds with a staff member. If the client reached either one of the two highest levels, silver or gold, it implied that the probability of any risky behaviors, specifically AWOL, self-harm or aggression was low. If the client had recently engaged in any of the above risky behaviors, supervision was around the clock. Thus, given Emily was on a formal suicide watch, she needed to be supervised by staff at all times, which typically meant remaining on the unit unless engaged in therapeutic activity. However, Barry did not see it the same way.

I continued. "Furthermore, she was restrained last night because we screwed up. She should have been able to call her mother. If she had been given the opportunity like she had been told, this whole mess could have been avoided. We're the ones who made the mistake, not Emily."

Despite his arrogance, Barry did not like being confronted. "She could have just waited and called her mom today. I don't see what the big deal was."

"The big deal was-" I began.

"She gave our staff a really hard time and she should think about her actions." Barry interrupted. "You're just reinforcing her behavior."

"Well Barry, as much as I appreciate your re-educating me in the principles of behavioral psychology, I really must be going. I'm taking Emily to the family room." I said curtly.

Barry yelled after me, "As the clinical director you should be more supportive of staff. After all, we do the brunt of the work around here."

I turned to look at him, "My job is to advocate for my clients not the residential staff. By the way Barry, you're three weeks late on your unit reports. I'll have her back after morning group." I opened the door and led Emily off the unit.

We entered the family room on the first floor. It was painted a soft, pale yellow and always reminded me of springtime. Emily and I sat opposite each other on overstuffed, faded blue sofas. She immediately reclined, placed her feet on the coffee table and tilted her head back, her eyes tracking the long cracks in the white plaster ceiling. She shifted her focus to her hands as she chewed the dry skin around her cuticles, pausing briefly to examine them, and continued gnawing until they bled.

"Before we start, is there anything you want to review from

your intake session? Any questions about confidentiality or my role?" I paused.

"No. I've been through this before. I understand you have to break confidentiality if I'm going to hurt myself or somebody else."

"OK. I know we spent a long time last night talking about your placement here, the restraint and your behavior. I want you to understand that since last night, I've read your file and spoken with your foster mom and county social worker."

Their take on Emily's situation had been consistent. She had been placed in the foster home about seven months ago, following her initial discharge from the hospital. She had done well initially, seeming grateful for the stability and routine. Emily's mother, Maggie, had been in a drug treatment program at the time, and she was in frequent contact with her daughter, calling almost daily and visiting regularly. Emily was a model foster child, compliant with requests, always willing to complete her chores and homework. Her grades at school were average and she did well socially with peers and adults alike.

However, Emily's demeanor had changed after her mother was discharged from drug treatment. Maggie promised she would visit, but never did. Always having excuse after excuse as to why she couldn't make it. Emily called her mother daily, but her mother rarely answered the phone. Emily started to become anxious, frequently asking her foster mother if her mother had called or stopped by. Her mother never did. Subsequently, Emily increased the frequency of her calls to her county social worker, often calling multiple times a day searching for answers.

Unfortunately, Maggie's behavior didn't change, and Emily's did. Emily started to retreat socially, showing little interest in her peers and even less in school. Her grades dropped. Threats to complete her homework and chores were ineffective. Instead, she chose to retreat to the darkness of her bedroom. She refused to attend outpatient therapy and was defiant with her foster mother. Finally, her foster mother gave up. Exasperated and not knowing how to proceed, she contacted Emily's county social worker. It was decided if Emily did not choose to make any changes, she would be removed from the foster home and placed at Ellis House until a more structured placement could be found. Emily had called their bluff and lost.

"Emily, I wanted to let you know, you made a good decision last night. I'm glad you changed your mind and were willing to speak with me."

"Yeah, all I needed to do was talk to my mom. I know she was probably sleeping when I called. I'm sure she'll call back as soon as she can. She moved into her own apartment a while ago, after she got done with her inpatient treatment. Her county worker helped her find a place. I'm hoping I can move in with her soon. I just don't know why I couldn't call her last night when I wanted to. That's what set me off. Made me start thinking about hurting myself. I felt so trapped."

"Sounds like you wanted to get some control back." I interjected.

"Sure. I never really wanted to kill myself. I'm not saying I haven't thought about it and that I'm not depressed, but last night I felt like I had no power. Couldn't even do something simple like make a phone call without it being a huge deal."

"And today?" I asked.

"Better. I mean it's not like I had anything planned last night. I just took advantage of the situation when those kids took off. There was no staff around, so I left...not really knowing what I'd do. I know it's no better on the street. I just needed to get out for a while. Once I did manage to get outside, I saw the fire escape and it seemed like the perfect solution. But once I got up there I still felt trapped. I knew I'd catch shit. That's when I started cutting, but I couldn't make myself cut deep. I've known other kids who can do that, but I can't. I did it once before and that's when I wound up in the hospital. I still have scars. See." She rolled up her sleeve exposing several, pink, puckered lines on her forearm. "These were the worst." She said, showing them off like old battle wounds.

"Emily, where'd you get the knife?" I asked.

"I smuggled it in. It's from my foster mom's house. My stuff wasn't really searched when I checked in last night. I brought it with me because I thought if they found it when I got here, they'd send me back to my foster mom."

"Why aren't you with your foster mom anymore?"

"I don't really know. Well, I guess I do. I think it was mostly because I was keeping to myself and kind of being rude to her. I wasn't doing my chores and stuff, like I used to."

"That's pretty much what was communicated to me as well. I understand you were checked out by medical last night and none of your cuts were more than superficial."

"Yeah. Like I said, I couldn't do it. I'm sad and frustrated with stuff, but I don't want to die."

"So, you're telling me you won't hurt yourself?"

"Yeah."

"I'm glad to hear that, but you know you're still going to be kept on suicide watch."

"I've been told." She rolled her eyes. We spent the next twenty minutes discussing her safety and she agreed she would let staff know if she ever felt like hurting herself again.

"Getting back to why we're here. I meant what I said last night. I really would like to know more about you. I thought we could spend some time talking about your life and how you got here from West Virginia."

Emily was silent for several minutes. Finally, she looked at me and said, "If you really want to understand things, I guess I could talk about stuff."

I nodded. "We can start where ever you want."

She sighed. "I grew up in Buckhannon, West Virginia. It's a small town in the northern part of the state, closer to Pennsylvania than Virginia. It's the kind of town where everybody knows everybody." she paused, "You know what I mean?"

"Yeah, I do." I said.

"I remember being happy when I lived there. We lived in this old farmhouse. It was white with green trim and had a really huge wraparound porch. My brother John and I used to sit on it for hours in the summer, playing cards, drinking orange soda and eating watermelon. Then we'd have seed spitting contests. See who could come closest to hitting my mom's rose bushes. Sounds kind of disgusting I know." She smiled. "Anyway, we'd always wait for my dad to come home. He managed a grocery store, so he'd always sneak us candy before dinner. Peppermint patties and peanut butter cups were our favorites. He'd tell us not to tell mom because he'd get in trouble, but she always knew. I guess the chocolate smears on our faces gave us away."

Emily continued to reflect on her memories and then her expression changed drastically. She disclosed, "Everything changed so fast. I know you probably know about what happened - what's in the report. But that's only some of it. It was a lot worse than what anybody knows...my mom knows though and that's what made her crazy, turn to booze and try to off herself. She couldn't handle it. She's not as strong as I am."

She looked down at her shoes and whispered. "That's all I want to say right now, but let's just say my life has turned to shit."

Chapter 4

I pulled into our gravel driveway just after 6:00 p.m. Our house was a red brick bungalow perched on a sloped periwinkle covered yard. In the summer, it was a thick, dark green blanket speckled with purple flowers. Only vestiges of its past splendor remained. Now, it was no more than a dry mass of brown, crusty leaves courtesy of our neighbor's oak tree. A single wrought iron railing flanked four steps to our fire engine red front door, which was framed by two small white arched windows on either side.

Elliot and I had lived here since we married four years earlier. It had been one of the few houses we could afford and we were willing to complete the necessary home renovations to leave the cramped quarters of apartment living behind. In the past, our home had always seemed cozy and warm, but recently it was beginning to feel frigid and uninviting.

As I entered, the hardwood planks creaked beneath my feet and I surveyed the space. Our kitchen, dining and living areas all bled into each other, not defined structurally as separate rooms. Instead, it was a single open space filled with furniture, primarily donated from family and treasures unearthed at yard sales. We had a wood burning fireplace at one end, encircled by a sofa and two arm chairs. Our kitchen area with the dining table was at the opposite end opening up into our backyard via a sliding glass door. The house was messy, last night's dinner dishes still stacked in the sink, a reflection of our hectic lifestyles.

I put down my briefcase, briefly stopping to pet Snowy as he snaked between my legs. I went through the mail, the typical junk, and then changed into jeans and a t-shirt. I assumed Elliot was going to be late at the lab working on his dissertation, so I meandered into the kitchen, examined the contents of the fridge and scrounged up dinner. I plunked myself down in front of the television and channel surfed while munching on a turkey sandwich and leftover potato salad. It resurrected my taste buds to eat at least one meal which hadn't come out of a vending machine.

My eyelids felt heavy and soon I succumbed to sleep despite my will to watch the end of *Casablanca*. Several hours later, I was roused by the scraping sound of the front door as Elliot returned home. I propped myself up on my elbow with some effort as he entered.

"What time is it?" I mumbled.

"After twelve. I decided to stay until I got all my data analyzed. I have got to get this thing defended before I go on internship next month." Elliot stated.

He threw his black, gore-tex Eddie Bauer jacket on the chair and I followed his large frame into the kitchen. He was six feet tall, solid and when he hugged you, your whole body was enveloped in warm, protective armor. His face was square, with a strong jaw and a full mouth that revealed white, almost perfectly straight teeth barring one that veered left and helped form a crooked smile. His eyes were hazel, with flecks of gold, which looked the color of leaves in autumn and always betrayed the intensity of his emotions. He stood hunched over the sink, filled a glass with ice water and took a long gulp.

26

"You eat?" I said, yawning.

"Greasy, cold pizza." he responded, putting his finger in his mouth pretending to gag. He stretched his arms up in the air almost touching the ceiling.

"Sorry about the whole key thing. I found them in my jacket pocket. I forgot I put them there." He stated.

"No problem. Things have been stressful lately." I said.

"Yeah, they have." He replied. "Speaking of which, you actually look tired tonight. Why don't you go to bed? I'm going to screw around on the computer before I call it a night."

"I was just heading to bed, but do you have a minute? I really wanted to talk to you tonight."

"Grace", he said with the slightest hint of irritation creeping into his voice, "I'm tired. I just want to relax. I don't have the energy for one of your intense discussions."

I looked at him without responding.

"OK…What is it?" he surrendered.

"Well, I've been thinking that maybe I could go to San Diego with you...get a job there." I suggested.

"Can I ask why you are bringing this up again? We've already exhausted the topic. I thought we agreed you going is not an option?"

"I know we agreed upon that initially, but why can't we revisit the issue? It's not an impossible scenario."

"But you're licensed here, in Michigan." He protested. "You just got a good job...a decent paying job. Getting licensed in California for the year is impractical. It would be different if we were planning on moving out there, but internship is only a year and then we're not sure where we're going to end up after that."

"I know, but I worry about splitting up again." I confessed.

We had lived apart when I was completing my internship out of state. Elliot had remained in Michigan and I had moved to South Carolina for the year. The result had been the acquisition of, not only a PhD, but a marriage that was on the brink of dissolution. It had taken vast amounts of strength and commitment to resuscitate it.

"Last time it didn't work out too well and I'm worried about everything falling apart again."

"Shit Grace! I can't believe you're bringing that up? Anything else you want to throw in my face." Color started to crawl up his neck and change his face from white to crimson. "It's not like our marital problems were just my fault. You did play a part."

"I know." I answered, raising my voice. "But how you dealt with things was lousy, depressed or not."

"Look, I'm not going to talk about this right now and by the way, thanks for stressing me out. Like I don't have enough pressure already. I just wanted to enjoy the rest of my night."

"Sorry, but our relationship has been tough lately and I don't think splitting up is the answer. Too bad you don't think it's worth talking about."

"That's not what I said. What I said was that I didn't want to talk about it right now. And our relationship is strained because we have a lot of stressors. Throwing away our only stable income won't help matters. Maybe you're OK with it, but I'd like to do more than scrape by and struggle to pay our mortgage." He fired back.

"I know." I said, my eyes starting to well up.

"And by the way, the next time you spill dirt all over the living room, how about cleaning it up. That crap was hard to clean up - all that dirt. I had to throw the plant out."

"I was in a rush, but I didn't knock over the plant. It was like that before I left. Snowy must have..."

"Yeah, blame it on the cat. It amazes me how you can take on all this responsibility at work, but at home it's always someone else's fault. I can't trust you to do a damn thing around here." Elliot responded.

He turned and left the room and I saw the bedroom door shut. My tears started to flow, reflecting my anger not only at Elliot, but myself. There were always so many things I wanted to say, but didn't. I held back and then I ended up bringing them up at the worst possible time. I knew there was no point to confront him any further right now, things would just escalate. We were both tired. We'd have to make attempts at resolution tomorrow. Things typically seemed less complicated in the light of day.

Treatment team meetings were held weekly and were mandatory for all clinical staff including myself, the therapists, the staff nurse and the two consulting psychiatrists. The residential director, intake coordinator, residential supervisors and assistant supervisors also attended, providing information regarding the behavior of the clients on the units. Unfortunately, instead of being a constructive forum for reviewing cases and programmatic issues, it usually ended up being a three hour bitch-fest. This was only tempered when county social workers, family members or program administrators made an appearance, which was an infrequent occurrence. Most of the time, it was a free for all for rude and whiny behavior.

The reasons the clients' county social workers rarely attended the meetings were threefold. First, they were provided with a faxed copy of the treatment team report the same day and could dispense with the hassle of leaving their offices. Second, their caseloads were enormous and much of their time was already spent in the car traveling to placement or school visits. Third, inevitably they were asked about whether they had found a long term placement for their client. The incorrect response brought a certain scrutiny.

This was particularly painful if Barbara, the residential program director, was attending the treatment team meeting. She typically started off oozing with charm and interest, appearing to listen intently during the case presentation. This would be followed by a more authoritative stance asking about what progress was being made to move the client to their permanent placement. Regardless of the social worker's response, short of having a placement finalized, Barbara made the same comments. She discussed how the county needed to remember that Ellis House was a short term placement and that she had carte blanche to give a seven day notice at anytime she saw fit. This was all, of course, said with the utmost care to maintain her reputation as a team player.

A seven day notice was an all too common event in this business. Any placement, be it a foster home or group home, was able to let the county know they were no longer able to maintain a child with seven days notice. It was typically done if the child was making no progress, too difficult to manage or falling apart emotionally. It was also used as a threat in instances where a client had been maintained in a short term placement for an extended period of time.

Today, the conference room was stuffy and smelled like stale air. There was very little leg and elbow room which added to the general discomfort of attending the meeting. The chairs were narrow, brown vinyl with silver legs and little padding. Recently, three ceiling fans had been installed, but they had done little to ease the discomfort.

"Let's get started." I stated, raising my voice to compensate for the increasingly loud chatter in the room. "We're already ten minutes behind schedule and we have a lot of cases to review today given we had eight new admissions last week. Our four priority cases today are as follows," I said, looking briefly around the room. "Nate Jackson admitted on October 1st. He's an eight-year-old Caucasian boy removed from his mother's home. Father's whereabouts are unknown. No extended family living in Michigan. The county social worker is doing a search for viable out of state placements. Nate is experiencing symptoms consistent with Posttraumatic Stress Disorder including frequent nightmares, flashbacks, intrusive thoughts, irritability and hypervigilance. He witnessed his mother place his 18-month-old sister in the oven, turn on the heat and prop a chair against the door so she couldn't get out. Nate's mother threatened he would be next if he made any attempts to help his sister.

"Jesus Christ." I heard somebody say.

"Did the girl die?" Max, an assistant shift supervisor asked.

"Yeah, she died." I replied. "Following the incident, Nate was immediately removed from his mother's care. She's currently detained at the county jail awaiting sentencing and is not allowed contact with Nate under any circumstances." I reported.

"Piece of work she is." One of the therapists, Steve, stated. Steve was a good therapist, but a bit of a loud mouth and a bit of a clown. That's probably why the kids loved him.

"Steve, do you mind?" I said, and continued. "Case number two is Jacob Brown admitted on September 30th. He is a nine-year-old African-American boy who had been living with his grandmother. Both parents are incarcerated for drug use and possession. The grandmother recently contacted Child Protective Services after he stabbed the family cat to death with a knife. Prior to that, he had been torturing small animals. The grandmother said she found several crudely dissected birds and squirrels in his bedroom closet. He has also been sneaking out of the house at night and has engaged in fire setting. The most recent fire was started in a trash container in the bathroom. His grandmother managed to put it out before it got out of control."

"What is this place, a breeding ground for serial killers?" Steve asked.

I shot him a stern glance and continued. "His behavior at school parallels his behavior at home and his teachers describe him as a bully. He was recently suspended for pulling a knife on a first grader because she stuck her tongue out at him. Jacob's grandmother has been authorized by the county to continue to have contact with him." I concluded.

"Case number three is Raymond Reid admitted on September 27th. As we all know, we've been dealing with him for the last couple of weeks and he's a challenge on the units, very influential with his peers, disrespectful towards staff and not motivated to work his program. He's a seventeen-year-old, actually almost eighteen-year-old, biracial male. He turns eighteen in May. We need to get him transitioned to another placement no later than his eighteenth birthday. Obviously, he can't just walk out of here without a plan. I know we've all been working hard to coordinate something with his county worker. However, despite how hard it may be, I am not willing to extend his stay past his eighteenth birthday. His county worker has already asked if this was an option.

For anyone who isn't aware of his history, Ray lived with his maternal aunt for almost five years. She stated she couldn't manage him. He came and went as he pleased. She reported she found weed in his room and there were allegations he had molested a neighbor's daughter. Over the course of the last six months, he's rotated through four placements because he AWOLs. He typically returns to the facility several weeks later. Needless to say, by this time, his bed's been closed and he is placed where ever there is an opening."

"Where does he go when he AWOLs?" John, one of the therapists asked.

"He says he hangs out with friends." I continued. "His father is incarcerated for dealing meth and he was removed from his mother's care after she stuck his hand on a hot plate as punishment for smoking weed. He experienced first degree burns on his left hand. Scarring on his hand is still very apparent. Mom doesn't seem to have any remorse for her actions. She says she doesn't want her son to end up being a dealer like his father."

"Original..." Steve mumbled.

"Ray stated he started drinking and smoking pot when he was eight to cope with his father who was physically and emotionally abusive with both Ray and his mother. Ray was frequently woken up in the middle of the night and forced to do housework, sometimes to clean out the fridge, or wash the floors, and on one occasion he was made to trim the lawn with cuticle scissors. Unfortunately, after his father was incarcerated Ray's life didn't get any better. Mom had a steady trail of boyfriends in and out of the house. They treated Ray no better than his father had and his mother became more abusive over time in an effort to manage his acting out..."

Corrine, a residential shift supervisor, interrupted. "Can I ask why we admitted such a high risk kid to the facility? There's no way to successfully manage him. I mean what if he AWOLs and takes another kid with him? Things could get ugly. My guess is when he AWOLs, he gets high, has sex. We had that happen before, remember?"

Several years ago, before I started working at Ellis House, a seventeen-year-old boy AWOLed with a thirteen-year-old girl. She became pregnant. Ellis House was almost shut down because staff hadn't provided adequate supervision. Several staff who had been employed at the group home at the time nodded their heads. Corrine went on, "It was a mess, licensing, the media, everyone talking about what a shoddy program we were running. County workers wouldn't refer any cases so we housed only the toughest kids, kids who should have been at juvie. And they were right. The whole mess was our error. We screwed up."

"I understand that's why the AWOL procedure was made more stringent." I responded. Corrine nodded.

"OK, we need to move on." I suggested. "Finally, Emily Rowan who was admitted to the facility yesterday. I'm sure you are all aware of the incident which occurred last night. Briefly, she was able to sneak out of the building and climb…"

"Excuse me Dr. Morgan," Susan announced knocking on the door as she entered. "Barbara says she needs to see you immediately."

"We're in treatment team."

"I know, but she says it's urgent."

"Let her know I'll be there momentarily." I said, irritated.

I turned to Jamie and asked, "Could you take over?"

"Sure." She answered. Jamie was my second in command. She had completed her Masters degree in clinical psychology and was licensed accordingly. She was only a semester away from defending her dissertation and despite her hectic schedule was able to commit twenty hours a week to the group home.

Her physical appearance was a direct reflection of her personality. She wore minimal make up, dressed in neutral colors and her chestnut hair fell straight around her shoulders in a blunt cut. She was efficient, reliable, had an excellent work ethic and a seemingly endless reserve of energy.

"Excuse me." I stated as I left the room.

Barbara Levy did not look pleased as I entered her office. She was a heavy set woman, with pale, almost translucent skin which was emphasized by her lack of makeup and dark clothing. Her eyes were dark and looked like tiny currants stuffed into soft, white dough. Her lips were thin and colorless. I tried to remember the last time I'd seen her smile and couldn't.

Barbara was the director of the residential program and masterfully fueled the antagonistic relationship between clinical and residential staff. However, she would die before admitting it. Her battle cry was, "We all need to work together as a team." However, she flew solo most of the time. Barbara was extraordinarily careful as to how she presented herself publically, but within the confines of her office her agenda became more apparent and she typically dispensed with any pleasantries.

"Grace, sit down." An order, not a request, but I obliged.

She continued. "I heard you met with Emily last night after her AWOL. My understanding is she was making some rather derogatory statements regarding our residential staff. Specifically, she was making comments that she was unjustly restrained? Is that correct?"

I knew she was already aware of the answer and thought to myself. Not this bullshit again.

I responded. "Apparently, she was told upon admission she could contact her mother that evening if she was having a difficult time. She chose to do so, however, when she made the request it was denied. Subsequently, she became distressed and verbally aggressive with staff on the unit. She also made a derogatory comment to one of the staff." Barbara started to speak, but I cut her off and continued. "Specifically, the verbal aggression started when Tristan attempted to de-escalate her. His attempt failed." Tristan was a recently hired child care worker with no previous experience using his night shift position to pay his way through college. "The shift supervisor was called and made the decision to restrain her and place her in one of the quiet rooms."

Quiet room was a misnomer because when it was serving its

purpose, it was rarely quiet. There were six in the facility. Two containment areas were provided for each unit. They were approximately eight by eight feet, with dark, blue carpet on the floors and walls. There were no windows except for a small wired pane in the door to observe the client. They functioned to maintain clients who had become dangerous to themselves or others and were separated from the rest of the unit. They were most frequently used for clients who had become physically aggressive and required physical containment until de-escalation could successfully occur. Needless to say, there was typically a lot of kicking and screaming to be heard until the kids calmed down.

Clients who had reached this point of aggression were typically escorted by two staff to the quiet room if they did not make the choice to go voluntarily. In Emily's case, she was escorted to one of the quiet rooms and staff had shut the door. According to Emily's report, it was to avoid listening to her scream and to punish her for her verbal aggression. According to staff, it was to maintain her safety.

"Don't you think Ana did what was needed?" Barbara asked.

"I believe if you tell a client you will allow them to do something you need to follow through. I don't think she should have been denied the opportunity to speak to her mother when she was told she could regardless of her behavior and it is my-"

"It sounds like you're taking a client's word over that of the supervisor?" Barbara interrupted.

"I believe staff should be consistent with what they tell the clients and this-"

"So, you're saying staff is not consistent?"

"I'm saying this all could have been avoided if staff had communicated with each other and we wouldn't have ended up with a restraint and a kid threatening suicide on our roof. I also think we should look into the fact the building was essentially unmanned for a significant period of time"

"That's a separate issue." Barbara said abruptly. "Our staff would not restrain a client unless they absolutely had to."

"I think in this circumstance it could have been avoided and staff didn't need to restrain her. No one even called for clinical back up to help diffuse the situation."

"Well, Grace, you have only been at the facility for a few months. You have no idea how it all works. I would caution you not to take the word of the client over the word of the staff or to minimize our ability to manage crises without the aid of the therapists. We always follow protocol here and if there is any deviation it would be approved by administration."

She looked up from the paperwork on her desk and continued, "I'll be blunt. I don't like your attitude and you must remember the residential program drives this facility. It is clearly the priority over clinical work."

"Are we done?" I asked. "I need to get back to treatment team. Maybe if nothing else, you could have maintenance clean up the quiet rooms? They smell like urine." I rose without waiting for a response and left the room.

Barbara quickly rose and shut her office door. She picked up her phone and dialed. She spoke into the receiver, "We've got a problem."

Chapter 5

Corrine left treatment team with a knot in her belly. The anxiety she felt was not about AWOLs and the management problems at the group home. That was typical fare. However, she wished it could have been that simple. Corrine had a problem that should have never been hers, but circumstances dictated differently. Now the question was, how best to handle it?

She had played numerous scenarios out in her head. Initially, she had thought about direct confrontation, but this would accomplish nothing.

If she were to follow protocol, she would seek advice from her supervisor, Barbara. However, she guessed talking to Barbara would go one of two ways, neither of which would be positive. She would either be quickly dismissed as a nuisance or, worse, she would be fired for spreading rumors. Corrine knew Barbara would not tolerate the program's reputation much less her own being tarnished in even the slightest way.

Going above Barbara's head was unlikely to be any more

effective. Administration would pretend the problem didn't exist and hope it would go away. After all, like in any business, people didn't like complications, particularly those which had potentially damaging consequences. However, the problem was, she knew what she had seen. There was no mistake.

Corrine had become fairly well acquainted with Dr. Morgan over the last couple of months. She seemed to be invested in the program and it was obvious she cared about the kids. Dr. Morgan needed to know what was going on and deserved to be told, but this...this was different. She didn't know her well enough to know how she would handle it...maybe she would tell Barbara...who knew?

She'd considered going to the police, the licensing board even directly to Child Protective Services. Maybe she could file an anonymous complaint? But would they take it seriously? And who would blame them if they didn't? Even if her allegations were taken seriously, would there be anything anyone could do about it? After all, there would be no way to substantiate her claims. All they would have is her word. Before she did anything else, she needed proof.

Corrine was a strong woman who had learned to survive at an early age. She had been an only child raised in poverty on Chicago's south side. Unfortunately, she had suffered more after the death of her mother than she ever thought imaginable. Her mother, who had been employed as a clerk at a local convenience store, had caught a stray bullet in a drive-by-shooting walking home from work. Wrong place, wrong time. Simple as that. Corrine had then been left with her father, who was only motivated by one thing - alcohol. Looking back, she couldn't remember a time either before or after her mother's death when he hadn't spent most of his day sitting in the powder blue recliner in their living room, drinking from a seemingly bottomless jug of Wild Turkey. Desperate to find a way to support his habit, he had prostituted his daughter to his friends, acquaintances and anyone else he could find. She had kept their secret for years before finally breaking down and telling her friend as they smoked pot on her front porch.

A week later, she watched her father being taken away from their home in shackles and shoved into a police cruiser, while she, Corrine, had been dumped in a county facility awaiting placement to a foster home. She sat there for almost a year until a paternal uncle had rescued her and given her hope. For that she was grateful. For the other, she had become a survivor with a steely disposition who believed she could manage almost anything.

Corrine knew she couldn't ignore what she had stumbled upon, even though she sometimes wished she could. After all, why couldn't it have happened to someone else? She knew it was terrible to think like that. It just made her life so much more complicated. However, right now was not the time for self-pity, she needed to figure out how best to move forward.

Following my meeting with Barbara, I decided to discuss the concerns raised in treatment team with Sam, our residential intake coordinator. Sam was the facility's gatekeeper. He chose the admissions to Ellis House. Corrine was right to be concerned about admitting Raymond Reid. My guess was that Sam had knowingly made a poor choice just to make sure the beds were full before he left for the day. He had a tough job, no one would argue that. There was pressure from administration to keep the beds at full occupancy to maximize revenue. Leaving a bed open even for as little as twenty-four hours was a significant financial loss.

Unfortunately, it wasn't as simple as accepting a referral and admitting the client to the program. The problems associated with obtaining appropriate referrals were numerous. Clients were occasionally referred directly from foster homes, families or other group homes, but the vast majority of referrals came from the county holding tank which housed children who had already lost a placement and had no other place to go. The county facility was so overcrowded that sometimes clients had to sleep on the floor of the cafeteria. There were no mental health services, no recreation services; it was nothing beyond a place to eat and sleep. Additionally, the facility was unattractive, built of depressing grey cinder block surrounded on the outside by cracked uneven paving set off by a chain link fence. Despite years of talk, even minimal improvements such as laying down sod, providing a playground, and adding services which extended beyond the basics, never happened.

Thus, county workers who had no choice but to place clients in county holding became desperate to get their clients out and placed in short term programs like Ellis House. Unfortunately, clients who wound up at the county site were typically the most difficult to manage. This is where the tug of war began. The county workers made desperate pleas to have their most damaged clients admitted and the residential intake coordinators wanted only to admit those clients who were least likely to disrupt the stability of the unit. The high risk kids who were dangerous and frequently AWOLed were a challenge to maintain and required intensive round the clock one-on-one supervision.

This was why to ensure the stability of the units, residential intake coordinators needed to be assertive and know how to negotiate. It was difficult because typically no more than 24 hours notice was given before a client was discharged. Even worse, county workers sometimes just showed up on the front steps and demanded clients to be discharged to a new placement. This left the residential intake coordinators scrambling to fill the bed. Unfortunately, Sam was a poor residential intake coordinator. Initially, he had worked hard, but after several years in the position he became lazy, preferring to take the heat for a poor referral rather than make the effort to gain a good one.

I knocked on Sam's door. As I entered I saw him quickly pull the plug on his solitaire game. "Just so you know we spent time in treatment team focusing on Ray. Remember admitting him?" I commented visibly irritated and made a point to stare at his computer screen. "Do you have any idea how hard it is to manage a seventeen-year-old boy on a unit filled with significantly younger kids, six of whom have been sexually abused? Are you aware that he was accused of molesting his thirteen-year-old neighbor?"

"Had no choice. I had to admit Ray. He was the only referral I got. Besides that sexual abuse stuff, it was never proven, just speculation." Sam responded flatly.

"But why take the risk at all? Not to mention the guy's always on the unit throwing around crass sexual comments, and we found porn stashed in his dresser...Oh, yeah, and he reports that he AWOLs so he can get high and have sex."

Sam said nothing.

I continued. "Like Emily, he came in with no paperwork, so there's no indication of what else may be going on. And my guess is that he's not the most accurate with his self-report. When a client is admitted, we need their medical records, school reports and background information...do I need to go on?"

Sam didn't bother to respond; he just let me continue talking. I had a stray suspicion that although he was looking at me, he wasn't listening. Short of being fired, I don't think he really cared much about anything.

"Come on Sam, paperwork." I pleaded. "Even if you can't get a decent referral and take only what is handed to you, please get the paperwork done. So, we can do our jobs, so the staff can do their jobs, so we have the pertinent information to help the clients as much as possible and know what we are dealing with."

"Fine." Sam finally responded. Unfortunately, my hunch was that he would continue to do what he always did, almost nothing. That's why he didn't even bother to argue, just too damn lazy.

Following my exercise in futility, I returned to my office to find Jamie hunched over her desk working on a report. She looked up as I entered and managed a weak smile.

"What's the matter?" I asked sitting down at my desk.

"Nothing really...well, actually, do you have any idea what it's like to run treatment team when you're not there?"

"I could take a guess?" I said.

"Everyone's so rude. Not the clinical staff, but residential."

"Such as?"

"OK, we're doing case presentations and nobody even bothers to listen. Paul had to compete with everyone else's conversations when he was doing his case presentation. When I addressed it, people just rolled their eyes and continued talking. Oh, excuse me, some people were courteous enough to stop talking and start writing notes back and forth instead. And when recommendations were made for how to facilitate treatment on the units people got so defensive. The same old excuses are made. They are short staffed and overworked, so if the therapists want anything done, we should drop everything and help out on the units."

"We'll address it at the next treatment team, but unfortunately the behavior at the meeting is a reflection of how the clinical program is viewed, irrelevant and expendable," I said.

"I know. Honestly, it's hard to deal with. Sometimes I wonder why I even bother." Jamie responded.

There was a knock at the door and Ana stuck her head in. She was a recent staff addition who was enrolled in the social work program at the university. She was new to residential work and her intentions were good. However, her expectations were frequently unrealistic and she expected too much from the clients. She had also been accused of having some problems with boundaries and sending mixed messages to the clients. It was a common failing to people new to the field, wanting to be a friend, but having to be a disciplinarian to the client. The bottom line was she openly disclosed her emotions and personal information whether or not it was appropriate to do so. My understanding was that it was being addressed by Barbara before it became a major problem. My guess was Ana would not take the criticism well.

She was tall, bottom heavy, with long brown hair and chocolate brown eyes. She had a loud voice and laughed frequently which made her whole body shake. I did not care for her. I gestured her to come in.

"Dr. Morgan, I just finished speaking with Barbara and she told me you disagreed with my decision to restrain Emily."

"Yes." I responded.

"Really!" She said incredulously. "Well, I think that's ridiculous. I don't know how you can even make a statement like that. You weren't even there. Emily was aggressive."

"My understanding was it was only verbal."

"It was more than verbal."

"Really? How?"

"She called Danny a buffalo."

I saw Jamie suppressing a smile. "That's only an insult, Ana." I said.

"She was threatening me." Ana replied.

"Still only verbal." I countered.

"I thought she was going to assault me."

"Let's say she did. How did you justify doing a wall restraint when she was already contained in the quiet room? You could have just backed off and left her in there. She would have likely started to calm down on her own, but instead you just kept antagonizing her. Not to mention, none of this would have ever happened if you had just let her call her mom in the first place."

"She hadn't earned the privilege yet."

"She shouldn't have to earn that. It's her right. It's like her right to speak with her therapist confidentially or her right to call her attorney."

"Yeah, I know all about the attorney. I already talked to him." She paused for a moment. "It really surprises me that you have no idea what it takes to run a unit. And moreover, life would be a lot easier around here if we ever got any help from the therapists. But whenever we ask for help, all we get is resistance."

"Nobody even asked for clinical intervention." I stated.

"That's because you guys give it so grudgingly, we might as well do it ourselves." She turned and stalked out of the room.

"That was pleasant. I liked the buffalo bit though." Jamie commented and went back to her report.

I looked at the work which had piled up on my desk. I could at least try to make some headway. I planned to remain in my office for the rest of the day and called Susan to confirm I had no more appointments scheduled. As I was hanging up, I heard a clicking sound. Had someone been listening to my conversation?

"Hello?" I asked. No response. I shrugged and went back to my paperwork. Immediately, my phone rang and I picked up.

"Hello." I said again.

"Hi. It's Corrine." Corrine had started at the group home the same time as Barry. They had grown apart professionally because of their different supervisory styles. Unlike Barry, who was strict and extremely rule governed, Corrine was flexible with clients and made significant attempts to work with the clinical staff to benefit each clients' progress. Corrine was a petite African American woman with flawless skin who carried herself with grace and confidence. Looking at her, it wouldn't be expected she could run a unit as seamlessly as she did, especially with as few staff as she typically had to run her shift.

"Did you just try to call me?"

"No. Why?"

"Never mind." I said.

"You better get up here," she said. "Emily's on her way to being restrained."

I quickly hung up and hurried to the unit. This time I didn't notice the faint clicking as I put the receiver on the cradle.

As soon as I got to the second floor, I could hear Emily screaming "Don't touch me you asshole! Don't touch me! You can't make me do anything I don't want to do." There were three staff positioned outside her door and as I reached her bedroom, I could see three more inside, including Barry who appeared to be the focus of Emily's anger. I entered the room and was greeted by his furious stare. There were clothes thrown all over the room and there was a large hole in the plaster where she had successfully kicked it in.

"We can handle the situation," Barry snapped. "I didn't call for any clinical intervention."

"You didn't, but Corrine did." I turned to Emily who was still screaming at Barry.

"I don't want to go to the quiet room and you can't make me! Everybody get out of my face. Just leave me alone!" She yelled.

She had a point. Residential staff sometimes got overzealous. More people than necessary got involved in a crisis and instead of providing the client with a sense of support, it had the paradoxical effect of making the client feel ganged up on and trapped. The unfortunate result was an escalation in the aggressive behavior rather than the intended reduction.

"Emily?" I said, but she didn't look at me. "Emily?" I repeated. Again nothing. "Emily?" I repeated a third time, again slowly and calmly attempting to make eye contact and get her attention.

"Emily, if you can stop screaming, you can stay here and calm down. You have to stop disrupting the unit."

"I'm not going to the quiet room. Get out of my face!" she screamed.

"Emily, look at me." I said. Finally, she turned to look at me.

"Just listen to me. Tone it down. Stop disrupting the unit and you can stay here. You can get what you're asking for. Just calm down."

She became quiet and I asked staff to leave. They did, with the exception of Barry who maintained his position.

"OK, Barry, I can take it from here."

He didn't move and I repeated myself. Finally, he left mumbling something under his breath which sounded remarkably like, "Stupid bitch," and "Mind your own business."

"What was that all about?" I asked Emily.

She was now sitting on her bed, chewing on her fingernails.

"I got mad."

"I can see that. Why did you get mad?" I asked.

"Because they said they were going to take away my phone privileges. And I'm stressed out because my mom still hasn't called. Then Barry came in and threatened to restrain me if I didn't calm down."

"Are you sure that's what he meant? Were you physically aggressive?"

"No, I was just really mad and cussing."

"And throwing stuff around your room and kicking the walls." I clarified.

"I wasn't going to hurt anyone, but I guess I was screaming and throwing stuff around."

"Is that why your phone privileges were threatened in the first place?"

"Yeah."

"Emily, we've talked about this. I know you have a lot to be angry about and you're going through a really hard time, but you're not going to be respected unless you show respect."

"I know." She said, sullenly.

"You know you're going to have to clean up your room and fix the damage."

"I know. But I'm so worried. I still haven't heard from my mom. She usually calls me back right away. I haven't actually talked to her in almost a month. I've just gotten the messages she's left. I called my social worker to see if she could find out what's going on, but I still haven't heard from her. What if something happened?"

I resisted the temptation to tell her everything would be alright. Who knew if it would be? However, we did agree she would focus on working her program for the rest of the day and I would attempt to contact the county regarding her mother. We would meet for therapy the following morning. Hopefully, I would have some answers by then.

I left Emily in Corrine's capable hands, returned to my office and contacted her county social worker. Half an hour later I received a call back. Unfortunately, the news was not good. Emily's mother, Maggie, had been found by her neighbor early this morning. The neighbor had let herself into the apartment after there was no response to her repeated knocking. Immediately, upon entering the apartment she had noticed the foul smell and saw the apartment was filthy. Trash containers were overflowing, the toilet was full of urine and vomit, and empty liquor and beer bottles we scattered everywhere.

Maggie was found unconscious, lying face down. Blood had trickled from her wrists to form pools on either side of her body. She had used a small paring knife which was still within her reach on the dirty, blood stained linoleum floor. The paramedics had rushed her to the E.R. Once stabilized, Maggie would be transferred to the psychiatric unit. My guess was she would be there for a while. I certainly hoped what Emily told me during our first session was true. That she was stronger than her mother.

Chapter 6

By the time I returned home, my head was throbbing. I anticipated it would only get worse as Elliot and I had not communicated since our argument the previous day. I didn't know if I had the energy to sift through all the emotional garbage which just seemed to keep piling up.

My body ached, and I turned on the shower making the water as hot as I could tolerate. I peeled off my clothes and enveloped myself in the cubicle of steam. The hard burning drops of water waged war on the knots in my back and neck, dissolving much of the tension which lingered from the day. I felt rejuvenated and strong enough to face Elliot when I finally came out thirty minutes later.

He was sitting in the backyard when I walked into the kitchen, his back to the door. He sat in the faded brown wicker chair we'd purchased at a yard sale earlier in the year. His lap was covered with a wool blanket as he watched the blazing fire. A book rested on his lap, a beer on the arm of the chair.

The backyard was the best part of our property. It wasn't a large yard, but it was extremely private with a six foot fence blocking any possible view of the neighbors. There were two sugar maples which glowed different shades of yellow, orange and deep red in the height of autumn. I stepped through the screen door onto the broad, uneven stone patio. A cool breeze touched my face, but was tempered by the warmth from the fire.

"Hi." I said tentatively.

"Hi." Elliot replied.

He turned around to face me and I said, "Look before you say anything, I'm really sorry about our fight yesterday, especially since you're leaving in a few weeks."

"Me too. I meant to call you today, but you know how it goes. Seems like most of the hours of the day are swallowed up by some giant black hole. It never seems like there's enough time to get anything done."

I sat down beside him and said nothing. We didn't speak for what seemed like hours watching the flames of the fire lick the grate. Elliot took my hand and we sat a while longer.

"You're right about us separating. It's not practical for me to go with you. It's just sometimes I think that even if I could go, you wouldn't want me to." I confessed.

"It's not that. Do you have any idea how expensive it would be? We're in so much debt already and I know you want to have kids someday."

Children. It was a sore spot in our marriage. When we married, I wanted children right away. Elliot wanted to wait, so we waited. We waited until I finished internship, until we worked out our problems, until I was licensed and until I had a stable income. Now, it would be until Elliot completed internship and until he became licensed. My fear was that we would just continue to postpone it. After all, was there ever a good time? However, there was no point thinking about that right now and I shifted my focus back to Elliot.

"Remember, it's just a year." He said.

Just a year. The phrase kept reverberating in my head. A lot

49

could happen in a year. It did last time.

"A lot can happen in a year." I said skeptically.

"Doesn't have to." He said a slight edge to his voice now.

He was right. I needed to have a little more faith. "I guess you're right. There is no reason why we can't do it."

"Right." He said cheerfully.

"I can fly out there and you can come out here on your breaks." I stated optimistically.

He put his arm around me and kissed the top of my head.

"Come on. Let's get dinner ready. I'm starved."

Elliot may have had his faults, but cooking wasn't one of them. We ate grilled salmon with wild rice and steamed asparagus for dinner. I indulged in two glasses of Chardonnay which immediately made me sleepy.

I stretched out on the couch and Elliot soon followed, leaving the dishes for later. I put my head on his lap and he played with my hair and gently kissed my face and neck. He moved to my mouth and kissed me gently then more deeply.

He whispered, "We can do this Grace. We've done it once, we can do it again." Then, he eased me off the couch and guided me to the bedroom.

Later that night, the dream descended on me like a vicious storm.

Instead of subsiding, the pain in my head only intensifies. He keeps me on the ground as he gags me. Then, he tightly binds my wrists and ankles with a thick, stiff cord. After what seems an excruciating eternity, he pulls me to my feet and drags me in the direction of his truck. I'm on the edge of panic. My heart is pounding, ready to explode. I can't fall apart. Then, I'll have no chance. I keep telling myself I have to control my breathing. Tears run down my face and my body shakes of its own volition, goose bumps forming on my flesh.

The film in my head repeats and I visualize my husband bound, gagged and bleeding . . . Stop it! Stop it! Stop it! Stop seeing things like that . . . you don't know that he's not alive. Get those pictures out of your head . . . Out! Out! Out! But they do not go away.

I feel my stomach churning and taste the remains of my dinner as it climbs up my throat. I choke it back as I'm forced into the bed of his truck. The metal is ice cold on my back and I feel my legs pulled toward the rear as he binds me to the vehicle.

He climbs back on top of me and slips his rough, cracked hand up my shirt and under my bra, cupping my breast. I squeeze my eyes shut and cringe. He smiles in response. "Aw baby, don't do that. We're just getting started. But if you insist, we can save the fun for later. How 'bout now we go on a little trip? We need to take you back home."

With that, he throws a wet, slimy tarp over me which has the strong aroma of manure. I hear him jump down from the truck bed. The door slams as he climbs into the cab. I can smell the fumes from the tailpipe as he turns on the ignition and pulls out onto the deserted road.

My night's sleep had been riddled with anxiety. The following morning wasn't shaping up to be any better. I took several gulps of coffee as I sat down beside Emily and passed her a box of tissues. She took one look at my face and her lower lip began to quiver, eyes welling up with tears. "I knew it. I knew it." She sobbed, hunching over in her chair and covering her face with her hands. "I knew something was up because it had been so long. She usually calls me back." Tears rolled down her cheeks. I sat back in my chair and waited, watching her shoulders heave. Eventually, my gaze began to wander and I scanned her current living quarters.

The rooms on all the units were virtually identical, square boxes painted a creamy white. A tall, broad window drew one's eyes to the rear wall as you entered. On either side of the window, rested light colored pine beds covered with heavy blue and white checked wool blankets. Beside each bed sat a matching desk and chair, with the desk doubling as a night stand. A dresser was placed at the foot of the bed leaving enough room for the connecting door to the bathroom to easily swing open. In each room, a large, hand knotted, multicolored carpet struggled unsuccessfully to disguise the well worn wall-to-wall carpet underneath.

While the common rooms and hallways were plastered with murals, art work, and calendars of events, the bedrooms were left virtually untouched to allow clients to express their individuality. Emily, like many girls her age, had covered her walls with posters of Hannah Montana, Justin Timberlake and animals - lots of animals, carefully cut from the pages of magazines and previous years' wall calendars. Her side of the room, unlike her roommate's, was orderly with teddy bears and stuffed animals neatly arranged on her bed. Her clothes, the majority of which were jeans and sweatshirts, were hung up in the open closet. At the bottom rested several small cardboard boxes and two pairs of dirty beige tennis shoes.

None of the closets in the facility had doors, as this allowed staff to efficiently keep track of clients and complete head counts quickly in times of crises. Prior to the doors' removal, the closets were a favorite hiding place. This happened for a host of reasons including avoiding therapy sessions and visits with county social workers. It was also a private place for the use of contraband, typically cigarettes and marijuana which had been smuggled into the facility.

Emily kept two photographs on the top of her dresser. The first showed a couple, presumably her parents, standing side by side. Her mother was dressed in a white, sleeveless blouse adorned with mother of pearl buttons and a red, floral print skirt. The starkness of the white blouse was a sharp contrast to her light coffee colored skin. Her eyes, bright green, were hopeful, and full of energy. Her dark hair was pulled back tightly in a ponytail, highlighting an elegant forehead, straight narrow nose, and a beaming smile full of perfect looking teeth. In her arms, she held a chubby cheeked girl dressed in pink.

Her father stood on her mother's right. Tall and heavy set, he was wearing a blue and yellow plaid, short sleeved shirt and olive green pants. His arm was draped comfortably over his wife's shoulders. His hair was a light blonde, almost white, which was cropped close to his scalp. He had deep, wide set eyes, full of life, and a short, slightly bulbous nose. In the photo, he smiled as though he had just stolen a date with the most popular girl at school. As the shutter clicked and captured the moment for eternity, all of them appeared content with the world.

The second photo was likely of Emily and her brother. They sat on a forest green wooden swing on a large white porch. Emily looked about eleven or twelve, dressed in an orange t-shirt with pink seersucker shorts and brown sandals. She smiled for the camera as she held a yellow Popsicle. Her brother held the same in his opposite hand and wore denim shorts and a lime green t-shirt. His red baseball cap partially covered his face but not enough to hide a large mischievous grin. I looked at Emily and was momentarily startled to see this grief-stricken girl sitting before me and wondered at the unpredictable nature of our lives. I handed her a box of tissues so she could dry her tears.

During our last conversation, we had agreed to meet for a therapy session early this morning. When I came to her room, no words had been exchanged, but she had known as soon as we made eye contact that all was not well with her mother. After there were no tears left, I provided her with a rough outline of what had happened. I gave no specifics about the condition of her mother's apartment or the circumstances under which she had been found, but Emily had been through this before and was easily able to fill in the blanks.

"She makes me so damn mad!" Emily yelled, now vacillating from sadness to anger. "She always lets me down! She can't even take care of herself. How can she possibly take care of me?" She exclaimed. I remained silent, letting her vent. "I get tired of the same old shit all the time, worrying about my mom. My life blows! You see? You see why my life blows? Hell, you don't even need to say how it all went down 'cause I know. Probably no different than the last time." She was quiet for a moment, but eventually moved her gaze from the floor to my eyes and told me about "last time."

After they left West Virginia, Emily and her mother had moved to Michigan to live with Maggie's younger sister, Olivia. It had seemed like a wise decision. Remaining in West Virginia was out of the question as there were just too many memories. Moving to a new place provided an opportunity for a new start.

Olivia and Maggie had been close growing up. They were strikingly similar in appearance and had often been mistaken for twins. However, that's where the similarity stopped. Unlike Maggie, who had married after high school and never pursued interests outside the family, Olivia was career oriented, content with her single life and ambitiously preparing for medical school.

Initially, the arrangement among the three of them had functioned well. Olivia was a registered nurse and typically worked the three to eleven shift at the hospital. This meant Maggie and Emily had the house to themselves from the time Emily returned from school until they went to bed at night. Maggie had quickly found employment as a receptionist at a local law firm. The income allowed her to help Olivia with some of the household expenses, with enough left over to start saving for a home of their own.

However, despite the change in her environment, Maggie couldn't escape her demons. She started having problems sleeping and became increasingly depressed. As the depression intensified, Maggie began to self-medicate with alcohol. Though she continued to work, when she returned home in the evening she would lock herself in her bedroom only to emerge the next day.

Emily knew there was a problem. Though Olivia had been supportive, it was often apparent she was exasperated with Maggie's behavior. Emily tried to carry her mother's load around the house, preparing meals and cleaning. She worried if she didn't, they would be asked to leave. After all, a person could only do so much - family or not.

But Maggie did not improve. She became habitually late for work, if she showed up at all. Several weeks later she was fired.

Maggie didn't tell Olivia she had lost her job, but it became clear when she was unable to contribute financially. Shortly thereafter, Olivia asked them both to leave. She said she had done all she could and wasn't willing to help someone who wasn't willing to help herself.

A week later, Maggie and Emily were living in a small one-bedroom apartment downtown, where they managed to survive for two months. That was the last time Emily had lived with her mother.

Emily took a deep breath and continued, "Last time she got really drunk, I mean smashed, and took a whole bunch of pills. Anyway, I visited her a lot when she was in the hospital." Maggie had used different means this time, but the pattern was the same, I thought to myself.

Emily continued. "I think she took a bunch of Prozac or maybe Paxil. It started with a 'p', anyway. She was taking them because she was depressed. The doctors said she was lucky she didn't die. That was after we had moved out of my aunt's house." She paused. "I had left the apartment that day to go to school. But halfway there, I realized I had forgotten my backpack and walked back home. That's when I found her." She stared quietly out the window for a moment and continued, "At first I thought she was just sleeping but when I got closer, I saw the empty vodka bottle and an empty pill bottle beside it. I called 911."

She looked at me again, "The ambulance got there and the paramedics did a whole bunch of stuff to her and then they strapped her on a stretcher, wheeled her out to the ambulance and took her to the hospital. She stayed in there for a couple weeks. She tried you know?" I nodded my head and she continued. "When she got out she went to AA and saw a shrink twice a week. She tried. I even went with her sometimes, but then she started drinking again." She stopped again for a minute and said. "I really should see her. I'm pissed though 'cause she promised me. She promised me she would never leave me. Over and over again she promised. I guess she's nothin' but a liar." Emily began sobbing again.

"I can't imagine how difficult this must be," I said.

"I just wish there was someone who could help us." Emily said. She kicked the chair with her foot and crossed her arms over her chest. "My mom needs someone to help her, but nobody will. I guess I'll have to be the one to do it, again. I've helped her as much as I can and look where it's gotten me, living in this shit hole." She sat back in her chair and looked at me.

"Emily," I said gently, "your mom needs to learn to take care of herself."

"I know she is supposed to take care of herself and take care of me, but obviously she can't."

"It's not your job to take care of her. You're not the parent. You need to take care of yourself and if she can't take care of herself now, she'll learn to again with some help."

"What if she can't?"

"Maybe she will, maybe she won't, but you have to focus on yourself. I know that probably sounds harsh, but you need to become strong again." Emily's history clearly indicated she was a parentified child who had shouldered the burden of her mother's care since moving to Michigan and perhaps even before that.

"How's she doing?" Emily finally asked.

"I spoke with her caseworker, Mr. Broussard, this morning. He told me your mom's stable now."

"Can I go see her?" Emily asked.

"I don't want to make you any promises, but let me call Mr. Broussard." I replied "You'll have to try to be patient though, it may take some time."

She nodded. From what I knew of Jacques Broussard, he would have no problem agreeing to the visit. He was a strong advocate of family reunification and generally had an agreeable disposition.

Emily had provided me with a further glimpse into her life and I resisted the urge to ask for more. Clearly, this was not the time. I needed to know more about both herself and her family. I was flying blind working with only her self-report. I had called Kim

56

and made numerous requests for any history she may have, but she still had not accommodated my request. I decided upon returning to my office I would try again.

Chapter 7

Following our session, I returned to my office pleased to have finally received at least one report from Emily's social worker, Kim Howe, about her hospital admission eight months ago. I had worked with Kim on several cases since I had taken my position at Ellis House and had enjoyed getting to know her. She was a short, heavy set African American woman with a wonderful sense of humor. Her only apparent, if understandable, flaw was her avoidance of paperwork and tardiness returning phone calls.

Emily's previous hospitalization had occurred following her mother's first suicide attempt when Emily had briefly returned to live with her Aunt Olivia. The psychological intake provided an abbreviated history of the trauma this young girl had suffered during the previous year.

PSYCHOLOGICAL INTAKE

PATIENT NAME: Emily Rowan
HOSPITAL NUMBER: 67834157

DATE OF BIRTH: 4/12/94

DATE OF EVALUATION: 2/9/08

REASON FOR REFERRAL: Emily is a 13-year-old female who was admitted as the result of a recent suicide attempt. The patient developed acute depressive symptoms in response to her mother's recent drug overdose and continues to have chronic difficulty adjusting to the death of her father and brother last year.

"Death of father and brother?" I inquired aloud. I put down the report and picked up the phone. I dialed Kim's number and after a fruitless attempt, I dialed zero and tracked down her supervisor. Within five minutes, I could hear Kim's voice on the end of the line.

"Kim," I said unable to stop myself. "Why didn't you tell me Emily's dad and brother were deceased?"

"Sorry Dr. Morgan. I thought you knew."

"How would I have known? You're the only person I get any information from besides Emily."

"Sorry, we're just so busy over here."

"I'm sure you are, but I'm trying to keep this kid out of the hospital. I feel like I don't understand what I'm up against. I can't believe I've worked with her this long and just found out half her immediate family's dead."

"Look, if that's all -"

"One more thing, please fax me the rest of her paperwork, social studies, court reports, evaluations, anything and everything you got."

"OK."

"Today, please."

"OK, OK." She said sounding frazzled.

I hung up and hoped that Kim would be reliable. I quickly

shifted my focus back to the report in an attempt to develop a better understanding of Emily.

PRESENTING PROBLEM: The primary presenting problem is Emily's depressive symptoms. She recently took a razor from the bathroom and made several deep cuts in her inner left arm. She reported that she wanted to slice her wrists, but despite drinking several beers to "get up her nerve" was unable to follow through. She disclosed that immediately following her self-mutilation, she felt relief. However, when she saw the blood, she panicked and called 911.

The patient reported she feels sad almost every day. She stated she feels hopeless and does not want to get up in the mornings because she knows she will "hurt" all day. She expressed her mother doesn't love her otherwise she would have never overdosed. She stated that within this last year she has lost her family, her home and the life she loved. She further reported she doesn't have any friends in Michigan. She feels worthless and knows that she is a burden to her aunt.

Emily reported she is frequently tired and does not have interest in anything. She reported it often takes her more than two hours to fall asleep at night and she can't sustain sleep for more than several hours at a time. There is no reported change in appetite. Further, Emily stated she could not remember a time since the death of her father and brother when she was not sad. However, her depressive feelings intensify when she sees things which remind her of her family.

Emily's aunt reported her niece has low self-esteem and is frequently irritable and moody. She also stated Emily has made statements such as "I wish I were dead," and "maybe I just won't wake up in the morning."

BACKGROUND INFORMATION: The patient lives with her maternal aunt in Kalamazoo, Michigan. Emily's mother, Maggie Rowan, age 36, was hospitalized approximately four weeks ago for a drug overdose. She had been living with her daughter in a one bedroom apartment and had been applying for disability. Emily's father and brother are both deceased. They died four months ago in a car accident.

Emily's aunt reported that Emily was born four weeks early via a C-section. She indicated that Emily's mother's health was fair during the pregnancy, she ingested some caffeine, but no prescription medication. Developmental and heath history were unremarkable. There was no concern regarding achievement and timing of developmental milestones (e.g., walking, talking, toilet training). Emily's aunt reported the marital relationship between Emily's parents was good and supportive. Maggie has been in no relationships following her husband's death and often stated she would never consider remarrying out of loyalty to her husband. There is no report of physical or sexual abuse, or alcohol or drug use by Emily. However, when Emily was interviewed separately from her aunt she discussed her mother's problems with alcohol in depth. Emily indicated that since they had moved out of her aunt's house, her mother drank everyday and always had an open bottle stashed somewhere in the apartment. She denied that her mother had ever been depressed or had a drinking problem prior to the loss of her husband and son.

SCHOOL: Emily is in the ninth grade at Blackwell High School. Her grades are higher than average, primarily A's, which is consistent with previous years. No learning problems or special class placements reported. Peer relations are poor. Emily was suspended from school for two days. She wrote a letter to a classmate which included foul language, insults and statements such as, "I am your worst nightmare. Watch your back." Emily's aunt noted that there were no known difficulties with school prior to her move to Michigan.

SOCIALIZATION: Emily indicated her peer relations are poor and have been since moving from West Virginia. Her past relationship with her brother was described as extremely good and she described him as her "best friend." Emily reported she would like to spend more time with her mother, but is unable to due to the current circumstances. She stressed she had close friends in West Virginia, but has not met anyone in Michigan. She indicated her peers at school often tease and make fun of her accent. Emily likes to read and has always wanted to dance, but because of financial restrictions she has not been able to enroll in ballet classes.

PSYCHOLOGICAL/PSYCHIATRIC HISTORY: Emily's first contact with mental health professionals occurred in November when she was seen at the Oakridge Hospital Crisis Clinic. This was approximately 2 months after the death of her father and brother. The evaluation revealed suicidal ideation and depressed mood and she was transferred to Eastwood, a psychiatric hospital in Charleston, West Virginia. Emily was initially brought to Oakridge because she had tried to kill herself by hanging herself with rope from a beam in the family's garage.

Following discharge, she had four outpatient sessions at Jackson Mental Health. During this time, she was placed on the anti-depressant Paxil. Emily reported her outpatient therapy was discontinued because the last time she was scheduled to attend a session she locked herself in the car and refused to get out. Her medication was subsequently discontinued because she was not compliant with treatment and refused all follow up medication visits with the psychiatrist, Dr. Morris. She has had no mental health treatment since that time.

Emily's mother was diagnosed with Major Depression. She has received treatment for substance abuse following a drug overdose. Emily's father had been diagnosed with depression by his general practitioner and had been taking Zoloft.

MEDICAL HISTORY: Emily is not currently prescribed any medications. Her physical health history is unremarkable.

BEHAVIORAL OBSERVATIONS: Emily was well groomed and appropriately dressed for the intake. Initially, she was downcast, quiet and bit her nails. However, she became more verbal as the intake progressed and talked more openly about issues which concerned her. Emily's aunt readily discussed her concerns about her niece. When Emily was seen in the absence of her aunt, she was very verbal and demonstrated insight regarding her circumstances.

CASE CONCEPTUALIZATION: Emily is a 13-year-old female who presented with a history of depression and suicidal behavior. Currently, she is exhibiting many depressive symptoms (feelings of hopelessness, sadness, irritability, suicidal ideation, and sleep difficulties). The duration and severity of the symptoms are consistent with Major Depressive Disorder. These symptoms are recurrent, as she was previously diagnosed with Major Depression in November, 2007.

Several factors which likely contributed to the development and maintenance of her depressive symptoms were identified and included the following: the death of her father and brother; poor peer relationships at school; and her mother's recent drug overdose. Emily reported she will likely always remain depressed over the loss of her father and brother.

RECOMMENDATIONS/PLAN: Current treatment plan includes the use of Cognitive Behavior Therapy to treat depressive symptoms, the development of a support system, bereavement counseling and medication management. Discharge plan includes a referral for outpatient therapy and follow up appointments with a psychiatrist.

The report ended with the signature of Associate Professor, Janine Dean, Ph.D. Emily had stayed in the hospital for two weeks. During her hospitalization, Emily's aunt reported she was unwilling to provide further care for her niece, given the circumstances. She then became part of "the system" being placed in a foster home following discharge.

Clearly, this evaluation provided a window into Emily's life and I could understand why she was so concerned about her mother. She was all Emily had left. However, what I didn't understand was her mother. Sure, she was bereaved and lonely, but she still had a daughter who needed her. I knew I still didn't have a solid understanding of what had happened. Emily told me herself that the reports only scratched the surface. The idea nagged at me that there was something else. There was something which had caused Emily's mother to fall apart, to be desperate enough to want to take her own life. But what was it?

I spent the rest of my day conducting clinical supervision and playing catch up. Documentation was such an essential component of clinical work, but the first casualty of a busy schedule. My inbox was jammed with evaluations and treatment plans which required both my review and signature. Additionally, there were requests, suggestions and information about upcoming audits, workshops and new demands set by the county. I buckled down and managed to address most of the work by the end of the day. One of the final papers in my box was a request from Tori Ridgeway stating that she wanted to speak with me. I made a note to myself to make sure I took care of it before I left for the evening.

Tori was the most recent addition to our clinical team. She had enthusiastically responded to my request for an interview and had performed well answering questions regarding crisis intervention, diagnosis and treatment planning. Jamie had followed up by checking her references. Two days later, Tori had promptly and without hesitation accepted the position. Her arrival was greeted with applause and I could see relief on the faces of several of the therapists. We had been struggling to provide services and another staff meant a reduction in therapists' caseloads and the luxury of having a co-facilitator for some of the more difficult groups. The therapists were tired and it was nice to provide them with some good news.

The size of our clinical team had been one of the largest challenges I had encountered since starting employment at Ellis House. Several positions had been vacant when I had accepted the job and two more therapists had given notice and had been scheduled to leave the week I started. My first clinical meeting had been incredibly uncomfortable, filled with negative and sarcastic comments from angry therapists. Every positive statement I made was greeted with cynicism and mockery. I tried not to be judgmental. They had been functioning without a clinical director for over a month and the entire clinical team was comprised of only eight members, including the nurse and two psychiatrists. The therapists reported they felt bullied by Barbara. This was in direct contrast to residential team members, be it supervisors or childcare workers, who were provided with incentives including paid days off, gift certificates and frequent opportunities for advancement.

There were fifteen therapist positions budgeted and to date only ten of the positions had been filled. But, if nothing else, at least progress was being made and there was hope that in the not so distant future we would be functioning at full capacity. The therapist's role was difficult under the best of circumstances, the pay and benefits were tolerable, but it was difficult to hold onto good people because of the great divide between the residential and clinical programs. One of the longest-standing complaints from the therapists was the resistance they encountered when attempting to implement their treatment plans on the units.

I was confident Tori would not be easily rattled by the challenges she would face as a therapist and would maintain her position at least long enough to accrue her hours for licensure which typically took two years. In addition to myself and Jamie there were John, Paul and Steve. They were the only long timers left. They had all been employed at the facility since it opened. All were from the same clinical program at Western Michigan University and all had been friends for years. I believed their support for one another was part of the reason they continued to stay through the highs and lows. John was close to accruing his supervision hours and I was concerned about being able to provide him with enough money or opportunity to remain on staff once he passed his licensing exam.

Sean and Marcie had been working at the facility for about a year, a relatively long time in this line of work. Christina and Toby were both new recruits completing their eighty hours of mandatory training. Once completed, they would be ready to start working on the units and to start carrying a caseload.

Mandatory training occupied eight hours a day for the first two weeks of employment. The training was similar for clinical and residential team members and included safe transportation of clients during off site outings, cultural diversity, first aid and CPR. The most intense was a four day workshop on the use of manual restraints. Manual restraint training focused on verbal de-escalation of dangerous behavior which typically manifested itself as aggression towards staff and peers. When verbal means were exhausted, there was no choice but to intervene physically. The training focused on how to use hands on techniques effectively without negatively impacting the client. The most frequent manual restraint used, was escort and containment. When a client continued to engage in unsafe behavior and verbal interventions had proven ineffective, the client was physically escorted by two staff members, one on each side, to the quiet room. The door was then closed and the kicking and hitting of the walls could commence. This was all under continued supervision.

There were other physical restraints, including wall restraints, standing restraints and prone restraints. Prone restraints, which involved holding a client face down to the ground, all four limbs secured by staff, were used only as a last resort. These were potentially dangerous and had been used more liberally in the past by overzealous staff members. Several months earlier, a 16-year-old boy in Northern Michigan had been placed in a prone restraint. Eventually, he had been released and escorted back to his room where he fell asleep and soon after stopped breathing. He never awoke. His admission paperwork had been incomplete and failed to address his asthmatic condition.

Restraints at Ellis House continued to be frequent, but their reduction had been a focus of both programs. It was hoped with earlier intervention, the use of any manual restraint would be a rare occurrence.

On my way out, I stopped by Tori's office. As I approached, I saw the light streaming through the crack at the bottom of her door. The square window that offered a peek into her office had efficiently been covered with a piece of black paper and she had placed a silver nameplate under the window with Victoria Ridgeway, M.A. in bold letters. She would have this office to herself until the next therapist was hired.

I knocked on her door thinking her request to speak with me had something to do with one of her newly assigned clients. "Tori?" I asked as I knocked on the door and entered. She sat at her desk, hunched over paperwork. She did not lift her eyes from her paperwork to look at me.

"Tori." I repeated. She took a moment to shift her eyes in my direction. "I got your message about wanting to see me. Is this a good time?"

"No, not really." She said, still looking at the papers on her desk.

"OK. Would you like to schedule a time to meet? I know you probably have some questions about how things work."

My statement was greeted with immediate hostility. Finally she looked at me with her piercing green eyes, "No, I don't." I said nothing, but she didn't have any difficulty reading my expression and said, "The note I left you, ignore it. I already answered my own question. If I need anything, I'll let you know."

I left her office feeling like a school girl dismissed by the principal.

Chapter 8

The following day was Wednesday which meant being stuck in treatment team for the entire afternoon. I stopped by my office on the way to the meeting to find a yellow piece of paper neatly folded and taped to my mailbox, which hung outside my office door. It read:

Be careful who you trust. Things are not always as they seem. You don't know how this place works and what's gone on here. Some people want you gone.

I reread it to make sure I had read it correctly. I looked around the hallway, wondering who had written the note. Not really knowing what to do with it, I stuffed it in my pocket. I walked to the conference room and sat down beside Jamie. I continued to think about the note. Was it a joke? Could it possibly be serious? I thought about mentioning it to Jamie, but decided against it. Right now I needed to ignore it and focus on my job.

Barbara was attending the meeting today, which meant she had heard we would be spending time focusing on the negative attitudes which seemed to be flourishing on the units. However, we started the meeting as we always did, with case reviews.

The first case, Nate Jackson, who had been diagnosed with Post Traumatic Stress Disorder had made little progress since his admission. His trauma was constantly apparent in the flashbacks, intrusive thoughts and nightmares he experienced day and night. Both revolved around watching his sister die or being burned to death himself.

This had been a particularly difficult week for him. A staff member had attempted gently to coerce Nate to the dining hall, which he refused to enter. The staff member became frustrated and threatened negative consequences. Unfortunately, he was unaware of Nate's history and did not realize what seeing the two industrial sized ovens in the dining hall would do to him. After a terrible scene, it was agreed to allow Nate to eat his meals in the lounge with a therapist or staff member until he stabilized.

Case number two, Jacob Brown, was currently in the Separation Unit, which was used if a client's behaviors were destructive or aggressive toward themselves or others. The Separation Unit was a stark, white room, void of any color. No pictures hung on the walls and there was no carpet on the floor. It was furnished simply with a white dresser and a pine bed which was covered with white blankets and white sheets. There was a brown chair in the corner with a thread bare seat and scuffed legs.

In addition to the physical drawbacks of being placed in the Separation Unit, there was no contact with other clients on the unit. Occasionally, there was the opportunity to earn desired activities, but most of the day was consumed with homework and therapy. Meal times were no more pleasant as food was presented on a soft orange plastic tray, free of knives and forks. The client was, however, provided a plastic spoon with which to eat his/her food, which had already been cut into bit sized portions.

The stay in the Separation Unit typically lasted no more than 72 hours, but could be extended depending on how responsive the client was to his or her individualized program.

Jacob was a budding antisocial personality and it was

anticipated his stay would extend for some time. He was also a child who should have never been placed in Ellis House. During the course of his first week, he had assaulted his roommate. Jacob shoved him against the wall when he refused to play with him. Two hours later he threatened to cut a client in the dining hall with a plastic knife unless she gave him her cookie. At school, he told his teacher she should "watch her step" or she might find her classroom "burned to the ground." Reports from all shifts about Jacob were consistent. He threatened adults, assaulted his peers, and made makeshift weapons which he typically hid under his mattress.

His behavior on the Separation Unit had been uncontrollable. He had initially been defiant and aggressive. He threw his food trays against the wall and refused to clean up the resulting mess. He refused to do any homework and instead would stand on his bed and scream foul language at anyone who would approach his room. One of his favorite activities was urinating from the chair onto the floor and telling the staff member who was supervising him to "lick it up."

Tori had been his assigned therapist and had spent many hours seeking consultation about his case. During her case presentation, she stated Jacob had been misdiagnosed. While she agreed he presented with many symptoms consistent with Conduct Disorder, she also believed he was experiencing hallucinations. Apparently, Jacob had recently revealed to her he was hearing voices. These voices were telling him to "be bad." The voices were responsible for his behavior, not him. He simply couldn't help it.

Several staff members pointed out to Tori that Jacob was a behavior problem not because he was mentally ill, but because he was a bully. However, Tori explained that Jacob was "misunderstood" and had opened up to her because she made him feel safe. She believed the Separation Unit made things worse by exacerbating his depression and psychosis; what he needed instead was unconditional support, not rules and structure.

I was taken aback. It was clear to me, and to most everyone else in the room, Tori was being manipulated by Jacob. More alarming to me was that changes in diagnosis or treatment planning were addressed in individual supervision and needed to be approved by me before being presented in treatment team. We had met for individual supervision two days ago and she had agreed with the diagnosis of Conduct Disorder. I had approved her plan for the Separation Unit. We had also agreed to maintain him at the facility for no longer than possible. In the interim, his county social worker needed to understand the urgency of his diagnosis and expeditiously obtain a placement for him at a treatment facility specializing in Conduct Disorder. Obviously, we were not equipped to provide adequate treatment for his symptoms given their severity.

I knew I would have to address this lapse in protocol with Tori, but now was not the time. I interjected and confirmed her original diagnosis, Conduct Disorder. Tori shot me a look from across the table and I knew she felt undermined, but I ignored it.

Our third client was Raymond Reid, one the few clients who had made progress during the previous week. He had adjusted to life on the units, attended school and completed his homework. It was likely he was just biding his time before his eighteenth birthday knowing he would soon be free to do as he pleased. The challenge was preparing him to start life on his own and making sure he was well linked to community resources.

We then moved on to Amanda Carter, and Jasmine Rowe, both of whom had gone AWOL recently. Jasmine had several foster home interviews scheduled and had had no more behavior problems since the AWOL.

Amanda, given her history, was a more difficult client to place, and her county social worker continued to look for a placement. She had even extended her search out of county because she wanted Amanda to stabilize and remain in a long term placement instead of shifting from placement to placement every several months.

Finally, we discussed Emily. She hadn't been restrained in the past week. However, she had kept to herself and there was concern she was becoming more depressed. She presented as more lethargic and had little motivation to get up in the morning. She typically wore the same clothes from day to day not caring about her appearance. Her appetite had decreased and she complained she felt nauseous throughout the day. She continued to worry about her mother and frequently asked staff if she had called, or if her county social worker had called. The team agreed it would be beneficial for Emily to visit her mother in the hospital. If her county social worker was unable to take her, I would step in.

Having completed case reviews, we took a five minute break before moving on to discuss what was happening on the units. I looked at Barbara as she left the room. I knew she would not support any discussion which addressed problems involving the residential program. She was defensive and biased about her position and the role the residential program played, always pointing fingers at the clinical team for any failures. On the other hand, she readily accepted responsibility for any successes.

After everyone had reassembled, I began, "Before we wrap up today, we need to address what's been happening on the units. I'm sure it's not news to anyone that things have been particularly tense lately."

I saw several staff members roll their eyes. I wasn't feeling particularly diplomatic to start with and said, "Let me say what I need to and then you will have the opportunity to respond. However, the eye rolling, note passing, and chatter when we are in this meeting is unacceptable and unprofessional. If you don't want to be here, then leave. If you intend to stay and do your job, then show some respect." Faces reddened and I saw anger flash through several sets of eyes. I cleared my throat again and continued, "In fact, there has not only been a lot of disrespect observed on the units, but a lot of complaining and whining as well. What's worse is that most of the time it's done in front of the clients. Consistency between the shifts is poor and has contributed to the clients' increased acting out because they don't know what rules apply from one shift to the next."

Jamie interjected, "I just have to say that it has been really hard for some of us to do our jobs."

Unable to restrain himself any further, Barry interrupted. "Do your jobs? I mean, what do you guys really do? You're never on the units. We have to hunt the therapists down to get any help. There are always so many excuses..."

"Excuses?" John asked. He was typically quiet and listened, rather than speaking. He was well respected and could frequently be found on the units eating lunch with the kids. "Do you recognize what our role is? It's not to help residential staff. We're not additional staff. Our primary responsibility is to provide therapy to our clients and this is incredibly difficult at times. It's not an excuse, it's a fact."

Ana jumped in. "Well, we have a tough job too and we never have enough staff."

"Everyone recognizes that you have a difficult job, but it's not our job to pick up the slack when you don't have enough staff. We don't ever ask you to do our jobs." John responded.

"God, I'd love to be able to sit in an office all day and do paperwork and talk." Barry said sarcastically.

"Obviously, you don't have any idea what our job entails." John snapped.

"Well, I know it's easier than our job."

Corrine spoke up. "That's exactly why we are having the problems we're having," she said, looking at me. "There is so much disrespect." She looked back at Barry. "You know Barry the therapists do help out on the units and do a lot they don't have to. And John's right, you have absolutely no idea what they do or you wouldn't have said what you did."

Rather than accepting this, Barry chose to fuel the fire, "Well, you all know we have three people leaving my shift, so I'll need lots of help from the therapists on the units especially next week. We still don't have any new staff hired."

I spoke up. "Staffing is always a problem and it is not the clinical team's responsibility to fix it. The residential program is never fully staffed nor does there seem to be much of a push to get it that way. We, as a team, are not responsible for completing your job responsibilities and have no expectations for the residential staff to help us with ours. In fact, we are not fully staffed either, but we are making progress. We have interviews scheduled and review resumes the day they come in."

I continued. "To respond to your request Barry, next week you will have to find a way to manage without the help of the therapists. We have our yearly state audit and really need time to prepare."

I then turned my attention back to the entire room. "I believe we also need to pay attention to Corrine's point about respect. We need to be respectful of each other and respect that we are doing the best we can. If we need help from each other we should ask, but not take it personally if the person asked says they are too busy. Finally, I think each of our programs should focus on becoming fully staffed because then some of our daily problems could be eradicated."

I stopped and looked around the room. Some faces were vacant, some, like Barry's, were red with anger, but others appeared to be listening. "Any questions?" Barry grumbled something unintelligible. "OK, I wanted to thank everyone for their time."

As the staff began filing out of the room, I dropped my eyes to the table and looked at the stack of papers in front of me. I could hear various voices complaining about what had just transpired. I knew it would take time to make progress. Maybe the programs would never mesh, but regardless, staff members needed to be aware that the therapists were not required to pick up residential responsibilities despite the staffing shortage. There was a lot of anger and resentment floating around and I didn't see it changing without some hard work. I picked up my stack of papers, glad to be done with this three and a half hour meeting and pushed back my chair.

As I was standing up, I noticed Barbara was still seated. "Dr. Morgan, don't rush off." She said, her southern drawl dripping off every word. "I need to speak with you regarding the units."

Oh no, I thought. Get ready for another lecture about the laziness and ineffectiveness of the clinical staff. I pushed my chair back to the table and tried my best to look non-defensive. Barbara sat with her legs crossed, leaning back in her chair her left arm on the table. She picked up a white Styrofoam cup filled with the grayish brown swill which passed for coffee at Ellis House, took a sip, and locked her eyes on mine.

"That was quite a presentation during treatment team. I've never known a clinical director to have so much interest and motivation on the residential side of things, especially one with so little experience."

She smiled slightly, obviously trying to bait me. I tried to ignore her comment, knowing that this was her style, confronting people privately to maintain her image, and couldn't help but respond. "If you had something to say during the meeting, why didn't you say it?"

"Oh, I'm not fond of confronting people in public. Uncivilized, don't you agree?" She asked, looking briefly at her coffee cup and then raising her eyes to me. She slowly stirred her coffee with a red plastic stick. "Anyway, I guess it'll all work out with time. Don't need to rush these things you know." Her eyes returned to mine, the fluorescent lights reflecting briefly off her brown irises.

"What do you mean?" I asked.

"Given your inability to appreciate subtle southern politeness I'll be direct. Though I must say I would prefer not to do so. Dr. Morgan, your therapists will be required to help out on the units at my discretion. Your naivety about how this place has been, and will continue to be, run surprises me. We've talked about your role before. It is to supervise your clinical staff and support the residential program. However, you seem to have a difficult time appreciating this." She sat back in her chair, her hands folded on her lap.

"Excuse me?" I said not quite believing what I was hearing.

"Come Doctor, you heard me." She shuffled some papers in front of her and did not look up at me as she said, "Now about Barry. He is a great supervisor, don't you think?"

Barbara was slow to speak and liked the sound of her own

voice. When I had first started working with her, she had spent forty-five minutes discussing her childhood and upbringing in Georgia, noting repeatedly that it was a far superior place to live than the Midwest. She had married a medical supplies specialist, moved to Michigan and had chosen to stay following her divorce. She stayed, she insisted not because she liked Michigan, but because she believed she was indispensable to Ellis House. In fact, she stated the administrators refused to let her go.

Barbara cleared her throat and said, "I need to clarify what I've been hearing about the interactions between you and Barry. He has brought it to my attention that you have been questioning him and have been undermining his authority. Is this true?" She looked at me questioningly, but I said nothing. "This simply is unacceptable. It is difficult for me to believe you have already forgotten our recent discussion about not biting the hand that feeds you." Again she looked at me, and I stared back, silently.

"You see, Dr. Morgan, I don't want you to get too confident. Perhaps it would be in your best interest to stop being so idealistic and to start focusing on your career rather than your clients." I was fuming inside, but said nothing. My career was my clients, how could she not understand that?

"I don't want you to become frustrated and force us to rotate through yet another clinical director." She let the not-so-subtle threat hang in the air waiting for my response. I didn't give her one. Instead I gathered my papers and silently left the room. Talking to Barbara would accomplish nothing, but there were other ways to handle this.

Chapter 9

Barbara was motivated by being in control. She had been controlled by others for most of her life and now it was her turn. After a messy divorce, she refused to leave her fate in the hands of others. Over the years, she had observed how individuals in positions of power functioned, how people respected them and how others made efforts to please them. Her father had been a powerful man. His subordinates fawned over him to obtain raises and end of year bonuses. She had seen the same dynamic at Ellis House. She despised those in positions of authority, including the CEO Houseman, but in public she appeared respectful and gracious. She couldn't care less about those she considered beneath her, especially those working in the field of mental health despite the years of training they may have accrued. It wasn't a field that deserved respect as far as she was concerned.

Barbara had attended marital therapy with her ex-husband which she had determined to be an absolute waste of time. She would have rather spent the hour cleaning a toilet, even though she found the act of scrubbing anything, beneath her dignity. She had employed a maid for years. The marital therapist had accused her negative attitude as being directly responsible for the demise of her marriage. He had told her she was "emotionally detached" from her husband, more focused on material possessions than human relationships. She had made it clear to the therapist she had married a lazy bum who had shown a very different side when they were dating. She left the third therapy session and her husband on the same day and vowed never to enter a therapist's office again. The therapist was a stranger who had no right to tell her how to live her life. She deserved to be respected, regardless of her actions.

Barbara also knew that with power came financial stability. Barbara didn't need to be rich, not that she would have objected, but she required comfort which meant enough cash flow to support her lifestyle. She appreciated the finer things in life and, despite not having a formal education beyond high school she realized she could advance quickly by paying attention and providing her supervisors with what they wanted most, loyalty and silence.

Barbara considered herself a traditional southern woman who didn't favor the directness of northerners or their general impatience to accomplish tasks in haste by skipping lunch and running around constantly doped up on caffeine. She also frowned on casual dress, taking great pride on her appearance. Weekly trips to the beauty salon for manicure and hair dressing were considered just basic grooming.

She had been raised in Savannah, a place of incredible loveliness. There she had never suffered the bleak, miserable winters of the North. This town was flat and unattractive. It was all so functional with its strip malls, drive through banks and wide concrete streets, unlike the beauty steeped south. She knew she just needed to be patient for things to work out and over time she could return to glorious Savannah and have the lifestyle she deserved.

Barbara was raised with her parents and a younger sister. Her mother was a classic southern belle who had taught her about proper decorum. Barbara had always dressed like a lady, never dressing in jeans and t-shirts, opting instead for skirts and heels. She was a tidy child who stayed out of any grime. She chose not to participate in sports, crafts or any outdoors activities that involved creating a mess. Barbara had blossomed into a very particular young woman who meticulously kept all her possessions in their place and insisted on nothing less than perfection.

Her desire for formality was highlighted in her office. It was full of deep red cherry furniture which echoed the era of Ellis House when it functioned as a single family home. Her desk, the focal point of the office was a massive, intricately carved cherry monstrosity. Beside it, also intricately carved was a tea trolley showing off an elaborate silver tea service. Her daily tea ritual was sacred regardless of what was occurring at Ellis House. Two wing chairs and a matching Victorian bench with curved legs and a tapestry inlay added to the room's atmosphere. There were also plants, lots of plants in blue and white pots, dracaenas, palms, bromeliads and aspidistras. Entering her inner sanctum was like taking a step back in history.

Barbara sometimes had a hard time believing that someone with the education of Dr. Morgan would tolerate her dingy little office filled with chipped and dented furniture. She couldn't help but chuckle whenever she walked by Dr. Morgan's office, knowing that Morgan's furniture had essentially come from the dump. It puzzled her why Dr. Morgan never complained about it, it was beyond comprehension, but she never did.

Installing the surveillance equipment had been a good idea. Initially, Barbara had been skeptical and all she was able to monitor were phone conversations. However, she had recently installed equipment which allowed her to hear all that occurred in Dr. Morgan's office. It certainly was superior to listening outside her door whenever a viable opportunity presented itself. So far, all the conversations she had heard had been benign. All she and Jamie had discussed were clients and how to benefit their team, a gallant effort, but futile. Dr. Morgan was genuine and wanted to do what was best for the clients. However, she was naive in thinking she could make the program more stable. There would always be a rift between the therapists and staff because Barbara liked it that way.

She looked at her watch and tapped the fountain pen on her desk. Late. Disrespectful. She'd have to talk with Barry about the importance of punctuality.

Barry didn't like Dr. Morgan. In fact, he had preferred the previous clinical director. Sure, he had been lazy as hell, but he hadn't cared about anything but his paycheck. He offered minimal resistance unless it impacted him directly. A lot of group homes didn't have separate clinical programs. In fact, they barely had a clinical team at all and they functioned solely with social workers who were budgeted through the residential program answering to the residential program director. That was how he wanted things to be at Ellis House.

In these situations, social workers functioned as case managers. Their job was to set up off site passes, help with long term placement, schedule and provide transportation to appointments, and help out on the units. The clients still had therapists, but they were off site and sessions were conducted at their offices one a week. It was so much easier when you didn't have to deal with therapists onsite much less a clinical director who was focused on issues other than helping on the units. He still couldn't believe that the therapists didn't "get" that spending two to three hours on the units a day was nothing.

The attitude of the therapists at Ellis House incensed him. He meant what he said in treatment team; all the therapists did, as far as he could see was sit at their desks, talk, shuffle papers and undermine residential staff by not being at their beck and call. Dr. Morgan was no different from the other clinical directors, once you got past the surface and looked at her agenda. Like all of them, she believed she made a difference. Which was horseshit, but she really did believe it and so did the therapists. That's why they were so self-righteous when they talked about their positions and their goals for their clients.

Barry had not come by his insight overnight. There was a time he wanted to be a psychologist, but never made the grade. He had applied for three years straight to numerous doctoral clinical psychology programs and was never accepted. Out of desperation, he had taken a job at Ellis House.

No one could argue he hadn't worked hard. He had started as a childcare worker, often working evenings and weekends. He picked up the slack for others and stayed late if there was a problem. He was reliable and his supervisors, including Barbara had noticed. Within a year, he had been promoted to assistant supervisor and later to his current supervisory position. Initially, Barry followed protocol to the letter. However, over time, to perform efficiently, he needed to cut corners here and there.

Barry smiled to himself. He knew some would call him a lackey, but who cared. Thanks to hard work and kissing a little ass, he was probably pulling down more than Morgan, especially if one included all the bonuses he received from Barbara.

Barry stared at the computer screen and completed the incident report on his most recent restraint. That kid, Jacob, had lost control again and he'd walled him in the quiet room. Stupid little punk, Jacob thought he could threaten him and swear at him. The little bastard didn't think Barry would touch him. Surprise. Surprise. Well, maybe he twisted his arm a little too hard, but no one would ever know. Besides, even if he did tell, the kid was a lying little creep. He had cried wolf too many times before.

Barry looked at his watch and realized he was running late. He grabbed his clipboard and shut the door to the unit office. As he left the unit and walked down the hall to Barbara's office, he saw the door was open, but he knocked anyway. Barbara waved him in and motioned for him to take a seat. He obliged and sat across from her the large carved monstrosity forming a barrier between them. He was always mildly annoyed trying to interpret the intricacy of the carved pattern. Were those representations actual birds or somebody's idea of phoenixes just before their resurrection? It was difficult to tell. Then there was this odd undulating trunk or branch, or was it a snake? Barry wondered if he would ever figure it out. Didn't really matter, but it was more fun than watching Barbara execute her tea pouring ceremony. Barry watched in silence as she finally poured tea from the lumpy Victorian pot that sat on the trolley next to her in the two fine delicate porcelain cups. She placed two lumps of sugar in his and handed it to him with a tiny silver spoon carefully balanced on the saucer. He took it, thanked her and leaned back in his chair. As long as he had worked with Barbara as a supervisor, this had been the ritual.

"Fifteen minutes late. Not like you Barry. Remember what I told you about punctuality." He knew she wasn't going to accept his tardiness even before he stepped into her office and even though he had already apologized he did it again that much more profusely. She appeared satisfied with his response and continued talking.

"Be a dear and shut the door." Barbara ordered.

He complied and she asked, "So, what new tidbits of information do you have for me? Any new ideas about how to better manage our current problem?"

Barry smiled and started to talk only too happy to oblige.

Chapter 10

The day had finally arrived. I looked at his bags packed and placed by the front door. I already felt alone. What made things even more difficult was that we had been spending more time together over the last few weeks. We had agreed to make more time for each other before his departure and had done so. Three nights ago, we had celebrated the successful defense of his dissertation. We enjoyed a long, quiet dinner together at our favorite Italian restaurant, feasting on pasta primavera and tiramisu. After, we had returned home, built a fire, and enjoyed a quiet, romantic evening.

The start date for his internship was December first. However, Elliot had made the decision to leave a month early and take advantage of his cross country trip. I didn't agree with it, but who could blame him? Several evenings ago, we had mapped out his route and I was envious of his upcoming freedom. It would be two to three weeks before he arrived in San Diego. His plan was to leisurely traverse the prairies, the mountains and the desert, finally arriving on the California coast.

He had found a one bedroom condo in a complex in University City which was a short commute from the medical center where his internship program was located. The pictures reminded me of so many of the complexes in Southern California, cream structures covered with red clay tiles. Bougainvillea, hibiscus and birds of paradise were abundant and the complex grounds were impeccably manicured.

I looked over at Elliot, eating his cereal, and couldn't keep the tears from welling up in my eyes. He looked over at me and smiled.

"Gracie, everything will be fine."

I nodded my head, made no attempt to smile back and let the tears flow. He reached over and took my hand, but that just made me cry harder.

"I don't want you to go." I sobbed.

"I know, but we'll be fine. Really."

"It's just so hard."

"I know and I know it's always harder for the person who gets left behind. But remember, Christmas is just around the corner. We'll see each other then."

He walked over and held me for a long time and finally said, "Help me load the car."

We had promised each other we wouldn't make this day any harder than it already was and I wasn't doing a very good job holding up my part of the bargain. I wiped my face with my sleeve and followed him outside. After we crammed everything into the trunk and rear seats, he said, "Well, I guess this is it."

He hugged me one last time, climbed into the car and waved as he pulled out of the driveway. I watched until the car disappeared around the corner and then went back inside. The house immediately felt deserted. So many of the things which reminded me of Elliot were gone, his favorite books, CDs, clothes -toothbrush. Gone were all the things which said I didn't live here alone. Well, now I guess I did.

I stayed in bed most of the day, alternating between sleep and feeling sorry for myself. When the evening news came on, I decided the best thing I could do was get out of the house even if it was just to pick up dinner. I drove around for a while and finally opted for a local burger joint. I was too lazy to leave my car. So I didn't, choosing the drive through instead. Three minutes later, I had my meal. Not being able to resist the aroma permeating from the paper bag, I wolfed down the cheeseburger and fries on the way home, chasing them down with a vanilla milkshake. I felt better by the time I pulled into the driveway and decided to just take it easy for the rest of the evening.

The answering machine was blinking when I walked in the door. Elliot had called me from the road. He had had a great day and was going to keep driving. His goal was to make it to the Illinois/Missouri border by tonight. He'd call me tomorrow to check in. I settled into bed early, looking at the empty spot beside me and started to feel sad again. Despite all the stress which had been placed on our relationship over the course of the last few months, I missed him and I knew I would diligently be crossing the days off on the calendar until I saw him again. In the back of my mind, I was hoping he would be doing the same.

I watched a rerun of *Six Feet Under* on HBO as I flipped through a home decorating magazine. I must have nodded off around midnight. I wish I hadn't. My sleep was intermittent and restless at best.

We start down the gravel road, churning up thick clouds of dust. I'm so thirsty. My throat feels like sandpaper. I have to swallow, but can't without extreme effort, like trying to swallow a cotton ball. As we pick up speed, my body is bounced up and down on the cold metal, bruising my back. My head slams against the truck bed repeatedly, sometimes so hard I see stars.

When the wind catches the tarp right, it teases me with brief glimpses of the night sky. It is no longer a deep black illuminated by the stars, but a slightly lighter shade; in a few hours it will be morning. I try not to think where I will be then. Stay positive, focus on the here and now and hope you will be done . . . done with

85

all of this.

I know my chance to escape is soon. Once we get in the house it will be over. He has a gun and I will be no match for him physically. If only I can loosen these ropes. I must find a way. They are tightly knotted, but I begin twisting and wriggling my wrists. I want to use my teeth, but I am so tightly gagged it is impossible. If I can just get untied, break free from where he has secured me to the truck bed, then maybe . . . and he'll have to slow down . . . if I can just get loose . . . I keep twisting . . . and pulling. I guess even if he doesn't slow down, it doesn't matter, I will have no option. Don't think that far. Just focus on now.

I can't see the road, but I can feel the truck snaking its way around the lake. I was right. No traffic passes. I know we will be there soon. I keep focused and finally . . . finally, I feel the rope give. Just a little, but that's all I need. My wrists are bloody and raw from where the cord has broken through the skin, but I keep working the rope. Then, my left hand slides out, followed by my right. As quickly as I can, I yank the gag down to my chin where it falls around my neck. It feels good to breathe through my mouth. I go to work on my legs, my hands throbbing as they strain to create some slack around my ankles.

Then, I feel the truck start to slow. The brakes squeak as we start to pull over to the side of the road. I keep working at my ankles . . . faster . . . faster . . . We stop and everything is still for several minutes. Keep working . . . maybe he fell asleep. I pray to God he has. Then, I hear the door creak open and slam shut, footsteps on the gravel.

I look for something, anything to use as a weapon. There is nothing, nothing at all. He will see the ropes are untied, the gag. I can't get my ankles loose. Hurry! Hurry! Hurry! Put the gag back on. Tie up your wrists. I yank the gag up to my face and wrap the rope around my wrists. Almost done. Almost done.

He lifts up the tarp. Too late. He sees what I have done. He says nothing. Instead, he scrambles into the back of the truck and slaps me hard across the face. My head twists and my cheek burns. I feel blood dripping from my nose, salty as it drains into my mouth. I yelp as he tightens the gag and ties my wrists. I can feel my hands turning numb. As he jumps down from the truck he says, "Bitch, I got plans for you. I don't know where you think you're going."

He gets back into the cab and we are back on the road. Soon after, the road turns from gravel to nothing more than tracks in the dirt. It is bumpy and narrow with not enough room for another vehicle to pass. I can hear tree branches brushing against the side of the truck. We are close. The truck slows and turns to ascend the steep drive. I want to scream. My house is my place of peace, my sanctuary. And what I used to love about my home was its quiet isolation. Now it is what I dread most.

I could hear my phone ringing as I entered my office the following morning. Kim Howe was on the end of the line. Emily was scheduled to visit her mother, but an emergency had come up. Could I take her? Kim had already made arrangements to meet with Jacques Broussard, Maggie's social worker, at St. Mary's. I was still fighting sleep given my interruption from the night before, but I also knew Emily would be disappointed if she couldn't go, so there was really no alternative. I cleared my calendar, made some phone calls and asked Jamie to hold down the fort until I returned. I grabbed my coat, walked back to the staff office and signed out one of the mid-sized company cars. The keys jingled in my pocket as I made my way up to the girls' unit, two steps at a time. As I approached Emily's room, I deduced she had been waiting rather impatiently. She didn't even give me time to reach her doorway before she met me in the hall. I guessed that her apparent enthusiasm was as much about getting off grounds as it was about visiting her mother.

She looked better than she had in weeks and had clearly taken time with her appearance. Her hair was neatly combed into a ponytail and it was the first time I had ever seen her wear makeup. But she still wore her usual uniform, jeans and a sweatshirt. I smiled and without any words exchanged, we walked down the stairs to the parking lot.

Despite the several inches of snow that Mother Nature had dumped the night before, the roads were already slushy, melting furiously on this bright, sunny November day. After a tedious twenty minute drive, during which conversation was restricted to small talk, we parked and made our way to the main entrance of the hospital. At the entrance, the doors automatically opened blasting our faces with warm, dry air.

Emily had not said a word since we left the car. Her expression had become stoic, almost blank. She was building mental fortifications. She began to chew and pick at her cuticles and efficiently shredded her thumb and index finger to the quick. I had spent the day before preparing Emily for her visit, discussing her expectations, fears and ambivalence. Her feelings of anger and disappointment toward her mother were becoming more apparent in addition to her continued belief she was somehow responsible for her mother's welfare. She had reason to be concerned. Her hopes of ever living with her mother again were falling apart.

Jacques had given me a brief rundown before we met this morning and Maggie's prognosis was not rosy. She had stabilized and was partially responding to treatment. This was her second run through detox and inpatient drug treatment. However, her motivation was poor and she continued to be hopeless about the future despite having her body pumped full of antidepressants. The suicide attempt that landed her in the hospital was not the typical "cry for help"; it was a well executed effort to end her life. If not for her neighbor's intrusion, she would have accomplished her goal.

Jacques reported that after sifting though Maggie's apartment in an attempt to find her wallet and some essential documentation for her hospital stay, he had found a shoe box neatly placed on the kitchen table, a severe contrast to the rest of her home which was nothing less than chaotic. It had been carefully sealed and when opened contained an apology note to her daughter for her actions and for being the kind of mother she had become. It also stored several framed family photographs and two sleepers, one pink and one blue which she later explained to Jacques had been the outfits that Emily and John first wore when they were brought home from the hospital. There was no question that she had every intention of ending her life.

The lobby of the hospital was what you would expect, quiet with soft muzak wafting down from small, round speakers embedded in the ceiling. Visually, it was bland. The waiting area was filled with small, round, chipped wooden tables with beige coffee stained cushioned chairs. Magazines were abundant with an unusual glut of Golf Digest. The walls painted a pale peach were adorned with nondescript prints of flowers and landscapes framed in black. The beige carpet was well worn and looked like it was in need of replacement. All of it screamed "institution." A long desk, composed of dark, pressed wood was strategically placed in front of the wards, where the patients were housed and it was manned by two efficient looking, elderly receptionists both wearing small, reading glasses complete with silver chains.

Jacques was slouched in a chair, legs crossed, thumbing through a magazine. I had spoken with him numerous times over the telephone, but this was our first face to face meeting. He saw us immediately and rose from his chair. The first thing I noticed was his size. He was just shy of 6'4" and must have carried a solid 260 pounds on his frame. My first impression was that he had played football in college. He had widely spaced blue eyes, a long narrow nose and thin lips made more interesting by a moustache and a goatee.

He extended his hand and I shook it.

"Bonjour. Comment ca va?" I asked.

"Bien." He responded and laughed. We had determined during our initial phone conversation that we had grown up literally across the river from each other, I in Ottawa and he in the neighboring town of Alymer. We took the elevator to the second floor.

Maggie's room was directly across from the elevator. Jacques knocked on her door and the three of us let ourselves in. Maggie was sitting in a chair dressed in a navy blue sweatsuit as we entered. Her appearance was a dramatic contrast to the photo that sat on Emily's dresser. She looked like she had aged about thirty years. Her dark hair was short, spiky and flecked with white. Her skin was mottled and grey. Her green eyes now appeared dull, poking out of a sunken face. Her body was rail thin - a shadow of the woman she used to be.

When she saw Emily, she stood up with considerable effort and came to hug her. Emily hugged her back and within moments, her body started to shake. Her mother held her and kissed the top of her head until she stopped crying. Emily wiped her face with her sleeve and sat down on the bed.

"So, how's my girl?" Maggie asked. Girl came out like *"gurl"* and it was immediately evident than despite her departure from the Appalachians, the Appalachians remained deeply embedded in her. My guess was Emily had worked hard to sound like her peers given that she had endured so much teasing for her accent when she started attending school in Michigan.

"I'm alright." She said minimizing the truth. "Are you OK?"

"Yeah, you know me. I'm hanging in there. They got me on some real good depression drugs. Think that should help."

"Really?"

"Yeah. Well, maybe. You never know. They got me on some different ones this time. My doctor, well, she's been takin' real good care of me and she thinks this Effexor will help me better than the Prozac." The dance of superficial and forced optimism continued. "Maybe once I get myself together, we could get a place." Emily didn't respond. Maggie repeated herself and Emily finally appeased her with an obligatory nod and a halfhearted "sure." Her fantasy of living with her mother was just that and continued to unravel.

"So", Emily demanded, apparently through with the small talk "why'd you do it mom?"

"I don't know. No good reason." Maggie replied unconvincingly.

"No good reason." Emily scoffed, shaking her head.

"I know this is hard baby. But where's that get up and go attitude of yours?"

"I can manage. Don't worry about me. I just wish you'd care enough to worry about yourself."

"I take care of myself when I have to. You needn't be telling me what to do." Maggie snapped. "How can I-" Maggie stopped herself. "Sorry. It's just that everybody tells me that. It's hard. I do the best I can. And I struggle knowing it's not good enough."

Emily's tone softened. "You gotta understand. It's just that I worry about you."

"So, how's that place you're staying now...that, um, what's the name of it again?"

"El-"

"Yeah, Ellis Home."

"House."

"House. Home. Close enough. Well, how's that?" Maggie asked apparently relieved to have shifted the focus from herself. Too many guilt feelings. Too much pressure.

"What do you mean?"

"The food? Have you made any friends? Do you have a roommate?"

"Yes, I have a roommate. She's OK."

"That's good honey."

"But the food sucks. I hate the staff. They're all power trippers. Get off on telling you what to do. And I don't like a lot of the other kids. Some of them are even more fucked up than I am."

"Watch your mouth. You know how I feel about you cussin'. And there is nothin' wrong with you."

Emily ignored her mother's comments and continued. "You can't really make friends. Kids are just biding their time 'til they get transferred someplace else. This one kid last week was only there for three days before she was shipped to a foster home. Wish that was me."

"I'm sure you'll get a spot soon and then once I get better . . ." Maggie's voice trailed off. "Maybe you could go back and stay with your old foster mom for now."

"Mom, don't you get it. She kicked me out. It's not like I

have a choice to go back." She said becoming irritated.

"Kim needs to find a place for me to stay on a permanent basis."

"Kim?"

"Kim Howe? Remember? My county social worker?"

"Oh, Yeah. OK, but what about your aunt. I bet-"

"Mom just stop it. She told Kim that she couldn't take care of me either, so I have no place to go OK. No place. No relatives. You're here and Kim won't let me be emancipated." Emily reacted with pronounced frustration. "I need a foster home and it is not likely that anyone will take a kid who's so fucked up."

"Don't talk about yourself like that baby!"

"Well, it's the truth. Who wants a fourteen-year-old depressed kid who's tried to off herself?" She became teary and asked for a tissue. Her mother pointed her to the dresser. Emily rose and walked over to the other side of the room. She stood there, without taking a tissue and remained for several minutes back turned. When she turned around fresh tears were running down her face.

"How could you? How could you . . . keep . . . that picture? She asked between sobs. "How after everything, after everything could you keep it?"

"Because he was part of our family too."

"He wasn't part of our family after what he did. Damn asshole."

"Don't you talk ill of the dead. He had problems, but never meant to hurt no one."

"What the hell do you know? You think he was better than daddy or something?" Emily screamed accusingly.

"No one was better than your daddy. He was the best. And I still miss him every minute of every day. Him and John." Maggie responded quietly.

"It's your fault they're not here." Her face had turned bright red, her fists clenched white. Tears continued to roll down her face. Maggie remained quiet and expressionless as Emily turned to face her. "Sometimes I hate you mom...for what you did. If you had just taken the time to listen to me that day, everything would have been alright."

Emily had opted to go to the cafeteria with Jacques and I remained with Maggie to await their return. Emily had requested some time to get herself together so she could decide if there was anything else she wanted to say before she left.

Maggie's expression did not change once Emily had left the room and she continued to stare out the window providing me with no eye contact. We sat in silence for a time and then Maggie spoke.

"I do love my daughter. I know what y'all must think, that I'm a rotten mom, a pretty bad person 'cause I can't seem to get it together. I mean what kind of woman can't control her liquor and tries to kill herself . . . twice? I can't even sit here and say I didn't want to die. But there's one thing you gotta understand. I never used to be this way. I used to be a pretty good momma and I have always loved my children. The thing Emily doesn't understand or maybe she does. I don't know . . . " She took a drink of water, her hand shaking as she put it to her lips. "A big part of me died when John did. You can't never recover from the death of a child. Me and Frank were close, had a decent marriage. I mean we had our problems. But we were alright, had gotten through some pretty bad times. But when you lose a child . . . How am I supposed to go on?"

"You have a daughter who needs you." I responded.

"I have a daughter who needs a momma. She doesn't need a broken shell. I'm all busted now." She continued to look out the window and didn't say anything else for a while. She sighed and said. "That day, that day was gorgeous, you know, picture perfect in every way. It was like something you'd see in a magazine, tourist ad for West Virginia."

She sat back in her chair, crossed her legs and began to tell her story. "It had started out like any other day. We'd gotten up around eight. It was a Saturday and we had this tradition kind of thing. It was the only day during the week we weren't rushed and could all get together, you know work and church on Sundays.

Probably hard for people to believe I went to church every Sunday. Had since I was a little girl."

"I'd usually make a big breakfast, fat potatoes, you know fried in bacon grease, scrambled eggs, toast, and ham. Me and Frank would usually polish off a pot of coffee and the kids a pitcher of juice. They liked that fruit punch, Hawaiian punch stuff, you know, it's that red junk. Anyway, we'd finished our breakfast and we were stuffed like tics. Frank went out on the back porch to grab a smoke. He was always real good about not smoking in the house. Funny thing is that's what I thought would kill him."

"Anyway, his brother pulled up in his old blue Chevy pickup pretty soon after that. His little brother Cam. He wasn't driving too straight and you could tell as soon as he got out of the truck that he was drunk. I'd never seen him drunk before, so I knew something was wrong. He was real mad too. Slammin' the door when he got out, kickin' the ground, cussin'. Frank walked out back to where his truck was parked out by the barn and I could see them from the kitchen window, but couldn't hear what they were saying."

"When they stood together, you could tell they were brothers even from a distance. They had the same coloring, fair and freckled. Same build too, only Cam was a few inches taller. Cam had always been considered the better looking of the two, probably because he was more muscular, took pretty good care of himself, worked out a lot. He also had this charisma, could talk to anybody. People loved him. He was friendly you know, made you feel at ease."

"I was still inside then and called to the kids to go upstairs. I didn't want them to hear the fightin'. Frank and I could fight like cats and dogs, but we tried to never let the kids see it. Anyway, I kept watching out the window. I was curious but didn't want to get in their business neither, not unless they asked. Cam was holding an envelope and passed it to Frank. He opened it and held it. I don't think he really understood what Cam was trying to tell him because he just shook his head. Cam seemed to get real frustrated and ripped it away and let out a high pitched scream, like something out of a horror movie. Frank just looked at him. Then, Frank started yelling too. It happened in a flash. Cam pulled out a gun and shot a couple times at the barn as if to get up the nerve, then swiveled, I thought he was gonna kill Frank, but he blew his own brains out instead."

Chapter 11

It was Thursday morning, the day before the audit and I had attended a mandatory law and ethics training earlier that morning. Under normal circumstances I would have enjoyed it.

However, the visit with Maggie continued to run through my head. Maggie had clammed up as soon as Emily returned from the cafeteria and I still hadn't developed an adequate understanding of what had happened in her family. Emily had told me upon exiting the hospital, she considered the past a dead issue which best remained buried, talking about it just made her feel worse.

Though I wanted to stay at the hospital and discuss the issue further, I felt pressured to return to the facility to complete final preparations for the state audit. I knew Barbara was watching me closely and nothing would please her more than to see the clinical program fail. Jamie and I had stayed until almost twelve the night before downing two pots of coffee and a box of chocolate glazed donuts. We left feeling a little nauseous, but confident about the charts we had reviewed. The assessments were complete and diagnostically accurate, the treatment plans were thorough and reflected changes in the clients' progress, required signatures had been obtained, and the progress notes were legible and concise.

As I entered my office, I threw my briefcase down on my desk and saw that Jamie already had Tori and John's charts on her desk. These were the final two therapists' charts which needed to be reviewed. It looked like she had already completed three of John's which meant we were ahead of schedule.

I decided to check in on the therapists before I started auditing to see if there were any final questions and wandered down the short hallway to their offices. Typically, the day before a scheduled program review or audit, the therapists were buzzing around their respective offices making sure their paperwork was completed and that everything that was expected of them was done. However, I was surprised to find as I knocked on each of the offices, they were empty.

I returned to my office and paged Jamie.

"Hi", I said. "Am I missing something or are we incredibly ahead of schedule."

"Hardly." Jamie responded irritably. "We've been stuck on the units all morning. Barbara said three childcare workers called in sick and since staffing was already short, it was now a safety issue. We had no choice - audit or no audit."

I was furious. It was a deliberate attempt by Barbara to undermine the clinical staff. I picked up the phone and called our program administrator Max Bertyl. He was out for the morning and could not be reached on his cell phone. All I could do was inform him of the situation and wait for a call back. I left my desk and headed straight for Barbara's office. I knocked on her door loudly. No answer. I tried again, still no response. I found Susan who informed me that Barbara had gone out. She could not be reached by phone and did not say when she would be returning. I knew I couldn't take the therapists off the units, it wouldn't be safe. I did the only thing I could. I picked up the phone and called Corrine at home.

Forty-five minutes later, Corrine arrived at the group home

with four additional staff members to help relieve the majority of the therapists. I thanked her and she waved as she let herself onto the unit. Jamie and I buckled down to audit the remaining charts and I was stunned at what I was seeing. Tori's charts were a disaster. Her assessments were sketchy at best, her treatment plans were generic proposing the same goals for each client regardless of diagnosis and she hadn't obtained the necessary signatures from clients, parents or social workers. I was flabbergasted.

I grabbed Tori's charts and walked back to her office. As I approached her desk, I saw she was crying. She made a valiant attempt to hide her tears, but her eyes were still watery and red. She avoided eye contact and continued to look down gathering up some papers on her desk. She kept her eyes averted and said with a dismissive tone, "Look, this is a bad time. I gotta go. I've got group."

I looked at my watch. The day had become a blur and I had lost track of time. My watch said 3:25 pm.

"Group was scheduled to start twenty-five minutes ago." I stated. Today was generating quite the tension headache.

"I just told you I had to go. I know I'm late. It won't happen again." She started choking back tears, her lower lip quivering.

"Tori, late or not you can't go on the units like this."

"Like what?"

"Upset. You've obviously been crying."

"It won't affect my performance." She stated.

"Sure it will. The kids don't need to see that. They don't need to worry about what's going on with you when they have enough to deal with already."

"I can leave my personal problems here."

"You should leave your personal problems at home."

I picked up her phone and called Jamie's extension.

"I know you're busy, but I need you to run anger management group immediately. It should have started at three." I hung up.

I turned back to Tori. Her expression had turned to stone. "You had no right. I'm capable."

"We'll talk about this later. But right now, we have bigger

problems. Your charts are incomplete. I know that you're aware we have the audit tomorrow and last time we spoke in supervision, you said everything was caught up."

"I think my charts are adequate given how much I have to do. The paperwork is there for the most part."

"Your assessments are not thorough and you don't even have the necessary signatures." I pulled out one of her charts and flipped it open. "This is your best chart and it is filled with errors."

She looked at me with daggers, obviously, no longer on the verge of tears. I plowed on. "First of all your treatment plan focuses on social skills and self-esteem building for a kid who is diagnosed with anxiety? You don't even address his symptoms."

"What the fuck do you expect me to do about it?"

"Excuse me?"

"We're so damn busy all the time. Hounded by staff. Huge caseloads. How do you expect us to get it all done? You won't approve any overtime."

Barbara who controlled the budget for both programs had refused any overtime for therapists citing that any overtime monies in the budget needed to be funneled to residential to manage staffing issues.

"You know Tori. I've had enough. You're not my peer and I don't care for your disrespectful tone. When I ask you to do something I expect it to be done."

She paused then confessed. "Look, I'm having some personal problems. Also, my last job at the counseling center wasn't like this. We were told to keep the paperwork generic and write brief progress notes to protect client confidentiality in case our records were ever subpoenaed. "

I had a hard time believing that a counseling center had operated as such. However, I gave her the benefit of the doubt and tried to look at it as a training issue. "Your documentation needs to reflect what occurs in session."

"The bottom line Tori is that personal problems or not, we're going to have to get your charts in order today. Our state audit is a big deal and over the last three weeks I have been a broken record telling the therapists that if they were having documentation issues to meet with me. You never did."

"Like I said before, I thought they were adequate."

"Well, they're not so I'm going to get the rest of your charts and we'll go through them and then you can catch up and make the necessary changes. It's going to take some time."

"Fine, but I can only stay until 4:00. I've got plans after work."

"Tori, you need to get this stuff done."

"I've got something I have to take care of. It can't wait. Anyway, my work day is done in 45 minutes."

"Could you come in early tomorrow?"

"What do you want from me?"

"I want you to do your job." I sighed knowing expending anymore energy was fruitless. "Look, your work day is done now. Consider yourself off the clock. Your lack of effort with your charts and attitude will be reflected in your upcoming evaluation."

I took her chart and returned to my office.

Ana slouched against the door of the blue Ford Explorer in the parking lot inhaling cigarette smoke deeply into her lungs. She stared into the night sky. What the hell had she gotten herself into? She wasn't stupid, but the problem was she was hooked. Stopping wasn't a choice she wanted to make, at least not now. She'd just have to find a way around all the existing minefields.

She had made one decision. No matter what, no one could know. Not under any circumstances. It would be the end of her career and this was not an option. She had worked too hard sweating it out at greasy hamburger joints to earn her tuition money. To this day, she could smell greasy patties and French fries permeating her nostrils and making her nauseous wherever she went.

All her life, she had been the dumpy, pudgy kid who always got picked last. In gym class, eyes would begin to roll when she approached the team which had been saddled with her presence. Constantly ridiculed and picked on because of her weight, curly mop and coke bottle glasses, life had become even worse with the addition of braces and the development of acne in junior high. She didn't bother making an effort to socialize, instead choosing to keep to herself.

In college, her physical appearance hadn't changed significantly even though the braces and acne were gone. She was still overweight and the buffets at the dining hall were no help. During her first semester at college, she had expanded another two pant sizes. However, despite her appearance, she felt more accepted by her peers, people more interested in what she had to say rather than how she looked.

In the middle of her second semester, she had met Martin, a tall, athletic, all American boy. It had been a Sunday night and they were both studying for an anthropology midterm at the library on campus. He cramming, she reviewing. She had helped him muddle through all the lectures he had missed because of his heavy partying and pledge activities. He had explained that pledging his fraternity had taken up much more time than he could have ever imagined. He had thanked her profusely for her time and said goodbye.

Miraculously, Martin had passed his midterm and the following week when he saw her in class, had asked her out to dinner. He had walked her back to her dorm that night and kissed her softly on the lips and she felt an electric current run through her body. She quickly reciprocated and he pushed her to go further, but she resisted and he honored her wishes. He had accepted her. But was he willing to wait until she was ready?

Their romance had continued for another three weeks before he had coaxed his way into her. He had eased her down on her bed, gently raised her skirt and moved into that warm wet place between her legs. It had made her feel so alive, so wanted and so beautiful. He had called her in the morning and asked her to dinner at the frat house. All the pledges were supposed to bring a date. Would she? She eagerly accepted and wore a soft pink chiffon semi formal dress the color of cotton candy. She had mingled, feeling rather uncomfortable noticing people sneaking glances and didn't know if it was more than her insecurities. She tried to ignore it and enjoyed the party. During the evening, both she and Martin had imbibed heavily; he so heavily that he had passed out. She ended up walking home by herself at one in the morning, cold, miserable with aching blistered feet.

Martin hadn't called the next day, or the next or the day after that. She knew he must have been embarrassed, so she gave him time. However, after a week had passed she finally broke down and called. The only response she got was the answering machine. She became annoyed. Even if Martin was embarrassed, that was no excuse. She finally got up enough nerve to visit the frat house.

A lanky freckled man who had also been pledging the fraternity answered the door. As she stood on the porch, she had politely asked for Martin. He shook his head stating that Martin wasn't available. She insisted. He continued to insist that he was not available and didn't want to see her. She was relentless until he had no choice but to confess.

The freckled man stated that the night he had seen her at the frat house, he thought she seemed intelligent enough to have figured it out sooner. Martin was an attractive guy, had girls falling all over him. No one would dispute that. But this wasn't about having a girlfriend. She had been his in, his last challenge before becoming a brother. It was "the ugly chick test," old as the hills. Certainly she had heard of it. The task was to befriend and date the ugliest woman you could find. You court her until she has sex with you and then invite her to the last pledge dinner so the brothers can judge which pledge had the ugliest lay.

Ana was mortified, not quite believing that Martin would have done this. He had appeared so genuine, the things he had said, the way he had touched her. However, after the disbelief wore off, she had cried and crawled into bed with all the junk food she could corral from donuts to potato chips. She had thought Martin had truly cared about her as a person, as his girlfriend. That maybe they even had a future. Instead, he had used her. How could he? And how could she have been so stupid?

Ana had needed some moral support and called her mother.

This was a bad idea. Instead of support, she got chastised. It was her fault for being so naive. All she had to do was look in the mirror. How could she have thought a good looking frat boy would have wanted anything to do with her? Then, she got advice. The same advice she had received for years suggesting that she would have to learn how to tolerate this kind of treatment. After all, hadn't she always been treated poorly by her peers? Why on earth would things be any different in college? She just needed to prepare herself for a life of misery and accept she would always be alone. She needed to realize she was just like her mother who had never married, conceiving her daughter following a brief encounter with her best friend's father in the back seat of his car as he drove her home following a high school dance.

The irony was, however, she was not like her mother. In fact she was anything but. Her appearance may have said mouse, but there was a cobra coiled up inside her. So, she decided to take charge. She became angry with herself finally deciding to fight against her lot in life. Following three months of rolling around in self pity, she had straightened and bleached her hair, changed from glasses to contacts, and lost 40 pounds, eating nothing but salads, apples and drinking diet soda.

The result may not have been supermodel, but no one could argue that she wasn't attractive. In fact, so much more attractive with her new wardrobe and carefully applied make up that many people on campus no longer recognized her, including Martin. He hadn't even seen her coming. Maybe if he had he would have been able to defend himself instead of having his life snuffed out before completing his first year of college.

Chapter 12

As the snow fell, problems on the units continued. Clients were more volatile because of the approaching holidays. They were painfully aware they would remain at the facility with no family willing or able to take them. Additionally, the clients were impacted by the holiday staffing shortage. There would be virtually no opportunities for any one on one time with staff during the holidays and many of the superfluous "fun" activities would have to be cancelled resulting in more room time. It was no surprise that restraints were up.

To add to the misery, the number of residential staff continued to dwindle. There had been more resignations in the last month and it appeared that hiring continued to be at a standstill. You could sense the frustration from the hardcore residential staff who continued to put forth what at times seemed like a futile effort.

The clinical team had agreed to chip in and spend as much time as possible on the units. We continued to be a team of ten, but more therapists' positions had been filled and there would be two new faces starting after the New Year. The state audit had gone exceptionally well. This was a combination of both hard work and luck. Charts had been randomly pulled. None selected had belonged to Tori. That was luck.

There hadn't been any evident change in Tori's attitude. She seemed to be cavalier about her position, always showing up a few minutes late for her shifts, and then exerting only a minimal effort. She had made some progress on her charts, but only enough to avoid any potential disciplinary action.

A second disappointment came in the form of the response I had received from Max Bertyl, the program administrator. He had avoided providing me with any concrete solutions or advice regarding Barbara, instead congratulating me for the audit and recognizing it was a success even though we had been stuck on the units for the majority of that day. When I asked him directly about Barbara and her bullying, he stated that she was a very opinionated woman who was good at her job. Max further stated that Barbara recently reported to him that we were working well together. I decided to cut my losses and move on to other things for the time being. I knew a brick wall when I hit one.

Emily had not fared well since the visit with her mother and had started to sink into a deeper depression. She had stopped asking about Maggie and there had been no further contact between the two. She recognized that she would be spending Christmas alone. This was particularly painful because it had been such a special time of year for her family in the not so distant past.

Emily had slowly isolated herself from her peers, demonstrating little motivation to do anything beyond sleep. Her appetite had significantly decreased and she would do no more than pick at her plate during mealtimes. I had bought some fast food to share with her before our most recent session. Emily had pushed the warm, greasy bag back in my direction stating she wasn't hungry. She commented she had come to terms with the fact that her life would be "shit." Her future would likely be filled with loneliness. She believed it was her fate to be poor and live alone in a dumpy apartment with no family to speak of. I had referred her to one of our consulting psychiatrists, Dr. Antonazzi, for a medication evaluation. She had said she would be able to meet with Emily in the next week.

It was just after 4 pm and I made my way up to the girls' unit to complete my daily check in with my clients. I peeked in on the latency age unit and noticed that all the lights were off save one that cast a faint light by the staff desk as you entered. I opened the door and could see all sixteen kids sitting in the hallway silent. There were being watched by several very solemn staff members. Drew saw me and waved me over.

"Hey, I just tried calling your extension. I just completed a unit shut down."

"I see that." I said.

Unit shut downs were an efficient way to contain and account for all the clients in an emergency or a situation that had potentially dangerous consequences.

"So?" I urged dispensing with any small talk.

"Well, it looks like we've got a missing pair of scissors."

"Great." I commented. "How did that happen?"

"It happened during art therapy. I guess they were making some kind of collage, cutting pictures of people out of magazines and gluing them on paper. Anyway scissor count at the beginning was eight and at the end during clean up it was only seven."

"God, just what we need."

"Preachin' to the choir Doc."

"Art Therapy today that's..."

"Tori's group."

"Yeah, when Heather was here and she used to do it she'd cut all the stuff out before group and not let the kids touch the scissors. I liked that plan much better."

"Me too. Where's Tori now?"

"Uh, she's still in the group room looking."

"Alright, I'll check in. You need any help or you got enough bodies?"

"Help? Yeah. Definitely. I'm just gonna keep the kids here until the common room is searched and then corral them in there until we search the rest of the unit. Hopefully, we'll find them. If not, some shit's gonna fly 'cause I'll have to explain it to Barbara."

Despite Tori's poor judgment and supervision, the shift supervisor was ultimately responsible for safety on the units. I opened the door to the group room to see her on her hands and knees looking underneath the couch. She turned to look at me as I entered and I thought I heard her say "shit."

"Hey, Tori, have you found them?"

"Well, obviously no, since I'm still searching." She responded sarcastically.

I ignored her comment. "Before you continue, are you absolutely sure you had eight pairs of scissors?"

"Yes. Yes. Yes. I already told Drew. I don't know why I have to repeat myself. I got them at the craft store this morning on the way in." She said in a very exasperated tone.

"OK then, looks like you'll need some help."

"You know, I'd prefer to do this alone. You being here well, frankly, I feel like I'm being judged, evaluated, whatever you want to call it. It stresses me out. And I know what you're thinking."

"And what's that?"

"Well, that I should have done things differently."

"Do you think you should have done things differently?" I said throwing the question back at her. She was right though, an ounce of prevention . . .

"No. I can't watch that many kids at once."

"What about not giving them scissors to start with? We've talked about that in treatment team?"

"What do you want from me? I didn't think it would be a problem. It's not my fault. Hell, I can't predict what those kids are gonna do." She was now rooting around in the couch. Tori was always defensive, so quick to react and was just plain disrespectful. Worst of all she never wanted to take responsibility for anything. I was tired of her attitude. I just wanted to fire her, but knew administration wouldn't support my decision. However, maybe at least I could extend her probation letting her know that her continued insubordination would not be tolerated. I excused myself. My energies would be better focused elsewhere.

I stayed and helped search the units. Nothing. Three hours later, we gave up. Either Tori had miscounted the scissors and they were actually all accounted for and this was just a colossal waste of time or, clearly the worse alternative was that they had been snatched and well hidden to be used later for some predetermined purpose.

It was after 8 p.m. before I stopped at Fazoli's, an eat-in or take-out, Italian restaurant to pick up a quick meal on my way home. Once there, I chose to eat in. I was ravenous. I realized when ordering my meal that I hadn't been anywhere besides work or home since Elliot had left for internship. I frequently refused invitations from friends to socialize. It wasn't like me to be so reclusive and I told myself I had to start making more of an effort to leave my cave.

As I ate linguine, mopping up the marinara with a bread stick, I looked around the restaurant. The tables were filled with families. There was constant chatter interrupted by shrill screams from the many babies and children who were present. It made me feel lonely and disappointed. There were couples who looked younger than Elliot and me dining with their children. It was hard to see what you wanted, knowing it may never happen.

I ended up feeling sorry for myself the rest of the evening. When I finally returned home, I called Elliot. No answer. So, I left a message, hoping he'd return my call. Then, I plopped myself down on the sofa and settled into my evening routine of channel surfing.

Despite my negativity, even I couldn't deny that there were two things that had been going right. First, my concern about the mysterious note that had been stuck to my office door had disappeared into the ether. My guess was that it had been a spur of the moment practical joke left by a client or staff member, certainly nothing to be taken seriously. Second, I had been sleeping soundly since the night Elliot had left, finally free of the intrusive, recurrent nightmare. I attributed it to the mounting anxiety I had developed prior to Elliot's departure and my fear of the "unknown". As I had established a routine, my worries lessened and even though all was far from perfect, things were more or less predictable and that provided me with a sense of comfort. My guess was the nightmare was gone for good.

I had taken my worries to sleep with me since I was a child, experiencing nightmares when faced with stressful situations which were beyond my control. When I was eight my grandmother had developed ovarian cancer and I had dreamed about her almost every night. She would be swimming in filthy, putrid water. I stood on the gray, weathered beaten boards of the dock watching helplessly. She begged me to help her. I tried throwing in a rope, but she couldn't hold on. I wanted to jump in. She told me no, so I respected her wishes, continuing to watch her struggle. I dreamt this until she died, worried and wanting to help her but knowing I couldn't.

When I was fourteen, my parents divorced. I had taken it harder than anyone else in the family. Initially, we had participated in family therapy, but the marriage was beyond saving. There was too much damage - too little motivation from my father, and maybe my mother, as well, but for different reasons. My father had met someone new and was excited by the prospect of a fresh start. My mother resigned to her fate hoped to put it past her as quickly as possible. My dream had occurred night after night and it was always the same. I had left the psychologist's office with my parents, younger sister and older brother. We were waiting for the elevator. The elevator doors opened and I fell straight down the shaft into blackness.

The last time I had experienced nightmares was when Elliot and I had endured a year of separation after an already volatile and painful summer of marital conflict. I had left for South Carolina not trusting him, but desperately wanting things to work. After all, I had vowed I would not end up like my parents. My sleep during that summer and the year of our separation had also reflected my anxiety. My dreams were repetitive and involved me walking from the psychology lab to my car after staying late to work on my dissertation. As I made my way to the parking lot I heard footsteps. I looked over my shoulder and saw a faceless man chasing me. I dropped my briefcase and ran. I never made it to my car.

At some point in the evening, I had fallen asleep. I awoke to the sound of the door bell. My watch said 11:30 pm. I must have nodded off watching the news. I rose and dragged my stiff body to the door. I looked out the peephole to see Corrine standing in the snow.

Chapter 13

It had been snowing hard with thick, sloppy flakes sticking to the ground like glue. Corrine shook the white fluff from her coat before entering.

"I'm really sorry to bother you Dr. Morgan."

"No. No. No bother. Please come in." I responded somewhat disoriented.

"It took a lot for me to come here, but I have a confession."

She continued to stand just inside the door and rejected my offer to come in and sit down.

"You have to understand I feel really awkward about this. I feel like I've been deceitful." Corrine looked around the room. "You've always been nice to me, really respectful, you know. I like you. You seem like a decent person."

"Thanks. I appreciate that."

"Well, I'm the person who put that note in you box . . . you know the one I mean . . . about watching your back. I wanted to let you know."

"Go on." I answered becoming more puzzled.

"At first, I was going to leave you another one, but I felt guilty because I walked by you in treatment team the day I left it and saw you looking at it. You seemed confused. Things at work are bad on most days and I didn't want to add to your stress."

"What are you trying to tell me Corrine?"

"It's not a joke and I'm not trying to be funny. I don't want to lose my job and that's part of the reason I've been scared to come and talk to you about things. I also don't want to be pulled into a big mess, like you confronting Barbara and expecting me to back you up. Besides, my opinion doesn't count for much with my lack of education. What I said in the note is true. You need to watch your back and there are things that you should be aware of."

"For example?"

"I don't even know where to start because I don't even understand it all, but I know more than I should and more than I want to."

At my continued prompting, she finally advanced to the living room and took a seat. I grabbed two sodas from the fridge and took the chair opposite her.

"Well, I've been at Ellis House since it opened with Barbara, Barry, Mr. Bertyl and Mr. Houseman. You've met him right?"

"Yes. Once, at a board meeting when I first took the position." I stated.

Mr. Houseman was the company C.E.O., with an MBA from Columbia and a Masters in Psychology from the University of Chicago. He had a formidable presence and I couldn't help but be impressed when I had made his acquaintance. He was indeed larger than life with a booming voice and a wickedly strong handshake that effectively cut off your circulation. He was handsome with piercing blue eyes that seemed to look right through to your soul.

"Well, first of all. Barbara listens."

"Listens? What do you mean listens?"

"I mean she has a phone in her office so she can listen in on other people's conversations. I'm not sure how it works. Anyway,

112

you can hear a faint clicking sound sometimes, so be really careful with what you say. She knows pretty much everything and records anything that she thinks is important and then uses it against you. That's how she got rid of Fiona May.

"And what did she use against her?"

"Oh, shit Fiona was saying about Houseman. I guess after a meeting she tore him up pretty good to one of the staff psychiatrists. They had a real bitch session about the management or should I say mismanagement of the program. She talked about how the clinical program always got screwed and that all Houseman really cared about was lining his pockets. He didn't give a shit about the kids. Next day she was asked to pack her things."

Fiona May was a first generation Japanese American woman who had put herself through graduate school in San Francisco while maintaining a 40 hour a week job at a local restaurant just down the street from her parents' tiny apartment. She had always been passionate about her job and was a strong child advocate. She wasn't afraid of hard work and had regularly been seen on the units during the weekend checking in with her clients and anyone else who seemed in need of attention. Fiona was also an extremely diplomatic woman and if she were to make any harsh comments, they would have been made discretely to someone she trusted in the privacy of her own office.

"She was the clinical director before Brian Crawford right?"

"Right. Don't even know what happened to him. He didn't even make it six months."

Brian Crawford, on the other hand, had never put forth an effort to exercise change and during his reign the clinical program suffered. He did, however, have a fiery temper and wasn't likely to censor anything coming out of his mouth. No wonder he was fired.

"So, getting back to Barbara." I prompted not wanting to get off track.

"Barbara eavesdrops, on phone calls, listens at doors, has her snoops around the building . . . who knows what else? Probably bugs the place. Has mini surveillance cameras set up. Hell, I don't know."

I continued to absorb everything I was being told.

"Make of it what you will. All, I'm saying is that people with authority who really advocate for the kids don't seem to last long. I'm sure Barbara would love the clinical program cut. Then, she could completely rule with an iron fist."

I found myself looking at my watch. Corrine asked if she should go and should we find another time to speak. I urged her to finish, deciding that all I had to do right now was listen. I could decide what to do with it later.

The story was that Barbara had left Georgia with her tail between her legs. Two minors had AWOLed on her watch when she was the residential director at Crestwood, a small group home in Savannah. It had resulted in the near death of a thirteen-year-old female who shot up and while high got struck by a car. She was in the hospital for months and never fully recovered mentally or physically. Barbara had been investigated by state licensing and the program had been fined due to their negligence. She had been fortunate to avoid any civil action given that the girl had no family to speak of. There were personal consequences, however, and the director of Crestwood gave her the boot in no uncertain terms stating that what had occurred was her fault. Barbara had no way to dispute it despite her efforts. She hadn't even been on grounds when the incident occurred, instead she had been enjoying a leisurely three hour lunch.

Barbara reluctantly moved to Michigan, her husband's home state and somehow managed to procure her position at Ellis House. One of the first suspicious incidents occurred just two months after Ellis House opened. Corrine took another sip of soda and said. "God, this still really bothers me. There was this 9-year-old girl called Cherry Jones, a psychotic kid dumped at the facility. When she heard voices, she went nuts, lost control. Obviously, we can't manage kids who are that severe, but we had to keep her for seven days until her county could find her a place to go.

One day she was in the quiet room cussin' and screaming for

114

God to help her make the voices stop. Barbara came back to the unit and told staff to leave, she'd handle it. So, they all cleared out and left them alone. Well, except for me. About five minutes after Barbara went in the room the kid stopped screaming. I peaked in the quiet room window and could see Barbara getting up off the floor, Cherry was still down there lying in a fetal position. Anyway, Barbara came out and told me the problem was solved and to get back to manning the quiet room. I went in and checked on Cherry. She wouldn't talk, just kept crying. I stayed with her and later noticed that she had a couple welts on her arms and there was a bump on her head. I had medical check her over.

I was enraged and called state licensing to make a complaint, anonymous of course. But, nothing happened. I still don't understand. An investigator came out and interviewed Cherry, but nothing happened. I never heard anything else about it. I called them back to see how the investigation had progressed because it was public record. They told me that the claim was unsubstantiated. What is so disturbing is that I can't tell you how many incidents like this have occurred, not always physical, sometimes verbal. Also, sometimes kids are conveniently forgotten about in the quiet room. How she treats the kids is awful, but she gets away with it and she's never caught. I just don't get it. It seems like the higher ups don't care."

What Corrine had told me, as ridiculous as it sounded, somehow made sense. Maybe she was little on the paranoid side, but it made me start to question my own job security. And I couldn't help but recall the numerous times during which I had been aware of that clicking sound on the phone. It seemed as if nothing else Corrine had helped raise my already existing suspicions.

Corrine sat in her car feeling the icy blast of cold air flow out the vents. Her hands were like ice, but she hardly noticed them. She was waiting, taking a little more time to decide if she should go back and tell Dr. Morgan. There were so many times during their conversation that she had wanted to blurt it out. She needed advice, but didn't know if she'd be taken seriously. She caught Dr. Morgan's expression several times when she was talking and knew she was skeptical. She didn't blame her. She'd eventually figure it out for herself, but at least Corrine felt like she had given her a heads up.

Dr. Morgan wouldn't believe her without proof. No one would. What was reality to her and her accuser was just conjecture to others, so she held back even though she didn't want to. She looked over at the red canvas overnight bag which she had packed only hours before. She was looking forward to tomorrow when she could take a day or two to gain some perspective.

Chapter 14

Despite heightened airport security since 9/11, I experienced no delays. Once boarded, I grabbed a pillow and blanket on the way to my seat to make myself comfortable. Finally settled, I examined the grey, drab landscape outside my scratched, dingy window. No question, I was looking forward to a long, yet relaxing flight to San Diego.

I was filled with anticipation. I would have a temporary respite from the mounting complications and pressures at work. There was still no resolution with Tori and I thought perhaps a break over the holidays would do everyone some good, especially me.

More importantly, I yearned for Elliot. It had seemed like a lifetime since our teary departure and I could hardly wait to see him, to be close to him. My whole body seemed an empty shell without his touch and warmth. I had been crossing the days off my calendar somehow hoping it would accelerate the date of our reunion. And now, it was here. California with him would be the next best thing to the vacation we'd both been desperate for.

Elliot and I had done a great job keeping in touch, corresponding multiple times a day typically by text messaging or by email. In the evening, as the day drew to a close, Elliot would usually call and provide me with a detailed description of his day and I would reciprocate. However, despite our efforts, it did little to satisfy my craving to be with him. I wanted to be held and to feel the warmth of his touch. I continued to stare out my window and started to reminisce, an exercise that had provided me with some satisfaction in his absence.

Elliot and I had met in graduate school. I was starting my third year and had returned to Michigan from Ontario where I had been granted approval to complete my external practicum. I had spent the preceding four months at Children's Hospital conducting evaluations and providing treatment for children who had developed cognitive deficits as a result of renal failure. The return to Kalamazoo, Michigan, the town in which my graduate program was located was extremely difficult.

I had grown up in Ottawa and loved the city and its surroundings. It was cosmopolitan with its museums, art galleries, National Arts Centre and upscale clothing boutiques and bistros, yet had not lost its small town charm as demonstrated by its narrow tree lined streets with local markets and bakeries. It had the distinct advantage of being a city where one could function easily without a car regardless of where you lived since so much was accessible in each neighborhood by foot.

Each season was distinct and offered so much. Spring brought renewed vibrancy to the outdoors. This was particularly evident with the hundreds of thousands of tulips which created an impressionist landscape in the parks, by the bicycle paths and all along the Rideau Canal. Summer lured people to sidewalk cafes, beaches, and lakes; the city was dominated by walkers, joggers and cyclists along the hundreds of miles of trails that wove their way through both the more urban and rural areas. Fall brought frequent visits to the open air markets and county fairs. The sugar maples turned shades of gold, auburn and scarlet and piles of firewood began to accumulate in yards and on porches. Winter came. First, the scant, powdery snow fell and then the more serious, burying the city in its cold, silent beauty. The festivals continued and the canal was frozen to become the world's largest skating rink. The lifestyle had been both comfortable and enjoyable. It was that familiarity and the comfort of my family and friends which fueled my reluctance to return to Michigan.

However, my return to Kalamazoo was inevitable and an obvious requirement for completion of my Ph.D. I arrived at my new apartment late in the evening letting myself in with the key my roommate Ralph had sent me a couple weeks earlier. Ralph, in his final year of the program had two vacancies in his three bedroom apartment.

My initial and desired plan had been to get an apartment of my own. However, finances dictated my lot, so here I was sharing my home-to-be with Ralph and Elliot Morgan, a fresh new face from the University of Massachusetts - Amherst. Unfortunately, my desire to share my space with anyone was tainted by my roller coaster ride with my former roommate who had finally been requested to leave the graduate program because of her continued lack of motivation and unstable behavior.

Elliot and I did not get off on the right foot and my dislike for him was instantaneous. My understanding from Ralph had been that since I was a woman living with two men, I would have the one bedroom with an attached bath and that the two men would share the second bathroom. This, however, was where my distaste for Elliot began. As I started to unpack my belongings, I discovered that Elliot had already procured the aforementioned bedroom with all its amenities and was happily watching television without any apparent apologies for the situation.

Ralph, who was an accommodating, passive soul told me he had informed Elliot upon his arrival that this was my room. However, Elliot responded by stating that he would take responsibility for any negative consequences and that if I had arrived sooner it wouldn't have been an issue. I was too tired to bicker and thus, without a word put my bags down in the small bedroom at the end of the hall vowing to speak with Elliot about the situation when I had more energy.

A month passed before we initiated more than small talk and forced greetings in the kitchen at meal times. I had by this time given up on confronting him about the room. We were both settled and what would be the point? One evening, we had remained at the house while Ralph, the social butterfly of the residence, had attended a "meet and greet" for the most recent class of graduate students. We had passed on the event commenting on how stiff and forced the conversation would be and agreed to go and see a movie together at the theater down the block. We spent the evening laughing and joking, a pleasant change from the monotony of books and lectures. The more time we spent together, the more fun we had and we became inseparable. Within three months, Elliot had gotten down on bended knee and proposed marriage while I sat on the tattered red couch in the living room.

My affirmative response to his proposal had surprised everyone, including me. Typically, I was a planner, deliberate in my actions and waited to see how things developed, but for whatever reason this time I dived right in. We were married seven months later at my family's cottage on Lake Muskoka followed by a hurried honeymoon in Las Vegas. We delayed our return to school until only several hours before making the mandatory appearances at our respective teaching positions.

Our marriage had progressed well, despite the constant stressors that always seemed to be thrown in our path. Within our first year of marriage we had experienced two deaths in the family, an automobile accident, the looming separation for completion of my pre-doctoral internship and a monthly existence on less than five hundred dollars.

Looking back, it seemed what held us together were our goals for the future. We had similar ambitions, both wanting to be successful with our careers and have enough financial flexibility to search New England for an old Victorian house in need of renovation. Our plan was to get our hands dirty and do most of the work ourselves so it could be something we created together. Massachusetts was the state of choice as this was where Elliot had been raised. I had loved the Boston area since childhood and could find no flaws with the idea. We were truly compatible in so many ways, expect one, children.

We had agreed that if it ever came to that, and this was a big "if" because of Elliot's hesitancy, I would be the primary caretaker making the sacrifices with my career. I had no issue with this, but it was about so much more than sacrificing my career. Elliot said that he had observed too many relationships fall apart after children. Babies changed everything and he was right. The unfortunate interpretation of this statement was that I saw the change being positive and he didn't. He said that with children you lose your partner and your focus shifts to diapers, night time feedings and constant responsibility. It wasn't a risk he wanted to take with "us," but if I continued to insist we could possibly consider it.

I knew if I didn't have children, I'd regret it. So, it seemed like Elliot was putting me in a position where I had no choice but to press the issue. I hoped Elliot would change his mind and see things differently over time. After all, many people did. But, what if he didn't? What if having children turned out to be for him exactly as he predicted? Then, where would we be? Nevertheless, it was an issue we needed to revisit and maybe San Diego was just the place to do it.

I was brought back to the present when the drink service interrupted my thoughts. I gulped down a can of cranberry juice followed by a glass of water. I decided to forego the pretzels, I'd just be thirsty immediately after anyway. I thumbed though the newspaper, scanned the most recent American Psychologist and soon became distracted. I pulled down the window shade, shutting my eyes. I drifted off to sleep and was soon in the midst of my nightmare.

The truck completes its ascent up the narrow drive and slows. I hear the squeaking of brakes as the truck lurches to a full stop. The engine dies. I know exactly where I am, at the end of the driveway only a stone's throw from my front door. I wait. I hear nothing, just ambient noise, the rustle of the wind through the trees, crickets chirping, sounds of morning starting to stir. It's still early and the sky is a dark grey, still time before the sun rises, but the stars have faded and light lurks on the horizon. My body hurts. It is stiff, sore and every inch of it aches. My wrists continue to throb from where I rubbed them raw exposing my flesh to air.

I hear the cab door open and slam shut followed by the now familiar sound of footsteps making their way to my metal cage. The tailgate is released and I hear sawing, the thick rope efficiently severed. The tarp gracefully sags and crumples continuing to cover my body. He reaches in, throwing the tarp to the ground. He jumps into the back of the truck. With a swift slice he frees my legs. Then, he pulls the gag down around my neck keeping my wrists bound. With one motion, I'm pulled to my feet and pushed off the truck. My legs are numb and my knees buckle providing me with no strength to brace my fall. I land with a heavy thud on the wet grass. I lie there only momentarily forcing myself to my feet as he orders me to rise. He shoves me in the direction of my home and I walk clumsily toward the front door.

The door opens and I immediately shift my gaze to the floor, afraid of what I might see. I remember what I heard when I escaped . . . the screaming, the glass shattering. I'm afraid of what awaits me. I know this man is capable of cruelty. And I shut my eyes thinking to myself, "Please don't make me look." Don't make me look . . . don't make me look if my husband is gone. I keep my eyes shut, having no desire to open them and learn the truth. He pushes me inside and I fall to the ground reflexively opening my eyes to guide me as I attempt to break my fall. I hit hard bruising my knees and jarring my wrists. I stay on the ground. No motivation to rise. What do I do? What the hell do I do? I keep hoping for a solution, a way out, but what? I still don't even know about my husband. God is he alive? How badly is he hurt? Can I help him escape if he's not mobile? I won't be able to leave him again.

I remain on the floor while he walks over to the kitchen. He peels off his mask exposing a flushed and unrecognizable face. I have never seen this man before, not that I remember. He has a long oval face with a pronounced dimpled chin, yellow horse teeth and a Grecian nose. His eyes are black, cold and lifeless and convey nothing to me, but inhumanity. He looks at me and stretches his thick frame to reach a pint of Jack Daniels from the small cherry cabinet above the stove. He unscrews the cap and takes a long swallow. He puts the bottle down on the granite counter and turns to face me. He crosses his arms and stares. He says nothing. I want to scream at him to leave us alone, but can't. He returns his focus to the whiskey taking several more swallows. He continues to hold the bottle, not bothering to put it down this time. Then, it hits me hard and fast. How did he know? How the hell did he know where we keep the liquor? The bastard had been in our house before.

I was jolted awake as the wheels of the plane touched the tarmac completing our descent into San Diego. My body was stiff and my muscles ached. My hands were sweaty as I wiped them on my jeans. I yawned and stretched shaking the sleep from my body. I peered out the window shifting focus from the unwanted dream to my new surroundings. The dingy, scratched window was now filled with light instead of grey. I shifted around in my seat not willing to join the urgent struggle to deplane. There was no rush to beat the clock and I'd have to wait on my luggage anyway. After the crowd of passengers had cleared, I made my way off the plane toward the baggage claim searching the crowds for Elliot. Then, I saw him in his usual casual Saturday morning garb, jeans and a t-shirt. My face immediately broke into a smile and I found my way to his arms.

Chapter 15

You could smell the ocean as soon as you walked into the parking lot. The palm trees were commonplace for Californians, but such a refreshing sight for me, a person who had grown up in Canada and now lived in the Midwest. Elliot threw my bags into the back seat of the jeep and drove a circuitous route through downtown to show off his new surroundings before starting the drive up the coast. Sailboats dotted the harbor and the skyline offered a view that was spectacular. As we drove north up Pacific Coast Highway, I couldn't help but be impressed. Even the highways were aesthetically pleasing with huge oleander and bougainvillea bushes growing along its side. I sat back, relaxed and enjoyed the ride. We followed the highway to the La Jolla Colony exit and turned off past Rose Canyon entering the condominium complex where Elliot had made his current home.

Just like the photos, the grounds were perfect, not a leaf out of place. The thick, green lawns were bordered by ice plants with bright pink flowers and waxy leaves. Birds of paradise were abundant and seemingly grew like weeds. The bougainvillea bushes were tall extending more than fifteen feet showering a spray of magenta and purple flowers. There was a beautiful aqua colored pool which sparkled. The pool extended to a large hot tub that was adorned with brown, yellow and blue Mexican tile. Royal blue umbrellas provided shade to the few who sought refuge from the sun.

I visually inhaled the surroundings and followed Elliot up the cement stairs to his second level condo. The interior of the condo itself was as visually appealing as its surroundings. It was airy with multiple skylights and floor to ceiling windows. The ceilings were vaulted and dotted with several ceiling fans which helped keep it cool even on the warmest of days, lessening the need for air conditioning. It was painted a creamy sand color with the faintest splash of yellow.

There was a tiny galley kitchen which opened up to a cozy dining and living area. A small balcony opened up from the living room and Elliot had decorated it with dwarf citrus trees and yellow and orange bromeliads. A black metal café style table with two matching chairs was positioned in the middle anchored by an oversized three wick white candle. Elliot had decorated well despite having a tight budget. I flopped down on the sofa.

"The place looks great." I said and smiled.

"I think so." He said and sat down beside me kissing me lightly on the lips. I kissed him back and immediately his hands slipped up my shirt. He kissed me deeply, playing with my tongue as he unbuttoned my shirt. His mouth followed a slow and familiar path down my body. I stretched out my hand and felt a hard knot as I unbuttoned his belt and freed him from his pants. We quickly found a rhythm and I could feel him pushing deeper and deeper inside me. Then, he momentarily slowed and I felt him release finding my own desire quenched seconds later. He rolled off me, dripping in sweat and smiled.

"That was great. God, I've missed sex. There are some days I don't think I can wait." He confessed.

"You better. It's no fun for me either."

He laughed as he picked me up, carried me to the bedroom and threw me on the bed. He stretched out beside me and pulled the duvet up over our naked bodies. We quickly fell into a sound sleep for the remainder of the afternoon.

We rose from our slumber around six in the evening feeling well rested. We showered, dressed and finally made it out of the condo by 8 pm. We took a leisurely walk through the park to the Ritz, a small Italian restaurant bordered by the park and Via Plata. Our table faced a wood burning fireplace that threw off a pleasant heat. The decor was casual and rustic. The food surpassed my expectations. By the time the evening was done, we had feasted on baked garlic, hot crusty bread and stuffed eggplant. We lingered over merlot and my eyes were drawn to an infant bundled up in a car seat several tables over.

"Isn't she adorable?" I said and gently nudged Elliot's arm. Elliot was quiet for a moment and the mood shifted from light to serious. He looked down at the table.

"You know Grace I have felt so disconnected from you lately." Elliot admitted.

"Where's this coming from and what do you mean exactly?" I asked completely taken aback, still focused on the infant.

"Like we've grown apart. I know we're living in separate places now, but even before I moved out it was as if we were just living in the same house but had parallel lives."

"I can't believe you're saying that. I've never felt like that." I responded defensively. "Is this a new thing? I don't understand?"

"No, I guess I've felt like this for a couple of years now."

"But we're close. We talk every day." I argued trying to convince him.

"Yeah, about superficial stuff. What's been going on that day."

"So, what you're saying is that . . ."

"Is that we struggle to find things to talk about. We've never really had things in common. Our sexual needs are different." He paused and looked down. "And the whole kid thing." He sighed, took a sip of wine and continued. "I know you want kids and well

126

I don't. You lose your whole life. All you have are dirty diapers, feedings, sleepless night and a messy house. It gets no better as they get older because then it just gets replaced with soccer games, music lessons, homework . . . It's constant work. Not to mention the financial sacrifices and that you have absolutely no time for yourself."

I started to feel on edge. "So, what exactly are you saying?" I asked

"I'm saying that I still want to take my time with this. I want us to work on ourselves this year since we are separated anyway and really find out what we want in life."

"I know what I want and I can't say that I'm too happy right now. I thought we'd have a nice relaxing week. Enjoy ourselves and each other. I didn't want to stress over our marriage which I thought was just fine. Obviously, you think otherwise. And why are you bringing this up now?"

"Relax. Don't blow everything out of proportion and get yourself all worked up. We'll have fun this week. But ask yourself what we'd be doing this week if we had kids - nothing. We'd be stuck inside most of the time. That's my point. See, where I'm coming from?"

I said nothing. He returned my stare and then continued.

"Look Grace, I guess that being in California has sort of opened my eyes."

"Opened your eyes to what?"

"It's shown me that you don't have to follow some predetermined path established by societal norms. It doesn't have to be marriage, a nine to five job, the white picket fence and 2.5 kids with a station wagon and golden retriever."

"So, what do you want then?" I responded with pronounced irritation.

"Well, I'm not saying that I don't want that."

"God El. OK, you may want that but . . . but?" I insisted pressuring a response.

"I'm saying that we don't need to rush it and all I need is time to digest things before and if I become a father. You've got to remember that I still want to experience things before I get tied down. Having kids changes everything. We'll both have our PhDs and no longer be tied down academically. I just want to have some freedom for a while before we jump on the idea of having kids again OK?"

"You know I want kids. I always have. I've never going to change my mind about that."

"I know. I know. And I don't want you to. I respect your feelings. I want you to respect mine too."

"Fine."

"Stop getting so pissy. We may have kids. I just don't want to rush it. I know you've been waiting, but what's one or two more years? I mean we could live out here for a while."

"Hell, Elliot, you told me coming out here wasn't practical, which made me stay in Michigan."

"I know but that was before I got out here. There's just so much to do out here – so many possibilities."

I looked at him without saying a word.

"You've got to remember Grace. You're older than me."

"Two years. That hardly makes a difference."

"Two years makes a big difference. You've had a lot more time to do the things you want to do. You've traveled a lot. You've had opportunities to do a lot of things."

"We've traveled too."

"Right somewhat . . . but, how can I say this? I still feel like I'm missing out. We got married so fast and young."

That was something I could agree with. His statement transported me to our engagement, a time that offered a fantasy of no conflicts, no stressors, just bliss. I quickly brought myself back to the present to focus on our conversation.

"But, it's not like we stopped living. We've traveled and had lots of fun. Remember when we went to Tortola. It was magnificent, so relaxing, the island was beautiful."

"I know. It was. I just want more of that. Sometimes I feel like I'm trapped being forced into a mold that I don't want to be in. Do you understand?"

I nodded and finally said, "I understand, but I don't like it. It feels like a step back."

"It's not, so, let's just not rush things."

"OK." I heard myself say. It was like this reflexive response that emitted from my mouth to accommodate others. I felt like Elliot was asking me to put my life on hold again and push back stability and children for some kind of bohemian life style. I sometimes wondered if despite our love for each other we'd ever get on the same page.

The topic remained buried for the rest of the week with the focus shifting to seeing the sights of southern California. Elliot had taken a few days off and we crammed as much as possible into seventy-two hours, even making it to Disneyland and hiking in the Anza Borrego Desert. Friday, my last full day, was spent on a walking tour of Coronado Island. We had milled around the Hotel Del Coronado for most of the morning admiring the architecture and the ornate holiday decorations. We walked along the beach dipping our feet in the cool ocean and fantasized about owning one of the beachfront properties. As we drove home that evening, I remembered that Elliot had to work and I had accepted an invitation to dinner. Earlier in the week, Leah Braden, Elliot's fellow intern at the med center, aware of his work schedule that evening, had extended an offer for me to join her and a group of her friends for dinner. Elliot had suggested I accept Leah's invitation, citing that since they were friends it would do me good to get to know her better, particularly given that there was always the possibility that we may choose to stay in San Diego following internship. Translation being that Elliot would not likely want to leave San Diego and that way I would have already started a social support network here.

Once back at the condo, I quickly showered and threw on a grey sweater with tailored black pants. I took the jeep letting Elliot struggle with public transit. I drove to La Jolla following the directions that Elliot had jotted down on a piece of paper. I found the brewery without trouble nestled between a Mexican restaurant and a French bakery.

I elbowed my way my way to the back of the restaurant since I hadn't been successful in locating Leah anywhere else. Leah waved me over as I turned the corner motioning me toward a large rectangular table with approximately ten women. I found an empty chair and she began introductions.

Leah was taller than I expected with plain brown eyes and a slightly crooked nose that she explained had recently been broken roller skating. Her lips were thin and even thinner when she smiled exposing large square teeth. She had long, stringy brown hair, wore minimal make up and lacked any style opting for a large green baggy sweater and loose faded jeans. This surprised me given the stereotype of the blonde, beautiful California girl who paraded around in designer threads.

The evening progressed well and I conversed with many of the women most of whom had lived in California since childhood. We ordered trays of beer samplers and platters of deep fried appetizers followed by overstuffed sandwiches. This was completed with fresh coffee and a creamy strawberry cheesecake.

Initially, Leah discussed her children. She had a four-year-old girl and six-year-old boy and had been married for 7 years. She quickly turned the discussion to the medical center and her relationship with Elliot. This dominated the conversation for the rest of the evening. She only stopped gushing about him long enough to shove hunks of cheesecake into her mouth. She talked about how they had bonded through various experiences, coincidentally had so much in common and could confide in each other about so many personal issues. She had even joked that they were close enough to fight. Initially, I was flattered and happy that they had such a close working relationship. However, I found myself becoming increasingly annoyed thinking that she should be flattering her own husband instead of mine. I left the pub feeling nothing more than irritation knowing that Leah and I were not destined to be anything more than mere acquaintances.

I didn't discuss my opinions about the evening with Elliott and brushed off questions about how it went answering with a vague "it was fine". I meant it, but there was just something about the focus on Elliot that made me uncomfortable, I found it rather inappropriate. Perhaps that was silly or perhaps these were just feelings of insecurity and paranoia filtering in from my past. I knew Elliot loved me, so what did I have to worry about?

When it was time to return to Michigan, I cried. It would be at least another month before Elliot would be able to fly out to Michigan. Initially, I had been frustrated with his proposal to put our potential family on hold to remain in California. However, after staying for just a week, I was beginning to understand his argument. It was a beautiful place with the sun, sand and surf. It certainly wouldn't take much getting used to. Also, it had been so good to see Elliot and I had missed him so much I didn't want to cause any waves. I just wanted to keep our marriage strong and do whatever it took even if it meant putting the white picket fence on hold for another year of two. After all, marriage was all about compromise and I was willing to do what I needed to keep my husband happy.

Chapter 16

The week in San Diego had flown by and I missed it horribly. I missed the weather. I missed relaxing by the pool, but most of all I missed Elliot. Returning home, the house had seemed like a tomb, cold and still. I had immediately turned on the television to get some feeling of companionship. It didn't help and all I wanted to do was catch the next flight out to California. To make matters worse, during my absence, piles of snow and a coating of ice had turned the city into a driver's nightmare.

The following morning it was snowing heavily again. Visibility was negligible and I was relieved to pull into the staff parking lot. Ellis House looked like a gingerbread house covered in huge mounds of white, puffy, cotton ball snow, icicles hanging from the eaves. I dreaded my return to work and already anticipated the numerous headaches and crises that had developed over the course of the past week.

As expected, my desk was overflowing with papers that could no longer be crammed into my mailbox. My inbox on Susan's desk was stuffed with phone messages and I already had three people waiting to see me. I wasted no time and plunged into the rough seas only pausing long enough to grab a cup of coffee.

By eight a.m., I had conducted two face to face meetings and sifted through a healthy stack of paperwork. Twenty minutes later, Jamie arrived. It was nice to see a friendly face.

"Welcome back." She stated. "I am so glad you're here."

"Thanks. I can't really say it's good to be back." I admitted.

"That's not surprising." She said nodding her head in agreement.

"So, how are you? What's been going on? Update me on last week's happenings." I asked.

"Well, you won't be surprised to know that things have been as crazy as usual. But last week was bad. I mean it was a really horrible week." Jamie admitted.

"How so?"

"Well, the usual crap, but I ended up having it out with Barbara. It was a mess. Still is really. Nothing has been resolved."

"Go on." I urged.

"Well, like I said, nothing has been resolved. It's so tense. I admit, I usually feel threatened by her, but she was really nasty, bullied me. That's probably the best way to describe it."

"She can be intimidating." I agreed.

"She made me feel like I wasn't doing the right thing, like I wasn't doing my job when I was right and I was doing my job. I was acting in the best interest of a client." She stated emphatically.

Jamie said the incident had occurred last Saturday night when clinical staff was gone for the weekend. Jamie had received a phone call around 9 p.m. informing her that Nate had escalated. He was aggressive, noncompliant and no one had been successful in de-escalating him. He continued to remain in the quiet room and they had been unable to get in touch with John, his therapist. Jamie had agreed to go in and given her long commute and the icy road conditions that night she arrived an hour later than she had hoped.

Once Jamie arrived, she met with Barry who provided her with a brief synopsis of what had transpired. As Barry talked, it became apparent to her that similar to past episodes, Nate's intention was not to be aggressive but rather a byproduct of his anxiety. She went to find Nate, but was unsuccessful. When alerted, the assistant supervisor immediately initiated a unit search. Soon after, Nate was discovered sleeping only partially clothed on the floor in one of the quiet rooms. As Jamie entered, she gagged in response to the overpowering foul stench.

Barry's story was that earlier that evening, in response to Nate's aggression, he had been escorted to the quiet room. However, he continued to escalate, and to minimize further disruption to the unit, they shut the door and held it closed. Nate kicked and screamed pulling at the door handle. He begged and pleaded with staff to let him out.

Obviously, the weekend staff had not bothered to read Nate's safety plan, which stated that under no circumstances should he be closed in a small space given it exacerbates his symptoms causing panic.

Eventually, Nate stopped begging to get out and requested to use the restroom. Staff interpreted Nate's request as manipulation. They ignored him. Nate kept asking until his behavior again escalated . . . kicking, screaming and hitting.

Nate was told if he calmed down and was silent for several minutes, he would be allowed to use the bathroom. He then became very upset, said he couldn't hold it anymore and had a bowel movement in his pants.

Jamie paused took a drink of water and continued. "Nate's report is that he yelled at staff to let him out, but they continued with the same mantra. "If you can calm down . . ." He finally gave up, took off his soiled pants and curled up in the corner. Eventually, the staff member monitoring Nate opened the door a crack and immediately noticed the smell. Instead of taking him to the bathroom to clean up, Nate was told to pick up his pants and put them in the laundry first. The same power struggle ensued and Nate wasn't allowed to leave the quiet room. My understanding is at that time, something else happened on the unit. Staff left him in the quiet room, forgot about him and Nate fell asleep."

"When I walked into the room, Nate got to his feet. His lower half was naked and smeared in fecal matter. His underwear and pants were still rolled up in a ball where he had left them. I wrapped him in a towel, walked him to the shower, and made sure he stayed in there long enough to get clean. Then, I helped him get ready for bed, gave him a snack and waited with him until he fell asleep. The worst of it was they had called me around 9 p.m. So, this means Nate had been in there since recreation time which is around 7:30 p.m. By the time I saw him, it was after ten. The poor kid had been in there for over two and a half hours." She concluded.

"Shit." I said. "Has licensing come to investigate the incident? If they haven't they will." I sighed. The licensing board was the gatekeeper, set the guidelines for what was considered acceptable conduct in group homes. There were rules group homes needed to follow with the physical plant, safety procedures, hygiene, diet, exercise and how the clients were disciplined. Staff was able to restrain a client if all other alternatives had been exhausted. Obviously in this case, the line had been crossed and some disciplinary action was mandatory.

"No, not yet, probably because it was Christmas." Jamie responded.

"This is a clear case of staff negligence. Power struggles are usual problems, but just forgetting about a kid? I mean come on. There's no excuse. No excuse." I repeated.

"Wait it gets worse." Jamie stated. "The next day Barbara calls me into her office to sign an incident report that is completely fraudulent."

Special incident reports or SIRs were to be completed following any kind of restraint or dangerous behavior including aggression, self-destructive behavior, or property destruction. It was a brief report citing who had been involved, what precipitated the incident and how staff responded. Generally, it was viewed as documentation to justify the use of restraints, be they physical or structural (i.e., use of the quiet room). In a nutshell, it was a risk management tool which could be used with disgruntled county workers, attorneys or licensing agents if a client were to make allegations against the group home.

In rare instances, clients who had been escorted to the quiet room could remain there at staff's discretion for considerable periods of time if they were unable to successfully calm down. In these instances, therapists were required to notify the client's county worker so he or she could be kept abreast of the situation.

There had been rumors that incident reports were sometimes altered as needed to present staff in a good light. However, in Nate's case, it was glaringly apparent the documentation that followed the incident had been manipulated. "You know how after the containment is longer than fifteen minutes you need a therapist involved." Jamie urged. I nodded. "Well, when I read the report it was completely inaccurate. They minimized the whole incident and tried to shift blame to make it appear like it was all Nate's fault. It really pissed me off."

"Ridiculous." I agreed.

"So, anyway, Barbara hands me this SIR and tells me to sign it. I told her no way because that's not what happened. Regardless of who else had already signed off on it, that's not what happened." Jamie stated convincingly. "Barbara looked at me for a long time and said nothing. Then she started with the threats. You can't leave this office until you sign it. You better not disagree with this documentation if you want to keep your job. I hope you're smart enough to keep this conversation between us. Blah, blah, blah . . ."

"So, how long did she pressure you?" I asked.

"Hasn't stopped. She made me so mad that as I left her office, I told her that she didn't give a damn about the kids. It's true, but I still shouldn't have said it. It was really unprofessional, but I had reached my limit."

"Did Barbara say anything else?"

"No. Except she reminds me of our conversation whenever I see her in the hall. She tells me to be wise."

"What happened with the SIR?" I asked.

"I have no idea. I'll call the county worker again and find out. Her voicemail said she was out last week. One thing's for sure, I'm not asking Barbara." Jamie answered.

"I'm really sorry you had such a tough week. Too bad it happened when I was gone."

"Me too." Jamie went back to searching through some papers on her desk and then looked back up.

"And I'm sure you know about Corrine."

"No. I haven't heard anything. What about her?"

"She's gone." Jamie announced.

"Gone? What do you mean gone?"

"I mean gone. Gone as in she doesn't work her anymore."

"What do you mean?" I asked, stunned. "Was she fired?"

"No. I don't think so. Well, now she is, but I guess she just didn't bother to show up for her shift on Monday."

"That's odd. That's not like her at all. Did she call in? Give a reason?" I questioned knowing how conscientious Corrine had always been about her job.

"Heck, I have no idea. It's not like I'm privy to anything that goes on around here. But the rumor is that she got fed up with the job and quit. Didn't give any notice so she could stick it to Barbara. Left Barbara hanging without a supervisor for the shift since Barbara always treated her like shit. It was no secret how she treated her, changing her shifts last minute, barking orders."

"Corrine wouldn't do that - just not show up."

"She hated Barbara."

"True, but she wouldn't have done that to the kids. Make things more chaotic for them, I mean."

Jamie shrugged. "I really wouldn't know."

"You never really spoke with her."

"No. Not really." Jamie admitted. "I'd see her in treatment team and on the unit every once in a while, but that was about it."

"Well, when she was growing up circumstances placed her in a group home for a while." I offered.

"Wow! I didn't know that." Jamie responded, surprised.

"Always told me if nothing else, she would be there for the kids. So, she wouldn't just leave. I really don't think she'd be able to do that. She believes what she does makes a difference. And that's the only reason she puts up with Barbara." I explained.

"Well, all I know is that she's gone. You're right about the kids though. A lot of them are upset. Some really pissed. And it's gotten worse the longer she's been gone. They're asking questions that no one can give them an adequate answer to because no one knows what's going on either."

"Normal reaction. They feel like they've been abandoned again by someone they trusted. And it's especially hard because all the kids respect Cory even if they don't like her."

"They sure do." Jamie agreed.

"So, how did you find out? Did Barbara make an announcement?" I asked changing gears.

"Not at clinical meeting. My understanding is Barbara told everybody at the residential staff meeting that Corrine quit and didn't even have the courtesy to give formal notice . . . how unprofessional she is . . . blah, blah, blah . . . you know."

"Did she say anything in treatment team?"

"Nope, she wasn't there. Anyway, I also heard Barbara called Corrine at home and left a message telling her that she didn't care what the reason was, but if she ever thought about coming back not to bother because she no longer had a job." Jamie concluded.

"Well, I guess that's to be expected given their relationship. Corrine's not coming back regardless of the circumstances. But did anybody ever find out what happened? Did anybody speak with her?"

"At home? No, not that I know of."

"I mean she's OK right?"

"I assume so. I mean I never contacted her if that's what you're asking. I don't know her well enough to call her at home, but I'm sure she's OK."

"Oh, I know it's not your place. I was just wondering if anyone had."

I said nothing more. Jamie took that as her cue to update me on the rest of the happenings on the units before she excused herself and went to conduct a therapy session.

I spent the remainder of the morning checking in on the units, returning phone calls, and tackling more of the paperwork that monopolized my desk. I had wanted to check in with Emily, but she was off grounds until lunch, so our session would have to wait until after treatment team.

Chapter 17

By one in the afternoon, I was back in the stuffy conference room reviewing the scheduled cases for treatment team that day. Of course, nothing had changed. Despite our charged discussion in treatment team about respect several weeks earlier, the eyes continued to roll, the notes continued to be passed and the therapists continued to compete with ongoing chatter. By the time we got down to discussing our last three cases, the disrespect was contained to note passing.

Nate Jackson hadn't made any progress and this was to be expected given the events of last week. His symptoms of Post Traumatic Stress Disorder continued to be glaringly apparent. This included his hypervigilance, flashbacks and nightmares. He had been avoiding going to sleep most nights and could frequently be found with a staff member sitting in the common room watching television into the early morning hours. His mother remained in prison. Nate's county worker had been successful in locating a paternal aunt in Indiana, just outside Indianapolis and was investigating whether this could be a possible future placement.

It had been a frustrating case presentation for John who had been working in concert with the psychiatrist and Nate daily to provide him with some symptom relief. He had developed a solid treatment plan which continued to focus on symptom reduction and stabilization. However, it was doubtful that Nate would ever fully recover from watching his sister burn to death and resolve his overwhelming feelings of guilt at not being able to save her.

"I would really appreciate if people wouldn't get defensive and jump all over me before I can get my concerns on the table. Please give me a moment to speak first." John urged, anticipating the response. "I have been working hard with Nate to help him make progress - any progress. The poor kid's gone through hell. No other way to describe it. What bothers me is that following everything we discussed last time and our in depth discussion regarding his safety plan, no one bothered to follow it. Instead what happened was - "

"We couldn't find it." Barry stated.

"Barry, don't tell me you couldn't find it. It's on the unit. I checked Friday evening before I left."

Each unit office housed a crisis folder which contained a safety plan for every client on the unit. The plans were individualized and provided recommendations about how to most effectively manage that particular client when in crisis.

"Well, it wasn't there. Ask my staff." Barry argued.

"If it wasn't there, it was removed. And Barry, you're a smart guy you know we have a master file, duplicates. Why not use that one?"

Barry didn't bother to respond.

"The point is the harmful response Nate received from staff made him regress. All his progress, albeit what little there was, is gone. And now's not the time to get into the incident itself, but it is something that needs to be addressed seriously with the parties involved. I've gotten backlash from the county worker and I can't say that I blame him. We didn't let him use the bathroom and let Nate shit all over himself. To make matters worse, then we forgot about him!"

In the interest of time, we finally shifted gears to Jacob who also had made no progress. He continued to be a bully, to be verbally aggressive and to manipulate people whenever possible. He had managed to refrain from being physically aggressive for five consecutive days which earned him an opportunity to start reintegrating into the community an hour per day. Jacob wasted this chance. He lasted only long enough to call one of the cooks in the dining hall a "fucking asshole" who didn't know how to boil water. Once he took his seat, he became combative plastering his former roommate with a plate of pasta and then pinning him to the floor. Needless to say, Jacob was quickly escorted to the quiet room and once again found himself back in his familiar surroundings of the Separation Unit.

Unfortunately, Tori provided no insight when asked for suggestions as how best to manage his behaviors on the unit. Instead, she minimized his problems, deflecting responsibility from her client to staff. She continued to believe he was erroneously diagnosed, though she would no longer admit it publically given the verbal backlash that would inevitably ensue. Challenging her resulted in an icy stare and curt acknowledgment that as a team we agreed on a strict behavior plan to manage his behaviors until his anticipated discharge the following week.

I presented Emily's case. Her progress on the milieu was nothing more than expected. She continued to lose ground since she had walked out in the middle of her evaluation with the psychiatrist, Dr. Antonazzi. She stayed only long enough to deny any suicidal ideation and refused medication arguing that it wouldn't remedy the loss of her brother and father.

Emily's behavior had become increasingly noncompliant. She had been escorted and placed in the quiet room twice for significant property destruction to her room. In the last few days, she had started restitution, plastering, sanding and painting the walls that had suffered numerous scuff marks and several holes. Emily had started to isolate herself from her peers and from community activities on the unit. She appeared to have lost interest in most things with the exception of animals because as she liked to stress, "You can always rely on your pets because they never let you down, not like people." Her depression was gaining strength and she had reached her breaking point. As far as anyone knew, there had been no further contact between Emily and her mother. Maggie's status remained unknown. I needed to get an update about her condition as quickly as possible.

I flagged Drew down following treatment team. I knew he and Corrine were close and thought that he might be able to shed some light on her departure. I offered Drew the chair across from my desk, but he declined.

"Thanks, but I've got to get back to the units. Shift change you know." There was always a temporary, yet inevitable staffing shortage for about thirty minutes during shift change with staff leaving promptly at the completion of their shifts choosing not to wait for the chronic replacement stragglers. It was a time during which kids knew there were the most chinks in the armor and they were more likely to AWOL, use contraband, and engage in sexual activity.

"Before I go, what's up?" He asked in his typically friendly way.

"Well, I'm concerned about Corrine. Did she give you a heads up about quitting?"

"No. But, I do know this she was going to see her uncle last weekend. She was having a really tough time with work. Her uncle, well he's her dad by all rights and my guess is that he convinced her to walk."

"That's not really like her though. Corrine's always been really responsible."

"Yeah, I know, but she was really burnt. She was so fed up and stressed out, she couldn't sleep at night. This place was eating her alive. I told her I thought she should quit. Not that it was really any of my business, but nothing is worth your health."

"True, but Corrine? I think Corrine would give notice."

"Knowing her, if she came back and saw the kids, they would

have just convinced her to stay. You know her, there's no way she would have been able to do it if she had to face them. Besides, it's a great way to make a statement to Attila the Hun." He smirked.

"Everyone knows Corrine doesn't like Barbara."

"Doc, that's the biggest understatement of the year. No one can stand her, but Cory, especially Cory. Barbara brought out the worst in her, really pushed her buttons."

"I know they locked horns a lot."

"Cory can't stand how Barbara treats the kids and how tight she is with the budget. She's always complaining about how little the kids get for crafts and outings." He looked at his watch. "Look, I'm sorry. I really gotta go. Don't worry about Cory. She's fine. Nice talkin' to you." Drew turned, waved and walked out to the hall.

I called and left messages for Kim and Jacques to get back to me with updates before heading to the unit to meet with Emily. As I was shutting my door, my phone rang and I picked it up. "Hello." I answered.

"Dr. Morgan its Ana. Could you get up here?"

"What's going on? You need help?"

"Yeah, help controlling your therapist." She responded breathlessly and hung up.

As I reached the top of the stairs and unlocked the unit door, I could already hear the yelling. I walked through the door to the quiet room area and saw Tori and Tristan posed in assertive stances, faces only inches away from each other. Tori's face was flushed and her neck strained, accentuating thick veins which snaked down her arms to her clenched fists. Tristan was pale, beads of sweat covering his forehead. He was holding his right forearm with his left hand. As I got closer, I saw red seeping out from beneath it. Ana was ignoring them holding the door to the quiet room shut. In addition to the high pitched screaming, you could hear the repetitive thud from where Jacob continued to body slam the door. I glanced over at Ana who flashed me a look indicating that she was OK, at least for the time being.

"What's going on?" I interjected.

"I'm so pissed right now." Tristan panted. "Tori -"

"Don't even start Trist -"

"Shut up and let me talk. Shit! I can't believe this! God, she's such an idiot! He stopped and took a deep breath. "She's so easily manipulated. Tori took Jacob back to his room to get a box of his toys and -"

"He didn't have anything to play with -" Tori interrupted.

"Shut up. OK. Just shut up and let me finish." Tristan switched his gaze from Tori toward me. "Anyway, she took him back to his room which is completely against the program rules and let him pick out a box of things he wanted to bring back to the Separation Unit. He must have planned it. Hell, I don't know, but he had hidden a pair of scissors in there. Well, they weren't scissors anymore. A lot sharper, he'd filed them down somehow. Anyway, she didn't bother to search the stuff that he wasn't supposed to have in the first place." Tristan stopped to catch his breath.

I looked at the red patch that was spreading under his hand and said. "You better see medical. This can wait."

"No. No. Actually, it can't wait. I need to say this before I go otherwise my story will get all twisted."

"You calling me a liar?" Tori responded accusingly.

He ignored her and stammered on. "I dropped off his lunch tray and told him to come and eat. He told me to go fuck myself and kicked the tray splattering the food all over the floor. I told him that I was going to tell his therapist and he said to go ahead that she would never take staff's side over his. I explained it wasn't about taking sides, but about keeping everyone who was involved in his treatment current about his behavior. I explained that he needed to learn to follow the program rules so that he could get placed. He told me to screw off and I thought that was it. But as I was cleaning up the mess I saw him coming toward me out of the corner of my eye. I saw the glint of something shiny and then felt the sting. He had sliced my arm right through my shirt. I guess I was kind of stunned. I mean he really caught me off guard." He pointed to his forearm indicating where he had been cut. "I think I need stitches. Anyway, I used force to protect myself. I know he's only a kid, but my arm hurt like hell. I was scared. I pinned him against the wall in a kind of one man wall restraint. I know it's not proper procedure, but there was no one to help me." He shifted an angry gaze back to Tori. "She was there, but refused to help. She just stood there watching."

"Is that true?" I asked.

"You know my thoughts on restraints, but that's irrelevant." She responded adamantly.

"Why?"

"Because I'm sure Jacob was provoked. He was fine earlier when I went to get his toy box."

"Toy box! Toy box! Is that what you call something with razor sharp scissors in it? What's the matter with you?"

"Look, Jacob was fine. He needed something to - "

I interrupted. "Tori, you see the blood."

"Yes." She replied reluctantly.

"You saw Tristan get stabbed?"

"Yes."

"And you still chose not to help? Even if you didn't want to do the restraint, why didn't you get help?"

"Because he seemed to be handling it just fine."

"Bull shit!" Tristan cried.

I looked down at his bleeding arm and he allowed me to lift his hand to examine the wound. It was a deep, long gash. I was no physician, but I was certain he needed stitches.

I said to Tristan, "I understand that you want everyone to know what happened, but you really need to take care of that arm. Why don't you check back after you're done with medical. Chances are you'll have to go to the ER to get stitched up. This will all be waiting for you when you get back if that makes you feel any better."

Tristan agreed and nodded to Ana who continued to hold the door to the quiet room and left the unit. I turned my attention to Tori.

"So, Tori getting back to this situation, why didn't you help? The client was clearly a danger to others. And what if he had become a danger to himself? What if he had tried to cut himself?"

"Jacob wouldn't do that."

"Maybe not, but best not to be so confident in your powers of prediction." I stated.

"I know my client-"

"Well, good for you. But you didn't know him well enough to predict this situation. And if you know him so well, then what do you suggest we do with him? He's still going off." I pushed her, already knowing her answer would be defensive.

"Do you blame him?"

"I blame you for managing his case so poorly, for being irresponsible and for ignoring the advice you received in supervision. All you do is enable the kid, bend the rules for him and excuse his behavior. You haven't made him take responsibility for his actions. You're always letting him off the hook. You may in some odd way think you're helping him, but you're not. You're hurting him. You're not helping him at all."

"He's hearing voices - "

"He's manipulating you." I emphasized.

"He's depressed, most likely with psychotic features."

"Tori, drop it. We have already talked about this. There may be some mood disturbance, but it's secondary to the conduct disorder and there are no psychotic features. End of discussion. So, let's just focus now on how we need to proceed."

"Let him out of the quiet room and - "

"Even though he's still going nuts? Look, you're completely off the mark. You obviously don't listen to anything we discuss in supervision or treatment team."

She glared at me, but this was no longer a democracy.

"This is what is going to happen. You are going to call Jacob's county worker. Explain the situation and let him know that either he or someone from the county will have to come and transport your client to Juvenile Hall ASAP. Definitely no later than 5 p.m. today. If you can't arrange it in the next twenty minutes, come and get me and I'll get in touch with his supervisor.

"I don't think - "

"Frankly, Tori, right now I don't care what you think. Just do it."

She stalked off down the hall and I wondered if I'd find her resignation letter on my desk by the end of the day. I could only hope.

By this time, Ana had managed to switch with another staff member and came over to unleash her wrath asking me if all the therapists I hired were so unwilling to help when things got rough. I knew she already knew the answer, but I understood her frustration. Despite the animosity between therapists and staff, we had always seemed to, albeit briefly, demonstrate a united front in times of crises. The situation had been bad, but it could have been so much worse. Jacob could have seriously injured one or even several clients if he had used the scissors while in a group session. Just look at how he had responded when he had been placed in the community recently; he had assaulted his former roommate. Razor sharp scissors would have meant a trip to the ER for the roommate instead of the minor bruising from Jacob's fists.

I was pissed. This was all so unnecessary, so preventable. I knew that I was going to have a lot of explaining to do. Tori was my responsibility since I was her clinical supervisor. Despite the fact that she knew how to proceed, she chose not to. It was clearly her problem with authority and my job was to manage her, ensure that she was responsible with her clients. She hadn't been responsive to feedback. I needed to speak with Barbara and Max, discuss options for consistent insubordination.

Tori returned to the units forty-five minutes later with Jacob's county social worker. By this time, Jacob had worn himself out and was sleeping back in his room. Jacob's county worker appeared somewhat irritated, but agreed with the decision. Given the circumstances, Juvenile Hall seemed like the best option. Ana immediately had staff pack and place his belongings in the reception area while Jacob woke to his county worker's disgruntled face and an explanation of what was to follow. Jacob seemed to take it all in stride. Tori hugged Jacob and cried as she watched him leave the building. Then, she took an aggressive stance regarding my decision.

"Don't push me Tori. You're on probation, remember?"

"Don't threaten me."

"I'm informing. This is your last chance to step up to the plate. I'm writing you up for the incident today and placing that in your file. One more step out of line and your employment will be terminated."

She further attempted to engage in aggressive dialogue regarding my decision. I was sick of her attitude and disrespect and sent her home for the remainder of the day.

By the time I had completed Jacob's discharge paperwork, it was well past the dinner hour. Jacob's county worker had called to tell me that he was sending over an aide to pick up his discharge paperwork, any remaining belongings and to let me know Jacob had successfully been transported to Juvenile Hall. Tristan had received eleven stitches, but later had returned to work to complete the incident report and speak with Barbara about the situation. I had also agreed to meet with Barbara and Max the following day. Administrators rarely became involved in clinical situations, but given the severity of the circumstances it was necessary. I also hoped to address some additional concerns during the meeting.

I still hadn't met with Emily, but needed to do so before the end of the day. Since Jamie had already left for the day, I called the unit and asked if staff could please bring her to my office for our session. Two minutes later, there was a knock at the door.

"It's open." I called. I was greeted by Jamie not Emily.

"Do you have a second?" She asked sheepishly.

"Of course, but I thought you'd left for the day."

"I did." Jamie took a deep breath. "I've been trying to work up the nerve all day to let you know . . ." She let the words hangs there and I already knew how her statement would end.

"I've been doing a lot of thinking . . . And you already know how hard it was when you were in San Diego for the week." Jamie started to build her case. "Well, my chair offered me a research position, twenty hours per week, flexible hours, higher pay and well, no stress. I mean I'm sure I'll have headaches, but…"

"I understand." I said.

"Really?" She said, the tension draining from her face. "I mean you're not upset with me for leaving?"

"No. I know you need to do what's best for you. You stayed longer than expected anyway." I said smiling.

"I could give you as much time as you need to hire someone, but I'd really like to get things wrapped up in two weeks, if possible." She responded hopefully.

"I'm sure we can work it out." There was a second knock on the door. This time it was Emily. Jamie quickly excused herself, obviously relieved that she had completed the dreaded task. Jamie's resignation wasn't unexpected. I knew I would feel disappointed and although I hated to admit it to myself, I also felt a little hurt. It was a great opportunity for her, but I knew her departure would weigh heavily on the clinical program.

Emily slid into Jamie's now empty chair and began to spin around. She had lost weight and the brief period of time during which she started taking more pride in her appearance had ended. As she sat across from me, she seemed not only tired, but combative. Her anger appeared to be building and I knew this session would be a bumpy ride.

"Have a good vacation Doc? I hope so." She stated angrily. "Thanks for pawning me off on that creepy psychiatrist. I thought that you were gonna help me, not ditch me?"

"I am trying to help you." I responded non-defensively.

"Well, you sure have a funny way of showing it. Leaving me and trying to force me back on drugs. Didn't I tell you when I got here the last time I was in the hospital they injected me with stuff? It made me feel like crap and it didn't even help."

"Emily, I told you I was leaving for a week. I had no intention of abandoning you or "pawning" you off on someone else. We prepared for it."

"I know, but I thought you'd call. Check in with me."

"Emily, I told you that I wouldn't talk to you until I got back."

"I know what you said, but I thought you'd call anyway. I thought maybe you cared about me."

"I do care about you. I want to help you, OK?"

"I guess. I mean I know what you said about helping me. But I thought it would be easier for you to just get someone else to deal with me." Emily admitted.

"Because you're grouchy and depressed?"

"Yeah." She said hesitantly.

"Emily, if I stopped being concerned about my clients because they were grouchy and depressed, I'd have no one to work with. Besides, I know some people who work around here who are crabby and irritable on their good days." I joked trying to lighten the mood.

Emily smiled.

"I understand your life is rough and you're angry. You have reason to be. Anyone in your situation would be. If you weren't angry, I'd be worried about you."

"I can't help it you know. Sometimes I just want to kick and scream."

"You don't have to help it. You need to work through your anger. I just want to make sure you go about it in an appropriate way. No more destroying furniture or punching holes in the walls."

She gave me a weak smile.

"I wish I could help you more. I know I haven't been able to do as much as I would like to and part of that is because I still don't have a really good understanding of what you went through."

"I said all that stuff that happened was a dead issue. No point in talking about it. I meant it. It won't help me."

"I think it will help. It will give me a better understanding of your concerns and of your previous circumstances. Our life experiences, both good and bad, shape who we are. It's obvious you have just turned away from what happened that day. You have not dealt with it. You believe your mother is responsible for something and you are extremely angry with her."

Unconvinced by my argument or possibly just trying to avoid the discussion, Emily switched topics.

"I haven't talked to my mom. I don't even know how she's doing. Maybe I should have called her, but I'm still so mad after what I saw."

"The photo."

"Yeah."

"About your reaction to -"

"I told you, I don't want to talk about it."

"It still is very troubling to you. Your reaction was strong."

"Just drop it. Please." She begged. "I just don't want to go back there. I don't want to talk about it now, maybe not ever." She forged ahead. "And as far as I am concerned, I've finally recognized that my mom will probably never get any better."

"Maybe that's true." I agreed. "Maybe you're mom will never be able to overcome her problems or maybe she'll have to try for years before she makes progress. You can't predict how it will go. But what does that mean for you?"

"It means everybody lets me down whether they want to or not. My parents did. I guess I'll always be miserable."

"Since you won't talk about it, I don't understand why you think both your parents failed you. Obviously, I know about your mom. However, I also know that you still have some control over how your life turns out. And probably more than you think."

"How do you get past the crap though?" She asked.

"Well, the passage of time helps, but it also takes a lot of work and commitment."

"What if I don't want to do the work and I just decide to give up?"

"Emily, I know you can't see everything clearly, and I know you've a lot to be angry about, but you still have a future if you want it. You told me when we first met that you are stronger than your mother, so prove it."

"Why bother?"

"Because you are worth it and you owe it to yourself. That day we went to the hospital to see your mom, you told her that she should care enough to take care of herself. I would think that the same would apply to you."

I could immediately see the irritation on her face. "If you're so damn smart tell me what to do."

"You already know. We've talked about it before. I believe if you weren't so depressed, you'd already be doing it."

"I'm too depressed, so that's my excuse?" She scoffed.

"Emily, before we had gone to see your mom, you had started taking care of yourself. You had taken time to decorate your room. You were doing your homework . . . now, you don't eat, you are constantly exhausted and distracted, not to mention how bleak you see your future to be . . . all I'm saying is that even if you wanted to focus on getting better, you're motivation is so low and you're so tired that it is really difficult to make any headway. I'm also worried about you ending up in the hospital. I don't want to see that happen and I know you don't. That's another reason why we had talked about giving the medication a try. Not because I was trying to pawn you off on someone else." I stopped and waited for her to respond.

"I already told you that I'm not letting anyone stick a needle in me."

"It's not a needle. It's a pill."

"I don't want to be forced. What if it's not working and it makes me feel like shit? Then I'll have a nurse forcing it down my throat? I've seen that happen a lot in the movies."

"It won't be like the movies, I promise. You'll have a choice whether or not to take the medication. If you're having side effects, talk to me or the psychiatrist about it. Think of it like taking medicine for a bad cold. Once you're better and you only have a little cough you may not have to take it anymore. It can be the same with depression. You don't necessarily have to be on medication forever. Some people choose to stay on it, others don't."

She looked at me skeptically.

"How about a test run? See how it goes and if you really don't think it's helping, we can talk about stopping it or trying something else. I'll even come to your first med evaluation with Dr. Antonazzi. Then we can all talk about it. Deal?"

"You know," Emily said, "if you really wanted to help me, you'd get me out of this place. I'd do anything to get back to a foster home. I blew it last time because I thought I'd get back together with my mom. But now I know that won't happen. I used to have pets, even at the foster home, I had a cat. It's so hard here because we're never outside and we can't have pets, not even a fish or hamster. That's the worst. The staff suck pretty bad too, well, except for Corrine and Drew. They're both pretty nice."

Emily raised her legs up and started spinning in the chair again. "By the way, any idea when Corrine's coming back?"

"Actually, I don't know, but once I find out, I'll tell you." I switched gears. "I was meaning to ask, how were things on the unit last week?"

"Well, I got restrained a couple times as you know, but to answer your question, it was miserable as usual. With Corrine gone, it's been even worse than usual 'cause we have to deal with Barry that much more. You really don't know when she's coming back?" She almost pleaded. "A lot of kids are wondering."

"Really, I don't know. I wish I could tell you." I shifted back to the issue of medication. After ten more minutes of pleading my case, she agreed to give medication a try. I just hoped she wouldn't back out on me once we were ready to start. I believed she'd benefit and it was the push she needed to get back on track. Or at least I hoped it would be.

As I walked back to my office, I wondered about Corrine. It was the same story over and over again from staff. Corrine must have quit after years of tolerating Barbara's mistreatment. She was done struggling with last minute changes to her schedule, working weekends, and never having holidays off because she was too "valuable" to the program.

However, it didn't make any sense. Corrine was a responsible person, perhaps too responsible. She was a person who didn't make impulsive decisions. That night she sat in my living room, she never indicated she would leave her position. When Corrine left my house, she remained in the driveway with the car idling for at least ten minutes before backing out. I almost went outside to ask if something was wrong, but stopped myself. Looking back, I wish I had.

A great number of possibilities ran through my head. Had she been threatened? Intimidated? Forced to quit or give notice like Fiona May? I finally dialed her home number after looking it up in the staff directory. No answer. Hearing Corrine's voice on the answering machine only fueled my concern. I decided to stop by her house on my way home from work. After all, it wasn't that far out of my way.

I knew where Corrine lived because a month earlier I had dropped her off when she was having car trouble. I took the interstate towards Albion and then took the first exit just before town. I followed the winding road another ten miles, finally turning left onto the dirt road which led to Cory's house. I noticed two cars in the gravel drive. The first was a forest green Chevy Cavalier dotted with rust around the door handles. The second, I recognized, as I pull up behind it. The roof, hood and trunk of Cory's fire red, Hyundai Accent were dotted with snow. As I walked past it on my way to the front door, I saw a "Live for Today" slicker stuck to her glove compartment and two plastic leis hanging from her rear view mirror. Corrine had always talked about going to Hawaii. My guess was that she hadn't been lucky enough to make it there. However, wherever she had gone, she hadn't taken her car.

The house was white clapboard, with a black, shingled roof. Much of the house was masked by trees and bushes which disguised the serious need for a paint job. The steps to the front door were also in need of repair, the wood bowed and uneven. I knocked twice on the dark brown door and waited. I knocked again, harder and then I heard a muffled voice respond something which sounded like "coming." The door opened and I was greeted by a young, freckled face.

"Hi." She stated. "Whatever, you're selling, I'm not buying.

Starving student you know."

"No, nothing like that." I heard myself say. "I'm a colleague of Corrine's from work."

"Oh," she said, mild surprise showing in her green eyes. "Come in."

"Is she home?" I asked.

"No, but come in anyway. It's freezing outside." She said, inviting me into the tiny, but warm home. It was small and cramped, made bright with a large sliding glass door that led to a porch. The walls were white, or what one could see of them. Most of the surfaces had been virtually plastered over with bright posters, oil canvases and batik tapestries. The floors were covered with both large and small area rugs. The furniture was a mish mash of unfinished pine and pressed wood. The only jarring note was that of an elegant dining room table surrounded by six matching chairs.

"From my grandmother," She said, noticing me glancing at the table. "We go for creative, eclectic decorating here." She smiled.

"So I see," I responded, returning her smile. "It's beautiful."

"Yeah, but it doesn't fit with the other furniture. So what can I do for you? Oh, and by the way, I'm Cory's roommate Janine." I shook her hand. She had long flaming red hair and was dressed in a long sleeved, pink dress that brushed the floor.

"As I was saying, I'm a colleague of Corrine's. My name is Grace. Since she hasn't been at work, I thought I'd drop by. I had a couple things to speak with her about."

"I'd love to help you, but like I said, she's not here."

"Any idea when she'll be back?"

"All I know is that she was going out of town."

"Do you know where she went?"

"Chicago. My guess to see her uncle. I didn't ask. She just told me she'd be gone for a few days and to enjoy having the place to myself. That was Corrine's weak attempt at humor because we never see each other anyway. We have opposite schedules. That's part of the reason we get along so well. You know Corrine, she's so serious."

"Didn't she drive?" I asked.

"I thought so initially, but her car is parked out front. She might have taken the train given the weather. Traffic's pretty miserable in the best of circumstances."

"The rumor at work is that she got fed up and quit. Do you think that's possible?"

"Maybe. She sometimes talked about it. Don't get me wrong, she loved the kids, but she couldn't stand the way things worked and how her boss treated her."

"Yeah, I know she had a tough time with her boss. No one would blame her for walking out. Has there been contact from anyone at the group home? Has anyone called?"

"Nope. Except her boss, she left a pretty nasty message. She told Corrine that she didn't care what the reason was, she missed her shift and she should consider herself fired."

"That sounds like Barbara." I said.

"Yeah, she has been on Cory's back for as long as I can remember. We've been roommates for a couple years. I answered the ad she posted on campus in the psychology department. We were both taking the same cognitive psych class at the time and agreed to give living together a shot. It has worked out pretty well. I remember when I first met her. She used to miss the class a lot, because of work, and she would borrow the lecture notes from me. School didn't work out too well for her though and she quit."

I recalled that quitting school was another frustration Corrine had mentioned. She initially had scheduled classes and worked around her set shifts at Ellis House, but Barbara made more and more demands as there were more and more staffing shortages. Corrine finally had to make the choice between keeping her job or pursuing her education. She had decided the only option for the time being was to put her education on hold. She felt like Barbara not only ruled her with an iron fist at work, but in her personal life as well. I could only imagine how resentful that must have made her.

"Would you ask her to please call me when she gets back? There are some things I really need to discuss with her." I asked.

157

"Sure. Man, I hear some of the stories about where you guys work. Sounds like a three ring circus."

"Certainly can be sometimes." I answered truthfully.

"I know Cory gets frustrated. A lot of the time she can't get into the house before the phone starts ringing. Then she continues to get calls at all hours of the night. People asking her to come back in, to cover their shifts or to manage some kind or crisis. That's the only complaint I've ever had about her as a roommate. Those phone calls. Really annoying."

"She's very reliable and some people tend to take advantage of that. I understand that it would frustrate her."

"More than that. You should hear her go off about the people she works with, especially her boss who calls her up with no consideration to her schedule. I know she feels jerked around and she believes that some of the staff do not treat the kids right."

"I know Corrine wants others to have her level of commitment and they don't. It upsets her on a personal level."

"Sure does. She does that job for the kids. That is the only reason she stays." She looked at her watch. "I'm sorry, but I've got to get going. I've got a date." She flashed a big smile. I shook her hand once again and let myself out.

Corrine left town to visit her uncle. The problem was, why hadn't she come back? Was Drew right in his assumption that she quit and didn't have the nerve to come back and face the kids? If so, why wasn't she back at home now? Did she extend her stay in Chicago? There were still so many unanswered nagging questions.

Chapter 18

During the course of the last month, my correspondence with Elliot had dwindled. Initially, we had corresponded daily. However, since my return from San Diego, the emails and text messages had become less frequent occurring only once every several days. And there were hardly any phone calls. This didn't reflect my efforts. Elliot no longer answered his cell phone and when I did speak with him, he sounded preoccupied and distracted. When I asked him what was going on, he cited internship, his increased workload and his presentations at two upcoming Grand Rounds. It all sounded reasonable.

Our correspondence continued to follow this newly established pattern with me being the person to initiate contact. However, over the course of the next several weeks, a wave of uneasiness began to wash over me. Elliot's behavior was very much like it had been when we'd had problems before.

Then, Elliot had just completed his Master's defense and was working on establishing a dissertation proposal. I was in the midst of preparing for my dissertation defense, the next to final step before completing my doctorate. We were both working in addition to school, Elliot twenty hours a week at a drug treatment center and I forty plus at a local community mental health clinic. Things were busy, chaotic and stressful. Elliot had grumbled we never saw each other anymore and I couldn't help but agree. However, we both knew it was short term as my defense was scheduled just several weeks down the road. The unfortunate part was that immediately following my defense, I was scheduled to go to South Carolina to start my pre-doctoral internship. Elliot would not be joining me because of his graduate school commitments. However, we agreed we could do it, many couples did.

Not spending any time together was unusual for us. Barring our professional obligations, we were inseparable. I knew this time was difficult. However, we agreed all the hours I was keeping at the clinic provided us with some financial stability to maintain two separate households during our upcoming year apart. This meant we did not need additional loans.

Given our schedules, Elliot started spending more time with his co-workers. He seemed happier, more relaxed and without question more occupied. Things continued to progress without incident until I arrived home one Saturday anticipating a quiet evening with Elliot. I planned on ordering some Thai food and thought we would watch as many comedies as we could cram into a night. Instead, I was greeted by an empty apartment. The red light on the answering machine was flashing. I pushed play to hear Elliot's voice inform me that he was going bar hopping with his colleagues.

"Great," I had thought to myself. I hadn't really wanted to spend the night by myself, but I'd deal with it. I ordered in anyway and watched some television topping off the evening with a hot bath and the most recent issue of "Martha Stewart Living." By the time I climbed out of the tub, it was slightly after 10 p.m. It was still relatively early for a Saturday night and I decided to call Elliot to see if I could meet him at a bar. I dialed his cell and let it ring. He didn't pick up and after the fourth ring, I opted not to leave a message. I called again several more times with no response and finally decided to call it a night. I was in a deep sleep by the time Elliot returned home and crawled into bed beside me.

Three evenings later, I returned home fatigued and hungry, to hear humming from the bathroom. I knocked lightly on the door and let myself in immediately ambushed by a thick cloud of hot steam. Elliot continued to groom himself as I entered and informed me of his plans. Tonight, he was going out with Sarah. He would see me later and reminded me not to wait up for him. He said that they would likely stay out until the bars closed and then sober up with some coffee before venturing home. There was no invitation to join them. As he left for the evening, unpleasant thoughts began to cloud my brain. I started to question why I was feeling suspicious and uncomfortable. I never had before. Was Elliot hiding something from me? I knew Sarah on a personal level and I trusted her implicitly. Elliot and Sarah had been close friends since starting graduate school. They often frequented bars to unwind and grumble about their shared dissertation advisor. Sometimes I joined them. Sometimes I didn't. However, I was always extended an invitation and it was always my choice to accept or to decline it.

I had met most of the people at Elliot's current work place. Most were married or in committed relationships, so why the concern? Just obsessing . . . maybe a little uncomfortable Elliot was doing so well without me? I convinced myself I was being ridiculous as I drifted off to sleep. However, after a fitful night that nagging feeling was still there when I awoke the next morning to an empty bed.

I had prepared for work washing back a multivitamin with a cup of coffee and made my way out the door down the two flights of stairs. I threw my briefcase on the passenger seat, put the car in gear and navigated my way out of the apartment complex parking lot. I passed the mall and followed the road through the commercial district and was about to exit to the I-94 when I made an impulsive decision to continue driving down Franklin Avenue.

Five minutes later, I pulled into Sarah's driveway and climbed the six wide, grey steps to the wooden porch. The screen door squeaked as I swung it open and gave the blond oak door three hard knocks. I stood there for several minutes. There was no response and I repeated my actions. Two minutes later, I heard shuffling and metal scraping as Sarah unlocked and opened the door.

She stared at me half asleep, black hair falling loosely around her shoulders. She wore checked flannel pants and a white t-shirt that was partially camouflaged with a red, terry cloth bathrobe. Her feet were bare, toes painted with glossy red polish. The left side of her face had lines that betrayed how soundly she had slept the night before. Despite her early morning drowsiness, she smiled. Her weak attempt to be polite. I quickly apologized for the intrusion and dispensed with any small talk asking her if Elliot was still there or if he had gone to work. I assumed that he crashed at her place. She looked at me confused. Further discussion revealed she had worked the previous evening not returning home from her waitressing job until after 11 p.m. when the restaurant closed. She and Elliot had never had any plans.

The knot in my stomach tightened. I kept trying to convince myself that there was some logical explanation for this lie. I cancelled my clients for the day and drove home. I walked into the apartment, picked up the phone and dialed Elliot's number at work. He answered on the first ring and his voice quickly changed from professional to personal when I told him my concerns. He walked into our apartment twenty minutes later and I knew as soon as I saw his face.

Initially, the relationship had been platonic, someone to share jokes with at lunch time when the stress of the job was too much. She was attractive, but that was a non-issue. He was married and she was in a committed relationship. She had been with the same man for five years. However, over time, things had changed. She had reached out to him when she started having problems with her boyfriend. She had needed support, a sounding board, so they went out to dinner. He ate and she talked, both imbibing several beers. He had provided her with support giving her ideas for how to improve her relationship. That evening as he walked her to her car, she hugged him and kissed him on the cheek slowly moving her way to his mouth. She continued kissing his lips softly, tentatively at first. He didn't try to stop her as he felt his body react. She urged him to follow her home. Her boyfriend was out of town. Elliott was drunk and had no desire to reject her offer. He confessed that she made him feel excited, alive and re-energized.

Their relationship continued. After all, the damage was already done so why stop? Of course, he didn't want his marriage to end. Half the fun was the thrill of it all. I was never supposed to find out. Chances are I never would have because I was leaving for internship. Furthermore, he knew the relationship would never last and would eventually fall apart. The plan was before I returned from internship, it would no longer be an issue or so he thought.

His ability to rationalize the situation infuriated me. He argued his point noting all the reasons why his behavior had occurred. We had no sex life in recent months and he was feeling ignored and rejected. Conversely, she made him feel wanted, attractive and she took care of all his physical needs. However, he knew he made a mistake and was willing to do whatever it took. I too was feeling sexually frustrated and alone, but didn't respond by initiating a new relationship. I was so angry, so hurt, so disappointed.

Slowly, we started working to salvage our marriage, living in separate spaces until my departure for internship. We surveyed the situation and seriously looked for chinks in our armor. We found lots and patched the holes as best we could. Finally, I was able to move on. However, there was a part of me that had always been dissatisfied with the final resolution. I wasn't assured despite Elliot's apologies and protestations that he had really understood the gravity of the affair. He had made me feel like I wasn't enough.

I struggled to bring myself back to the present. It was a place that I didn't like to go and once I did, it sucked me in and held me there. That had been an incredibly difficult time, but it was over. My anxiety about Elliot's upcoming conference in San Francisco was completely unreasonable. First of all, I knew Elliot loved me and that he would never again jeopardize our marriage. He had made that promise to me over and over again. But even more importantly, we were already living a world away. There's nothing that couldn't happen in San Francisco that wasn't already happening in San Diego. Elliot was scheduled to fly out the following week. All that garbage was history. I just had to relax.

Leah wasn't naive. She knew she had no control over how unfairly she was treated and how underappreciated she was at work. However, she wasn't going to tolerate any further mistreatment in her personal life. She was becoming frustrated. Usually, it didn't take this long to get things going, especially with someone who was already emotionally vulnerable. But everybody had their breaking point. She needed to continue to be supportive, stroke his ego, demonstrate empathy for what he was going through and build his trust. Eventually, they would have a sexual relationship and later everything else would fall into place.

Clearly, she had made progress, particularly in the last few weeks, and he was starting to trust her, she could tell. It was amazing how many times she could "coincidentally" be in his neighborhood or need to drop something off that she had forgotten to give him at work. Already, they had established a good friendship, the rest would follow. It was just a matter of time. Unfortunately, right now things were going far too slowly for her liking.

She recently had to slow it down with Daniel. They had been frequent companions at work never missing a lunch date. However, this relationship interfered with her current plan. Daniel was a decent guy, married, with two kids. However, he wasn't enough to sustain her long term. She knew he wanted something more substantial, and despite his lack of income, he did lavish her with attention - something she was sorely lacking from Bill, her husband.

Unfortunately, her life hadn't been going according to plan. This last year had been particularly disappointing. To add insult to injury, she had recognized she was no more than an old shoe to her husband. All those promises he had made when they married. No damn follow through except for the time she was in the hospital. What a load of bullshit he had given her. Wasn't he supposed to take care of her?

To her disappointment Bill had turned out to be strictly blue collar. He was stable, predictable and spent all his available free time with their two kids. He was dull. He craved absolutely no excitement and was pleased with the status quo. A working stiff Mr. Mom with no ambition to make it. That's what she was saddled with. Well, at least for the time being.

She, on the other hand, had ambition, thrived on excitement and wanted it all. She couldn't just let life slip through her fingers and be a passive observer of life. She wanted to no she needed to be recognized. Bill was the opposite, sitting on the sidelines of life, like a second string quarterback, content with being ignored. His ideal weekend was playing with the kids and watching football. That's the reason she had to be so active in the community. She needed to get out of the house, and to have outlets for her needs. They certainly weren't being met at home. She was involved in everything and loved the attention she received from others. Everyone saw what a well rounded woman she was, a professional mom who was cultured, well socialized, athletic, musical and an avid church member to boot. As long as she continued to receive so much external praise from others, she could tolerate her home life for the time being.

Over the course of her marriage to Bill, she had stepped out on him repeatedly. Cheating was such a nasty sounding word and she didn't suffer any remorse since she felt justified in engaging in said activities. Sometimes she carried on full fledged affairs, sometimes, only one night stands. Bill had never suspected and this had allowed her behavior to continue.

After a bitter end to an intense affair, she had been hospitalized. Although her husband had never understood the

165

reason for her breakdown, she had been indebted to him for being her knight in shining armor. However, once she had improved mentally and physically and settled back into the monotony of their daily lives, his constant attention had ceased. This infuriated her.

She had become upset. Threatened to kill herself and go back to the hospital. He had accused her of being too dramatic. So ridiculous. If she stopped to think about it, she had been the victim in their marriage because he had failed her. Not the other way around. He had failed to give her the lifestyle she deserved. He had given her no choice but to keep looking. After all, she deserved happiness. She had suffered long enough.

As corny as it sounded, she believed that she had finally found her real knight in shining armor. She reclined in the passenger seat, looked over, and smiled at Elliot.

Chapter 19

The following day had begun rather uneventfully. It was the usual, starting with morning meeting and continuing with the sorting of papers, the completing of forms and the spending of time on the units. However, late in the morning, I received a call from the school and was informed that Nate had been involved in a significant incident.

The school was a single story brick building with a black shingled roof set on the northeast corner of Ellis House grounds. It looked like a blemish when contrasted with the Tudor elegance of the group home. The contrast did not stop here. In fact, the only link between the two institutions was that they were housed on the same grounds. The school was a separate entity run by the county and held to different standards and regulations from the group home. However, despite the differences, the two institutions shared a symbiotic relationship, a generally peaceful co-existence. School personnel rarely asked for assistance, since they were well trained in managing severely emotionally disturbed children.

As I pushed open the door to the recreation field open, I remembered that licensing was scheduled to arrive at Ellis House in the afternoon to investigate the incident that had occurred with Nate. Bad timing. If the interview with Nate happened at all, it would have to wait. My guess was Nate's lips would be sealed tight like a bivalve. He would be unwilling to talk to anyone especially a stranger intent on asking him a series of questions.

Nate's incident at school had happened during art class. He had been painting, intent on mixing his once bright colors into muddy patches of greenish grey. Mrs. Diaz, his teacher, had been walking around the class supervising the project when she had heard, "Something around here smells like shit." Smirks, giggles and instructions to knock it off followed. Nate had thrown the first jar of paint narrowly missing the top of his roommate's head and splattered paint all over the wall behind him. His target had retaliated in kind. Then, not content with physical retaliation, his roommate said, "You chicken! You let your sister die. You could have saved her." The teacher's gaze had quickly returned to Nate. He was silent. Standing by his desk, covered in paint, Nate sat down and began to draw with manic intensity, an oven with a chair wedged tightly against the door sealing it like a burning tomb. The initial image saturated with pain, was drawn repeatedly while tears streamed down his face.

His fellow classmates were quickly removed from the classroom. Only Nate remained. Once alone, he began to gouge and bite his arms expressing his self-hatred. His energy reserves sucked dry he then curled up under his desk and held himself tight.

He was still holding himself when I entered the room. As always, it was difficult to see a child in such pain. I wasn't surprised he had fallen apart. It seemed like it was just a matter of time. His life on the units had been hell recently. He had suffered relentless teasing from his peers, the worst from his roommate who took every opportunity to remind Nate that he had "shit himself" in the quiet room. This was debilitating, it had eroded the last of his

168

mental strength and brought him to his breaking point. Of course, Nate's most daunting challenge was the anxiety and fear that permeated every aspect of his life. He was unable to sleep, feeling ever threatened by his recurring nightmares. His guilt would likely increase as it had now been validated by another child. It was clear he did not feel safe. It was also arguable he was no better off now than admission. This was a problem.

"Nate" I stated, poking my head under the desk.

No response, with the exception of a brief glance over his shoulder. He looked cold and had his arms curled up around his chest like a coat of armor.

"Nate." I said again.

A muffled, "Leave me alone." was his response.

"Can I get you something? Water?" I said quietly.

A quick head shake "No."

"OK. Well, I hope it's OK for me to sit beside you."

"OK."

I sat with him for a long time saying nothing, looking at his paint streaked hair. Finally, I spoke.

"I know you're upset and you've been through an awful thing." He turned to look at me. "But please come back to the unit with me so we can get you cleaned up and comfortable. We'll get John and you can spend some time with him, OK?" I smiled. It took time, but Nate finally crawled out from beneath the desk. He said nothing, but followed me back to the unit. When we entered his room, he walked straight to his bed, sat down and said, "My mom sent me a letter. Told me she was doing better. Asked if maybe I could come and see her sometime."

"Your mom?" I asked, knowing that any contact with her was forbidden.

"She said she's sorry and that she's changed, but just like all the kids think, she thinks I'm guilty too. She won't hurt me like she did Lydia."

"You got a letter?" I asked again for clarification.

"Yeah. She sent it with my grandma's mail."

"OK." I answered, now understanding how it had fallen into

169

his hands. Do you still have it?"

"Yeah."

"Do you think you could show it to me?"

Nate reached under his bed and retrieved a wad of paper. Nate showed me the letter from his mother. It read:

Hi Baby,

Hope you are being treated OK. Life here is hard but I get by. I hope you can find a way to come and see me sometime. Don't be scared. I'm sorry for what I did, but I would never hurt you like I did your sister. You've always been such a good boy. You always minded me. Never acted up. Never questioned me. Sometimes I wish you had. Maybe then I wouldn't have done what I did. I think about you all the time.

Love Mom

Lovely, I thought. Placing the burden of guilt on her son for doing well. I couldn't imagine how difficult his life had been before all this happened, but I also guarantee it would have been even worse for him if he had not "minded" his mother or had "questioned" her.

As I was handing the letter back to Nate, I heard my name on the overhead page. The page was quickly repeated requesting my immediate presence in the front lobby. I excused myself leaving Nate in John's capable hands.

I heard the booming voice before I completed my descent down the staircase and saw the expression of relief on Susan's face as I entered the room. Standing much too close and towering above Susan was a tall man wearing a black track suit. He glared at me through his wire, rimmed glasses and dabbed sweat from his bald head with a white, handkerchief he held in his left hand. In the other, he carried a black briefcase. I guessed he had made his way to Ellis House directly from the gym.

"This is Dr. Morgan, she'll explain . . ." Susan stammered.

"Name's Schroeder." He interrupted, abruptly introducing himself. "I need to go on the unit to see Nate. Your help, here,"

He said, dismissively indicating Susan, "doesn't seem to understand the situation."

"I'd be happy to get him for you, but he's with his therapist now. I'll call the unit and have him bring Nate down as soon as possible." I offered.

"No. I'll get him myself."

"As I'm sure Susan explained, that's not possible."

"Bullshit. I want to see where Nate lives and what he's complained about. I've talked to his county worker and to Nate himself. He called me today bawling like a baby."

"He's been having a difficult time."

"Yeah, you would be too if you were locked up in this dump. So, if you don't mind, let me on the unit."

"I have no problem letting you on the unit, but you'll have to wait until after lunch."

"So, you can clean the place up? Hide what it's really like?"

"No, because if I take you on the unit now, I'm breaking confidentiality for the other clients who reside here. Not to mention, it's not fair having strangers parade up and down the unit. It's no different than having a stranger wander through your home."

"Well, that's a nice excuse. I'm going to see Nate."

"I will get him and I will be happy to show you the unit after lunch when the clients return to school." I insisted. "I understand your frustration with his lack of progress, but I too want what's best for him."

"Fine. Suit yourself." He surrendered. "Be aware I've already expressed my concerns to licensing. Licensing is investigating when staff held Nate against his will in a locked room as we speak. Ms. Carter was extremely interested in what I had to say." I looked over at Susan who sheepishly said, "She got here about twenty minutes ago, and is waiting to speak with Nate." My gaze shifted back to Schroeder who appeared smug. I wanted to wipe the grin off his face. My guess was that Nate wouldn't be too willing to comply with the interview, but let Schroeder figure that out for himself.

"Is there anything else you need?"

"No, but I do have a question. Why do you allow yourself to work in such a shit hole? I'm sure I'm not the only one who's complained about this place and I'll continue to do so until this place is shut down or seriously overhauled. As far as Nate goes, I'm getting him out of here as soon as possible."

I consciously restrained myself and replied. "Well. I hope you can help him find a good home where he can feel secure and gets the help he needs."

He grumbled something and excused himself to go to the restroom as I retrieved Nate from the unit. Attorneys, at least the ones I had encountered recently, all seemed to be cut from the same cloth. They believed if they were aggressive enough, regardless of whether they were right or wrong, they would get what they wanted.

Schroeder returned to Ellis House with Nate two hours later. Following, Nate had refused to speak with Kendra Carter, the licensing representative. However, it was now a moot point as Schroeder demanded staff pack Nate's belongings. Schroeder had spoken with Nate's county worker who had authorized the move to another facility until Nate could be transferred to Indiana to live with his paternal aunt and uncle. I confirmed the plan with Nate's county worker, alerted John to coordinate all and within forty-five minutes, Nate was gone. This came, of course, after additional threats and criticism from Schroeder. I didn't argue. After all, it was in Nate's best interest to leave. My hope was that he would move to a place where over time he could heal and find peace.

On the way back to my office, I noticed that Barbara's door was still shut and her meeting with Ms. Carter continued. I wondered how the investigation was going and couldn't help but hope she was making Barbara squirm. Ms. Carter had not spoken with me because I had been absent during the incident. Nor had she spoken with Jamie, since she was no longer employed at the facility. Subsequently, her investigation was restricted to residential staff. Ms. Carter finally emerged from the office laughing and shaking Barbara's hand. My guess was that, once again, Barbara had managed to escape unscathed. It frustrated me that she continued to always come out on top of any situation, no matter how heinous.

Barbara was pleased. The meeting with licensing had gone smoothly. It typically did. Such meetings were simply a formality given that Kendra Carter was such a close friend of Houseman's. Regardless of what the incident reports documented or what the kids did, Barbara was always given the benefit of the doubt. Nate's case had been particularly easy. Nate had refused to speak with Kendra and Jamie, the only therapist involved had quit. Jamie's abrupt departure made her look suspicious. A therapist who knew she was in the wrong fortuitously left her position prior to the impending investigation. At least, that's how Barbara was able to spin it.

Barbara had explained that the residential program continued to be stable, maintaining the same leaders since its inception, but the clinical team had leadership problems. New clinical directors appeared every six months. Given the lack of leadership, the therapists were always trying to shift blame. Take, for example, the incident with Nate. Why hadn't there been clinical coverage over the weekend and why was the clinical director on vacation at such a crucial time? If a therapist had been working that night, perhaps this whole incident could have been avoided.

Both John, Nate's therapist, and his county worker had initially been insistent on justice, but given that Nate had now been discharged, they would cool down. There were too many other fires to put out. The bottom line was that the client was now being well taken care of. Anyway, John's opinion carried little weight. He hadn't even been there the evening of the incident. Like any other governing body, all licensing really wanted was all the t's crossed and the i's dotted.

A knock on her door roused Barbara from her thoughts. A glance at the clock revealed the time as 3 p.m. sharp. Barry had paid attention to her previous request for punctuality. He entered her office, slightly nodding his head in her direction and took the tea she offered him.

"I'm pressed for time today, so let's use it wisely. Update me on how it's going with the therapists and Morgan. Any rumors of her quitting? Could we be so lucky?"

"No. I wish. I don't actually have that much this week, but there are a couple things. First, there has been some dissension in the ranks."

"Go on." Barbara said impatiently.

"Well, Tori Ridgeway hates Morgan. She's been bitching about her all over the units to anyone who will listen. She's even gotten some of her clinical teammates complaining about her. I think she doesn't like Morgan because she believes she has set the bar too high for her. Tori is extremely lazy and definitely disrespectful. She's going to be a thorn in Morgan's side. Also, things seem to be coming unglued since Jamie left a lot more infighting. The team is less cohesive."

"That is lovely. Keep up the good work. You always seem to have something that brightens my day. Maybe over time Morgan will decide this place is too much and will finally dispense with the hassle she is forced to deal with every day."

Barry had been providing her with information for as long as she could remember. It was clear that he was a kiss ass, but the information was valuable and she had promoted him for his efforts. Initially, he had reported only about his staff, but as time went on the focus shifted to the therapists and lately to the clinical director. Along the way, they had acquired the common goal of making the clinical program appear incompetent. As she watched Barry exit the room, she decided to return to the surveillance tapes to see what other information was available.

Chapter 20

I returned home hungry and tired. It had been another long and grueling day. Without hesitation, I fell into bed and pulled the thick, warm duvet around my neck. Words could not describe the comfort I felt as my body became horizontal and the knots and tightness in my muscles fell away. Seconds later my eyes were heavy and I fell into a deep and heavy sleep.

He continues to drink the whisky. When he returns the bottle to the counter top, there is only a thin layer of amber liquid remaining. He stretches, says nothing and exits the room. I look around the living room. Paintings I love and bookshelves filled with books, some of which I have yet to read obscure the sand colored walls. Will I ever get the chance to read them? I want to disappear. I feel like melting into the mocha colored couch. Nothing appears changed or disrupted in anyway, but nothing is the same. I feel exhausted, dizzy and my eyelids are like lead, but I fight to stay alert.

I don't have to wait long before he returns. He walks over to me and removes the gag. He puts his face next to mine and says, "Scream as much as you want, ain't no one around here can hear you anyway. But you already know that, you live here. Wanted a place that was away from it all"

"What the hell do you want from me, from us?" I said, fighting back tears. "I'll do anything, anything, just leave and I'll get you money and..."

"Money? Don't you worry, I'll get my money. Just have to pick it up. Anyway, I'm just doing this for the fun of it. I got real bored in prison, you know? It's nice to be able to take control of things again. To express myself. As for leaving you alone, I'll be on my way soon baby, but I still need what you owe me. Remember all you gave me was a little tongue. You better pay up."

I lunge at him, driving my foot into his groin. He loses his footing, but recovers and grabs my arm twisting it hard and forcing me to the ground. I yelp in pain.

"You fuckin' asshole, where's my husband?" I scream.

"I'm sick of you bitch. You want to see him that bad, let's go."

As he yanks me across the floor, I hear a soft noise. Humming? Coming from the other side of the house, low and quiet, the sound of another person humming a song? The tune is recognizable, but I can't recall it. I realize now why he doesn't care if I'm not bound and sickeningly, the remaining hope I have evaporates.

He shoves me in the direction of the bedroom. The humming has now stopped and the house is silent. We make our way through the living room and kitchen to the narrow hallway that leads to our bedroom. The door is open a crack. As I approach, I can see the rod iron footboard of the bed. Then my eyes are drawn to red. Pools of glistening red.

I awoke panicked and sweaty, my heart pounding uncontrollably. My bedroom was dark and lonely. Immediately, I found myself missing Elliot. He had left me no choice but to comfort myself. The nightmare had unnerved me. I turned on the light and squinted. I made my way to the bathroom and splashed water on my face. I took a drink, a deep breath and returned to bed, where I arranged my pillows and picked up Dean Koontz's latest, a good read, but bad choice considering my nightmare. I started to read, but my thoughts wouldn't let me. After twenty minutes, I gave up. I dragged myself into the living room, stretched out on the living room couch and watched some late night television. Finally, I dozed off.

The shrill ring of the telephone startled me awake. I felt disoriented, but quickly enough I dragged my quasi numb body across the floor and managed to pick up the phone by the fourth ring.

"Hello." I said hoarsely into the receiver.

"Dr. Morgan, it's Ana."

Given the hour, I knew it wouldn't be good news.

"We've got two AWOLs." She said. "I wouldn't have called, but one of them is yours. It's Emily."

"Oh no," I said, my stomach sinking. "How's that even possible? What the hell happened?"

"We are really short staffed." She explained.

"Same damn excuse every time." I responded. "I'll be there in twenty minutes."

I was there in fifteen and was meeting with staff in thirty. Both Emily and Ray had AWOLed by getting out through the gate in the back recreation area. No one was sure if they had somehow stolen a key, managed to pick the lock or if the gate hadn't been properly shut in the first place. Regardless, they were gone. Ana had left the unit along with Drew and several other staff members in an attempt to find them. All that could be done was now being done, but it was too little too late. This all could have been prevented if more people took their jobs seriously. A missing person's report had been filed for each client. Attempts had also been made to notify Emily's and Ray's county workers. They were unavailable, but their direct supervisors had been notified and were aware of the situation. At this point, the best thing I could do was join the search. Knowing Emily, if staff tried to bring her in, particularly someone like Barry, she'd run.

No one was sure if they had planned on leaving to go some place together or if each had their own plan. My guess was Ray would follow his already established pattern of leaving for several hours, days or weeks to quench his desire for drugs, sex and freedom, returning to the facility when it suited him. He was well enough versed in the system to know that the consequences for AWOLing would be minimal. Since he was being discharged from the system in several months, what he did really didn't matter, and he knew it.

Emily most likely AWOLed to see her mother, return to her aunt's or to her former foster home. However, it was possible she planned to make the long haul and go all the way back to West Virginia. My best guess was she had left without a solid plan, just to get some space for a few hours. Emily, like Ray, knew the consequence for AWOLing wasn't particularly severe and that clients didn't wind up in the Separation Unit, unless the AWOL resulted in aggression. Most of the time, the consequence was simply to be placed on watch. If no fuss was made on return to the program, there would be no further consequence other than being under the watchful eyes of staff. And given the record of the program these days, those watchful eyes frequently wandered.

My guess was that Ray had been the mastermind and Emily had gone along for the ride. I got in my car and started down the wintery streets, thinking where Emily might go first. She and Ray weren't close, or at least I didn't think they were. However, would she stick with Ray? Doubtful but I hated to think of her alone wandering the streets.

I drove past the mall and combed the grocery stores, liquor stores and gas stations. I even searched the hotel lobbies, any place someone would seek shelter. I wanted to find Emily before anyone else did. I thought about Emily being confronted by the police, or staff and I didn't like what I saw run through my head.

I couldn't help but believe this was a kid who, despite having the bottom drop out of her world, would be able to overcome her problems in time. I didn't want her to face any more trauma than necessary. I didn't want her to go back to the hospital, to feel trapped and desperate.

I'd been searching for two hours, with no leads when I finally pulled into an all night diner for coffee. It was three a.m. The place was empty except for one waitress standing idly by the cash register. I asked for a large cup of coffee, two creams and one sugar. She sealed the steaming paper cup with a plastic lid. I paid and provided her with the same physical description I had given to so many others that night. Ray's description resulted in a vacant stare, but she nodded her head when I described Emily.

She told me she had seen a girl fitting Emily's description about twenty minutes ago. She'd been alone and the waitress remarked she remembered her because she'd thought it odd a young girl would be out so late. She had tried to engage Emily in conversation, but her words fell on deaf ears. Emily had bought a hot chocolate and mumbled something about being in a rush to get home. The waitress said that was the only reason she hadn't called the cops. She figured the kid had been out late partying, and was already going to be in a heap of trouble.

I thanked her, grabbed my coffee and ran back to my car. I turned left onto Nichols Avenue in the direction of Olivia Holgate's house. After ten minutes of crawling around side streets at five miles per hour and scanning the darkness, I saw Emily walking at a fairly rapid pace. I rolled down my window and said, "Emily, get in the car."

"Nope." She said, continuing to walk at a fair clip. "Nothing against you, but I told you that I was fed up with that place. Maybe my aunt will take me. She did call me at Christmas after all. More than my mom did. Maybe she's had a change of heart."

"Emily, please get in the car. You are considered a missing person. The police are looking for you, staff is looking for you and I'd really like to avoid having this become any worse than it already is. Not to mention, the streets aren't safe for a kid to be wandering around at this time of night."

"I'm not wandering."

"Fine. My mistake, you're not wandering. You're going to Olivia's, but please get in anyway."

She kept walking and I kept talking.

"Look, what if things don't go according to plan? Then what do you do? Please get in the car so we can talk."

"Fine. I'll get in, but just because it's freezing." She pulled the door open and climbed in. "Not to insult you or anything, but your car's no better than what my mom used to drive. I thought doctors were supposed to make lots of money."

"Well, if it's any consolation, Emily, you know that I don't drive around the streets in the dead of night looking for my clients because I get paid for it."

I saw a little smile form at the corner of her mouth. "Yeah, I guess in a weird way that gives me some comfort. Means you do care about me."

"I already told you I did."

Emily agreed to return to the group home if we could make some head way regarding her placement. I agreed to help her as much as possible. This was a kid who really knew how to negotiate for what she wanted. I couldn't blame her. It provided her with a sense of control and if nothing else I was beginning to see a little more fight in her rather than the apathy which had consumed her.

As we drove back to Ellis House, Emily stated that earlier in the day, she had seen Ray by the gate during recreation time. As she approached, she saw that he had a key that he was fidgeting with the lock. She had asked him where he had gotten it and he just smiled and said he had his sources. Initially, she was going to report him, but then he suggested they leave together. So she thought, if nothing else, she could have some freedom for a while. Later that evening when the night shift was coming on at 11 p.m., they had used the key to open the gate and to get out onto the street. She knew it was wrong, but it had felt so liberating.

Emily and Ray stayed together until they got to the 7-Eleven.

After buying some cigarettes, Ray had wished her good luck and said that he had to go, he had plans. It was then she had made the decision to go to Olivia's because going back to the group home was not an option. Emily stated that she felt kind of sorry for Ray because after all his planning and scheming, it appeared that his plan had been foiled. I asked her to elaborate and she said that she thought she saw Ray get into a car with Ana as she took off for Olivia's house.

I called the group home on my cell to let the staff know that I had found Emily. Drew answered and I could hear relief in his voice as I told him the news.

"Well, we were successful." I said. "Got them both in a matter of a few hours."

"What do you mean?" He responded sounding perplexed.

""Emily and Ray. We got them back."

"Emily. Yes. Ray is still AWOL. I thought you knew that. Ana and her staff are still looking for him."

"Oh." I responded. "That's weird."

"Why?"

"Emily said that she saw him get into a car with Ana."

"She sure?"

"I don't know." I said looking in Emily's direction asking her again. She shrugged.

"Well, she's probably mistaken, but I'll tell you this, if Ray got into a car with someone, my guess is that he probably planned it for a while and had one of his friends pick him up. You know what that means."

"Yeah, he's gone for good."

Emily and I arrived at the group home ten minutes later. We continued talking and I repeated that I was very glad she had agreed to return voluntarily. I could see that she was still running on adrenalin so I suggested a hot shower and some food. I told her I would say goodbye before I left for the night, or what was left of it anyway. I called the police and left a message for Kim informing her of Emily's return. I wandered back to the unit where I found Drew and provided him with my portion of the incident report for Emily. Ana would have to complete the initial piece since the AWOL had occurred on her shift.

As I was leaving the unit, Ana entered, Ray following closely behind. I looked at Drew and we both smiled. We had both made the wrong call on this one. Ray appeared cocky and arrogant as he swaggered down the hall past us into his bedroom like he had just returned from a relaxing weekend pass. His eyes were dilated and my guess was that the mandatory drug screen for Ray would be positive. Ana on the other hand looked tired and flustered.

"Hey." She said breathlessly.

"Hi." I responded. "So what's the deal? How did you track him down? Must have been dumb luck you found him."

"Yeah." She replied sounding winded.

"You obviously didn't tackle him. Couldn't restrain him alone? Unless you had staff with you?"

"No. No. I was alone."

"So, he came back voluntarily?"

"Yeah. Surprising isn't it." She answered still struggling to breathe. Maybe she should cut down on the smoking I thought.

"How did that go down?" Drew asked.

"Well, I really had to sweet talk him."

"So, what did you say? You promise him your first born?" Drew joked.

"That's ridiculous." She stated sounding offended.

"Hey, chill. I was only joking."

Ana appeared to have finally composed herself and was able to tell us what happened. She stated that she had left the unit only a couple minutes after she found out that Emily and Ray were AWOL. She had jumped into a car and started combing the streets. Finally, she had spotted Ray at a convenience store. She approached him diplomatically attempting to persuade him to return to the facility voluntarily. He declined and took off.

She followed him in her car and then when she couldn't maneuver down the back alleys with her car, by foot. She said that she had pulled out all the stops, first bargaining with him and then when that hadn't worked pleading with him that she would likely be fired if he didn't return.

Ana said he had agreed to return to the group home if she gave him forty bucks and one hour. She agreed even though she knew it was risky and against protocol. However, Ray had kept his word. He returned fifty minutes later and climbed into the car beside her.

"So, how many times exactly did you break protocol?" Drew asked.

"I don't know how many times but I did. I was desperate to get him back." Ana responded angrily.

"So, let me get this straight. You let an almost eighteen year-old kid, call the shots and get high with your money? What the hell's wrong with you? Are you high too?" Drew responded. "How the hell are you going to write that up in the incident report and not have everyone outside this agency on this program like a fly on shit?"

"I had no choice. What would you have done superman?" Ana retaliated sick of being chewed out a second time this evening.

"First of all, before I tell you how to do your job, you are aware that this program has been looking miserable lately and it's because of people like you. You know by doing what you did, you just got yourself in hotter water." Drew took a deep breath. It was the angriest I had even seen him. "About what you should have done, why didn't you call for help? That's why we carry cell phones. Then you could have just kept following him until someone else showed up. You could have called the cops to inform them of his location? You could have called here. I could have been there in five minutes."

Instead of yelling, Ana began to cry. "I forgot my cell. I know I messed up. I don't even know how to start writing that incident report. Things are a mess. How do I even write it?"

"You write it exactly as it happened. I know they'll be some pretty serious questions and don't be surprised if you are reprimanded. You made some pretty stupid decisions." Drew responded softening his tone a little.

"Ana," I said, "I just wanted to ask you one thing. Emily said she saw Ray get into your car at the 7-Eleven just about fifteen minutes after they had AWOLed. Did you almost get him into the car once and then you lost him again or what?"

"No, I already told you. I tried to convince him to come with me, but he took off. Look, I know Emily doesn't like me on a personal level and we started off on the wrong foot. She's still pissed I wouldn't let her call her mom and restrained her the night she was admitted, but God, get over it. I can't believe that kid's still trying to get me in trouble. Not to mention why she's AWOLing with a guy so old. What if they had sex? That would be an even bigger mess."

She stalked off down the hall. I looked at Drew and shook my head. Ana was right about one thing, this was a big mess, a mess that could have been prevented completely. As Drew and I discussed the situation, we both agreed we would be surprised if Ana wasn't placed on probation for her poor judgment and lack of respect for protocol.

The next morning, I sat across from Malcolm Jensen in the conference room. I tried to stay focused on what he was saying. It was difficult since I was not exactly alert. I was desperate for sleep. I got to work two hours later than usual and now I was confronting this detective, a middle aged guy who also looked as if he hadn't slept in a week. I could relate. His thick lips took a sip of Ellis House swill which masqueraded as coffee. He neatly folded his hands on his spiral notebook and made eye contact.

"Well, as you've probably heard, I've been interviewing people from the facility this morning. "You're," he referred to his notebook, "Dr. Morgan."

I didn't let him get any further. "I suppose you're here about the AWOLs we had last night. I'm sorry if the missing persons report for one of the minor's wasn't cancelled. They have both returned to the facility. I can tell - "

"No. No." He interrupted not caring to get off topic. "Nothing like that. I'm here about Corrine Duschene."

"Corrine? Why?" I asked confused before he was even able

to offer me an explanation.

"A missing person's report was filed on her. She didn't show up at her family's home as scheduled. We're trying to find out what's going on."

"Oh my God!" I heard myself say as my heart dropped into my stomach. Different scenarios started to fill my head.

"Anything you can tell me about her? Buzz around here is that you knew here better than most."

"Yeah, I mean I've gotten to know her pretty well over the last few months and I used to speak with her daily when she worked here. I don't really know her personally meaning than I don't socialize with her outside of work, but we get along pretty well."

"So, tell me about her. How does she get along with everyone? Enemies? Habits? Anything that stands out?"

"Well, she gets along with the kids just fabulously. And most of the staff love her, but she clashes horns with her supervisor, Barbara. Corrine is reliable, punctual. She's a very good employee, takes her job seriously."

"Clashes horns? How so?"

"Well, she feels Barbara could treat the kids better. And that she could treat her better as well. Barbara changes Corrine's schedule on a whim, she wasn't respectful of her desire to go to college. She treats her in a most reprehensible manner."

"That must piss her off? Why doesn't she quit?"

"Corrine is a very responsible person and never wants to do anything to let the kids down. However, the rumor is that she did quit."

"So, I heard. So, you think her supervisor could be involved in her disappearance?"

"Heck, I don't know. I responded sounding annoyed. "I don't like Barbara, but how am I supposed to answer a question like that?"

"One last thing, you said that you don't socialize with Corrine outside of work. So, could you tell me what you were doing at her house?" He questioned. "Her roommate says that you were asking a lot of questions."

"I stopped by the other day to make sure that she was OK. I was concerned." I responded defensively feeling like a suspect.

"If you were so concerned, why didn't you call the police?"

"I said that I was concerned, but not to the point of thinking there was something going on that required police involvement. I mean isn't that a bit of an overreaction?"

"Appears not given that we're sitting here talking about it."

"I thought she may have been forced to leave her job and perhaps she is keeping a low profile until she decides what to do about it. Like I said Corrine's really reliable. I thought it strange she would just leave."

"You think she's the type to sue?"

"I don't know, maybe . . . maybe figure out a way to let Barbara know what she thinks, go to admin. I'm not sure."

"Suing the agency would hurt a lot of people. Maybe she's threatening the wrong people."

"I think that's pushing it and I don't think Cory would threaten anyone. I just think she needs time to clear her head and gain some perspective. And like I said, I don't know much about her personal life, but from meeting her roommate it seems like they get along well. At work, same kind of thing, except for the rare few, she is well liked."

"That's the impression I'm getting."

"Is there anything we can do to help?"

"Several searches have been organized. They always need volunteers. And one more thing, the snooping stuff, pretending you're a detective, that kind of stuff, leave it alone, it could get you hurt." He stated condescendingly. "Let me give you some advice, this isn't an episode of Law and Order or CSI, you should stick to what you know."

"I wasn't trying to be a detective . . ." I started to say and stopped myself. No point arguing. He had already made up his mind.

"Fine. Fine." He responded with a dismissive wave of his hand. "You don't want to throw yourself in the middle of a potential murder investigation. You could really get hurt or worse." He let the words hang there. "You need to leave this stuff to the big boys."

"Murder investigation?" What are you talking about? She's just missing, right? I mean isn't it unlikely to assume there's foul play involved without any evidence?"

He shrugged and said, "I can't talk about details of an ongoing investigation, but who says we don't have any evidence?"

I returned to my office feeling rattled and not really knowing what to make of the situation. It sounded more severe than I had imagined and I couldn't quite believe it. Did her disappearance have anything to do with why she had sat in my driveway for so long that night? What the hell was going on? I sat in my office attempting to make sense of it all, but none of it made any sense, damn it! I hated not having any control so an hour later I switched gears to Emily. I had to keep the promise I had made to her the night before about finding her a good placement. The first step was to speak with Kim, Emily's county worker and see if she had made any progress.

My initial impression of Kim had changed. What I had initially interpreted as an easy going attitude was more adequately described as laziness. Since my return from San Diego, Kim had not bothered to return my calls about Emily's placement or provide any information about Maggie's progress. She hadn't even bothered to call back since Emily's AWOL. Emily had been at Ellis House long enough to have placement interviews scheduled. In fact, by now her discharge date should have been determined.

Since Kim wasn't answering and hadn't returned my numerous phone calls, I went over her head to her supervisor. I knew that with pressure from above, I would get communication, if not cooperation from Kim and very shortly I did.

"Dr. Morgan, this is Ms. Howe." Kim stated formally and assertively when I picked up the phone ten minutes later. "I understand that you have had difficulty reaching me. That's because I am extremely busy and continue to spend my days putting out fires. I am not lounging about in my office."

"I understand, but I have been calling and it was a fruitless effort until I contacted your supervisor. I hope by getting on the same page we can do what we need to actually prevent another crisis and improve life for Emily. Needless to say, Emily is desperate for a placement, information about her mother is essential and I wanted to let you know that she is extremely disappointed that you didn't bother to stop by over the holidays." I added dryly.

"There's no change with her mother." Kim said ignoring my last comment. "In fact, you probably know more than I do. As far as placement goes, there's nothing."

"What do you mean there's nothing? What plans do you have for her? Is she supposed to live here permanently?"

"You know my plan. Foster home or long term group home unless her mother gets better." She said throwing me the party line.

"Foster home or group home. Could you be more vague? You could have given me that same information the day we admitted her. I need specifics. What kind of foster home? What kind of group home? Do you have any placement interviews set up? And by the way, I wouldn't recommend a foster home."

"Why not a foster home? It could be short term and then she could go to her mom's…"

"She's talked to me about foster homes and like a lot of kids, perceives a foster family as attempting to replace her already existing family. She would be more comfortable in a long term group home, one where she can have access to lots of animals. Also, her mom is not a viable option. You'd know this if you'd checked into it."

"We stress family reunification."

"Who doesn't? I don't think anyone in the mental health profession has an agenda to keep families apart." I responded sarcastically. "Heck, I'd love for Emily to be able to go back with her mom, but her mom may never recover. That's a really strong possibility. And if she does, Emily will probably be a legal adult by then and we will be past caring for her." I paused and said.

"Look, I'm not telling you how to do your job, but it seems like you're extremely passive about everything. It's as if you expect a placement to fall in your lap or updates about Maggie to just magically appear on your desk. You haven't even bothered to find out what's going on with Maggie. You've never even spoken with her since Emily was admitted to Ellis House and you're throwing around a placement with her like it's a viable option."

"It's always an option."

"Perhaps theoretically in the distant future if everything goes without a hitch, but not now. And there's no point getting the kid's hopes up for nothing. You want her to sit here and pin her discharge date on her mother's recovery? It's ludicrous. I know you're swamped, but this kid needs something to happen fast. We need to help her gain some resolution with her mom, we need to find her a suitable placement and then maybe she can start to have some hope. She's been through hell."

"There's nothing out there."

"So you say." I replied sounding unconvinced. "And aren't you even going to ask?"

"About?"

"About her AWOL? Whether she's back at the facility? How she's doing?"

"I figured she was back and I guess I'll be informed once I get a copy of the incident report."

"You really frustrate me. You are her county worker. You're supposed to follow her case and look out for her well being until she becomes an adult, but it seems like you just dropped her to be frank. You are so disinterested in what's going on with her."

"I'm looking for placements."

"You say that, but then you say there's nothing. There's always something if you dig hard enough. Where are you looking? Tell me one place you've called? Just one place you've researched that would be good for her. Not to mention have you bothered to sit down and talk with her about what she wants?"

"I know my client." Kim responded huffily. "To answer your question, I called other group homes affiliated with your agency to see if I could get her placed there?"

"Where?"

"Wallace and Caldicott House."

"Those are short term level fourteen programs. She's in a twelve now. That's a much higher level of care than she needs."

"She has a significant history of self-harm. She's had numerous restraints recently. She needs more supervision. Not to mention her AWOL last night. That's already her second one since she's been admitted."

"Those programs are one step away from juvenile hall. She needs us to provide her with an appropriate placement, not any placement. Shuffling her around like that and sending her to a higher level of care will just make her decompensate."

"You know, it seems to me if you were doing your job, instead of pointing fingers, she'd be improving and I wouldn't have to look at a higher level of care." Kim responded condescendingly.

"Fine. You're entitled to your opinion, but regardless of your opinion let's start helping this kid. If nothing else at least you could see if her aunt would take her for the weekend. Get her some day passes, arrange for holidays, anything to get her off grounds sometimes. Come over yourself and take her out."

"I am helping her and next time you have a concern please call me directly, not my supervisor. It's a waste of his time." With that she said goodbye and the next thing I heard was the dial tone at the end of the line. I was irritated. There were so many good county workers. Why did I have to get a lemon? There was no denying that their jobs were difficult, and finding a placement for a client took work. Unfortunately county workers sometimes shifted their kids to different short term placements or placed them in whatever ones were available regardless of fit to make it look like progress was being made.

My meeting with Emily was brief because I had nothing new to tell her. She responded indifferently, but my guess was that it had been fatigue talking. She ended by saying that maybe I'd have more news for her tomorrow. I left the office that day feeling miserable and frustrated.

By the time I pulled into my driveway, my frustration had been replaced by worry for Corrine. This was only magnified when I turned on the 10 p.m. news. A picture of Corrine flashed across the screen. I immediately felt my stomach knot up. This was serious. I tried not to jump to conclusions. Instead I tried to focus on how I could volunteer in the search efforts.

Chapter 21

The following morning, I received a voicemail from Kim stating that she had spoken with Olivia Holgate. Olivia's answer had been firm and without hesitation. She wasn't willing to initiate any contact with Emily beyond phone calls because she knew eventually she would be asked to do more. She did not want to be "stuck" with having Emily live with her again. She had a life. She had goals beyond taking care of a screwed up adolescent girl who had attempted suicide - twice. Besides, why bother? Emily was destined to be just like her mother. Olivia was surprised her niece wasn't yet a druggie and six months pregnant. That was a cold and unfeeling verdict coming from a family member, but maybe Olivia wanted to have a fresh start and pretend she never had a sister. People sometimes became inured to the problems of others. Or could it be that she really didn't care about anyone beyond herself? If this was the case, it was just as well that Emily maintain minimal contact with her aunt, family or not, or she would be doomed to more disappointments.

This was an issue we'd have to address, but my concern today were the rumors surrounding the AWOLs and they were spreading like wildfire. The story was Emily and Ray had AWOLed to get high and have sex. I knew regardless of the veracity of the rumors, I had to confront Emily before my administration meeting. Her response would be outrage, outrage that I would be asking her about having sex and getting high especially since she had denied it the night before.

She sat in the chair opposite me and swiveled back and forth. She had bigger worries than these rumors, but it was a big problem for administration if the rumors happened to be true. Her drug screen had come back negative which indicated that she had not smoked any weed, but that didn't mean that she wasn't present when Ray did. His screen contrary to Emily's had been positive.

"Emily, I don't know if the nurse stopped by to let you know, but your drug screen came back negative." I informed her.

"I told you. Didn't I tell you? Why did you have to doubt me?"

"A drug screen is mandatory after an AWOL regardless of what has gone on. It's like the search when you return to the units from a pass or being placed on watch after any self-destructive behavior. Remember last time?" I reminded her.

"Well, I already told you everything that happened that night. I didn't smoke any weed. Doesn't mean I couldn't have gotten some if I wanted to." She boasted.

I ignored the comment. "Emily, I'll cut to the chase. We need to discuss the rumors that are floating around."

"Rumors?" She asked either truly not aware of them yet or trying to act like she didn't care enough to be bothered.

"The rumors about you and Ray having sex."

"Having sex? You've got to be kidding. Is that what he's saying?"

"Not exactly, but he is saying that he was sexually active that night, bragging to everyone who will listen. Your name has come up and when he's questioned about it, he says nothing. So either he's protecting you, or someone else, or maybe he's just straight out lying."

"Ray! I didn't have sex with Ray! Why would I? He's not even hot and I'm not really in the market to screw up my life anymore that it already is. In case you hadn't noticed, it's pretty fucked up already." She stated sarcastically.

"The way he talks about things, maybe he did have sex, but it wasn't with me. Such goddamn horseshit all this - like I'm being drilled or something! I've never even had sex! I've told you that."

"I know. I know. I'm just checking my facts."

"I don't even know why we have to talk about this again. I told you everything that happened. I AWOLed to get the hell out of this place hoping that just maybe I wouldn't have to come back, but you know the rest." She paused. "Knowing how all Ray thinks about is getting laid, he probably did have sex. I may do some stupid stuff, but not that stupid."

After further discussion, I decided Emily was telling the truth. I had never seen Emily sit with him during meal times, steal glances in his direction, or make any effort to speak with him. In fact, I had never seen them communicate before the AWOL even in casual passing. I went into my meeting an hour later confident that Emily's story was accurate.

The meeting had been called to get the party line on the AWOLs. A preventative measure given that licensing had just completed an investigation which in spite of how well it went was never good practice. I was the last to arrive and before I could even sit down, Barbara demanded, "What's going on with Emily's placement?"

I explained the situation and provided her with an update.

"Just so everyone in this room knows, Max already does, she needs to be discharged as quickly as possible. She's a huge liability to the program."

"How so?" I responded preparing myself for the onslaught.

"I've had in depth discussions with Ana. It's apparent that Emily lies frequently, is unstable and as we know, has significant problems. She initially lied about how she was restrained in the quiet room when she first got here and then accused Ana of having

Ray get into a car with her when he AWOLed."

"She didn't accuse Ana." I tried to explain. "She said that she thought she saw them get into the same car."

"That's a lie!" Ana piped up. "Emily's a vindictive kid who's had it out for me since the day she got here. She wants me to get fired."

"What do you mean she's vindictive? You make it sound like she spends her days figuring out ways to target you."

"Well, doesn't she?"

"That's ridiculous. She's just providing her perspective whether she's mistaken or not."

"Mistaken or not. You mean you believe her? Answer this then. Why would I pick up Ray and not bring him back to the facility right away? You think we were out joy riding?"

"I don't know what to think. I'm not making any judgments one way or the other right now. I'm trying to focus on what's best for my client."

"Do you think I spend my days trying to befriend all the kids on the units?"

"Would you just drop it?" I responded starting to get irritated. She couldn't and the harder she pushed the more she started to plant seeds of doubt. She had been so vehement that she had never had contact with Ray at the convenience store I started to think that maybe she had. Or maybe something else was going on or maybe she just had to save face since she had screwed everything up so badly. Whatever the case, time would tell.

I switched my focus back to Emily, "Why move her?"

"Like I said, too big a risk. I've spoken with Kim Howe and we both agree. Emily's behavior had deteriorated since she got here. Seems like your treatment isn't working doctor." I saw a smirk form at the side of Barbara's mouth and resisted the urge to say something inappropriate. "Kim explained the two of you are at odds with how to proceed. Kim and I on the other hand are on the same page. I spoke with the intake coordinator at Caldicott House. They say that they can take Emily by the end of the month."

I retaliated. "I'll need to speak with Kim's supervisor then and do what I need to do to get her moved quickly to a suitable placement, one where she can progress, but I will not sit by and see you destroy my client just to keep your hands from getting muddy. Emily is not a level fourteen client."

"According to Kim she is."

"What do you think?" I asked directing my gaze at Max.

"I can't determine given I've never met her, but according to the incident reports I've read, she seems to be a real handful?"

"That doesn't mean a fourteen though?" Max ignored my question and excused himself.

A level fourteen facility typically housed clients who hadn't been able to make significant progress in a level twelve facility. Clients at level fourteen group homes were provided with more structure, more intensive treatment and eventually they were moved to a long term level fourteen placement or Juvenile Hall. Most kids who were placed at this level had conduct related problems, propensities towards aggression and noncompliance. Some had bourgeoning personality disorders. They were manipulators with self-destructive tendencies. Once labeled a level fourteen, it was almost impossible to return to a lower level of care even if the client made significant progress. No one was willing to take a chance with an adolescent placed at that level. These were hardcore kids.

Despite the choices Emily had made, she was not a kid who fit the profile. She wasn't frequently aggressive toward others nor did she engage in self-destructive behavior as a means of manipulation. She was a kid who had been through hell and deserved the chance to get placed in any group home or foster home she wanted.

"Emily needs to be certified before she goes or she won't be admitted."

"True. True. But we have thirty days and Kim has already called Judge Dean to start the process."

I knew Barbara was right and I knew Judge Dean would comply. Kim could easily twist the facts to make it look like it was just the placement Emily needed, especially with this last

AWOL.

I ambushed Max on his way out the door. I could tell he was avoiding me and his response to my questions would likely be apathy consistent with previous interactions. Regardless, I confronted him about his apparent lack of concern and, as expected, hit the same brick wall I always did. About why he always supported Barbara? Or why administration continued to stall on hiring? And why was it mandatory for the therapists to help the residential staff but, this practice was not reciprocated? My questions were not answered. My mounting frustration was finally interrupted by the overhead page. Max took this as a convenient opportunity to exit the building.

The page was about Tori. She still hadn't started Art Therapy group. Unfortunately, this wasn't much of a surprise. My recent interactions with her indicated there had been no change in her negative attitude. She continued to push the envelope. Her blatant disrespect for her job and her clients had pushed me to the edge. I knocked on her office door and entered not waiting for a response. Her office was empty, but she couldn't have been far. Her chair and desk were draped with nightclub attire. There was a pair of black leather pants and a midnight blue sequined top on the chair. I picked them up and moved them to her desk. I shut off the radio, took a seat and waited. Five minutes later, Tori waltzed out from her adjoining bathroom wearing a candy apple red mini skirt with a sheer black tank. She knew she'd been caught but decided to brazen it out anyway.

"You're late for group?" I stated.

"I'm on my way. Lost track of time."

"Better think about changing before you do anything else."

"It's not that big a deal for the kids to wait for a bit."

"A bit? Group should have started twenty minutes ago. It's already half over."

"I said I was on my way."

"No. You're not. I've already got it covered. By the time you change, you'd be half an hour late. Besides what are you doing? Would you have bothered to show up at all or would you have just continued with your fashion show?"

"It's none of your business what I'm doing."

"It is my business when you're not getting your job done."

"I get two breaks a day. I stocked them up so I could take the time now to do what I needed to do."

"You get breaks, but not during group time."

"Well, you got it covered, so we're OK for today."

"No, we're not OK. You need to be responsible to complete your job responsibilities without being micromanaged."

"Fine. Write me up and put it in my file, but if there's nothing you want me to do now."

"Just go home. All you're doing now is creating a distraction. Your group is covered. We'll deal with this on Monday."

"Suit yourself." She replied focusing more on her stack of clothes than anything I was saying. I left her office and called administration. Max was out of the office for the weekend. I would need to get approval to fire her on Monday.

Chapter 22

I was still fuming about Tori and her insolent behavior when I opened the door for Elliott. He put down his duffle bag in the entrance hall, walked over to me and gave me a hug. He wore a midnight blue long sleeved shirt with carefully pressed khaki pants and his black shoes had been recently polished. His skin glowed, his hair and goatee were nicely coiffed and his hands beautifully manicured. He looked great. My suspicions rose immediately.

"House looks great." He commented already rummaging around in the fridge. He stopped when he found a soda.

"Thanks." I responded dryly. "How was your flight?"

"Decent, but I'm exhausted. Leah and I didn't get back from San Fran until early this morning. It was a long drive, even longer than I expected. Anyway, I dropped her off, went home, changed and drove straight to the airport to catch my flight."

"How was San Francisco?" I asked simply out of politeness.

"Awesome. Yeah, really, really great. Remember how we had always talked about going, well that's one thing we were right about. It's a place everyone should visit." He replied. I felt jealousy wash over me like a tsunami. It had been so long since Elliot and I had had any opportunity to travel together much less stay in an expensive hotel and eat at gourmet restaurants. We were always penny pinching, favoring local diners as our dinner spots of choice.

"Glad to hear it." I managed with effort.

"Well, hate to do this, but I'm exhausted. I'm going to bed." He retrieved his duffel bag and wandered into the bedroom.

OK. I thought to myself. What just happened? Elliot is obviously distracted. He's oblivious to my anger. I know he's tired, but that's no excuse. We've been separated for weeks. In the past he would have asked me to come to bed with him, exhausted or not. Feeling rejected and angry, I didn't follow him into the bedroom that night. The living room couch seemed like the better option.

The next morning I awoke to silence. I called for Elliot and there was no response. I meandered into the kitchen and turned on the coffee pot. A note was lying in the middle of the kitchen table. It read:

Grace,
Woke up early and went for a jog. Be back soon. Start breakfast without me.

El

Two hours passed and my frustration was mounting. I noticed that he had taken his cell phone and finally dialed his number. His line was busy and the knot in the pit of my stomach was growing. I grabbed my keys and jumped into my car. Pulling out of the driveway, I hit redial. This time he picked up.

"Where are you? Who are you talking to?" I demanded angrily.

"I wasn't talking to anybody. I'm jogging my old route by Silver Lake. In fact, I'm on my way back home now so calm yourself. What's your damn problem anyway?" He yelled.

"Don't tell me to calm down!" I shouted and threw the phone in the passenger seat. I turned around at the end of the block, pulled back into our driveway, stalked back in the house and waited for him to return. Several minutes later he entered looking furious. However, before he had a chance to say anything, I unloaded with both barrels.

"I'm not going through this again. I won't do it! If I find out you're cheating on me again, so help me God, I'll get a divorce."

"You're so fucking paranoid Grace. Look at yourself!"

"Shut up. It's Leah right? You probably fucked her in San Francisco."

"You keep her out of this."

"You keep her out of this." I mocked. "I will not. There's something not right with her. That night I went out with her. She's way too into you."

"She's my friend. She likes hanging out with me."

"Whatever. She married, with kids no less. Why doesn't she hang out with them?"

"She's having problems with her husband. I mean I shouldn't be telling you this, but he hit her once."

"So, it's your problem now. Shit! The woman's got a huge support system with her family, friends, and her church. I mean why does she have to drag you into it?"

"She's not really that close to anyone. She just knows lots of people. Look, she reached out to me."

"So, you're her savior? Why lie to me about it? I know you were on the phone. Why lie?"

"OK. OK. I called her. She's having a really tough time. Internship is rough. She feels she doesn't get enough credit for her work and her husband's an ass."

"So she says. Sounds like a pity play, the helpless female who needs your support and care. Besides doesn't she know you're with your wife this weekend? You see her all the time. Why can't you cut the cord?"

"I told you. She's in a tough spot, thinking of getting divorced. She really needs support and I'm the only one who knows."

"Hell, the writing's on the wall. She's wants you. What a weak, scheming, needy bitch."

"Grace, you're making a fool of yourself. You're so damn immature. I told you, we're just friends. I can't be accountable for your insecurities and poor self-esteem." He responded condescendingly.

"But you can be responsible for hers? You're a fool. She's a manipulator. I can't believe that you're so stupid to not see what's going on. I always thought you had a brain."

"Stupid! About what? Nothing's happened. Leah is my friend. We spend time together. I value her friendship. We went away for work. It's not like we went on vacation together."

"She wants a relationship with you Elliot. I thought about that when I was in San Diego, but it's so obvious now. Your friendship with her makes me really uncomfortable. Whether you see it or not, I can't handle something like that happening again. I think you'd care about me enough to show me a little respect."

"This has nothing to do with respecting you. I'm lonely there. There's nothing wrong with me having a close friendship with a woman. I'm not backing off that friendship just because you can't deal with it. Shit Grace! I'm perfectly capable of having friendships with women."

"If it makes me uneasy, you should stop."

"Not if your uneasiness has no foundation. She's the only friend I've got out there. And you think that I should make myself miserable because of your unsubstantiated jealousy and paranoia? No way! I wouldn't be all over you if you had a guy friend."

"Yeah, that's because I've never cheated and I have good boundaries. I never let things get as far as you do. You're always so emotionally involved, so into their personal lives. Can't you just have a normal friendship, talk about sports, movies, stuff like that?"

"I am perfectly capable of having appropriate boundaries with women."

"The hell you are. You have always had shitty boundaries

with women and the problem is that Leah's boundaries are even worse."

"Bullshit! She has good boundaries. She may be intense and emotional, but she's like that with everybody."

"She's a damn drama queen. Look at the cards she sends you about how she's there for you, anytime day or night. The Christmas card about how much you are cared for. Look at her relationship with her graduate training director. She screwed around with him and then acts like she got sucked into that relationship. She likes to play victim. Oh! And you told me when you started internship that she was cheating on her husband."

"Those were just rumors."

"Sure. If you ask me, *if* her husband is nasty to her it's because she brought it on herself."

"You don't have a right to say that."

"Sure I do, she's damaging my life. I can say anything I want."

"Stop berating her. She's done nothing but be nice to you."

"Sure. *Nice*." I responded sarcastically. "Nice is making stupid comments and pretending that she knows you better than I do? Trying to take my husband away from me? Muscling her way into my life when I don't want her in it?"

"Well, I want her in mine. God, Grace! There's no talking to you. You're like a child always pointing the finger at someone else. You're paranoid and suspicious and the only reason you feel threatened is because you are so insecure. Besides, you know Leah is religious. She wouldn't commit adultery."

"Yeah, she's a saint. I get it, but if she did it would be OK anyway."

"God, grow up."

I took a breath and attempted to speak in a normal tone. "If it upsets me so much, why can't you just cool off that friendship? You know how worried I have been since you started internship there. Why can't you do that for me?"

He took a deep breath and spoke slowly. "Doing that just feeds your insecurities. Besides she's my friend. I like spending time with her. We have a lot to talk about, psychology, relationships, camping, music . . . Our marriage has never been like that. We've never really talked. We always just did things together. I mean if we weren't fighting about this, what would we have to talk about?"

I felt the tears start to well up in my eyes and struggled to say, "So, you're saying we have nothing to talk about?"

"Yeah, I mean come on. Even you can't disagree with me on that. We've never really had anything in common. We were always together because we wanted to be, not because we had similar interests or saw things from the same perspective."

"But you and Leah ..."

"Yeah, if I'm being honest, we are really compatible, and if I wanted to be with her I could be. There would be no reason to stay with you. I'd just tell you I found someone else."

"Oh, that's lovely." I responded feeling particularly dejected.

"Well, it's true. You just have to back off and give me some space. I feel like I have to spread my wings a bit. I know you probably don't want to hear it, but I want to be honest with you. San Fran was the first time I had fun in a really long time. When we're together everything is focused on work and obligation. I guess maybe Leah has replaced a lot of what we used to do together and can't anymore. I'm sorry, but I can't stop living my life for you. We're thousands of miles apart and you can't expect me to just sit in my condo by myself feeling miserable night after night. I'm having fun for the first time in a long time and I'm not going to stop because you feel insecure about what happened in the past."

"So, I have nothing to worry about?"

He sounded exasperated. "Grace for the last time, if I didn't want to be married to you I wouldn't be and I certainly wouldn't be spending my morning talking to you about this. OK?"

"OK."

"Just stop being so insecure. You're driving me crazy. The past is the past."

He stood up and disappeared into the bedroom.

Elliot had tried to allay my fears, but I wasn't buying it and my instincts continued to tell me something was wrong. He had always been good at talking me into things. I just wished I could believe him this time. I heard the water running in the bathroom and the faint mumbling of Elliot's voice. Just let it go for now I thought. He'll just have another excuse.

The remainder of the weekend was tense. We attempted to pretend that nothing had changed, but it was impossible to maintain the charade. There was continued tension and our conversations were stiff and forced. Elliott kept his distance opting to sleep on the couch which just continued to my fuel my suspicions. Our conversations were terse and circular. My request for him to terminate his friendship with Leah was scornfully put aside. He kept up with his mantra that they were really close friend, and that his friendship with her was so valuable that it would continue despite my angst. He continued to assure me that my concerns were minor, simply fueled by my own insecurities and unresolved issues.

There were numerous times I attempted to talk with Elliot only to be interrupted by the seemingly endless stream of phone calls which were all conducted in muffled tones in the adjoining room or outdoors. Not only were the phone calls endless, but so were the text messages which seemed to occur throughout the night. I was astonished to see how quickly he responded to them.

The day of his departure, I finally got the nerve to go through his things. He had gone for a jog and his briefcase and duffel bag were strewn on the living room floor. I rummaged through them, finding Mary Kay moisturizer, lip gloss and a hair elastic. I grabbed the items and threw them in the garbage. I was furious. Was Elliot actually having another affair? Was that possible? I did not want to believe there wasn't a rationale explanation. He knew better. He also knew what it had done to me last time and how it had damaged our marriage. I had warned him about Leah and her intentions. He wouldn't stoop so low, would he?

Seconds later, I could see the red light on his cell phone begin to flash. Another text message? I flipped the phone over before I lost my nerve. It read:

Elliot,
    Thanks for the early morning call and starting my day so beautifully. I'm counting the hours before you come home.

Leah

I put the phone back and started to think. Making every attempt to reconcile this message with our past history and my suspicions. It didn't work. There was no other explanation. Elliot was back to his old shit. He was cheating on me. I told myself not to confront him right now. He'd just have another excuse. Besides, I was scheduled to fly out to San Diego in the next couple weeks. I could check things out for myself then.

Chapter 23

Sweet success. Finally, finally, her life was on the right track and she deserved it. San Francisco had worked out great. Initially, she didn't know if it would and she had been getting a little nervous. The drive up the coast from San Diego and the following two days had been fun. She and Elliot had spent all their time together, attending the conference during the day, sightseeing and frequenting the local clubs at night. They had even started jogging together, discussing their lives, and respective marriages. They had become very close in all ways but one.

Their last evening, they had decided to splurge and went to fisherman's wharf for a surf and turf dinner. They had binged on shellfish and steak, washing everything down with a dry California Chardonnay. Leah had asked Elliot for his advice and began discussing her problems with Bill. Bill didn't appreciate her. In fact, he actually mistreated her over the years. She told Elliot that unlike her marriage, which was a disaster, she could tell that he was happy with Grace. How lucky she was, to have a man like him…a man who was the complete opposite of her husband. Elliot was liberal, sophisticated, supportive emotionally, the type of man any woman needed, the type of man she needed.

Elliot disclosed that despite what she may think, his marriage was not without its problems, the biggest strain being his lack of desire to have children. Leah stated she understood. She had bore two children because Bill had pushed. She loved them, of course, but how her life was now, the monotony of it all, wasn't what she had wanted. She longed for adventure, excitement, and most of all passion. Elliot couldn't help but agree. In fact, he admitted this was the most fun he had experienced in a long, long time. No obligations. No responsibilities. No stress.

They took the trolley back to the hotel that night. He had opened his hotel room door and she had followed him in stripping off her sweater. She brushed up against him, kissed him and told him that nobody had to know. She also warned him that he would be crazy to become involved with her, but then again taking crazy risks made you feel alive, didn't it? It was worth it. She was worth it.

They day after they returned to San Diego, Leah made the decision to file for divorce. She knew Elliot would be getting one regardless of whether or not he wanted it. Elliot wouldn't file, but Grace would. Leah knew that he would be putty in her hands. She had had contact with Elliot almost hourly since he arrived in Michigan. She knew he was miserable. Grace had already confronted him and knew he was cheating. She just couldn't prove it. Well, not unless Grace had found some of the stuff she had stashed in Elliot's bag. Grace would be furious, obviously unable to provide him with any emotional support and so Leah was able to drive the wedge in deeper and deeper, calling to offer her support, letting him know everything would work out fine. As far as she was concerned, they had each other now and they could start to build their life together.

After Elliot returned from his miserable stay in Michigan, Leah knew he would want to be with her, to escape the memory of his angry, nagging wife. She also knew if Elliot ever had second thoughts about their relationship, all she would have to do was become depressed and check herself into the hospital. Bill had rescued her in the past and she knew Elliot would too. He was extremely responsible. So even if Grace wanted to work things out in the future, Elliot was hers now.

When I pulled into the Ellis House parking lot on Monday morning, I had an agenda - terminate Tori's employment. She had left me with no other choice. Her behavior the previous week had been the final straw. I had received approval from administration earlier in the morning. The good news was I had documented all her problems including her lack of response to any corrective action. I had conducted all my disciplinary meetings in the presence of a neutral observer and she couldn't tell me that she wasn't fully aware of what the expectations were.

As Tori stepped into my office, she took a seat across the table from me and Barbara. Despite Barbara's lack of involvement in the clinical team, administration liked her to participate in any program changes or budget issues. Tori stared at me with a blank expression and I decided to forgo any niceties, and be direct. There was no room for negotiation anyway.

"Tori. You have had numerous opportunities to rectify your actions. You have failed to do so. Your actions have become increasingly reckless and disrespectful."

"You mean-"

"Your behavior last Friday was inexcusable. You were already on probation and that kind of blatant disrespect . . ."

"You don't deserve any respect." She interjected.

Keeping my temper in check, I continued, "As your supervisor, you need to respect what I ask you to do, but that's not the issue. The issue is your job performance. Effective immediately, your employment is terminated. I don't want you to say goodbye to your clients. Just pack your personal belongings and leave. Your final paycheck will be mailed to you as soon as it becomes available." Tori said nothing. She stood up, kicked her chair and slammed the door on her way out. I was surprised she hadn't fought harder, but my guess was she saw it coming. I asked Barbara if she or a supervisor could escort Tori out, but she refused.

I followed Tori back to her office to the sound of drawers being slammed and personal belongings being hurled into cardboard boxes. As soon as she saw me, she started her tirade about what a lousy supervisor I was. As the other therapists began to trickle in from group, she shifted her demeanor and began to cry. When she finally left the building, I breathed a sigh of relief. I had been rushed when hiring her and I had made a mistake. It was a tough lesson but one I wasn't likely to forget.

Later that afternoon, I walked into clinical meeting and was met by a heavy silence. I knew what the issue was and expected a rocky ride. Steve piped up before I could begin.

"I always thought we were a team. So, who's next or do you always just fire at a whim?"

"I had my reasons."

"Would you mind sharing them? Let us in on how you make decisions that so profoundly affect a person's life. Then we can all prepare ourselves for the chopping block?"

"I don't want to go into specifics. But I can assure you that no one in this room has made any errors which places them at risk for losing their jobs."

"Tori was good at her job." Steve insisted as he looked around the room for support with several others nodding in agreement. Marcie bucked the trend.

"She was really negative. That was tough to deal with."

"She was negative, lazy and didn't take her job seriously enough." John remarked, supporting Marcie and earning an icy stare from Steve.

"Oh, I see how it goes John. Now that you're filling Jamie's shoes, or at least trying to fill them, it's time to suck up to the boss." Steve stated sarcastically. John ignored his comments.

"The bottom line is we're down two team members with Jamie and Tori gone. We all have to pitch in and -"Steve cut me off.

"Here we go." Steve responded oozing with even more sarcasm. "Pitch in and do what we need to for the team. You know, I've had enough." He abruptly pushed back his chair, picked up his belongings and left the room. No one else followed and the meeting continued.

An hour later we had hammered out how we would compensate for Tori's absence and completed case reassignments. At least something beneficial was accomplished today. I walked out to the parking lot and saw a large scratch down the side of my car where someone had keyed it. I didn't have to think too hard about who committed the act. I was just happy she was gone. It would simplify my life. Simplicity and peace was what I needed more than anything else these days.

Elliot's flight had left early in the morning and I breathed a sigh of relief as I entered to a quiet, empty home. My relief seemed like a betrayal to Elliot, but with stressors pounding me from all sides, I would take respite wherever I could get it. He hadn't bothered to leave me a goodbye note and I was disappointed, but not surprised. Unfortunately, the only thing he had left me was a mess. The fridge door was wide open, the sink was full of dishes and the back door unlocked. He definitely did not have my best interests at heart. This juvenile form of revenge made me wonder how much he had loved me in the first place, if even at all. I tried to keep my thoughts from floating in that direction. Instead, I curled up in my arm chair with Snowy as my blanket and drifted off to an exhausted sleep.

The red is a dramatic contrast to the clean white sheets. As the door opens wider, I see him, my eyes transfixed on the blood soaked clothing. I react physically, gagging, then vomiting. I keep retching bile unable to stop, even though there is nothing left in my stomach. Finally, the heaving slows. I keep my hands on my knees, keep my head hung low. I can feel the bile soaked strands of hair clinging to my face. Eventually, I raise my head and see movement.

I stare in disbelief. Somehow attempting to reconcile the image before me with what I cognitively know to be true. He, my husband, sits up and swings his feet over the side of the bed. He looks at me and says, "Surprise!" A wicked sneer spreads across his face. "You should see your face. Sure did spook you. Pretty good trick if I say so myself."

He looks through me while peeling off his shirt. He crumples it into a ball with his hands and lets it fall to his feet. He gets off the bed and walks over to the armoire pulling out a t-shirt from the top drawer. He pulls it over his head and says, "Hey man, we're all paid up as he looks in the direction of my captor. Check it if you want." My husband throws the man an envelope. "You need anything else before you get outta here?"

The man shakes his head while examining the bills in hand. As the man turns and leaves the room, my husband yells after him, "Hey, did you have any fun with my wife?"

"Would have if the bitch hadn't thrown up all over me. Don't like the stink of vomit. She don't have enough fight left in her anyway. Should have done it sooner." He leaves the room. Minutes later, I hear the sound of an engine and the crunch of tires rotating on gravel.

Chapter 24

The morning was overcast and dreary - the sun, obliterated by a thick blanket of grey, looked drained of all its fire. Storm clouds had started to form to the north, a sure sign snow would soon powder the landscape with a new coat of white. Today I had decided to forego putting out fires at work. I had risen at dawn to join in the latest search effort, now one of many that had been organized for Corrine. I tried telling myself I was helping. That I was somehow making a difference. But the harder I tried to convince myself, the more it felt like my actions meant nothing. I constantly battled the morbid thoughts surging through my head, the feelings of helplessness and the silent understanding that the search today was focused more on recovery than rescue. No one could argue the odds were against finding Corrine alive, for as the days and weeks continued to pass, hope continued to diminish.

Corrine had now been missing for well over a month. Though I never thought it possible, I had started to become inured, surprised if I didn't see her face plastered on the television screen, in the local papers or stapled to lamp posts on street corners. According to the police, there was no change in the status of the investigation. Another way of saying there had been no progress or at least none they were able to share with the public. The only thing which had become more apparent was Corrine hadn't just walked out on her job. No one, absolutely no one - friends, family or stranger, had reported seeing her since the night she had appeared on my front doorstep. She had vanished and I, like many, believed she had met with foul play. She had been gone far too long.

As I drove down the icy streets, bordered by dirty snow, I kept thinking about what could have happened to her. Was it possibly work related? Did it have anything to do with a client or a client's family? As an employee of Ellis House, threats from family members were part of the job description. Corrine had discussed some of her suspicions with me about the staff, but it seemed unlikely that selfish motives could have resulted in her disappearance. I couldn't imagine Barbara or anyone else hurting her. Or could I? More likely it concerned her personal life. All she ever showed me or her co-workers was what she wanted us to see and I wondered what burden of secrets she carried. After all, everybody had secrets.

Hard pellets of snow began to bounce off my windshield as I pulled off I-94 and turned into a well marked site a half a mile down the road. The search command center had been set up in a clearing just before the flat ground turned to sloping hills covered with thin, bare maples. It was devoid of any conifers. I pulled into a spot close to the other cars and noticed the large crowd of volunteers which had already assembled. They were huddled together as much for warmth as for conversation before they fanned out across the landscape. I put on my hat and gloves as I slipped out of the car. I felt the icy wind slap me hard across the face. The air was damp and frigid, the kind of cold that chilled you to the core. This only made me admire the volunteers who had consistently participated in the searches that much more.

As I walked toward the woods, I saw a tall, African American man bundled up in a red ski jacket and matching red hat. I recognized him as Corrine's uncle from the photo she kept on her desk. I walked over to where he was standing and introduced myself.

"Hi. I'm Grace Morgan. I work with Corrine."

"Yes, Grace. Corrine's speaks fondly of you." He said taking my hand. "I know you worked with Corrine, uh, work with Corrine. Need to stay positive you know." He looked down at the ground averting eye contact. I could see pools of water begin to well up in the corners of his eyes. "Thanks. Thanks for coming." He said regaining his composure and facing me again. He took a breath and continued. "I'll tell you the same thing I tell everybody. I'm still hoping against hope all will turn out OK."

"I'm praying too . . . everyone is." I said, jumping in, not willing to radiate anything but hope.

"She's my little girl, even though she's not little and she's not actually my girl." He smiled. "I did raise her for a long time. Her father was a low-life, you know, almost destroyed her. I know you know that. But when her mother was alive, God bless her, she did everything she could to take care of Cory. Doesn't seem right. Now this? I mean hasn't she suffered enough?"

"It was really sad, what happened to her mother." I responded quietly. "Everyone's pulling for Cory."

"I was really proud of her, you know. There I go speaking of her in the past tense again. But I am really proud of what she is trying to do. She wants to go back to school, become a therapist, so she can continue working with kids, especially those who are so damaged. She thinks with more education, she'll be able to accomplish more with the kids."

"I'm sure she'll be a great therapist. All the kids at work really respect her. She'll be great." I shifted gears. "I am so sorry for everything you're going through. I guess I can't really believe it and I can't imagine being in your shoes. I'm just so sorry. I wish there was something I could say or do."

"I guess there's nothing really to say. Thanks for helping today and thanks for caring about her."

We shook hands and I turned to walk away.

"Excuse me, Grace?" I looked back in his direction.

"Yes?"

"Did you by any chance have any idea what was bothering her?"

"You mean with work?" I walked back in his direction. "She and her boss..."

"I know all about Barbara and Barry and their alleged practices. We've had lengthy discussions about them. But I'm talking about something more."

I looked at him blankly. "Sorry. Beyond work conflicts, I really have no idea. I didn't know too much about her personal life."

"It's just there was something going on."

"Meaning?"

"You see Cory usually planned her visits, but sometimes she just showed up at my doorstep when she really had something on her mind. She always considered me her sounding board, her voice of reason. Last time I spoke with her was the day she was scheduled to visit. She had called me earlier in the day and said she was coming to see me in Chicago for the weekend."

"So, you think..."

"She was coming to discuss whatever problem she was having. I just keep hoping somebody will be able to tell me what it was."

I nodded. "I'm sorry. I wish I knew."

I said my goodbyes for a second time.

I had spotted a couple of childcare workers from Ellis House earlier and now saw Ana making her way in my direction. She said hello and I noticed that she had mellowed from the last time we spoke. My guess was she was able to set aside her anger at least for today and focus on the issue at hand. Since the AWOL, Ana had been increasingly vocal in her outrage. My unconditional support for Emily and lack of support for her was inexcusable in her eyes. Even worse, my recommendations for remedial training following her recent lapses in protocol were unwarranted and insulting. However, I had stuck with my beliefs. She had made several poor judgment calls lately and even though I was not her supervisor her decisions significantly impacted the well being of the clients. For whatever reason, she seemed to have a hard time understanding this and took every negative comment as a personal attack. I had tried to explain it wasn't who she was but the decisions she had made and I sincerely believed that much of that came from inexperience.

"So, have you heard anything about the investigation?" Ana asked.

"Nothing except what's been plastered all over the news." I replied. Our conversation remained focused on Corrine, then shifted to small talk and finally dwindled to nothing as we spent the rest of the day searching culverts, ditches, frozen fields and barren woods. We had stopped intermittently throughout the day to seek warmth and fuel our bodies with sandwiches and weak coffee. But by the time the day was over and dusk was arriving, my hands and feet were frozen blocks of ice and my face as numb as a porcelain mask. Not unexpectedly, the results of our efforts were fruitless.

As I crawled into my car and turned on my engine, I felt the aching in my joints and the tingling in my extremities as they began to feel heat and circulate blood. I felt discouraged. I felt disoriented. The whole experience had seemed nothing less than surreal. Emotionally, I had tried my best to detach myself from the task, protecting myself and not allowing myself to become too involved. I tried to focus on being rational - logical. Logically, I knew bad things happened to people. I wasn't ignorant. I had frequently followed missing persons cases in the news. The cases that involved children were always the most devastating. During recent years, there had been so many that stood out. Some had had unspeakable and heartbreaking conclusions. For others, prayers had been answered and tears of relief had been shed.

However, the situation with Corrine had provided me with new found insight and helped me better understand what anguish people must experience when trying to find a missing loved one. It was indescribable, so much desperation, so much pain, the families so frantic. I sometimes found my eyes welling up for these strangers whom I had never met.

Darkness had descended by the time I arrived home. Quickly, I changed from my damp clothes to my workout gear and braved the elements again. Though thoroughly fatigued, I thought a run would help clear my mind and deplete the nervous energy my body had been housing. As I exited the house, the icy air refreshed me, providing the motivation I needed to run in spite of the slick streets and clumps of snow which littered the sidewalks. The weather had been colder than average for this time of year. Last week's ice storm paired with frigid temperatures had turned the landscape into a skating rink. My legs moved awkwardly as I attempted to develop an even pace on the icy sidewalk, finally finding solid footing on the road where the snowplow had created some traction.

I completed my usual circuit around the neighborhood, enjoying the solitude of the dark, empty streets, save the occasional dim light that illuminated my way. By the time I rounded the corner and completed the last three block stretch to the house, I had slowed my pace to a brisk walk and felt more relaxed than I had all week. I followed the driveway to the side door and retrieved the spare key from under the recycling box. I noticed the door was already open. And not just unlocked - ajar. I hadn't recalled, but I must not have latched it well when I left. However, to be safe I made my way in cautiously. All the lights were on as I had left them. As I looked around, nothing appeared to be out of place. Soon, Snowy made his way to greet me and I immediately felt my body loosen. Despite this assurance, I still spent the next twenty minutes sweeping the rest of the house, looking through closets and under the bed, my paranoia getting the best of me. Satisfied with the results of my search, I checked and locked all the doors and windows. Finally feeling secure, I headed for the shower to scrub off the grit of the day.

The following morning when I was back at my desk,

yesterday's events continuing to cloud my thoughts. The whole experience continued to be nothing less than unsettling. As much as I had promised myself I would remain detached emotionally, it hadn't worked and I struggled to keep my emotions at bay. I felt desperate to help Corrine, but knew I had no control over her fate. It made me feel inadequate.

Additionally, my feelings were magnified once I got off the phone with Max. He managed to demonstrate even less effectiveness over the phone than in person. Theoretically, he was meant to function as a program advocate, but during each successive encounter, he felt more like an adversary. Max had just unloaded both barrels, first by saying the powers that be would likely be requesting Ellis House to take on another crisis case. I had argued we were not well suited to handle it, especially given the situation with Corrine.

Then, Max had made my day even worse. He informed me Tori had contacted administration the day I fired her and requested her job back. She had met with both he and Houseman, they agreed to give her a second chance. When I asked why they had rehired her despite both Barbara and I supporting her termination, Max stated I was mistaken. Barbara had been Tori's biggest supporter. His comment was no surprise. My hands were tied. I knew I didn't have any control over administration's poor decision or about doing anything to help Corrine. So, I managed by taking control of a situation I could do something about.

I picked up the phone and dialed Jacques who was able to provide me with the latest regarding Maggie. Not surprisingly, Maggie had convinced herself that since her most recent visit with Emily had gone so poorly, she should just leave her daughter alone. She loved Emily but had failed her repeatedly. Emily deserved better. Emily was resilient and would learn to manage without her. If nothing else, she would then be free to focus her energies on herself rather than on a mother who was at worst a burden, at best an embarrassment.

The staff at the treatment facility, the therapists and Maggie's fellow patients kept telling her she would change her thinking once she recovered. Maggie knew differently. To her, the future was irrelevant and whether she recovered or not, the past was the past. Maybe over time, she could be a responsible person again, but she could never change what she had done. She had destroyed everything. The worst of all being that she had ultimately destroyed her daughter's life. That's why she couldn't see Emily at Christmas.

Despite her guilt, Maggie had been able to maintain her sobriety, primarily because she had no access to drugs under the watchful eye of the treatment center. In a few days, despite the risk of decreased supervision, she would be stepping down to outpatient treatment. There was one positive aspect to Maggie's life. She had developed a good relationship with her psychologist. It was hoped her accountability to him would help keep her fighting her demons without abusing alcohol.

I also explained to Jacques the situation regarding Emily's placement. Jacques assured me he would make it a priority to shake the bushes from his end. He agreed that despite how difficult it was to place Emily, shifting her to a level fourteen was out of the question.

As I sat across from Emily in her room, I finally believed she had some hope. She had been taken off AWOL watch and for the first time since her admission was becoming involved in treatment. She continued to make baby steps and responded well to the medication she had been prescribed following her psychiatric evaluation. She had now started to take responsibility for herself rather than her mother and didn't see her entire future as hopeless any longer.

As I was getting up to leave, Emily reached into her pocket and pulled out a crumpled piece of white paper. She carefully unfolded it and began to read the script.

Dear Mom,

I may never build up the strength to send this, but just writing it helps. So, I guess I'm writing it more for myself than anyone else. Maybe it's a way for me to finally start sorting out some of my anger. See, most of the time I don't even know what I'm feeling. The sadness, worry and anger just seem to keep getting all mixed up. One thing I am sure of is that we haven't talked in a long time, not since I came to see you in the hospital. Why haven't you called me?

I feel like I'm always the one who has to be strong because you can't hold it together and that's not fair. You are my mom and you should take care of me or at least try. I'm sick of taking care of you. Sometimes I can't believe you don't even try. You don't even bother to try. It's like you don't think life is worth living anymore because you lost everything. Well, hello, I'm still here and your lack of effort to get better has made me feel worthless. Why won't you fight for me? Stay away from the booze. It makes me crazy.

I didn't turn into a drunk because of everything that happened. And in case you forgot and I think you must have, I lost my family too. I know I have had my problems and still do but the main reason I've had such a hard time getting better is because of you. I feel like I continue to be punished even though I was the only one who was aware of what was happening that day. If you had paid attention to me that day both dad and John would still be alive. However, despite all your bad decisions you're supposed to be my mom. You're supposed to be strong for me like a mom should be. You're supposed to provide me with a home and take care of me, but it's been the other way around and I'm sick of it. If you had been strong, I wouldn't have been forced to live in a group home. I'd be at home, in my room, with my things, like I should be. We could have stayed in West Virginia and I could have even gone to the same school. I know we could have never stayed in that house, but we could have stayed in the same town.

I can't help but always go back to that day and think how easily it could have been stopped. How I tried and how Uncle Cam started the sequence that wrecked my life. I understand, but I still get mad about you keeping that picture of him. He was a screw up. Just like you and daddy always said. I can't help but look at myself and recognize how much less important I was to you and daddy than John.

Understand that I am angry and do place a lot of blame in your direction, but you are not the only one I blame. Unfortunately, you are the only one left to hear it. Despite everything though, what I'm angriest about is what I told you earlier. You are not doing anything to help yourself. I can't believe that after everything and after all this time, you'd let me rot in a group home, but like I said I guess that shows me how little you must care about me. You're weak, too weak to be my mom. You should start acting like my mom again and get it together. I know your feelings will be hurt when you read this letter, but you hurt me every day.

Love Emily

It was clear that Emily had taken this task seriously and had written a well thought out letter. I expressed to her that I still did not fully understand what had happened to her. Emily agreed it was time for her to fill in the blanks.

Chapter 25

Houseman sat back in his chair and looked at the snow falling outside his window. His life had become complicated and he didn't like it. He had always excelled, succeeded professionally and still managed to set aside time for a personal life. However, things at Ellis House were becoming too unstable. To make matters worse, things were even worse with that missing staff member, Corrine Duschene. He didn't care to have the police and reporters hovering around the group home. Barbara already brought enough negative attention to the program. It didn't need any more.

He understood Barbara was a big fish in a small pond and that she ran the program as she saw fit. It was a tool to quench her thirst for control and her need for respect, but she sometimes pushed things too far, letting her ego get in the way. He hoped she would be able to manage things well enough for now. Manipulating the budget and writing out overtime checks for Barbara was easy when she asked for extra here and there.

However, it made him bitter. He couldn't remember when she had even come close to working a full week. He resented her laziness, her poor work ethic, and her simplistic way of seeing the world. She was really such a stupid woman.

Unfortunately, fate had delivered quite a blow and as a result he was right where she wanted him. He hated being held hostage by someone he considered inferior. He had always worked hard, built the agency from the ground up through sheer will; but everyone had secrets, things that could destroy you. Luck hadn't been on his side when Barbara discovered his. If only he'd been more careful. If only she hadn't dropped by to see him that day. But he hadn't been careful and now he had to pay.

The current problem was Barbara's ego. It was out of control. Barbara had made some bad management decisions recently - use of restraints was up, complaints from the county were constant and there was that ridiculous incident with Nate. Barbara just had to stop drawing attention to Ellis House and refrain from threatening the psychologist. He had already spoken with her about it, but he knew Barbara. She would continue to do things her way. She had called him that very day and told him she had a problem with Dr. Morgan's attitude.

Houseman knew the problem for Barbara was Dr. Morgan. She wasn't as easy to control as the former clinical directors had been. Dr. Morgan was dedicated to the program and was not a complainer, despite her horrendous workload. She was a good director. She was what was needed at Ellis House. But Barbara wanted the complete opposite. Barbara sought deliberately to create chaos and make Dr. Morgan's days at work as miserable as possible. She tapped her phone line in case she could find a useful tidbit. However, she had come up empty handed and had no choice but to keep Morgan's life as unpleasant as possible in hopes she would quit. Barbara had loved it when Ellis House was between clinical directors. There was no therapists' advocate and she could push them around however she wished.

Houseman also knew he had to figure out a way to pacify Max. He had been working with Max for almost ten years. He trusted Max and knew he was loyal to the company. However, Houseman also knew Max's frustration with him was becoming quite pronounced. He was painfully aware Max was seeing the program at Ellis House unravel and didn't understand why changes weren't being made. Max had urged Houseman to allow him to make small changes to boost staff morale and he frequently complained about supporting Barbara when she was clearly in the wrong. Max repeatedly stressed no matter how Barbara tried to spin it, there just wasn't enough staff. Sooner or later if something wasn't done, someone would be seriously hurt.

Obviously, Houseman couldn't tell Max the truth. He couldn't let Max know why Barbara was in control so he had to stonewall him, create excuses which were flimsy at best. He couldn't honestly answer the questions Max posed almost daily. Why did Barbara have so much power? Why didn't she suffer the consequences of her poor decisions and why were they never overturned? Why did she control the clinical budget? And why had she been able to overturn Dr. Morgan's decision to fire Tori Ridgeway, especially since it was evident she was detrimental to the clinical program? For now, he would continue to pacify Max. Barbara on the other hand was a problem. He needed to brainstorm and find a way to be done with her and her threats once and for all.

Elliot had been gone two weeks. Our last parting had been strained at best and as I had started to put the puzzle pieces together. I didn't like what I saw. Regardless of how Elliot tried to convince me my suspicions were unfounded, I knew better. As our telephone conversations became more abrasive, I accused him of adultery and he accused me of mental instability. My trust continued to dwindle. Finally, I decided to dispense with the speculation once and for all and hire a private investigator. This would provide me with answers and eliminate any twinges of self-doubt I had been having. I got online and looked up private investigators in the San Diego area. There were many, but I continued to scan the biographies until I found one I liked.

Aloha Investigations: Law enforcement trained and experienced. Providing confidential and professional consultation.
Kate Nguyen: 12611 Casa Avenida, Poway, CA 92064
Phone: (858) 663-8000
Email: KNAloha@cox.net
Established in 1994
Aloha Investigations has grown to earn a reputation of getting the job done efficiently and has earned a reputation for success throughout San Diego county. Known as a surveillance specialist, the agency is expanding to Riverside County to meet demands further north. Quality investigation starts with establishing a foundation before surveillance is conducted to minimize cost and maximize results. This agency has had ten solid years of experience focusing on infidelity, missing persons, fraud and background investigations. Focus on data collection with video surveillance, GPS tracking, and evidence photography.

I wasted no time and dialed her number. She picked up on the first ring.

"Hello. Kate Nguyen. Aloha Investigations. How may I help you?"

"Hi. I'm a potential client." I just spit it out. "I'm sure my husband is cheating on me. He's done it once before and I think he's doing it again."

"OK."

"It's the same behavior pattern. He says he needs his space. Well, I already live in Michigan and he in San Diego. He says he feels tied down being forced to speak with me on the phone every night. I can't ever reach him. He never picks up his cell. He ignores me, and says I'm paranoid and suspicious. He recently came to visit me and I found a woman's moisturizer in his duffle bag. He's always in contact with the same female co-worker." I confessed.

"Look, I've been doing this for twelve years. I'll be blunt. From what you've told me, it sounds like infidelity is a likely explanation. Can I ask why the need for a private investigator?

"Well, I don't want to throw away my marriage if there is the smallest probability that I'm wrong. I still love him, but I don't trust him at all."

"OK, so you want surveillance data to confirm the possible infidelity. My guess is the data will confirm your suspicions."

"Yes. That's what I need. You do video?" I asked.

"Yes, you'll get a video and a written report." Ms. Nguyen responded.

"Great."

"Now, let me tell you how I work. I charge seventy-five dollars an hour plus mileage. You tell me the dates and times during which you want him monitored and I'll set that up. I usually get there twenty minutes early to make sure I have all the equipment operational. OK?" Ms. Nguyen questioned.

"OK." I agreed.

"Also, I need a one thousand dollar retainer. I have learned from experience. I got stiffed a lot in the past. We can also figure out a cap if that makes you more comfortable. Most clients have a budget and can't exceed ten or fifteen thousand dollars."

"Whoa, I won't be able to exceed two or three." I admitted, somewhat embarrassed.

"That's fine. Just like to get everything figured out up front. So, you want to go ahead with things?"

"Yes." I responded hesitantly, thinking if nothing else Kate Nguyen was efficient and didn't waste any time on small talk.

"Can you give me your husband's name, a physical description, and a rundown of his daily routine?"

"Elliot Morgan. He's 5'11", about 180 pounds with green eyes and brown hair. He wears a goatee and recently had Lasik surgery, so no more glasses. He's usually casually dressed for work, khaki pants and a dress shirt, but no tie." I stated.

"Keep going." Ms. Nguyen prodded.

"He usually leaves his condo around 7:30 a.m. to make it to the medical center by 8:00 a.m. He's typically there all day and gets home around 5:30 p.m. After work he jogs and then after that

I don't really know. He calls me sometimes, but it's on his cell, so he could be anywhere." I stated.

"What does – "

"Oh," I interrupted. "I think they've been carpooling recently."

"Your husband and the co-worker?"

"Yeah."

"Before we talk about her, what kind of car does your husband drive and what are the plates?"

"It's a 1997 Jeep Cherokee, candy apple red with Michigan plates. The license is LSV 303." I concluded, feeling like a traitor.

"I need the same information for the woman he's having the alleged affair with."

"Her name is Leah Braden. She's about 5'8" with long brown hair, usually loose. I think her work schedule is the same as Elliot's. I know they jog together, but that's about it. I think she drives a 1998 white Toyota Tercel, but I don't know the plate number. It's a California plate though.

"OK, I can get the rest. If you can email me dates and times when you want your husband watched and a recent photo of your husband and the woman if you have one, I'll start as soon as I get the retainer." Ms. Nguyen concluded.

I already had the dates and times picked out in my head. I provided her with those, all the necessary addresses and concluded with letting her know I'd email her a picture of Elliot and Leah later that afternoon.

Elliot called later that evening. I had attempted to get in touch with him numerous times earlier that day, but was never able to reach him. This was becoming the norm.

"Nice of you to finally call back." I said coldly.

"What's that supposed to mean?" Elliot responded, immediately on the defensive.

"I can never get in touch with you."

"I'm busy. I just got back from my jog."

"Did you go by yourself?"

228

"No, why should I?"

I felt my throat tighten up. "Leah go with you?"

"Yeah, we've been jogging together since San Fran. It makes it a lot more fun."

"I bet." My voice betrayed my emotions. "Why do you have to do that? Why can't you jog by yourself like you used to? You know how much it bothers me."

"Grace, how many times do we have to go over this? You're like a broken record. All I ever get from you is this controlling wife routine."

"I'm not controlling."

"Yes, you are. You're a damn harpy."

"If you don't like how I'm acting, you can make me stop."

"Only if I give in to your demands."

"So, why not try to make me feel better?"

"Because your demands are irrational and why should I acquiesce? It just reinforces your behavior."

"I'm not controlling, just threatened and disrespected. I feel like you've replaced me." I admitted.

"That's ridiculous." Elliot scoffed.

"Is it? You said that she had replaced me in many ways."

"What I said was that she replaced what we used to do together - not you as a person. The jogging is just a lot more fun with someone. You know that. I always hated doing that by myself."

"And the carpooling?"

"Yeah, and the carpooling . . ."

"God, El, why can't you be without her . . . is there anything you do on your own ?"

"Grace, she's all I've got out here. You know how hard it can be to make friends. We're good friends."

"You know what she told me?"

"What?"

"That you guys are close enough to fight."

"Well, we are, I guess. Like I said, we have a strong bond."

"God, like I want to hear that."

"It's all innocent."

"Innocent as the text message she sent you the morning you got ready to fly back to San Diego?"

"What?"

"I'm sure you remember. The message she sent you. You know, thanks for starting my day off so nicely . . . I'm counting the hours before you come home." I said angrily.

"What are you talking about?"

"The message *Leah* left you on the phone. The day you flew back." I pushed.

"It's not what you think." He responded irritably. She was happy I was coming back. Stuff at the med center had been tough. It's a really stressful internship. We're under a lot of pressure and rely on each other for support. I had called her that morning to give her some support because I knew she'd have a tough day ahead. She's not very well appreciated at work, not to mention all her personal problems."

"So, you speak with her daily, multiple times a day? You can't put that relationship on hold even when you come to see me after I hadn't seen you for two months? It seems like you have some pathetic co-dependent relationship."

"She needs support and has reached out to me."

"She's lived in San Diego most of her life. She's got a husband, family, brother and sister, friends . . . why does she have to be so needy with you?"

"She reached out to me."

"So you said. She's so weak and needy though. It's pathetic."

"Shut up. I hate this side of you. I haven't seen it in a long time and it's less flattering the second time around."

"You don't like how your wife acts when you're cheating on her. Surprise! Surprise!"

"Hell, it's not like you have a hotel receipt. I'm sick of you not trusting me."

"I have no reason to trust you. I found woman's moisturizer in your bag when you were home. How did that get in there?"

"Hell if I know. I never put it there. But, I'll ask her."

"Sure, ask your stupid girlfriend. I'm sure the two of you will concoct some ludicrous story." Before I could say anything else, he hung up.

He called back and left me a voicemail later that evening explaining that she must have left it in our car on the way back from the conference. He must have placed it in his bag for safekeeping and forgotten about it. I didn't bother to call him back.

Chapter 26

The next day, I found Emily in my office sitting on my chair spinning back and forth in half circles. Emily kept her word and as promised relayed the events of what she termed the demise of her family.

It had been a typical Saturday morning, just as Emily's mother had described, one that had resulted in altering if not destroying the lives of them all. Emily had opened her eyes and stretched to the smell of coffee and bacon grease wafting through her doorway. As she jumped out of bed and rushed to the kitchen, she banged on her brother's door with her fist to rouse him from sleep. She inhaled a plate of sausage and biscuits chasing them down with orange juice on her way to the living room to soak in a morning of cartoons. John joined her several minutes later and they snuggled on the couch, eyes affixed to *Tom and Jerry*. They barely noticed when Maggie stuck her head in from the kitchen letting them know their Uncle Cam's truck was coming down the road.

Emily and John loved their Uncle Cam. Their parents were

sometimes critical when they spoke of him discussing how irresponsible he was. Would he ever grow up? But she and John didn't care what their parents thought. All they knew was Uncle Cam always made them laugh. Typically, they would have rushed to greet him. However, Maggie had urged for them to stay inside until the adults were done talking.

Several minutes later, Emily and John decided to pry their eyes from the screen long enough to wave "hello" to Uncle Cam from the back porch. Maggie stopped them from leaving the house to greet him. Instead, she asked them to go upstairs since their dad and uncle were in the middle of what appeared to be a small disagreement. They agreed grudgingly, went upstairs and immediately, with their curiosities peaked, raised Emily's bedroom window.

Even though they were not able to hear the words, it was clear that this was nothing less than an emotionally charged battle. John soon became impatient, telling Emily he was going to find out what was going on. She discouraged her brother and persuaded him to go to his room. This he did, but only until Emily turned her back and he was able to slink downstairs. John evaded his mother who was eavesdropping with fervor at the kitchen window and sneaked outside to do some investigating of his own.

Emily saw John from her bedroom window. She yelled ordering him back into the house. However, his mind was made up. John did not want to miss the action. He was crazy about his uncle and loved to be in the thick of things. Being on the sidelines was just no fun. Emily begged him one more time to come indoors tempting him with peanut butter cups, but he refused and ran around to the side of the house.

Emily ran down the stairs and hollered for her mom. Maggie ignored her cries as she continued to stare out the kitchen window. She told Maggie John had run off into the fray, but her mom had continued to hush her. She finally used colorful curse words to gain her mom's full attention. Maggie dashed out the back door and left Emily standing in the kitchen.

Maggie had almost made it out to the barn where Cam's truck

was parked when she froze. She had seen the shiny glint reflect from the metal of the gun. She had seen Cam swivel and take several shots at the wall of the barn. Then with the slightest hesitation, he looked to his brother, put the gun in his mouth and pulled the trigger blowing out the back of his skull. The blood, bone and grey matter fanned out, coating the weathered barn board. She had seen it form a grisly graffiti. She stood motionless for several minutes. Cam's body lay crumpled on the ground, a large sticky mass of red collecting beneath him. Frank held his brother and wailed. He looked to his wife, his eyes pleading for help.

Maggie stood paralyzed for several minutes. She didn't react until she caught Emily out of the corner of her eye coming toward her. She shrieked and demanded Emily return to the house. But Emily kept moving toward her. Maggie repeated her demand, yelled to Emily her father was OK. But Emily kept screaming. As Emily came closer to her mother, Maggie finally heard the words. Emily was screaming for her brother.

Emily became hysterical. She screamed until her throat was raw, desperate to find him. Her screams turned to silence when she entered the barn. A bullet had gone though the barn wall and hit John square in the chest. He lay on his back, the deep crimson pool spreading furiously. Frank picked up John's limp, lifeless body and screamed at Emily to call 911. Maggie fell to the ground and silently started to pray. Emily ran back to the house shaking and trembling.

Frank carried John to the car. He tenderly laid him down in the backseat and covered him with a blanket. He said he couldn't wait for the paramedics. John still had a pulse. He needed to drive him to the hospital. It was his only chance.

Maggie remained on the ground where John had been shot. Her arms were wrapped taut around her legs, knuckles white. She wouldn't speak. Emily paced back and forth across the yard waiting for a phone call. She waited for her dad to roll into the driveway creating a large cloud of dust, and take her to the hospital to see her brother. However, he never came.

Emily waited outside late into the evening. A police cruiser finally pulled into the driveway. As the policeman approached, he removed his hat and told Maggie he was sorry to inform her. Inform her that the accident had taken the lives of both her husband and son. Frank's car had been found wrapped around a telephone pole. He had been crushed by the steering column and John had been ejected through the windshield. The car had lost control. Neither had been wearing seatbelts.

The autopsy results indicated John was dead before impact having never survived the initial gunshot wound. He bled to death in the barn. Emily speculated her father knew John was dead before he placed him in the car. She believed her father had made the decision to take his own life.

Emily took a long drink of water and concluded, "I look back at that day and I blame my uncle. If he had never shown up, if he had never fired his gun, if he had been able to talk to my dad and not lose control, my dad and brother would be alive. I blame my mom too because if she hadn't ignored me when I begged her to listen, John would still be here and so would my dad. I blame my dad too. Because he left me and didn't care enough to think about what my life would be like without him. Maybe that way, I would have never wound up in a group home.

That picture my mom keeps, the one with my uncle . . . well, she keeps it because she feels sorry for him and believes he deserves to be remembered too. After he died and everyone in the family knew John had caught his stray bullet, no one bothered with him. He was cremated and no one bothered to pick up his ashes or hold a memorial.

And that fight between my dad and uncle, well, it wasn't really a fight. Uncle Cam had cancer. Really bad and it was eating up his insides. He had just found out and was falling apart. Uncle Cam had always prided himself on taking care of his body and joked that he was healthy as an ox. Then, life gives him shit and at thirty-five, he finds out that he has liver cancer and only three months to live. He hadn't gotten married, didn't have any kids, hadn't accomplished anything. No legacy to leave behind. Everything had been taken away from him before he even got started.

I guess over time my mom started to feel really guilty about Uncle Cam. You see, if she had been paying attention to us and kept John in the house, Uncle Cam would have only shot himself. Not good, but he never meant to kill John. But mom felt badly because she took away from him the only thing he did have and that was how well he had treated us kids. He had been blackballed for doing something he wasn't even aware of. People only remember him as a child killer.

I feel like I did nothing wrong and paid an awful price, a much higher price than my mom. We both left our home, but she was so fragile I had to become her caretaker. Because she was so weak, I wound up in here. I still hope my mom has some fight left in her. There are a lot of people who have survived extraordinary circumstances. Look at me. I absolutely consider myself broken, but what if you can glue it back together? There will always be cracks, but with enough glue maybe it can all stick."

As I pulled my office door shut for the day, I couldn't help but feel some peace. The last several days at work had gone smoothly and there had been progress. Jacques had kept good on his promise, successfully beating the bushes for placement options. As a result, Emily had several placement interviews scheduled later in the week. He had ruffled some feathers, Kim's primarily, but a bruised ego was well worth the price. Emily had been ecstatic to know she finally had options and her stay at Ellis House would soon be coming to an end. Drew's cheery voice broke through my thoughts.

"You sure have a cozy clinical team." Drew stated as he caught up with me on my way out the door.

"Come again?" I asked.

"Oh, come on Doc. You know what I'm talking about."

"Drew. It's five-thirty in the evening. My morning coffee has worn off and I'd rather not attempt to decode any of your cryptic messages right now."

"Sorry, I forgot about your crutch. But anyway, you're usually pretty observant. I'm sure you've noticed."

"Noticed?"

"Tori and Steve."

"Yeah, I know who they are." I responded sarcastically. "So, what about them?"

"They're very friendly if you know what I mean. Touchy when they pass each other in the hall. In fact, I just saw them doing a tongue dance out in the rec field. A couple clients saw them sucking face too. Pretty poor boundaries. Think you'd better get it under control."

Tori had only been back a couple weeks, and it appeared there was no change in her behavior. She had no more respect for her position than she had before. So much for second chances. I cursed Max and Houseman for being so naive as to trust Barbara and to be sucked in by Tori's charm. She was never going to make any effort to change or take her position more seriously.

I knew they were both working late shifts and wasted no time in using the overhead page to request their presence in my office - pronto. Several minutes later, Tori entered my office with Steve in tow. Steve was dressed even more casually than typical, bordering on unacceptable. It was true that given the nature of the job, casual dress was acceptable, with jeans being the most popular clothing item. However, Steve's jeans were frayed, with a strategically placed rip on his upper thigh. His t-shirt was tight, several sizes too small and accentuated the small roll of excess that sagged over his belt. His look was completed by the uneven stubble decorating his chin and his shaggy mop which had recently been crimped. Tori's outfit mirrored Steve's except instead of tennis shoes, she sported three inch chunky open toed shoes. Big gold hoops hung from her lobes and her hair looked like it had recently been highlighted from a box with thick strawberry streaks falling around her face. They were both chewing on large pieces of gum and acted put out. I couldn't help but be immediately irritated.

"You have any idea why I called you both up here?"

Tori turned to Steve and smiled bumping his leg with her hip.

"Yeah, I've got a good idea." Steve answered. "My guess is you're going to tell me that now we can't even date on the units."

"No. I don't really care who dates whom, but the message here is do it on your own time."

There was no reaction. Steve and Tori just continued to chew their gum.

"Let me refresh your memories. You were just seen kissing on the rec field . . . about twenty minutes ago." I said looking at my watch. "Not to mention, this happened in front of clients and staff. You both know better than that."

"So, who told you? Drew? Drew must have told you. Yeah, Drew. I saw him out there. And of course everyone knows you two are buddy-buddy."

"It doesn't matter who told me. That's irrelevant. The point is I need for you both to understand that that kind of behavior is unacceptable. And that it won't happen again." I looked at Steve who nodded. Tori was chewing on her thumb and shifted from one leg to another. She avoided eye contact and looked ready to blow.

"I'm going to give you a chance to correct this." I stressed focusing the majority of my attention on Steve. "So this is what I expect. Of course, the clients are the most pressing issue…"

"Who are you? My mother?" Tori finally piped in, unable to maintain her silence any longer. "Man, I mean this is no different than when I was a kid. Telling me what to do? Trying to push me around when you're not even my supervisor anymore." She continued shaking her head.

"I may no longer be supervising your assigned clinical cases, but I continue to be in charge of this program, thus your conduct on the units is my business whether you are willing to accept that or not. And just to be absolutely clear, your conduct was out of line."

It was true. I was no longer supervising Tori's caseload. Houseman had asked her to meet with Dr. Jackson, a psychologist who worked at Caldicott House and had stepped in to help out at Ellis House when they were between clinical directors. It felt like a slap in the face initially, but it was also a relief. I preferred to minimize stressors whenever I could and her presence in the program continued to be a thorn in my side. Let someone else deal with it.

"Out of line? A show of affection isn't out of line. Besides you didn't even see what happened. You're just taking somebody's word for it. If the situation had been reversed and I had come to you and said the same thing about some staff member, you wouldn't take me seriously."

"I certainly would take you seriously." I responded feeling like I had to defend myself. "It's a problem period. I wish you could appreciate that."

"Of course it's a problem. Everything's a problem with you. I'm sure Dr. Jackson wouldn't have overreacted like you did hauling us both up here. The reason this is such a problem is because I'm working with you - an obsessive, rule governed dictator who takes her frustrations out on others."

"Watch your tone." I growled.

"You know. No. I'm not going to watch my tone. In fact, just in case you haven't figured it out, you're a goddamn bitch. And the reason you're a bitch is because you're going to make a big deal out of this, like when I was trying on clothes during my break or when I was a few minutes late for group or whatever. And you know what? I won't let you throw this in my face." Tori had become more agitated and her face had turned red. She was screaming now. "I have more important things to do than eat your bullshit. I am a goddamn good therapist and I won't let you take that away from me. And I won't give you the satisfaction of writing me up and rubbing your hands together as you put one more piece of paper in my personnel file. So fuck you. I quit."

She turned, grabbed Steve by the arm and left. Twenty minutes later I got a hand written resignation letter stuffed in my mailbox. I wasted no time in contacting Max and bringing him up to speed. Surprisingly, for the first time I could remember, he backed me up and said with that type of conduct, the program was better off without her. I breathed a sigh of relief knowing she wasn't coming back and she had blown her chances.

There was a knock on the door a few minutes following.

"So, you happy now?" Steve barked as he let himself into my office. "Happy now that you're rid of her? Well let me tell you, you lost a really good therapist." He looked at me teeth clenched, eyes challenging to dispute his statement. "I'm really surprised too. We're so short staffed and you throw gasoline on an already burning fire. Great management."

"Lower your voice and watch what you say. As I mentioned before, you don't know the circumstances and you can't deny you have a personal bias."

"You know, if I weren't so hard up for money, I'd quit too."

"Well, no one is forcing you to stay. As I see it, you have two choices. Quit and follow Tori's lead or stay with the understanding that this incident will formally be written up and placed in your personnel file. Your response to the corrective action will also be noted. Barring this last month, I've been happy with your performance and you've been a good employee, but I think you are aware your behavior today was completely unacceptable. I need to do some paperwork. Please shut your door on the way out."

Steve turned and left the room without saying another word. I wondered if his decision making was clouded enough by his relationship with Tori to resign from his position. Barring Steve's poor judgment recently and his never ending string of smart assed comments, I would hate to lose him. He had always worked so well with the client population. I again returned to wrapping up my work for the evening.

Ten minutes later, I was pulling on my coat and exiting the backdoor to the parking lot. As I started to cross the pavement toward my car, I started to feel a little paranoid. I reminded myself I was being irrational. But my mind kept shifting back to the first time, I had fired Tori. I couldn't prove it, but I had convinced myself that she was the person who had keyed my car. She harbored so much hostility toward me and I had witnessed her act on her impulses over and over again. My guess was that Tori's hostility wouldn't carry her beyond verbal aggression and mild property destruction, but then again, you could never truly predict someone else's behavior.

I thought back to one of the conversations I had had with Elliot prior to his departure for internship. I had invited the clinical team to our home for an evening. Elliot had strongly advised me against it suggesting the function take place at a neutral location. He said I was playing with fire. Did I really want my employees to know where I lived? What if I needed to let someone go and they held it against me? What if boundaries started getting blurred and my staff started viewing me as their friend instead of their boss. I had told him that I didn't mean it to be anything but an opportunity to socialize. He insisted that regardless of how I meant it, others may not perceive it the same way. I had vehemently disagreed with him, but now, living alone and having such volatile, angry relationships with two employees, I wish I had listened to him.

I opted for a bath in the evening, not deviating too much from my typical routine. I watched the steam rise from the column of hot water that filled the cool tub. Once full, I slid into the steaming pool and felt my muscles begin to loosen. I shut my eyes and let my mind wander. Unfortunately, it wandered in an undesirable direction, one which required too much energy - my marriage to Elliot.

Once again, my marriage was unraveling. My phone conversations with Elliot were sporadic, filled with anger, insults and accusations. I had so many questions and needed to converse with him face to face, but knew right now it was out of the question. However, I also knew it couldn't wait. Finally, I dragged myself out of the bath, the cool air unpleasant to my skin. I quickly wrapped a heavy, terry cloth robe around my body, pulled on some socks and did what seemed most reasonable. I decided to email Elliot because, unlike a telephone conversation, I could more successfully communicate what I wanted to say.

Maybe if he had some time to fully digest my point of view, then we could make some headway. Anyway, it was worth a shot and I started typing.

Elliot,

As you know, things have been really difficult between us recently. I want to be honest with you in hopes we can come to an understanding, maybe even gain some resolution. I know you don't want to talk about Leah, neither do I, but I need to get this off my chest. We didn't cover a lot of ground we should have last time you came home and because of that our marriage continues to fall apart.

Understand I have felt threatened by Leah ever since I first spent time with her in San Diego. I didn't tell you then and maybe I should have, but I don't really believe it would have made a difference. But, reverse our roles. How would you feel if some guy talked about me all night and then I spent every waking second with him? You tell me I'm paranoid, but that's part of the problem. You're minimizing my feelings, but at the same time you don't say anything to allay my fears. You tell me you're close with her emotionally. This worries me because despite what you say, your boundaries are poor and hers are clearly even worse. You told me the first week you met her, the rumor was she was cheating on her husband. She doesn't respect her marriage. Why would she respect anybody else's? Ask me why I shouldn't worry? Anyone would in my shoes.

You say you love me and maybe you do, but you don't show it. You have no desire to touch me, have no interest in anything I say if you hear me at all. I get the impression I am intruding on your life not even feeling comfortable calling you on the phone anymore. I also know when I do speak with you, you're not happy to hear from me. I can hear it in your voice and that really hurts.

I know something is going on, but you won't tell me. And when you say you're detached, it's from me, not her. If there is something going on, I'm asking you to let me know. I'm not going to live in an empty marriage, one where I'm the only person exerting the effort. The bottom line is I'm uncomfortable and if you cared about me you would do something about it. Maybe you are not cheating on me physically, but I have no doubt you are emotionally. You put your relationship with her first, before our marriage and that's wrong. If you don't want to be married to me anymore, let me know. At the very least, you owe me that.

Grace

I reread it several times before I pushed send. It gave me the satisfaction of knowing that he knew how I felt and that I wasn't keeping it a secret. Ten minutes later, the phone rang.

"Where the hell do you get off sending me an email like that?" Elliot barked. "Man, I'm so sick of your shit Grace. You make me feel like you're breathing down the back of my neck when you're halfway across the country."

I was immediately on the defensive. "Goddamn it Elliot! All I'm trying to do is find out what's going on with you. Find out if you give a rat's ass about me or making us work anymore." I snapped.

"You want this marriage to work?" He responded.

"What do you think? But it seems like I'm the only one who cares to put forth any kind of effort. You can't do anything except be pissy all the time."

"Well, antagonizing me isn't the best way to keep me invested in making things work. By the way, did you ever bother to read that trash you sent me?"

"Of course I read it."

"So, you just spew forth whatever crap comes from your mouth and send it to me? Nice! Thanks for wrecking what would have otherwise been a good day. Why can't you just get off my back?" He snapped.

"See! This! This is what I hate. You make me feel like I'm an intruder on your life."

"Maybe you are."

"What do you mean by that? Why are you so nasty?" I pushed.

"Because I'm married to a paranoid harpy."

"Yes. I'm married to you. You're supposed to be able to talk to me. I shouldn't have to pry information from you."

"I told you when I was out there. You need to give me some space. I feel like you're suffocating me."

"Yeah, I know, spreading your wings and all that shit. Too bad you don't need any freedom from Leah. She's a real piece of work. Needy bitch." I spewed.

"You know. I'm not doing this -" Elliot responded.

"Doing what? Talking about the biggest problem in our marriage? Talking about what a hypocrite you are? Discussing how you need all this space from me, but it's OK to be suffocated by a cling on. You carpool, jog and work with her. Can she take a shit by herself or do you have to hold her hand to do that too?"

"You're a bitch."

"So you tell me all the time."

"God, I can't believe I marr..." Elliot stopped himself.

"Married me? Well, obviously you're sorry you did. And I'm sorry all I've gotten from you is pain and grief. I was under the false impression that marriage was about loyalty and teamwork. Don't worry. I'll get out of your way so you can focus your energies on your life with that bitch." With that, I slammed down the phone and hoped he wouldn't call back. I knew he wouldn't. What made me the angriest was I knew he was already dialing Leah's number so he could vent. I guess I could have tried to show him some compassion, but he didn't deserve any. I wanted him to find out for himself the type of woman she was. I knew I'd be flying out to San Diego to gain some closure after I heard back from the private investigator, but the results were irrelevant. I already knew the truth

I flopped down on my bed and shut my eyes. Even my eyelids seemed to ache and it felt wonderful to have my body motionless. The phone rang startling me and I jumped off the bed and ran to the kitchen managing to grab it after the third ring. I never thought

Elliot would call back. I braced myself for an ass chewing.

"Grace."

"Yes." I answered, caught somewhat off guard. I expected to hear Elliot's voice on the other end of the line.

"It's Drew."

"Drew. Hi. Sorry. I didn't recognize your voice. You sound so serious. Is something wrong? Something going on at work?"

"Yeah, something's wrong. Just not work. Turn on the TV. Channel four."

"Bad?"

"Yeah. Bad. It's Cory. Sorry. Gotta go." He hung up and I could hear his voice break.

I knew Cory was dead even before I turned on the television. As I picked up the remote, and turned on the set, I braced myself for what everyone had been afraid of. Cory had been missing for months and everyone had been hoping against hope. I remembered how her uncle had tried to stay positive throughout his ordeal, praying and wishing and hoping . . . but sometimes it's not enough and this was one of those times.

The reporter was standing in a densely wooded area in Southern Michigan close to the Indiana state line. This was where Cory's body had been discovered. She would have been missing for longer if not for the last several days of sunny, clear weather. A welcome break from what had seemed like an endless assault of freezing rain, subzero temperatures and snow since the beginning of the season.

Two students from Indiana State had found her while camping. Cory's foot had become exposed as they broke off pieces of the underbrush to use as kindling. Initially, confused, they had kicked aside the snow and the brush finally exposing the bone and the flesh of a partially gnawed leg.

They hadn't released many other details. We were left to fill in the blanks. I wasn't able to grasp what I was feeling, nothing beyond confusion and utter disbelief. I moved back toward the couch, my eyes still glued to the screen and tripped over the ottoman. What the hell? I said as I kicked it. How the hell did that damn thing get in here from the bedroom? I picked myself up from the floor hand over my mouth as I felt my stomach heave on the way to the bathroom.

Chapter 27

As Ana ascended the steps to the church, it had started snowing, more ice than snow. The hard pellets hit her face and made it sting. She wrapped her arms around her body hugging herself tight. The barometer was plummeting; she could already feel the chill. The temperature was forecasted to drop well below zero this evening and remain there for the next week. It appeared as if the weather was intentionally compensating for the recent unseasonable highs which had produced the temporary thaw. Ana would have never predicted the weather to be such a formidable adversary. It was a variable beyond her control and was becoming a spoiler for her plans.

Ana was late. She had hoped to be on time, not wanting to draw any more attention to herself than necessary. Cory's memorial service had started at noon, fifteen minutes ago. As discretely as she was able, she pulled open the door of the church and entered. She quickly walked down the aisle. She squeezed herself between two generously proportioned elderly women in the nearest available pew, unwrapped the damp scarf from her neck and peeled off her wet gloves. She unbuttoned her navy overcoat, and took a deep breath, eyes focused on the sea of faces around her. Some were easily recognizable, colleagues from work, but many were strangers. She found herself surprised by the vast number of people in bulky coats who had crammed themselves into this tiny, overheated building, filling it to the rafters to pay tribute to Cory. Silent tears streamed down many faces as Cory's uncle extolled the virtues of his "daughter" and of a promising life cut short. Ana was sweating now, but it was more than just being cramped and overheated. She had felt her anxiety start to build even before she set foot into the church. However, now, assaulted with vivid reminders of Cory's memory, she felt as if a raw nerve had been exposed. The problem was, she had never thought Cory's body would be found, especially so soon. It had seemed improbable events would have come together as they had. If only the weather had cooperated this mess could have been avoided. If it had just remained cold and miserable like it had been the night Ana killed her, those college students would have never gone out to the woods for a hike much less to camp for the weekend.

Enough! She needed to stop obsessing about how things were falling apart. No point torturing herself. She could not let it wreak any more havoc in her life. She refused to let that happen. Instead, she needed to focus on damage control. She was too close to making things work. So now, here she stood, pretending to care deeply about someone who she considered expendable and who had reaped just what she deserved.

Ana used a glove to dab the sweat from her brow and shifted around in the pew, jockeying for more space. She returned her focus to Cory's uncle who had just announced how he would be returning Cory's body to Chicago to bury her next to her mother whose life had also been unjustly ripped away. Ana's full attention was suddenly diverted to the man who stood at the end of the pew directly in front of her. She did a double take. That damn cop. He attempted to be casual, hands tucked in his pockets, as he continuously scanned the crowd. Detective Jensen certainly seemed to take his job seriously, perhaps too seriously. Not only did he show up today, he had returned to the group home several times since the day he had first interviewed staff.

Her interview with Jensen hadn't gone well. She recalled her feelings of discomfort when interviewed; he was condescending and belittled her position as a supervisor. Maybe he had issues with women in authority. She remembered noticing his hands. No wedding ring. However, this was not surprising given his thick, rimmed glasses and his polyester pinstriped suit accessorized by a brown bag lunch. He had asked her if eating his lunch at her desk was a problem, she had shaken her head. Consequently, she watched him unpack an orange soda and a foil wrapped sandwich which he promptly swallowed in three bites. But what Ana recalled most vividly was the anger he had brought out in her with his apparent lack of respect. Not only because he couldn't refrain from eating in her presence, but because he had repeatedly kept asking her the same question.

Ana had seen Jensen discretely glance in her direction several times, sizing her up, just as he had the day he had first interviewed her. She knew she needed to remain calm because as far as she knew, he couldn't prove anything. Or at least he hadn't been able to, but maybe with the discovery of the body . . . She felt hot and her chest started to tighten. There was no way to deny the discovery of the body was a huge problem. She wiped more sweat from her forehead. Why did he have to keep poking his nose around? Did he suspect her or was she just being paranoid? She felt sweat trickling down her neck, now. She wanted to leave, but knew how it would look. Instead, she forced her body to remain still.

Ana's mind wandered back to the weather. If the weather could have cooperated for another month, she could have risked moving the body, disposing of it properly. Maybe she had been sloppy when she killed Cory. She should have planned it better. However, despite any mistakes she may have made, she had been right to confront Cory. Cory didn't need to admit she knew her secret. Her lack of response betrayed her.

The day the confrontation happened, Ana had overheard Cory telling Drew she was leaving for Chicago in the evening. Ana knew she had to act fast. Immediately following her shift, she drove to Cory's house. She was frustrated by the time she found it, taking numerous wrong turns along the way. Ana had never understood why Cory lived there. Sure the rent was cheap, but it was so far off the beaten track and, worse yet, no bigger than a shoe box. Ana recalled the supervisors get together at Cory's place the previous autumn. There hadn't even been room enough to turn around in the galley kitchen and Cory's bedroom fit no more than a bed and small night stand. The only area which afforded some space was the living and dining area, but it was cramped with furniture including a large, gaudy dining room table. It felt claustrophobic. She didn't know how Cory could tolerate living there - much less with a roommate.

The second time she drove by the house it was dark. There was only one visible light shedding a dull, yellow glow from the bedroom. Ana pulled off the road, at the end of the long driveway, cut the engine and waited. She pulled a cigarette out from her jacket pocket, lit it and in its soft orange glow slowly inhaled. She smoked one cigarette after another to pass the time, her patience wearing thin. It had started snowing, first just a light dusting. But now, the snow was falling heavily, coating her windshield.

An hour later, the house went dark. Cory emerged seconds later, carrying a red canvas bag. Ana took one last puff of her cigarette before she extinguished it in the ashtray. She zipped up her jacket, opened the car door and slipped out into the wet snow. As she approached Cory in the driveway, she paused and momentarily second guessed herself. That is, until Cory turned and Ana saw her body stiffen. It was then she knew Cory would never appreciate the circumstances.

Ana gave Cory an excuse for coming to see her. As they parted ways, Ana returned to her car and grabbed the crowbar which lay on the passenger's seat. She moved quickly and quietly behind her prey who was placing her bag in the trunk. This time, Ana didn't second guess herself. With a steel grip, she brought the weight of the crowbar down on Cory's skull.

Cory's body lay in a heap on the snow. She had likely died instantly and hadn't suspected a thing. Looking at the body, Ana had felt the panic start to well up inside her. The panic didn't evolve from any feelings of remorse she had toward Cory. All she felt towards Cory was hatred. However, the panic rose from how to dispose of the current mess. She had worked too hard and come too far to let anything stand in the way of her happiness.

She wrapped Cory's body in a tarp and carried the still warm corpse to her car, depositing it in the trunk. Cory's skull had caved in, creating a disgusting mess. Ana had wrapped several plastic bags around the body to keep the blood, fluids and grey matter from leaking all over her. She grabbed Cory's canvas bag and threw it on the passenger seat. Then, she returned to the driveway and used her feet to shuffle the snow. She examined the area where the body had fallen and was surprised to see how undisturbed it looked.

Ana then climbed into her car, turned on the ignition and pulled onto the road. As she looked out her rearview mirror, she half expected to see some sign of life. She drove around the back roads and looped past Cory's house one final time on the way to the interstate. The snow continued to fall. Cory's driveway now appeared completely undisturbed, a betrayal to the violence that had occurred. As she turned from the main road toward the interstate, she was relieved she had not seen a soul.

Despite her initial stroke of good fortune, she hadn't planned this as precisely as she would have liked, not like with Marty. That had been a flawless execution. However, she needed to do damage control. First thing she needed to do was to get rid of the body. If nothing else, she just needed to keep driving. She'd find a place to dump it eventually, the further away the better.

She drove for what seemed an eternity, slowing her speed to a crawl because of the deteriorating weather. The roads had become treacherous and the freezing rain was turning the I-69 corridor into a skating rink. She had already seen several cars lose control to join those already lining the ditches on either side of the interstate. Others, the cautious ones parked on the shoulder. Occasionally, she'd pull up behind a set of red tail lights inching along at ten miles an hour. She'd pass carefully so as not to send her car into a tailspin. That was the last thing she needed. So, she kept her eyes focused on the road as the wipers cleared the slop from her windshield.

Ana looked at the clock and knew she was running out of time. She had to get back to work for the a.m. shift. She couldn't be late. That would only draw suspicion to herself. She finally eased the car off the highway and drove down the circuitous back roads to a thickly wooded area. There were dense evergreens, primarily balsam and spruce, where the road had narrowed to almost nothing. She pulled on her gloves and went to work. The ground was hard, frozen solid, so burying the body was out of the question. But she couldn't just leave it lying on the snow. She walked through the dense brush feeling the small branches snap beneath her feet. An outcropping of rock, masked by bushes, presented itself a half an hour later. She used her hands and feet to clear the snow and felt a space underneath the rock large enough to accommodate most of the body.

She returned to the car and climbed in, her body numb. She turned the heat on full blast and rubbed her stiff, frozen hands to revive them. Several minutes later, she retrieved Cory's body from the trunk. It was a struggle to maneuver the weight onto her shoulders. Every step was a grueling test of her strength. Her pace to return to the rock outcropping seemed interminable. She had made little progress before her knees buckled, her arms went slack and she lost the battle to hang onto the body. Cory's corpse lay still on the wet snow and she fought the urge to leave it. Perhaps no one would find her. There would be no reason to look for Cory in this part of the state. If anything, the search would be expanded towards Chicago. Or if Cory's exposed body was found, maybe it wouldn't be until the spring thaw after being ravaged by the elements and scavengers.

However, Ana knew despite her body's will to rest, it would be best if the remains were never found. She had to force herself to keep going. She picked herself up, brushed the snow from her now wet clothing and grabbed Cory's boots. She used her body weight to drag Cory's frozen corpse through the woods arriving at the rocky outcropping an hour later. Ana stripped Cory's body of all clothing and buried it in the snow. Satisfied, Ana rolled Cory's clothes into a ball and made the return trip through the woods to her car.

Ana stumbled into her apartment at five a.m. running on nothing but fumes fueled by the last flames of adrenalin. She was exhausted and knew the events of the night had taken a toll on her body. Her muscles were tight, her joints ached and her head was throbbing. She wanted nothing more than to collapse into bed, but she had come this far and knew she needed to finish the job. So, she pushed herself to finish, gathering up the blood stained trash bags and tarp that lined her trunk along with Cory's personal belongings.

She placed the trash bags in the grate of her fireplace along with kindling and newspaper. When the match ignited the paper, it immediately generated a foul smell and thick orange flames which soon began to lick the plastic, curling it into tiny, then nonexistent remains. Ana then burned the tarp, Cory's clothes and systematically burned the contents of Cory's overnight bag, piece by piece, books, wallet, clothes and make up. Some items proved resistant, but with patience and some extra effort, the fire destroyed almost everything.

As she reached the bottom of the canvas bag, she touched something hard. It was a thick, black bound notebook. It was about to meet its fiery fate, when she hesitated. Her curiosity piqued, she opened it and flipped through the pages. It was a journal, but not in the traditional sense. Instead of discussing her life and feelings, Cory had maintained a journal of what went on at Ellis House. The entries started about a year ago, initially more as queries to herself. Things she needed to monitor with staff or actions others had taken on the units she had issue with. A way to vent her frustration or problem solve without experiencing any repercussions. However, as time went on the tone of the entries changed. Instead, of an internal dialogue, they became a detailed record of who the employee was, what position he or she held and of most interest, the practices in which he or she engaged.

Most of the earlier entries centered around Barbara. There were multiple references to how she threatened and belittled the clients to coerce compliance and minimize complaints to outside governing bodies. It also included how Barbara all too frequently shaved funds from the budget to line her own pockets and to reward loyalty to her few faithful comrades.

And then she found it, pages and pages about her. She was appalled. Cory had always acted like she respected her, but her entries indicated otherwise. Cory hadn't even believed she was competent. The last several entries were about the night Cory had walked in on her. Cory had struggled with how to act on her new found information. However, one thing was clear. Cory was not going to ignore it. Cory would have destroyed her. Ana was now convinced, beyond a doubt, she had made the right decision. Cory had deserved to die.

Chapter 28

It came in a plain brown envelope three weeks to the day I had initiated my contact with Kate. I stared at it resting on the kitchen counter while I ate and thought about how the contents of the envelope might irreversibly change the course of my life. I had thought about my marriage frequently since hiring the private investigator. Despite all our stressors, I didn't want it to end, but I knew it would if infidelity was once again an issue. After all, how could you live with someone you didn't trust?

After all was said and done, I had dropped three thousand dollars to gain data, all my savings from before I had married. I now hoped this exercise would at least provide me with some answers. The report was written on salmon colored paper and read as follows:

Kate Nguyen
Aloha Investigations
12611 Casa Avenida

Poway, CA 92064

Dear Grace,

Enclosed is the videotape evidence, along with a case report, surveillance report and an invoice showing the balance due. I'm sorry that things ended up the way they did, but at least now you know your instincts were correct. Now, you can focus on moving on and making a new life for yourself. Remember to hold your head high and don't blame yourself.

I wish you luck, and hope in the future you will meet someone who will appreciate you. If I can ever be of service again, please call.

Sincerely,
Kate Nguyen

My heart sank and I read the report that followed:

Aloha Investigations
Case Report
Infidelity

Case Number: 06-00135
Client: Grace Elaine Morgan (07-10-71)
193 Jeffrey Avenue
Battle Creek, MI 33068

Subject: Elliot Jackson Morgan (04-21-73)
Address: 15125 Rosonda Court Apt A/12
San Diego, CA 92110

Subject: Leah Braden (06-05-65)
195 Sunburst Avenue
San Diego, CA 92110

Evidence: Item #1 and Item # 2, a Sony, standard grade, high durability, 8 hour VHS format video tape.

Narrative: On February 24th, 2005, Dr. Grace Morgan contacted me to report that her husband Mr. Elliot Morgan, may be involved in an extramarital affair. Dr. Morgan told me she suspected Ms. Leah Braden, who works with Mr. Morgan as a fellow intern at the medical center in San Diego, California.

Dr. Morgan told me her husband has access to a red Jeep Cherokee. She also said that Ms. Braden has access to a small white Toyota. She didn't know the license plate number of Ms. Braden's vehicle, but provided me with the plate on her husband's Jeep (LSV 303). Dr. Morgan said her husband arrives home from work around 5:30 p.m. and she wanted me to conduct surveillance March 10th through March 18th from the time he arrived home until there was no contact between her husband and anyone else that evening.

At 4:40 p.m., on March 10th, I arrived in University City and drove to Elliot Morgan's condominium at 12515 Rosonda Court. The carport was empty. At 5:00 p.m., I set up surveillance on Mr. Morgan's residence. At 5:21 p.m., a red Jeep bearing Michigan license plate LSV 303 turned into the carport from the street and parked. A man wearing a long sleeved, royal blue shirt and khaki pants exited the car. He was approximately 6 feet tall with brown hair and a goatee. I was unable to see his eye color because he was wearing sunglasses.

He walked over to the passenger side of the car, opened the door and extended his hand to help a woman exit. She was approximately 5'6", wearing blue pants and a purple and white floral shirt. She had long, thin, brown hair and her eyes were masked with oversized sun glasses. The man and woman matched the physical descriptions provided by Dr. Morgan and the photograph I had received via email.

The male subject retrieved two briefcases from the rear of the jeep. He slung the straps over his shoulder and held the woman's hand while ascending the steps to the condominium. I maintained surveillance on the condominium until 3:00 a.m., but there was no movement outside or around the condominium. Lights were on in the dwelling until 1:00 a.m.

At 5:00 p.m., on March 11th, I set up surveillance outside Elliot Morgan's condominium. At 5:10 p.m., the same red Jeep turned into the carport and parked. It was carrying the same two passengers as the day before. They quickly retreated to the condominium to exit at 5:20 p.m. wearing athletic clothes. They walked through the complex parking lot, crossed Randolph Street and initiated a thirty minute jog through Rose Canyon returning to the complex and ascending the stairs to the unit. At the top of the stairs, the female subject put her hands around the male subject's neck and kissed him, first on the cheek and then on the mouth. They remained embraced for several minutes prior to entering the complex at 6:30 p.m.

I continued surveillance with no apparent movement until 8:30 p.m. when the subjects in question exited wearing evening attire. The male subject was dressed in a white shirt and blue tie with black pants and shoes and she in a purple loose fitting dress and brown sling back shoes.

I followed the Jeep through Rose Canyon Boulevard to Lincoln Street where they parked and made a short walk over to Ruth Chris Steak House. They remained there for two hours. They exited the restaurant at 11:00 p.m. and returned to the vehicle. He had his arm wrapped around her waist until she entered the Jeep.

They returned to the condominium at 11:21 p.m. and entered. I continued surveillance until 8:00 a.m. when they both exited wearing what appeared to be casual work clothes. I followed them to the medical center where they parked and entered the building.

I continued to read through the remainder of the report. The rest of the week was consistent with the first two days. There was no way to dispute Elliot's involvement with Leah was beyond that of a friendship. That night I drove back to Ellis House, chugged three cups of coffee and caught up on my paperwork. I didn't have much choice. I had booked a flight to San Diego for the coming weekend and needed to have all my loose ends tied up at work.

Chapter 29

Today, treatment team was no more than an exercise in distraction. However, as soon as it concluded and I pushed back my chair to leave the conference room, my mind was back to my train wreck of a marriage. So, as I climbed the stairs to the unit, I distracted myself again and replayed treatment team in my head. Ray, Nate and Jacob were gone with Ray being the most recent discharge. Jacob continued to reside at Juvenile Hall and Nate had started to adjust to his new surroundings in Indiana. They both had expressed no regrets leaving Ellis House.

However, Ray was a different story. His resistance to leaving the group home had been surprising. Despite almost being eighteen, he had been fortunate enough to have been accepted for placement at a transitional living program. I thought he would have been thrilled with the opportunity to share an apartment with a roommate who was already established in the work force. However, instead of being pleased with the offer to live independently and earn a wage, he had balked at it, only agreeing to go after intense pressure from his county worker. Ray's county worker had arrived early yesterday morning to transport him to his new home.

I walked down the unit hall to Emily's room. I knocked and entered. The posters were all down, exposing an irregular pattern of nail holes. The bed was made and most of Emily's personal items were already neatly stacked in cardboard boxes and clear plastic storage bins with the plastic lids clipped on tight. Jacques had come through, finding a placement at a long term group home for girls who had been victims of trauma. However, this wasn't what made it stand out, what did was its location, a farm where some of her daily responsibilities would include taking care of the animals. Unfortunately, Emily's mother, Maggie, had not improved and her prognosis remained poor. She had returned to inpatient treatment, unable to stabilize in a less intensive environment. Emily had been able to recognize that the chance of living with her mother in the future was nonexistent, through no fault of her own. She had been able to let go of much of her anger toward her parents. She still had struggles and would always grieve the loss of her family, but she finally had something she hadn't had in a long time - a future studded with hope.

I finished helping Emily place the remainder of her belongings into the boxes. We then made several trips back and forth until her side of the room was empty. Emily didn't bother to look back as she left the room for the last time, now, a blank slate for the next admission. She was ready to go. I hugged her goodbye and waited by Susan's desk until she pulled out of the parking lot with her county worker.

"You must be sad to see her go." Susan commented.

"I am. I mean I'm glad she's going, but I'll miss her." I replied. Susan nodded in agreement.

"Nice to see something go right for a change. It's been tough around here lately." I said.

"From what I've been hearing, it's going to get even tougher." Susan stated.

"Meaning?"

"Emily's replacement."

"The new admit?"

"One of your former clients."

"Who?"

"Lisa..."

"Lisa Hennicke! Barbara knows about this?"

Susan shrugged her shoulders.

Lisa Hennicke had been the first client admitted under my watch when I started at Ellis House, arriving only several days after I did. She had been an attractive girl with thick black hair and hollow icy blue eyes that said she didn't care. She was angry at the world, had a right to be, but her anger didn't discriminate. She took it out on anyone who crossed her path. She had grown up in an abusive home, suffered extensive physical abuse at the hands of her mother and had been forced into sexual activity by her father when she was eight. Then fate had delivered her another blow, an unwanted pregnancy just after her thirteenth birthday. She had been removed and placed in her maternal aunt's home only to relive her past with her aunt's live in boyfriend. The boyfriend reported Lisa came on to him, adamant that he was not the aggressor. Her aunt picked sides and Lisa was again shuffled to a new set of temporary quarters.

I knocked on Sam's door and let myself in. Sam sat at his desk with a bag of chips in one hand, the other maneuvering the mouse, eyes glued to the computer monitor. He was playing solitaire. Good to know some things remained stable.

"Sam, I know I'm interrupting, but just wanted to let you know our milieu is completely unstable and no thanks to you even more so. I just heard you admitted Lisa Hennicke. You know her rep. Everybody knows her rep. How are we supposed to manage her?" I argued. He stared at me, seemingly apathetic. I kept going.

"I knew her reputation even before I started working here. She's histrionic, aggressive as hell and just tried to start a riot at county overflow."

"I know. I know. It's a tough case. But I did get all her

paperwork. It just came in over the fax." He answered pushing a stack of papers in my direction.

"Thanks." I responded flatly.

"I know you're invested in this program. It's what we need around here. However, you're always asking me about whether I see what's going on. The answer is yes. How could I not? It's been staring me in the face a lot longer than you. I was as motivated as you, if not more, when I got here, but quite honestly I don't give a shit anymore. I'm burnt out." Sam confessed.

Sam's line was beeping. He picked it up and quickly put his call on hold. He turned to me, still holding the receiver and said, "Hey, I've got a call from a prospective employer, better pay, better benefits, regular work hours and I'm sure a lot less shit to deal with on a day to day basis. So, if you'll please excuse me." I took the paperwork and left his office.

Lisa didn't even last an hour on the unit before she lost control. I could hear the screaming as I entered the unit and made my way to the dining hall. Lisa was being restrained against the wall by four staff members, but just barely. She was heavy set and tall to begin with, but had ballooned, now bordering on obesity. Staff were making every attempt to contain her, but it was difficult given she now had a target for her rage.

"Just calm down and we'll walk you to the quiet room." I heard someone say.

"Fuck you cocksucker." Lisa screamed. "Let me go or you'll be sorry."

"What's going on?" I asked a staff member who was clearing the dining hall of the remaining clients."

"Flipped out when she found out they were serving enchiladas. She said they smelled like dog shit and asked the cook to fix her something else. He refused. She went ballistic, smashed him in the head with her tray. Then she started smashing stuff until we could restrain her." I looked over toward the serving counter where chunks of broken glass were mixed with pickles, ketchup and salsa.

"Yeah, I made a goddamn mess, shrink! So, why don't you get down on your hands and knees and suck it up." Lisa spat through clenched teeth.

Well if nothing else, at least she remembered me. I walked over in her direction. Her long, black hair was pulled back in a loose ponytail exposing multiple silver hoops which hung from her left ear. She was wearing a worn, burgundy track suit which was awkwardly stretched over her large body, exposing the loose flesh around her abdomen. Her nails had recently been manicured, each studded with a diamond rhinestone which matched those on her white sneakers.

"Are you coming over here to feed me some bullshit?" Lisa taunted, the veins in her neck bulging as she strained to look in my direction.

"I'm here to discuss your options." I replied. "Because as I see it, you can't be too happy with your current situation."

"No, I'm not happy. Girl's gotta eat and I didn't get no dinner. Then these pigs shove me against the wall when I didn't do nothing."

"You were offered dinner. You refused. You then became destructive and left staff with no choice but to follow the restraint protocol."

"Yeah, well how about I follow protocol and call my attorney and file a fucking complaint about my personal rights being violated! I'll tell him how abusive the staff is and he'll get this place shut down."

"Your choice."

"OK. Let me go then."

"As I said, look at your options, you can continue to be unsafe and restrained against the wall or you can agree to walk to the quiet room escorted by staff and remain there until you are calm. Once you are calm, you can ask staff to use the phone and go ahead and call your attorney."

"I'll go, but I don't want them to be touching me anymore."

"Fine." I replied. Staff agreed and released Lisa reluctantly. She tossed her hair, gave everyone a dirty look, but held her tongue as she walked down the hall and entered the quiet room. When she was settled, I left the unit and returned to my office thinking about how things had gone with Lisa last time. She was sharp and had full control over her behavior. When she escalated and became destructive and aggressive, it was deliberate. She could turn it on or off depending on what she believed best suited her agenda. She was clearly a manipulator and I believed we were in for a rough ride.

Fifteen minutes later, I was paged to return to the unit. Lisa had quickly earned the privilege to use the phone, but became enraged when she was unable to speak directly with her attorney. She pushed the phone off the desk and only made it several paces further before she kicked over a cleaning cart, took an open can of Lysol and sprayed it in the face of the cleaning lady. She then grabbed a stray bottle of glass cleaner and ran toward the end of the hall tossing it at the exit sign and smashing it to bits, sprinkling plastic all over the floor. Still holding the can of Lysol, she refused to relinquish it, spraying it at everyone who tried to approach her. Finally, she was tackled and escorted back to the quiet room. Staff had shut the door to help drown out the constant high pitched stream of curse words with threats of personal rights violations echoing behind them.

As I entered the unit, Lisa had been in the quiet room for several minutes. She continued to be unresponsive to any clinical or residential staff and there had been no weakening in her ability to disrupt the unit. Her county worker had been contacted several times and after discussion with Barbara it was agreed we would terminate care and return her to county overflow. We were clearly not equipped to handle her. She didn't want to be at Ellis House; and our policy dictated that if a client posed a risk to other clients or staff it was an option we could exercise.

I could still hear her screaming as I came to tell her about her impending move to county, but the body slams against the door had stopped. I stuck my head in attempting to maintain my distance.

"Nice shirt." She laughed as she looked at me. I didn't

respond.

"I wanted to let you know your worker is coming over to take you to county holding. So, once you're able to maintain control staff will take you to get your belongings and take you to the lobby." I stated bluntly.

"Figures." She responded and a thin smile formed, curling her lips to expose pearly, white teeth.

I started to close the door. "Yo!" I heard Lisa say. I stuck my head back in. "I just wanted to let you know my opinion . . ." She let the words hang in the air. "I'm glad that bossy, black bitch who used to work here is dead. I told her she was going to get what she deserved if she wasn't nice to me."

I held my temper in check. "You know something? If you do, you need to speak to the police."

"Nah, all I'm saying is that maybe I would have done something like that if someone else hadn't beat me to it. So, now maybe you need to watch your back." She looked at me and smiled again. I turned and left the room hoping I'd never have to lay eyes on her again.

Forty-five minutes later I received a call from Houseman. "What the hell are you thinking sending Lisa back to county? You have no right to make that kind of decision without the proper authorization."

"Do you have any idea how out of control she is?" I said defending my decision. "We had no choice."

"You always have a choice. You just made the wrong one." Houseman barked.

"She's putting herself and others at risk. We can't maintain her."

"I don't care. Find a way."

"OK." I said between clenched teeth.

"And by the way, why did you decline Barbara's earlier offer to help manage her?" Houseman queried.

"Barbara is in agreement with me. She asked me to help move her."

"Bullshit! Stop trying to cover your ass. This was your

decision and yours alone. I just talked to Barbara and she had no idea what you were up to. So, a word of advice, next time consult with someone before you pull a stupid stunt. And for now, fix this mess. I refuse to have county threaten to stop sending us referrals because you think we can't manage one kid. Fuck this up and you can start looking for alternative employment."

He hung up without saying another word. I remained in my chair staring at the ceiling. There was no point confronting Barbara about what had happened. I knew the drill. Instead, I would probably be most wise to follow Houseman's advice to start looking for another job. I knew Barbara would be ecstatic if I quit and I thought maybe granting her wish wouldn't be such a bad thing. I was getting tired of the fight.

As I picked up the phone, I heard familiar clicking. My mind immediately jumped to Cory and the night she showed up on my doorstep and warned me about Barbara. I had forgotten about it, pushed it to the back of my mind. It seemed so irrelevant in the light of everything else that had been going on. But with all the bizarre recent events and the ever growing number of people who seemed to be gaining an increased dislike for me, I decided to give in to my paranoia. I started searching my office for anything metal or plastic that didn't seem to belong there. If Corrine had been right, and the phone conversations were being monitored, there was a pretty good chance that it hadn't stopped there. I played detective until I finally found something round and metallic under my desk. I crushed it with the heel of my shoe and tossed it in the garbage on my way out the door.

I could barely stay awake on the way home, my eyelids heavy, my body exhausted. It had been an extremely tough day. When I got home, I walked straight into my bedroom, stripped off my clothes, climbed under the sheets and fell into a deep sleep.

He strips off his pants and pulls on an old, ratty pair of jeans. He continues to engage in the task of dressing. No emotion registers on his face. His eyes are expressionless, his face a stone mask. I sit watching not knowing what to say, wanting to speak but incapable of putting what I am feeling into words. This man in front of me is my husband. But all I see now is a monster.

"*Guess I fooled you pretty well. Should've seen the expression on your face.*" *He says this smugly as he slips on his old tennis shoes and leans over to tie them. He sits across from me and continues with his monologue.* "*Cat got your tongue tonight, huh? That's rare. Well let me try to explain things. Obviously, you have been too naive to catch on. I've had all this planned for a while. Oddly enough, I was even worried for a while you might figure it out. Lucky for me you're so stupid.*"

I start to detect emotion in his voice now and begin to see it paint his face. "*You're nothing more than a ball and chain to me and I mean that in the most classic sense of the expression. How could you not know? How could you not know that I've been trying to get rid of you for years. My life with you has been excruciating . . . However, I have tried, tried to ease you out slowly . . . tired to convince you to leave, get a divorce. Hell, how many times have I cheated on you? Three, four and you're always so forgiving. I forget important dates and you're so accepting of being treated like shit. Are you a moron? Sometimes I think you must be . . . coming back for more and more when I keep pushing you away, insulting you and giving you the same message loud and clear.*" *He starts ranting and I block out the words fixated on the flapping of his lips and the hatred in his eyes.*

He takes a breath and aggressively puts his face in mine so he knows I hear him. "*Really, I'm asking . . . how stupid are you? I mean what else could I have done to show you that you weren't wanted? Don't you have any pride? Are you such a sniveling co-dependent loser as to need someone to be with that badly? Pathetic you know. You are really pathetic. So pathetic you have left me no choice.*" *He grabs me by the arm and tells me to get moving. He pushes me in the direction of the bathroom. I enter and see the tub. It is lined with plastic. He binds my arms and hands but doesn't bother to gag me. It doesn't matter how loud I scream. No one can help me. Now I know, I'm going to die.*

Chapter 30

I was sitting in the living room when I heard the keys rattle and saw Elliot step into the foyer. His expression clearly betrayed his surprise.

"Grace." He said astonished. "What are you doing here?

"I really needed to talk to you." I said.

"We do live in a society with phones and email you know?" He said jokingly, attempting to act casual.

"This wasn't something I could speak with you about over the phone." I replied dryly.

"OK, let me get changed. I'll be right back." He retreated to the bedroom and I heard the water running. I waited for several minutes and he still hadn't returned. Tired of waiting, I entered the bedroom, knocked and entered the bathroom. Elliot was on his cell and I didn't bother to ask to whom he was speaking.

"Elliot get off the goddamn phone and cut the cord to your selfish, needy whore for five minutes or are you too co-dependent to manage that?" I barked.

He turned and looked at me with a cold stare and stated flatly.

"Can't you give me any damn privacy? This is my house. I was just getting off the phone. It was a work related call anyway."

"Like hell. I know everything. Just grow a damn spine and admit it."

"If you flew out here just to piss me off you can catch the next flight out and leave me the hell alone." Elliot retaliated.

"I'm so sick of you turning this around on me." I yelled. "You're the one who's in the wrong. I'm not paranoid. You're cheating."

"Bullshit."

"I've got proof."

"Oh yeah, what? Stupid text messages? The fact that I'm on the phone a lot? What?"

"Where were you Thursday night?"

"Here."

"By yourself?"

"Yeah."

"Liar."

"I was here by myself!"

"You were not."

"Yes, I was."

"I have proof. So you may want to change your story."

"So what, you've got people spying on me now?"

"I know for a fact that you were with Leah Thursday."

"OK, she came over and -"

"And you lied to me again."

"Do you blame me? You're all over me like a fly on shit." Elliot said defensively.

"So, lying is better?" I argued.

"At least I don't need to deal with this shit all the time."

"So, tell me the truth."

"About what?"

"About having Leah over Thursday. The day you said she wasn't over."

"At least now it's confirmed." He grunted.

"What's confirmed?"

"That you've got people spying on me."

"You're an idiot."

"I knew you had people spying on me. I just couldn't prove it."

"Yeah, I hired a PI and she found *lots*."

"Like?" He challenged.

"Like you guys are always together. Like you guys carpool and jog. That the bitch stays over at all hours of the night. You eat together. That you hug and kiss her."

"OK. OK. OK." He sighed. "Fine." He ran his fingers through his hair and began to pace around the room. "I shouldn't be telling you this and I promised her that I wouldn't tell anyone, but like I said she and Bill are having problems, really bad ones. Much worse than what I told you in Michigan. She really needs help and I've been doing that. She says he's disconnected, doesn't care about her. She's filing for divorce. He's even hit her"

"Sorry, smells like shit. So, convenient she needs your help. Like I said before she's got a support system. That bitch just wants to break up your marriage and from the looks of it she's doing a bang up job."

"Don't call her that."

"I'll call her whatever I want. That woman has you snowed. She's so controlling and you are so protective of her. You should be protective of me, your wife, yet you continue to disrespect me with that relationship."

"You're crazy. This isn't about her. It's about us. I've been unhappy for a long time."

"Thanks for letting me know. It would have been nice if you would have let me in on your secret a little bit sooner. I'm sure you've been telling her the whole sob story."

"I have. You'd think you would have paid enough attention to pick up on that."

"God, you're so self-centered. You told me the only issue we had was kids and I compromised on that, again. Besides you're getting off topic. Tell me to my face you're screwing her. After all, at least I deserve some honesty."

He looked at me and said nothing, but his expression said everything. Finally, he provided me with an admission. "It only happened once . . . when we were in San Francisco. We had been drinking . . . didn't get back to the hotel until four in the morning. It was awful, just sex and not good sex at that. It wrecked everything. I mean we were friends and ever since then I've been trying to do damage control."

"Shut up Elliot. I guess I don't really want to hear it. And for the record, it doesn't seem like you are doing any damage control. You're with her all the time and if you're not physically with her, you're on the phone with her. And to top it all off it sounds like you want me to feel sorry for you like you're in a bad spot."

"Well, if you hadn't been so preoccupied with work - I've felt so ignored and she's been after me for a long time. I was drunk."

"So now it's my fault?"

"Our sex life has sucked for a long time, even before I left for San Diego and..."

I cut him off. "You're justifying your behavior. I work all the time. I support this family right now. I pay for this condo, the Jeep and your cell phone. I work so I can send you an allowance every month. You cheated on me once already and act like somehow I'm supposed to work that much harder to set things straight. But what about you? Shouldn't you be making some kind of effort? You think having sex with someone who's cheated is somehow desirable? It's a turn off."

"We did have our problems Grace."

"You're pathetic. Everyone has problems, but there is no excuse to cheat, you piece of shit. You think just because you're not getting attention constantly and your ego isn't being stroked every minute of every day that gives you the right to fuck the first sleaze who spreads her legs."

"Shit, it's more than you do."

"Fuck you. You're a pig."

"Well, you're a goddamn frigid bitch."

"I'm done. Get out. I'll be gone in the morning."

Five minutes later Elliot walked out the door with his overnight bag in tow.

Elliot had sounded awful on the phone, crying, confused, asking for advice about what to do. Grace had finally confirmed her suspicions by hiring a private investigator and had ambushed him by flying out to San Diego, confronting him about their relationship and letting him know she was filing for divorce. His marriage was over. What was he going to do?

Leah had taken charge. She told Elliot to meet her at the Super 8 off Poway Road. She would book the room. Elliot arrived twenty minutes later looking like a tired, lost puppy. He seemed like he wasn't quite sure what to do. He knew he didn't want to stay in the condo, but shouldn't he fight for his marriage? He was confused.

Leah had told him to get comfortable. She handed him a shot of Jack Daniels. He sucked it down, and she refilled his glass several more times before it took the edge off. She kissed him and whispered she understood. She unbuttoned his shirt, unbuckled his belt and stripped off his pants. He responded and she slipped off her clothes and took him to bed.

Elliot had talked and she had listened, making only those comments which would hopefully help sever the last few remaining ties to his wife. She had to be careful to watch what she said, keep her true feelings in check. She really wanted to express how she felt about Grace, how she despised her and how he was so much better off without her. She wanted to know what had possessed him to already waste so much of his life with her, a woman so focused on responsibility that fun wasn't even a word in her vocabulary. She wanted to tell him she believed Grace was a fool for letting him move to San Diego. After all, what did she expect to happen? He needed to start seeing Grace like she did, a nuisance, even less, an afterthought. However, as she lay beside him and watched his chest rhythmically move up and down, she thought about how negative comments about a man's wife had backfired last time.

The last time had she had been in a similar position was during graduate school. She had been living in Del Mar, a pricey beach community just north of San Diego. This was courtesy of her roommate Jill who had invited her along with two other young women to share her family's beach house for practically nothing. This was a definite step up from student housing. The snarled traffic faced during the morning and evening commutes was a small price to pay for waking up to the sound of the surf and the smell of salty air.

She had been there for six months before becoming involved with Jill's father, an MBA with a knack for good investing. He regularly stopped by to visit his daughter and had become friendly with all the women in the house. They had become social and found they had lots to discuss including their shared passion for the arts, theater and dance in particular.

Leah had invited her roommates and Jill's father, Marcus, who happened to be by that day to her modern dance recital. Everyone had politely declined with the exception of Marcus who appeared intrigued. She knew he was attracted to her, but was unlikely to make a move given his marriage. She had little restraint that evening as he walked her to her car and quickly made her feelings known. They spent that night at a beach side hotel; he left before midnight to return home to his wife.

Leah had made Marcus feel important, attractive, like there was no one else. It was no wonder their relationship intensified. She had made him feel sexy and wanted. She loved how much he needed her. Their relationship was an escape with no responsibilities. Nothing mattered except being together and they focused on nothing but weekend getaways, secret rendezvous and meeting their selfish needs. However, this type of relationship could only survive so long in a vacuum before extinguishing itself or moving beyond fantasy with boundaries set by responsibility. She had finally expressed her wishes, stating that she wanted more. She wanted him completely. She wanted him to come home to her every night.

Marcus had told her he really didn't know what he wanted. He hadn't really been thinking long term. He told her to be patient. However, it wasn't what he said that worried her, but what he didn't say. She wanted to give him the benefit of the doubt. She tried to be patient. Time passed and nothing changed. He refused to commit.

She convinced herself the relationship was unraveling. Marcus was going to leave her. It was only a matter of time. All her relationships seemed to end that way, men making excuses for why they couldn't commit. It didn't seem to matter if they were single or married, educated or not. It was an expected outcome when she dated college guys, but Marcus was a catch. A man who could commit, had committed. A man with money and status. A different breed from that of her usual bedfellow. She had higher expectations of him and it looked as if he was going to let her down.

Leah prepared herself for Marcus' inevitable abandonment self-medicating with prescription drugs and alcohol. An acquaintance had doled out prescription tranquilizers on an as needed basis for a hefty price, but it was worth it. It calmed her, functioning as a temporary bandage to keep her from crawling out of her skin. Despite this, she still had difficulty sleeping, often waking up drenched in a cold sweat, but it was better than not sleeping at all. She was distracted at school, not able to focus on anything other than Marcus. Her grades reflected this and she started failing her classes.

Leah was at her breaking point and finally pushed Marcus, telling him she didn't understand why he stayed with his wife. Why didn't he just leave her? Why would he stay with a woman who was so boring and repressed? Why would he stay in a passionless marriage? After all, his daughter was grown up. He didn't need to feel guilty about breaking up a family.

She saw the expression on Marcus' face as she vented and knew it was over. If she had been more subtle, not berated his wife then maybe, just maybe, he would have surrendered himself to her. She had made a mistake, coming out fighting instead of painting herself more like the victim she was, a woman who needed him. Instead, his reaction to her criticism had been to come to the support of his wife. How dare she speak of his wife in such a way? His wife had never hurt her. Why was she being so cruel and vindictive?

Leah understood vindictiveness and retaliated by telling Jill the next day about the affair with her father. Jill cried, yelled and let her know what a whore she thought she was. It was the reaction Leah expected. She didn't care about her relationship with Jill. It was of no value. She only cared for Marcus. She prayed to God Marcus would come back to her after his wife left. They could move past this. They needed to. After all, she had already started planning a life with him.

Leah's prayers were not answered. Marcus' wife did leave him. However, Marcus had become distraught, so distraught he overdosed. The paramedics couldn't revive him and he died on the way to the hospital. Shock had been her initial reaction, but rage soon washed over her. All she could think about was how angry she was. Angry because in the end, he had victimized her, used her and then left her all alone.

Leah looked over at Elliot and watched him sleep. Elliot reminded her of Marcus in many ways. The Marcus she remembered when they first started seeing each other. Elliot was, as Marcus had been, her equal. Someone who could take care of her and give her what she needed. She knew that right now, he was hers because he had no other place to turn. Eventually, he would be strong again, more decisive and this is what worried her. This was a man who was able to commit, had lots of potential, and was the star of the internship program. She couldn't lose him.

Elliot was vulnerable right now and easily influenced. He trusted her and was relying on her to make the right decisions. She knew she could convince him that his decision to leave Grace was best. They wanted different things out of life. He was actually being selfish staying with her if she wanted children and he didn't. They would both just be miserable in the end. Besides, she was still young enough to meet someone else and have children. Why take that away from her?

Leah knew she had to be smart about this and do whatever she needed to make the relationship work. She knew getting angry at him was a sure way to lose him. If she became angry, she would have to funnel it in different ways, feign sadness. Elliot couldn't stand to see a woman cry. She had managed things poorly with Marcus. She needed to be smart this time. Find a way to keep him at all costs, even if it meant going back to the hospital. She knew in that situation, Elliot would never abandon her.

Chapter 31

I sat at the café table and surveyed the grounds of the complex for one last time. This is the last time I'll be sitting here I thought. This is the last time Elliot and I will be a married couple. What a waste. What a shame we didn't make it. I felt the tears start to well up and I started to weep. I wept for myself and for the memories of happier times. I cried out of frustration because I didn't really understand. I didn't understand why my husband was not willing to make the effort. Why he quit. Why he didn't care. He had tossed me out like trash and I started to think what was wrong with me until I stopped myself. I wasn't going down that road again. Despite the circumstances, I was content with the person I was and how I conducted myself in my marriage. I also knew I was strong enough to stand by myself and take the next step.

My future was unpredictable. I knew I was taking a different path from the one I had initially carved for myself. And even though so many things in my future were unpredictable, I knew that I would take time for myself and grieve the loss of my marriage. Really be ready before I became involved in a relationship again. It infuriated me that Elliot was moving so fast. Leah's toothbrush, some t-shirts, essentials for spending the night all scattered around his bedroom. He had given me so little respect and also so little respect for the life we had shared. I pushed those thoughts away, composed myself and shifted back to tying up loose ends.

I reread the letter I had written Elliot, satisfied that it conveyed my thoughts
.

Dear Elliot,

You've put me in a situation where I've had to struggle and make a tough decision. One you promised, I would never have to make. Well, I've finally made my choice, one that I believe is best for me and I guess for you too, but it makes me sad to let go of our life together. Unlike you, I was never looking for something better. Unlike you, I never thought our marriage was bad. I never believed the problem was anything more than us not having time for each other. I was content and willing to ride out the good and bad. But as you know, this bad is just too much.

I met you at 23 and fell in love naively and without thinking beyond the fairytale life I wanted to live. Unfortunately, our life together was fraught with stressors even before we were married and they have continued to bludgeon us. However, despite our difficulties, I always knew you loved me. After you had your affair the first time, I felt worthless and broken. I don't really know how else to explain it. However, I desperately wanted our marriage to work. I loved you like I still do today and could say to myself that your transgressions were few. I could rationalize it by saying to myself you didn't realize how much it would hurt me and you would never do it again because nothing would be worth losing me. I knew I could heal and move beyond the pain and I did. Of course, there were still scars, and today many of my memories are tainted by that experience. Over time things changed for the better. The constant intrusive memories faded and as the days turned into months, I became happy with you again and regained my trust in you.

The fact that you see our marriage as stale and have left it for something new wounds me deeply. I could go on and on, but the bottom line is, I can't be treated like this and I can't live in fear of being betrayed again. I need to start a new chapter in my life. I need to become strong again and surround myself with people I can trust. Hopefully, one day, I'll be able to look back at our marriage and remember the good. However, I need time to heal and forgive. Forgive you for your actions and for not caring enough about us to even try.

Grace

I folded the letter and carefully placed it in an envelope. I put it on the dining room table, grabbed my overnight bag and pulled the door shut behind me. That part of my life was over.

Barbara hadn't been surprised when Grace found the bug. If she were the betting type, she would have thought the discovery would have been sooner. However, given all Grace's marital problems, she wasn't her usual self. She was distracted. Barbara wasn't concerned with Grace's discovery. It was irrelevant. The surveillance equipment had done its job and helped Barbara accomplish her goal. She knew Grace had weakened and was on the verge of quitting. That's all she had wanted. She had just finished listening to the conversation where Houseman belittled Grace and threatened her employment. In fact, she wouldn't be surprised if Grace resigned when she returned from San Diego.

That had been the plan, to keep the clinical program functioning weak. It meant more control, more power and most of all more money. She could easily shift the budget around and funnel more into her pockets. She could throw some bonuses to staff like Barry who continued to demonstrate his loyalty and Houseman would cover for her like he always did. He had too. He had no other choice. She knew Houseman despised her and because of that she loved to watch him squirm. He deserved to, given his proclivities. She would always remember the day she had walked in on him.

It had happened only several months after she started working at Ellis House. She had risen early, showered and dressed leaving the house before seven in the morning to quench her craving for bagels and coffee. The bagel shop was quiet, with only several of the small round tables occupied. She read the paper and relaxed while eating her breakfast. After enjoying two cups of coffee and a jalapeno bagel slathered with cream cheese, she decided to extend the same favor to her new boss, Mr. Houseman. She knew he worked Saturday mornings, always bragging he rose early to make it into the office and get a start on the week ahead. She bought a dozen bagels, several tubs of flavored cream cheese and a large cup of Columbian coffee. She weaved her way through traffic, pulling into the administrative offices twenty minutes later.

Mr. Houseman's shiny, black Mustang was parked in the driveway along with a foam green Sebring. Already hard at work, Barbara thought as she walked up the steps and used her key to enter the building. The lobby was dark, undisturbed this morning, unlike most days when it was full of chaos and activity. She walked down the hall, past his secretary's desk, knocked on his door and let herself into his office.

Houseman sat in his office chair, feet up on his desk smoking a cigarette. His necktie was loose around his neck, shirt unbuttoned. His eyes were drawn to the couch where a middle aged man was lying with a teenage boy. Both were naked. The man was kissing the boy's neck and stroking his chest. The man's expression was one of excitement and desire. The boy's body was stiff, his face like stone. Barbara recognized them both. The boy was eighteen, a recent discharge from Ellis House. The man was someone with whom she had just become acquainted, Marlin Probst, an administrative higher up from licensing. In fact, he had just been out to follow up on a complaint at the facility the week prior. He had found the complaint unfounded, and now she knew why.

She felt disgust, turned and fled the room. Houseman immediately bolted from his chair and followed. She dumped the bagels and coffee in the first trash can she saw as she hurried down the hall. She heard the door slam and Houseman's footsteps approaching from behind. He yelled and demanded for her to stop. She did. After all, she'd have to face him sometime. She leaned against the wall and spent the next forty minutes listening to what he had to say.

Houseman disclosed he had met Marlin a year earlier, following Marlin's move to Battle Creek from Des Moines. The attraction has been instantaneous, Marlin wasting no time in showering Houseman with attention. Houseman had been flattered, if not somewhat taken aback by Marlin's persistence. He had let Marlin know he wasn't interested in a relationship. However, Marlin disagreed and finally began to erode Houseman's will. Their initial affair was torrid. They met frequently under covert conditions adding to the excitement of their relationship.

However, over time, Marlin began to lose interest. He started hinting at seeing other people and allowing them to have an open relationship. The problem for Houseman was now, not only was he hooked, emotionally and physically, he was deeply in love and willing to pay whatever price he needed to keep Marlin happy.

Marlin had offered him a price, a high price. But Houseman couldn't see how high the price was at the time, when his mind was clouded with desperation. This desperation made Marlin's argument to spice up their physical relationship acceptable. Houseman agreed their sex life was stale, and that it was his fault, since he was the one typically balking at trying anything new sexually. However, Marlin suggested their sex life could be better if another party was involved. Lots of people did it, why should things be different for them? Houseman had access to young men, those who were discharged, older and had no place to go. It was a given that many of those boys were going to prostitute themselves on the streets anyway. Why not let them do it in a safe environment and pay them well for it? Initially, Houseman refused. His punishment was swift and Marlin ended their relationship the next day.

Houseman's desperation grew. Feeling lost and alone he finally recruited a boy. The boy had resided at Ellis House only for several weeks before turning eighteen and was discharged to the streets. Houseman had seen him begging, hand outstretched, as he pulled into a downtown parking lot. He stopped to speak with him and within several minutes had made him an offer. Houseman explained to Barbara there had only been a handful of boys and that technically he hadn't done anything wrong. He had paid them well to do something they had been doing anyway.

Houseman continued to talk and Barbara no longer heard the excuses. What she did hear were his verbal pleas for her silence. So, Barbara left there that day, not disturbed by what she had witnessed, but rather pleased with her good fortune.

Chapter 32

My journey to San Diego hadn't given me the closure I'd hoped for. Instead, I returned home with a headache, feeling frustrated with myself for assuming Elliot still gave a damn about our marriage, much less my feelings. He had moved on - a long time ago. I now knew I needed to do the same.

I pulled into the Ellis House parking lot hoping things had been going more smoothly at the group home than they had in my personal life. As I walked up the front steps, I flashed back to my last interaction with Lisa Hennicke. It had been ugly. I decided to prepare for the worst. I walked into my office and paged Drew. He called my office within seconds.

"Hi Drew. It's Grace."

"Hey Grace, you made it back. How was your trip?"

"Don't ask." I said, immediately switching topics. "I was just calling to see if you had any bombshells to drop on me before I came on the units. Any crises? Or more specifically, how's Lisa?"

"No. No crises. It's been pretty quiet. A few escorts,

complaints about staff . . . you know the usual."

"You mean Lisa's been OK?" I asked somewhat perplexed.

"I know it's a shocker. I mean it's not like she's been an angel or anything. She's still mouthing off at staff, but she hasn't been restrained since the day you left."

"Really?" I responded, revealing my surprise.

"Yeah Doc, we're miracle workers remember?" Drew laughed. "Seriously though, I think the reason she's holding things in check a little better is because of Ray. She knows he was discharged from here to that transitional living program. She's telling everyone they used to date and that they'd still be together if it wasn't for the system splitting them up. I guess she's been all over her county worker begging her to put Ray on her phone list and saying she'll do anything to get placed there. Of course, then she threatens her county worker with contacting her lawyer if she doesn't do it because that's Lisa's modus operandi. Nevertheless, since she heard Ray cleaned up his act and is now "free", she's been doing what she needs to. I know it won't last and that she'll never function in that kind of environment, but hey, if she's able to comply with staff better now, then what do I care?"

"Thanks." I said hanging up the phone.

I opted to tackle the mound of paperwork that sat on my desk later. I ran up the stairs two at a time and opened the door to the unit. As I shut the door behind me, something felt off, something more than the rhythmic pounding on the wall of the quiet room. The pounding became louder, more forceful, as I approached the unit office. Then, the pounding was replaced by screams - long, bloodcurdling, shrieks which just faded away to be replaced by more. I immediately left the staff office to discover the source.

As I approached the quiet room, I couldn't help but notice that staff still hadn't changed their strategy. Despite the unit barely being manned to begin with, most staff were hovering around the door of the quiet room. Barry was at the helm.

"Who's in there?" I asked.

"Jasmine." Barry mumbled not bothering to look in my direction.

"Jasmine?" I asked again for clarification. Jasmine had never been restrained before and was a model client. I couldn't help but wonder what had precipitated her behavior.

"Yeah, Jasmine." Barry snapped.

"Why? What happened?" I pressed.

"All I know is by the time I showed up she had kicked two holes in her bedroom wall. She wouldn't redirect and refused to walk to the quiet room. We tried to de-escalate her verbally, but she wouldn't budge. We finally had to escort her, but only after she shattered her bedroom window with an iron. Lucky she didn't use anybody head as a bull's eye."

"Did it have anything to do with Amanda?" I thought perhaps Jasmine had argued with her roommate.

"No. Amanda's not even around."

"Well, maybe.."

"No. They were together earlier at lunch, same as usual. Everybody knows they're friends." Barry responded sarcastically.

"I know they're friends. I'm just trying to understand why she decompensated. She never has before. "

"Frankly, right now, I don't care why she lost it. I just want her to calm down."

"You want me to talk to her?"

"No, I can manage." Barry answered with a look that said, "Go fuck yourself."

I left letting staff know I was available if needed. Jasmine continued to vacillate between screaming threats at staff and pounding her fists on the wall.

My review of shift reports in the staff office took longer than anticipated. It was impossible to ignore Jasmine's continued rant. Occasionally, silence prevailed, but it was always punctuated by screaming after the respite. After several more attempts to offer my services to staff, I walked down the hall to the common room to sit in on group. Typically, there were staff posted outside the common room, but not today.

John was running anger management group today. It was an especially difficult group to manage given it included not only the adolescent girls from the unit, but also the adolescent boys. John typically did not have a co-therapist and instead had one or two staff members sit in to curb any acting out. I decided to attend today to offer him a show of support which was well deserved given how successfully he had managed to fill Jamie's shoes. However, I first made a detour to the kitchen to forage a snack. I was ravenous, not having eaten since leaving California.

As I left the kitchen, still savoring the last juicy bite of a tuna sandwich, the common room door flew open narrowly missing my face. The metal handle made a heavy thud as it bashed into the wall smashing a hole in the plaster. It was followed by an eruption of clients who charged down the hall pushing, kicking and slamming their fists into the walls. The pushing immediately escalated into verbal aggression and hand to hand combat with their foes. A handful of clients who were not involved in the physical and verbal altercations took advantage of the mayhem to engage in property destruction by knocking over chairs and ripping down posters from the walls.

I knew trying to stop anyone physically was impossible. I shouted for help as I ran down the hall in an attempt to alert staff. I didn't wait for a response and hustled into the staff office paging all available staff to the unit. Then, I picked up the phone and dialed Susan.

"Susan," I blurted out, "there's a riot on the adolescent girl's unit. Get everybody up here immediately and call the cops." Out of the corner of my eye, I could see orange flames. I grabbed the fire extinguisher from under the desk and ducked as I ran out of the staff office, the window beside me shattered by an airborne chair.

I focused my gaze on the shift desk which was being licked by a column of deep orange and amber flames growing from the metal trash bin beside it. Amanda, Jasmine's roommate, stood in front of it, with her arms crossed and with an expression that said she was its protector. As we made eye contact, she picked up a telephone book and fed the flames. I positioned the fire extinguisher.

"Move." I screamed.

"Let it all burn, bitch. I ain't moving."

"Move." I repeated.

"Don't or you'll be sorry." Amanda threatened.

Fed up, I shoved her with the extinguisher. Caught off balance, she stumbled and I immediately worked to quell the flames. Amanda glared at me as she rose to her feet. She watched as her fire suffocated, now nothing more than a weak plume of smoke.

In one swift motion, she lunged at me. I wasn't able to avoid her bulk and felt my body buckle as it hit the ground under her weight. I was gasping for breath, making every effort to squeeze out from beneath her two-hundred and fifty pound frame. It was impossible. Then, I felt the weight lifted as Barry and Drew pulled me to my feet, but not before I heard the crunching of glass and saw Amanda grinding my eyeglasses into the carpet with her boots.

Barry pushed her and said, "Move."

As Barry and Drew ran in the direction of the quiet room, I suddenly got a sick feeling in the pit of my stomach. We had experienced small "outbursts", for lack of a better word, on the units in the past, but this one involved the whole unit. It seemed orchestrated despite its chaos. And as I scanned the unit, I saw Jasmine, now quiet, remained in the quiet room peeking her head out to catch a glimpse of what was going on. I noticed other familiar faces, but the person I expected to see most was missing.

I ran back down the hall toward the common room. My head was spinning and the first thing that came to mind was that this riot had indeed been organized. Lisa had somehow manipulated this havoc as a means to AWOL. I knew she was long gone. I'm sure she had left the grounds as quickly as possible. I thought if I could get to the rec area and make sure that the back gate was secure at least we could prevent any further AWOLs. As I ran down the hall, I caught up with Barry and Drew. I heard Barry yell. "We need to get outside fast."

As I pushed open the door to the common room, I saw it had been trashed. The television had been shattered and shards of glass fanned out in a half circle on the carpet. Bookshelves had been

287

knocked down and the furniture had been pushed over. I walked through the destruction as I made my way to the door that led outside. The door was no longer latched and as I pushed the metal bar to exit, I noticed it felt sticky. I stopped and looked at my hand. It was blood.

Barry and Drew maneuvered their way past me. My eyes followed them to the back gate. The recreation field was deserted except for a form that lay motionless, stretched out awkwardly on the ground between two concrete benches.

Drew reached John and checked his vitals. As I approached, he yelled he was going to call 911. John's face had been shredded on the asphalt, loose gravel still embedded in his skin. I took one look at him and got light headed. He was bleeding from his scalp and a deep gash ran down the length of his face. The scrapes on his arms and legs mirrored his face. Apparently he had been unable to prevent himself from falling face down on the blacktop, but the cut on his face was no accident.

"Stay?" Barry said as he turned in my direction. I nodded. "I need to..."

"Go." I answered, knowing he needed to join the chase for the missing clients rather than wait with John. And with no more said, he made his way to the back gate, turned the corner and was gone from sight. Several minutes later, I heard the wail of sirens and the ambulance pulled in behind the facility. I watched the paramedics effortlessly and efficiently place John on the stretcher and shut the ambulance doors behind him.

Chapter 33

Following several days of rest, I settled into bed and reflected on recent events. It had been a week since the riot and despite the mess it had caused for administration, it had also generated progress. Lisa had instigated the riot and generated support from her peers with false promises and aggressive threats. She had been successful in eluding police and avoiding the confines of juvenile hall. I knew they would likely never find her. At least, I was happy I'd never have to face her again.

Houseman had swiftly instituted a policy to double the number of residential staff on the units. This provided the therapists with much welcomed relief. John was recovering well from two broken ribs, a concussion and numerous stitches, but was in good humor and willing to return to Ellis House. Most importantly, the clinical program was starting to stabilize. With Tori gone, Steve was back on board and the therapists had once again become a cohesive unit.

Undeniably, it had been a difficult few months. Losing Jamie had been painful professionally and even more so personally. It was still hard for me to adjust to seeing John's face staring back at me from across the room as he sat at Jamie's former desk. Needless to say, nothing compared to the pain of losing Corrine. She was truly an inspiration, a woman who had overcome so many obstacles. To think of her lying six feet under still generated a sickness in the pit of my stomach. Her murder was not only a despicable, cowardly act, but such a waste.

And last, but certainly not least was Elliot, my soon to be ex-husband. I had so many mixed feelings; so much anger for his betrayal and lack of motivation to save our marriage. Yet, also much sadness to say goodbye to the life I knew and the future I had planned. Earlier in the week, I had finally signed the divorce agreement.

I quickly shifted my thoughts from my marriage in hopes of avoiding the inevitable downward emotional spiral it would bring. I shut my eyes and attempted to visualize myself on a sandy, white beach in Aruba until my eyes became heavy resulting in a deep, sound sleep.

He forces me into the tub and I sit there motionless tired of the fight. My skin feels the cool plastic over the hard ceramic it coats. He sits on the edge of the tub and says, "Look, this is going to be as hard for me as it is for you. After all, I'm the one who's going to have to clean up the mess.

But before I do it I guess I should explain . . . or maybe you already know. I mean it's pretty self-explanatory. Obviously, you're smart enough to figure out I couldn't just divorce you. If we divorced, you'd get half. Well, more if you wanted spousal support. On the other hand, if you disappear, I get it all without any hassle. It's just simpler. Get it?

For the record, I cheated on you . . . treated you like shit because I decided early on I wanted out. The marriage wasn't going to work for me. I thought you'd walk out on me . . . I hoped. I mean, what woman in her right mind would stay? I thought you'd have enough self-respect to divorce me and then feel so guilty about abandoning me that you'd just leave without giving me much hassle. I mean getting married was a mistake, even you can agree with that. I mean couldn't you read the signs? Didn't you see it? We don't even have anything in common. He said becoming furious. I betrayed you over and over and over again. I thought you'd have a little self-respect, a little backbone, but no . . . you're a fucking doormat. He is physically shaking now. His body stiff, his knuckles white. You left me no choice! You made me do this!" He picks up the gun, points it at my forehead and pulls the trigger.

I woke in a panic. I was drenched and the sweat had soaked through the bed sheets to the mattress. It was like I had taken a bucket of water and thrown it on my bed. I sat up, flipped my legs over the side and turned on my light, my heart still pounding. The light forced me to squint as I put on my glasses and cracked open the window. The rushing air revitalized me and cooled my damp face.

I eventually made it to the bathroom and almost felt alive after a long, almost scalding shower. I slipped into an old t-shirt and shorts, stripped the bed and threw the soaked mess into the hamper. I stretched fresh, dry sheets onto the bed, fluffed up my duvet and headed to the kitchen. I hoped after a soothing cup of tea, I'd be able to put the nightmare behind me.

I filled the kettle with water and placed it on the stove to boil. I wandered over to the back door and flipped on the outside patio light. The light had originally been installed for entertaining during the summer months, but more recently evolved into a security measure. I scanned the patio and was suddenly overcome with sadness. All the hopes and dreams that had been mused about in those two worn wicker chairs by the fire pit. For all the bad there had been so much good.

I returned to the sound of the whistling kettle. Even the smell of the peppermint tea was not enough to sooth my frazzled nerves. I went into the bedroom, placed the hot mug by my nightstand, and contemplated whether to call Elliot. No need to torture myself. I picked up my mug of steaming hot tea and slowly made my way to the living room.

As I walked toward the couch, I noticed that the front door was slightly open. How stupid I thought. That's the second time I had done that in the last two weeks. I knew I hadn't been myself lately, I'd been so distracted. But regardless, there was no excuse for carelessness. I quickly flipped the latch, returned to the couch and resorted to the comfort of a good read. After ten minutes, there was no respite and I continued to focus on my nightmare. It had been the worst I had ever had. Even worse, it had seemed so real. I was no dream interpreter, but it was easy to make sense of why I had continued to have it over the course of the last several months. It was driven by anxiety, like many of the nightmares I had experienced throughout my life. There had been so many indicators of Elliot's discontent even before he left for internship. We had made the best of things, but I had still been so anxious given our history. I had managed it all by keeping busy, pushing my anxiety away and minimizing its importance. However, my anxiety was expressed at night when I slept. As my marriage crumbled, the dream intensified. Elliot taking my life in my dream paralleled my belief that he had taken away my life as I knew it.

I started to feel drowsy. I placed my book on the floor and pulled a plaid wool blanket up to my neck and fell asleep. Immediately, I was back in the middle of a nightmare. I was struggling, my legs bound rubbing together at the ankles, my hands were tied securely across my chest and my eyelids were so heavy I couldn't open them. I felt dizzy and nauseous. As I continued to struggle, I came into consciousness and it became apparent that this was no dream. I forced words from my mouth, but none came. For what seemed an eternity, there was only silence, until a voice broke through.

"Guess some people would say I took the coward's way out. Drugging you and tying you up when you were sleeping. Not much of a challenge I know. But I needed to be sure. I couldn't take any chances."

That voice. I knew that voice.

"You may as well stay comfortable and chill 'cause you're not going anywhere."

If I could just place that - "Ana what the hell are you doing?" I slurred.

"Considering you work with me every damn day, I'd have to say that you were a little slow on the uptake. I'm surprised you couldn't tell it was me right away. Maybe it was those meds I put in your tea. Sure is nice working in a place where you have access to all those psychotropics."

"What did you give..."

"Just a little concoction of goodies. It'll help keep you sedated. I saw you looking all confused when you first came in here. To answer your question, no, you didn't leave your front door open. I let myself in. Guess I didn't latch it this time. I thought I had, but oh well, it doesn't matter anyway. I've been hanging out in your guest room tonight trying to figure out when to get the party started. Thought I might have to wait until the morning, slip the drugs in your morning coffee. You always tell everyone how you have to make a cup to drink on the way to work. But you gave me the perfect opportunity.

"Huh?"

"By making your tea. I slipped the drugs in your tea. You sure are slow tonight. By the way, sorry about the problems with your hubby. I saw the divorce papers. Bad marriage. I would have never guessed. Must be tough; and here I always thought you were the perfect picture of mental health." My eyes were beginning to focus and I could see her propped against the entertainment unit, legs crossed, wearing a black fleece jacket and black jeans. She pulled a pack of cigarettes out of her back pocket, stuck one between her lips and lit up. She inhaled deeply.

"Yeah, I've been practicing for a while. You're pretty trusting or maybe just careless. But I walked right into your office one day and made a mold of your house keys that were sitting on your desk. I had my own copy by the time my lunch break was over. I have to laugh because all those times you scratched your head and thought something was different in your house or your office, you were right. I never wanted to do anything so extreme that you'd call the cops, but just enough for you to feel on edge. At first I tried to be discrete, kicking myself if I left anything out of place, like when I knocked over your plant. But then I figured out I liked messing with you. It was fun to watch you stress. And you deserved it. You always treated me like shit.

I've been in and out of this house looking for any shit you may have stashed that you could hold against me."

"What? Why?"

I looked at her blankly.

"Corrine." She stated as if a light bulb was supposed to go off in my head. "You know."

I said nothing.

"Corrine was going to wreck my life. She saw me. She saw me with Ray and knew about our relationship. I know you know so quit trying to act dumb."

She retrieved another cigarette from her pack and made the end glow red. "We have plans you know. He may be shy of eighteen on paper, but he's a real man. A man who wants to spend his life with me. I knew Cory wouldn't keep her mouth shut about it, so I killed her. She didn't even see me coming. Stupid cow! I bashed her head in like watermelon; hit her square in the back of her head with a crowbar." She raised her arm toward the ceiling and brought it down in one swift motion. "She had no time to react. I dragged her to my car and got rid of her body, dumped it, and well you know the rest. I was really lucky the night I killed her. We had ten inches of snow fall. Covered everything up beautifully, otherwise I would have had a lot more work to do. Guess luck was on my side. I knew that night it would be a while before they found her, if they ever did." Ana inhaled deeply and continued speaking.

"Cory was going to tell. I couldn't let her destroy everything. I worked hard to get into graduate school. I have a good life planned, career, kids and a good man. She would have taken that away. The last person who humiliated me and wreck my plans paid a similar price. I didn't want to do it again, but she was like Marty, my old boyfriend, and made me do it. It was her fault. Marty tried to shame me in college and he paid the price just like Cory."

"Cory never talked to me." I responded at a loss for what to say.

"Sure she did."

"No. I really didn't know anything about it."

"No point arguing. If you didn't before, you know too much now."

I stared at her blankly.

"Just so you know the rumor at work is that you quit. Believe me it was easy to spin that story. Everyone was surprised you lasted as long as you did."

Ana took one last drag of her cigarette, walked over to the fire place and extinguished it in cool, grey ashes. Then she approached me. I began to feel panic well up inside of me and began to struggle. This generated a smirk on Ana's face. She bent over, grabbed my feet and pulled me across the floor to the back door. I thrashed my body desperately, making every attempt to wear her down. It had no impact and my feet made a loud thud as she released them from her grip. She pulled a roll of duct tape out from her jacket pocket.

"I backed my car into your driveway, so it'll be easier to load you in." Ana stated calmly.

"You don't need to do this. It'll only make things worse for you." I begged, feeling light headed.

"Shut up. It has to be done."

"You'll get caught. People will piece things together. Whether you think-"

"I won't get caught. I haven't yet."

"But two people murdered, dead, from the same group home, come on?"

"I don't need to explain this to you, but I will. First, they'll never find your body. Second, if they do, no one will ever consider me a suspect. Ray will turn eighteen soon. We'll be living together and I will have advanced to another job. I won't be at Ellis House anymore."

Desperate, I tried another strategy.

"Please, Ana, we're colleagues. Don't do this. I'll go along with whatever you want and disappear. I'll sell this house, quit my job and pack my bags, go to California and never come back. I won't tell a soul. Like you, I want a happy life. I have dreams too." I felt hopeless.

"Are you on crack? How dumb do you think I am? You think I can trust you?"

"You can. You can." I pleaded.

"Sure. And once you're out of town, you'll send the cops after me and my life will be over. Yeah, sounds like a plan." She responded sarcastically with irritation in her voice.

"Think about Ray then."

"I am thinking about him."

"He's young, getting his life on track. You want to do what's best for him. Make him proud of you. You really want to get him involved in something that could put him behind bars? Risk destroying his life?"

"Shut up. I'm protecting him. Just like I killed Corrine to protect him. I am his one shot for having a better life. I love him and trust him and he loves me and trusts me."

"If you love him, do the right thing."

"I love him and I'm doing the best for him so don't try to take it away from me with all your psychobabble."

Ana started to pick at the roll of duct tape, finally ripping off a large piece with her teeth. She said, "Need to keep you quiet. No telling how much noise you'll make once we get outside. Just so you know, I could shoot you now, but I'd prefer later to avoid a mess."

She knelt down, put her face close to mine, to place the first strip over my mouth.

"Ana?"

"What?"

"One last thing."

"What?"

"You know how you said you trusted Ray."

"Yeah."

"Maybe you shouldn't."

"What the hell does that mean?" She asked.

"You really think he loves you?"

"What the hell are you saying?" Trepidation and fear seeping into her voice for the first time.

"Ray's playing you. That night he and Emily AWOLed and you got so upset because the rumor was they had sex . . . well, they did. I just told everyone they didn't to protect Emily. Ray AWOLed to be with Emily because he's in love with her. I know because Emily told me."

Ana looked as if I had just slapped her across the face. As she momentarily lost her focus I lunged at her. I opened my mouth wide and clenched her nose between my jaws and bit down - hard. I felt my teeth puncture her flesh and tasted the salty blood between my lips. Ana shrieked like a wounded animal and instinctively placed her hands around her nose. Adrenalin pulsating through my veins, I raised my feet and kicked her square in the face. She continued to shriek and I could see the blood dripping through her hands. I gagged down the bile I felt rising up my throat. I pushed myself up against the wall and hobbled to my feet. I hopped through the back door and welcomed the icy air on my face.

Ana was getting to her feet as I hopped through the backyard to the driveway screaming at the top of my lungs. Seconds later, I was grabbed from behind and forced to the ground. My head hit the cold hard ground and I could feel the duct tape being stretched across my mouth. She said nothing, but looked at me with hate, blood still dripping from her face. She grabbed my feet and dragged me through the yard to the stone walkway. My shirt had ridden to fully expose my back, which was being shredded to a bloody pulp.

She unlatched the back gate and pulled me into the driveway. I knew I was going to have to fight like hell because once she got me in the car I was dead.

She pulled me to my feet and I could feel the cold metal of something against my back. "Get in bitch or I'll kill you now." I thought it didn't matter where I died, so instead of making her job easy, I made it hard. I fell on the concrete. Every time she tried to move me, I squirmed and kicked and made my body heavy. Short of knocking me out or shooting me, she wasn't going to get any cooperation from me. Ana was furious as she tried once again to force my body into the trunk. I kept using my body weight and finally managed to knock her off balance. I heard her scream, "Fuckin' bitch." Then black . . .

I awoke to the sounds of sirens and a voice saying "I came by and. . ." I knew that voice immediately. It was Elliot's.

Chapter 34

Elliot had flown out on impulse earlier in the day, catching a stand by flight from San Diego. When he had arrived, he had let himself into the house and panicked when he saw the blood on the kitchen floor. He immediately called 911.

Although battered and bruised, I had escaped with only a broken wrist and a concussion. I was very lucky, considering what the outcome could have been. Ana had been cuffed, and after receiving medical treatment, she was taken to county lockup where she was booked. There she could wait to see if anyone would post bail. Doubtful, I imagined. The only support she had was a seventeen year old kid to whom she had made false promises.

I had been released from the hospital following a night of observation. Elliot had insisted on bringing me home and stayed for three weeks to help me get on my feet. He had worked hard to get the house ready for the market. He knew I wouldn't stay there under any circumstances. Before Elliot was scheduled to fly back to California, we already had two offers, both of which were reasonable.

The night before Elliot was scheduled to leave was difficult. He came and sat down beside me on the couch and offered me a glass of merlot.

"I know I wrecked everything we had Grace. But I wanted to let you know that I had a good time with you these past few weeks. It's been nice to hang out with you and not feel any pressure. Kind of like old times." Elliot confessed.

"Yeah, I know. Seems like what things used to be like before the pressure cooker blew the lid off our lives."

"Yeah, things sure have been hard between us. Sometimes I think there is still enough there to make it work."

"Are you still with her?" I asked.

He turned away and tears began to well up in my eyes.

"So, how on earth can you say that?"

"It's you I want. Not her. Sounds dumb I know, but I got in so deep, I didn't know and still don't know how to get out."

"You say that, but the bottom line is you're with her not with me."

"For one reason and one reason only . . . you're divorcing me and won't give me another chance. You tell me in no uncertain terms our marriage is over. Hell, I don't want to be alone. Why be miserable and lonely? Miserable is bad enough in and of itself."

"That's a copout."

I took a long, deep sip of wine and continued.

"How could I ever trust you again? You broke my trust so many times, I don't even know where to begin and this is the second time you've been involved in an affair. You promised me last time that you would never do it again."

"Shit Grace. I meant it when I said it."

"I know you meant it at the time, but if you had any idea how much it hurt me the last time, and how I've struggled with it, you wouldn't have done it."

He said nothing.

"I told you that I would leave if it happened again. Once the trust is gone in a relationship, you may as well kiss it goodbye."

"You're right. I knew you didn't trust me coming out to California and that really angered me. I resented you for it. You seemed so cold and distant before I left and that continued once I was out here."

"I get cold when I'm worried. I was worried and obviously had reason to be. But if you thought I was distant, why didn't you say anything?"

"I don't know. You know my ego. And the kid thing. That scares the hell out of me. I already feel old. In a few months, I'll be wearing a suit and tie, having a 9 to 5 job and be accruing vacation time."

"But if you're so stressed out about getting old and being forced into some mold filled with responsibilities, what are you doing with a woman with kids?"

"Hell, she never sees those kids. It's like dating someone in college who cares about nothing but having fun. The kids live with their dad anyway."

"It seems like you're moving fast for someone who wants his freedom. My guess is that's you'll be remarried in less than a year.

"Grace, I'll never marry anyone else."

I started to cry.

"I just wish there was some way."

"Elliot I love you. And don't get me wrong I wish it could work, but the damage is done."

"Do you think maybe one day?"

"One day?"

"One day, if I keep the wedding ring."

I didn't respond. He didn't push for a reply.

The next day, Elliot was gone. The house seemed cold and empty. I stared at all the brown moving boxes piled high in neat stacks interspersed with the furniture. Only my essentials remained in their familiar spots, including my red chipped coffee mug by the kitchen sink. Everything was in order and I didn't really know what to do with myself.

The program at Ellis House had been permanently shut down.

It had a mottled history to start with. Ana's arrest for Corrine's murder and the exposure of Houseman's prostitution of young boys had been the final two nails in the coffin. Even new management and staff would never be able to shake it's now twisted reputation. I never did find out what happened to Barbara, but rumor had it that she had escaped unscathed and had plans to return to Savannah.

I picked up my bag of personal belongings and slung it over my shoulder. I stepped outside and felt ambivalence as I pulled the front door shut behind me. This year had been incredibly painful and I was happy for the fight to be over. However, I also knew I would likely never return to Michigan and would miss my former home which had been filled with many happy memories. I had already completed arrangements to move to San Diego and was looking forward to the adventure. Today, I was starting a new chapter in my life. After all, why should Elliot have all the fun?

ABOUT THE AUTHOR

Maria Channell is a practicing clinical psychologist. She lives
with her husband and two children in Leominster, Massachusetts.
This is her first novel.

Printed in the United States
210683BV00002BA/1/P

9 780980 178098